Jessica Garvie

PERIGORD

MARC LINDSAY

First published in Australia in 2015 by
Murder of Crows Publishing

First published in Australia in 2015 by Murder of Crows Publishing

Murder of Crows Publishing

Townsville QLD 4814

National Library of Australia Cataloguing-in-Publication entry

Lindsay, Marc, author.

Perigord / Marc Lindsay.

9780646937380 (paperback)

For young adults.

Great powers—Fiction. Suspense fiction. Young adult fiction.

A823.4

Printed and bound in Australia

Cover design by www.damonza.com

www.marc-lindsay.com

Acknowledgements

FOR ME GETTING this book into your hands has been a Herculean undertaking, the least of which was actually writing it. So before you begin your journey through Perigord there are a number of people I would like to thank, I appreciate your patience.

My kids Connor, Dylan and Dana who have had to put up with the endless questions and story updates and despite the busy and secret lives that teenager's dwell in, they were happy to indulge their father when required.

My mother who instilled in her three sons the love of reading and who has the unwavering belief that everything we do or are currently undertaking is sheer brilliance. Thank you for believing.

My wife Kate whom I was terrified to have read my first draft and was later relieved to find that she couldn't put it down, has been the level head through every difficult step.

My editor Julie who has had to endure my poor grammar, in particular a lack of apostrophes and questions marks. All I can say is hopefully I've improved on book two.

Ryan, my baby brother, whose critique I was truly dreading, has never let me get away with poor logic and made me strive to adapt a better story.

James, the middle one. He was the first, the one who saw the gem and never, ever stopped pushing, emailing, texting, phone calls late at night and most importantly nurturing the final product you see before you.

They say it takes a village to raise a child but in the case of a story it takes just one person to believe in what you're writing about, so to all the others who were involved in some way or another with this book ending up in your possession, thank you and for the uninitiated I hope you enjoy Perigord.

Prologue

HE MOVED WITH a confidence and speed that belied his age and the fact that there was little to no light on the forest floor would have made the journey precarious for anyone. Plato Wyngard was dressed appropriately for his surroundings in warm hiking attire and carrying a well-worn leather satchel over his shoulder. Plato was probably the most famous or infamous figure in the valley, depending on who you talked to. People were always speculating on everything from his past, the interior of his home or most importantly what he currently did with his time.

For those that hadn't met him before they would make the assumption that Plato was just a quiet but stern looking gentleman living peacefully in his twilight years. Yet despite his advancing age he kept himself physically and more importantly mentally fit and agile. What had him wandering the countryside in the middle of the night was a matter of grave urgency, a mission of sorts that he dared not entrust to another. He had been out here for the past twelve hours searching desperately for something that had been hidden in the forest years ago. Now in the darkness with his torch flicking over the trail, he was more than a little concerned that his efforts were going to amount to nothing. It was then that something caught his eye. A reflection from his torch that sparkled back at him like a wink in the night.

Plato stopped dead in his tracks and carefully retraced his flashlight to its point of origin. Nothing. He was just about to give up when he saw it flash again in the beam's light, a small circle of pressed metal the size of a man's palm embedded into the trunk of a tree. Plato moved forward cautiously, his torch trained onto the man-made object. As he approached he was now able to see an image engraved upon its surface. A large tree, a sequoia, which was native to the area. The engraving was amazing in its detail.

Plato was not only marvelling at his discovery but patting himself on the back as well, for now he knew he was on the right path. A bush rustled behind and Plato swung around. A figure cloaked in darkness stepped confidently forward. Plato was no stranger to confrontation. Without saying a word he raised the torch in an attempt to identify the mysterious individual. His eyes went wide.

"YOU!" Plato accused. His hand reached into his jacket in an attempt to free the glock pistol resting within. Despite his many years of training, his speed and reflexes were not able to protect him from the second and third figure who had moved up silently behind him. Before Plato could turn or react his world went black.

Chapter 1

THE SIGN STANDING at the top of the hill read 'Welcome to Perigord, population 3321, Home of the Black River Brewing Company'. The sky blue VW kombi sped past, its passengers studying the sign intently. The driver was an attractive woman in her late thirties. She wore her dark brown hair short, pixie style, which complimented her slender build. She had an anxious look on her face, but forced a smile toward her passenger, a teenage boy of sixteen years. His ash blonde hair worn short but ruffled from their trip, tall and lean with broad shoulders. He stared broodily from his window unsure of what awaited him at their destination.

As the van breasted the top of the hill both, its occupants stared wide-eyed at the view before them a small rural town nestled within a valley, surrounded by the Grey Cloud National Park. The national park was made up of beech, spruce and assorted varieties of pine trees, giving the forest a dark and mysterious aura. Beyond the town lay Greymeade Lake, the afternoon sun's reflection on the water, giving the impression of a glittering jewel. The view was breathtaking.

The woman was the first to break the silence.

"The pictures don't do it justice," she said. The teenage boy was also clearly impressed.

"Yeah," he replied simply. The woman observed him, happily.

"I don't know about you but I'm getting good vibes about this move," she said. The teenage boy didn't answer as he took in the scenery. The pair drove on in silence as their van skirted along the winding road.

The trees on either side of the road created a thick canopy giving the forest a dark and eerie atmosphere with small patches of sunlight finding their way through. A large river separated the town from the valley entrance with a simple timber and stone bridge accessing the only road in or out. The van slowed as it crossed, both passengers peering out at the rushing water below. Trout could be seen jumping from the crystal clear water.

"It's so beautiful," the teenage boy whispered. The woman didn't reply, but grinned to herself.

As they drove into the township they passed beautifully constructed homes made from timber and blue stone, and framed with white picket fences. The town's business and infrastructure surrounded an enormous park littered with elm and cypress trees. Elegant white gazebos stood out from under their shaded branches. Bronze statues of leaders and historical figures from Perigord's past could be seen amongst the thicket.

The blue kombi eventually found its way onto Main Street and after several minutes of navigating through the traffic, come to a halt outside a conservative looking shop front. Its black and white sign read 'Black River Realty'. The woman turned to the teenaged boy.

"Let's not keep Mrs Appleby waiting," she said eagerly. The sound of a bell chimed as they opened the front door.

The interior of the office was quaint and cosy, a fireplace in the corner was roaring nicely. Tasteful antique furniture lay within, and paintings adorned the walls depicting views of the valley region. The waiting room was lit by brass lamps illuminating the room in a pleasant glow.

The front reception desk was empty so they waited for a moment before the teenage boy leaned over and rang the bell located on the desk.

"Be right there," a pleasant female voice called out. Moments later, a plump woman in her mid-fifties appeared from one of the rear offices, her dark red hair arranged into an efficient looking bob. She was dressed neatly in a grey tailored suit, looking the epitome of professional.

The realtor smiled when she saw the younger woman and teenage boy. "You must be Doctor Page," she exclaimed stepping forward and offering her hand. The younger woman took it and returned her smile.

"Mrs Appleby I presume," Dr Page replied.

"Please call me Fiona."

"I'm Helen and this is my son Jason," Dr Page said. Her son gave the realtor a forced smile.

"Pleased to meet you ma'am," he said formally.

"Pleased to meet you too. Would either of you both care for a refreshment?"

"Tea if you have it," Helen replied.

"Of course, and would you care for a soft drink, Jason?" she asked. Jason shrugged.

"I hope diet is ok, I'm trying to watch my figure and it's all I have at the moment," she smiled sheepishly.

"Diet is fine," Jason replied. Fiona pointed to the nearest sofa.

"Please, take a seat and I'll be back with your drinks," she said warmly.

Helen walked over to the sofa and slumped into it with a groan.

"Come and sit down it's comfier than it looks," Helen offered. Jason however was studying one of the paintings on the wall.

"No thanks," he said, his interest piqued by the unusual art. Moving closer, his eyes roamed the painting intently, a forest scene, dark with subtle touches of light, a mist half shrouding a stone tablet of some description. Strange markings adorned its surface along with some other image Jason couldn't quite make out.

Fiona entered the room carrying a tray of drinks, a smile spreading across her face when she saw Jason appraising her art.

"I see you like my paintings," Fiona said proudly. Jason nodded in reply. "Yes, this one in particular. It's beautiful but kind of disturbing at the same time," he replied. Fiona placed the tray on the coffee table.

"It does have a rather unusual quality about it. The artist was also this town's founding father, Heinrich Perigord," she said, matter of factly. Helen sat up in her seat.

"How fascinating," Helen said with genuine interest.

"Brilliant or mad, take your pick," Fiona said candidly. Jason's attention was now firmly on Fiona.

"How so?"

Fiona pulled up a chair opposite Helen, clearly enjoying the audience. She continued with her story.

"Well Heinrich settled out this way in 1822, the minister of a small congregation, of what denomination no one really knows". She paused to pour herself a cup of tea. Jason watched her tip four spoons of sugar into her cup, a smirk appearing on his face remembering her comment about the diet soft drink. She settled back into her chair, and continued with her story. "Where was I?" she questioned.

"You were talking about Heinrich's church," Jason cut in. Fiona brightened. "That's right, Heinrich's church, or as rumour had it, his cult."

Fiona paused for dramatic effect, a naughty smile appearing on her face. "Heinrich was something of a pagan, the emblem of his faith a black tree, a rare black sequoia to be precise, one which can only be found in this valley."

"Sounds so sinister," Helen interrupted clearly intrigued.

"Oh it was," Fiona replied, then looking back at Jason, "If you're interested there are plenty of books on Perigord at the library." Jason nodded thankfully, his curiosity clearly aroused.

Fiona straightened the creases of her pants with her hands.

"I'm sorry, I've been babbling on, you're both probably tired from your drive," she said, adopting a more professional manner. She passed some papers to Helen. "As you're aware this isn't a sale as the house was bequeathed to you in your uncle's will. His solicitors left the transfer of his estate to my realty, making it an easier transition. These are your original copies, the last page is for you to sign saying that you have received the keys," Fiona said enthusiastically.

Helen nodded, but continued to read through the documentation, finally looking up at Fiona.

"It all appears in order," she said smiling, then retrieving a pen from her pocket, signed the last page of the document.

Fiona handed the keys to Helen.

"The phone and power were turned on earlier today, and I had a cleaner go through yesterday giving it a good once over. I hope you don't mind but I also took the liberty of having your pantry and fridge stocked with some bare essentials," Fiona said warmly.

"You're too kind," Helen replied.

"It's just our way of welcoming you both to our little community. You're both going to love it here."

"I'm sure we will," Helen replied giving Jason a wink.

Chapter 2

JASON STOOD ON the gravel driveway, his hands covering his face.

"You can open your eyes now," Helen said playfully. Dropping his hands to his sides, Jason's face clearly showed his displeasure at this childish game, letting out a sigh as he opened his eyes. Immediately his face changed from annoyance to utter surprise.

"I'm blown away," he said in awe. "I can't believe what I'm seeing."

"You haven't seen anything yet!" Helen replied as she planted a big kiss on his cheek. "Shall we have a closer look?"

The front driveway weaved its way through a vivid green landscape of lush grass and beautiful trees. At its centre an unusually large weeping willow standing close to eighty foot in height, its branches reaching out creating a large umbrella of vegetation. Under the green canopy, mounted within the willow's branches, as a magnificent treehouse made of sturdy timber, a multi-levelled structure complete with a roof, windows and a rudimentary lift with cables and pulleys. It was staggering in its attention to detail. Jason looked at his mother.

"I wish I were ten years old again," Jason says wistfully. Helen laughed out loud.

"I'm serious mum, this is where I'm living?"

"How about we spend our first night in the house and go from there," she replied.

"I guess," Jason said reluctantly as they continued their way through the grounds towards the house.

Like most of the houses in the valley, their new home was built from stone and timber, a two storey highset structure. The house was surrounded by mature elm trees that provided both shade and privacy. Jason walked up the stone steps that connected to a wraparound porch. Helen remained a couple of steps behind, watching his reaction closely. Looking up and down the porch, Jason was clearly impressed with the craftsmanship of the house's exterior, as well as its maintenance. Everything appeared to be freshly painted and in good repair. Approaching the front entrance was a large oak door beautifully engraved with runes and inlaid with iron strips, door handle and a wolf's head door knocker.

"I can't believe this is ours," Jason said amazed.

"I haven't been here since I was a little girl. It's sad to think that I was the only relative left of Uncle Plato's," Helen replied. Stepping forward she unlocked the door. "You haven't seen anything yet!"

Light filtered in through the dark house as the front door was cracked opened. Jason and Helen stepped hesitantly inside. What greeted them could only be described as amazing.

"Did I also mention the house came fully furnished?" Helen said proudly. Looking around the interior of the house Jason was stunned by the furniture arranged around the front lobby and sitting room. Drop sheets covered everything, including the paintings on the walls. Walking over to a large piece, Helen ripped the canvas cover revealing a beautifully carved writing desk.

"All this furniture is ours now, too?" Jason asked in astonishment.

"That's right, everything you see is ours. I don't know what Uncle Plato did for a living, but I know he was well travelled and educated. His furnishings are probably worth a small fortune." Helen said.

"There have been some problems with the power though, worst case scenario, the house may need new wiring."

"Even so, I can't believe our good luck!" Jason replied.

"Good luck? More like winning the lottery!" They burst out laughing. "Let's unpack the car and then we can organise something for dinner," Helen said touching Jason affectionately on the shoulder.

They sat at the large timber breakfast bar facing the kitchen, eating Chinese takeout from the cardboard containers, the room illuminated by candles.

"I'll call an electrician first thing in the morning," Helen said as Jason popped an egg roll into his mouth chewing enthusiastically.

"I kinda prefer the candles" Jason replied through a mouthful of food. Helen gave him a disgusted look. "Try and keep your mouth closed when eating, and yes the candles are nice but the novelty would wear off after a while with constantly having to light them and blow them out. Not to mention powering your cell phone would prove difficult," Helen said.

Jason smirked back.

"You always say I spend way too much time listening to my music, maybe this would be a good opportunity to sing instead," he said, proudly jumping to his feet and bursting into a hip hop song and dance number, his singing completely off key.

"Enough, enough," Helen complained. Jason feigned a hurt look.

"I could crack my knuckles with more rhythm," Helen said teasing.

"Really, you crack your knuckles to music? I'm thinking Beethoven," Jason joked. Helen smiled back patronizingly.

"Very clever," she said, then pausing. "Speaking of clever, I need to speak with your new school." Jason let out a loud groan.

"Can't we give it a couple of weeks or something," he grumbled.

"Poor baby, sending you back to the salt mines to do hard labour," she said. Jason rolled his eyes.

"Okay, okay, we'll talk about it tomorrow," Helen said.

Later that night Jason lay on his bed staring at the ceiling.

"Things will be different here, I'll be different here," he whispered to the darkness. Then sighing deeply he closed his eyes.

Chapter 3

HELEN WALKED DOWN the ornate timber staircase dressed in pink pyjamas and matching slippers. Descending the staircase she ran her hand down the smooth banister, the design of which looked like the exposed roots of a tree. She marvelled at its detail. Upon reaching the ground floor she could hear sounds eminating from the kitchen; the sizzling of the fryer, a fridge being opened, and finally her son's singing. Helen smiled as she entered.

Chaos was the first thing that crossed her mind as she watched Jason attempt to make scrambled eggs, bacon, toast, and coffee plus sing and dance all at once. She stifled a laugh and then as if on cue Jason whirled around to see his mother watching him intently. He grinned sheepishly, still moving to the beat in his head.

"You weren't meant to be up yet, you've spoiled my surprise," Jason protested.

"It's okay the removalists are supposed to be coming early, and…"

"And?" prompted Jason.

"And your eggs are burning," Helen replied deadpan. Jason turned to see a plume of smoke rising from the stove.

"Crap," Jason exclaimed, grabbing the pan and moving it from the stove to the sink in one quick movement. "I hope you like your eggs well done!" Jason asked, Helen wrinkled her nose in distaste.

"Um I think I'll go with the toast and coffee," Helen observed. Jason nodded in agreement as he tipped the burnt remains into the rubbish bin, and the pan into the sink.

"Yeah, probably for the best," Jason replied. Helen poured herself a coffee and the pair adjourned to the dining table.

"I appreciate the effort though," Helen said with a smile." Jason waved her off.

"I'm just glad Fiona stocked us with some essential items."

"I am, after all, a valued customer," Helen beamed. Jason looked dubious.

"Don't get me wrong mum, I'm really proud of you, but the way they're bending over for you, it's kinda unusual," Jason said diplomatically.

"I know it's a little weird but I'm trying to keep a positive spin on it, being the only vet in town carries a lot of weight in rural communities."

"When you're right you're right," Jason conceded. "Besides this place is unbelievable, I'm more than happy with this deal!"

The removalist arrived in a small white truck an hour after breakfast, an older man in his mid-fifties, balding, handlebar moustache and built like a tattooed tank. His partner was a younger man early twenties, blonde hair, big and beefy. His face bore a flushed complexion, he looked more like a butcher than a professional mover. The pair worked efficiently unloading the truck and with help from Jason, they were finished before lunch. Both men were polite and wished Helen and Jason good luck before they departed.

They ate a modest lunch before commencing the tedious task of unpacking boxes. After an hour Helen decided to send Jason for a walk as he was getting bored and becoming counterproductive.

"Why don't you get out of the house for a bit, stretch your legs and check out the town," Helen suggested.

"I don't think that's a good idea, we still have so much to do," Jason said.

"It's going to take us a week to get fully unpacked, so it'll still be here when you get back," Helen replied.

"You're the boss," Jason sighed. "I do want to check out the library Ms Appleby mentioned." he added.

"Then it's settled, I'll see you when you return," Helen said. Jason grabbed his phone and ear plugs before departing.

The sky was clear and blue, but chilly due to a cool breeze blowing. Luckily he had dressed appropriately, jeans, hoodie and canvas skater shoes. He strolled along the pavement listening to his music, a natural athleticism in his step. The way he was observing his surroundings, it was evident that he was new in town.

Jason eventually found his way to Perigord's central park and was surprised at its size. The park appeared deserted and after a couple of minutes of walking he stumbled across a man selling hotdogs near a statue.

"Afternoon, I was wondering if you could help me? I'm trying to find the library," he asked politely. The hot-dog vendor looked Jason up and down with curiosity.

"New in town?" He asked. Jason nodded.

"Moved here yesterday with my mum," Jason replied.

"Your mum wouldn't be the new vet would she?"

"How did you know?" Jason said, surprised at the vendor's apparent knowledge. The vendor laughed at his reaction.

"You know what they say about news and small towns."

Jason conceded his point.

"You said you were looking for the library?"

"That's right", where can I find it?"

The vendor pointed over Jason's shoulder.

"Go that way until you reach the Greymeade fountain then turn left, you can't miss it," he said helpfully.

"Thanks," Jason replied. He paused before leaving and pointed to the cloaked statue behind the vendor. "Who's that supposed to be?"

The vendor looked over his shoulder at the statue, then back at Jason

"Oh that's Heinrich Perigord," he answered. Jason looked at the statue sceptically.

"He really isn't what you would think of as a pioneer," Jason remarked. The vendor laughed good-naturedly.

"Thanks again for your help," Jason said then turned and walked away.

Continuing on down the winding cobblestone path he came to a small clearing with a fountain located in the centre. Atop the fountain stood another bronze statue of a soldier being mauled by wolves. The expression of fear on the soldier's face and the ferocity of the wolves appearing very real. The image was both gruesome and fascinating in its detail. Not the sort of image you would expect in a public place. At the statue's base a small modest sign read 'The Death of Greymeade'. Jason studied the sign intently, finding it strange that no other information was written on such an elaborate scene.

A short time later he found himself standing at the front of Perigord Library. The vendor was right, Jason thought. You definitely can't miss it. The Library was located within the park and nestled amongst dense vegetation. It was an entirely stone structure that would have looked more at home in a South American jungle. The architect had clearly been influenced by the Mayan period as it resembled one of their pyramids, but in shape only. There were no external steps to the top, only beautifully detailed stain glass windows depicting images of a giant tree. Two granite statues stood guard over stone steps at the buildings base that led up the entrance, framed by a large rock arch carved with ivy, and finally a simple but intimidating timber and iron door.

Something primal stirred within Jason. Despite its foreboding appearance, it felt safe and familiar. Slowly he made his way up and pushed his way through the door.

Chapter 4

THE INTERIOR OF the library was polar opposite to the exterior. Its outer shell was akin to an iceberg, with the vast majority of the structure located below the surface. Instead of walking in, Jason found a large staircase leading down. Standing guard at the top was a statue of a beautiful Greek goddess holding a bow and arrow at the ready. Jason read the name 'Artemis' on the statue's base. Now standing at the top he could see a giant maze of timber bookshelves below. As he made his way down the stairwell, colourful ambient light flowed in from the stain glass windows located above. From what he could guess there didn't appear to be many patrons within the library, but it was hard to tell with the sheer size of its labyrinth-like layout.

At the bottom of the staircase sat two giant stone gargoyles, vaguely cat-like in appearance but covered in reptilian scales. They had no ears and possessed massive club-like tails their eyes closed as if asleep. Running his hand over the head of one of the gargoyles, Jason could feel the smooth ripple of the scales and was amazed at the intricate detail. How long would it have taken the artist to accomplish such a piece, he wondered. Everything he could see had been painstakingly built or created from the shelves and furniture to the paintings and sculptures decorating the walls and tables. How could any of this exist in a small rural town when it rivalled anything that could be found in New York, London, or Paris?

Jason was so deep in thought he didn't hear the voice behind him at first. "Excuse me," the voice asked, followed by a gruff clearing of a throat. Jason turned around to see a giant of a man standing before him, easily six foot five and around two hundred and fifty pounds. He started to think of an old ballad about a drifter who saved a bunch of miners and died at the end. The individual before him definitely fit the description.

"Shouldn't you be in school?" he growled. Jason was still taking in the giant's appearance, it wasn't just the man's size but also the way he was dressed. Physically he looked like someone who would be more at home storming a beach with a platoon of men, or busting up fights in a biker bar. Instead, here he stood wearing a three-piece suit, bow tie and reading glasses perched on his nose. A name tag declared him to be the head librarian, bearing the name 'U. Walker'.

Walker ran a hand through his hair.

"Look kid, shouldn't you be in school?" he asked impatiently. Jason regained his composure.

"I'm sorry sir," he stammered. Walker raised an eyebrow and regarded the young man before him. "I just moved to town and wanted to check out the library."

"Okay slick you've got my attention," he said crossing

his massive arms over his chest. "What exactly are you looking for?"

"I was told there were books on Heinrich Perigord here."

Walker's jaw clenched again, clearly surprised by Jason's questions.

"What for?" Walker asked bluntly.

"Our realtor was telling me about him and I was curious."

"And?" Walker enquired. Jason's cheeks had begun to redden under Walker's cross-examination and he too, was getting irritated.

"I don't mean to appear rude or anything, but isn't this a library? Aren't you supposed to help me find books?" Jason demanded. From the look in Walker's eyes, he was clearly enjoying the reaction from Jason, his smile growing wider.

"Relax sport, I just want to know so I could help you with specifics." Jason seemed to deflate, not wanting to argue further.

"I just wanted some books, can you help or not?" he sighed.

"Follow me," Walker said, striding off without waiting for a response. Jason followed, remaining a couple of steps behind the big man. Walker paced robotically through the maze of books. Jason noted that he never looked where he was going. It was as though he had some built-in radar directing him, which was good, as there was no signage on shelves or coding's on books.

After several minutes of walking Jason come to two conclusions. One the librarian had no idea what he was doing, and two, they were both lost. "Hey, we might have to send up a flare or something," Jason joked nervously. Walker ignored the comment and after another minute of walking he stopped by a shelf, squatted down and looked intently at the books. Walker ran a finger along the spines before retrieving a thick tome. He did this five more times, after which he stood and faced Jason with a stare that could eat through steel

"Despite the fact that Heinrich founded this town and was a central figure in its history, the man was a complete dick," Walker said bluntly. Jason raised an eyebrow. "Keep an open mind and don't always believe everything you read on this subject," Walker added. Jason nodded, but it was clear he was only humouring the librarian.

"These books are fairly good accounts of Perigord, his early years, ideals, and some limited information on his church. If you need anything else come back and see me," Walker said helpfully as he handed the pile of books to Jason, who accepted them with a nod and a forced smile. "Thanks," he replied. Jason had a quick look around realising that he didn't know his way out.

"Um, Mr Walker?" Jason enquired, Walker pointed to the end of the shelf. "Just down there and turn left," he responded. Jason looked to where Walker pointed, total confusion plastered on his face.

"That can't be," Jason said puzzled, looking back at Walker only to find him gone.

Jason did a double take.

"Where did he go?" Jason exclaimed, then sighed. With books tucked under his arm he rounded the corner and found himself facing the reception desk opposite the staircase leading back out. Jason was dumbstruck.

"This isn't the way we..." Jason's voice trailed off as he turned back the way he had just came, only to find himself in a different aisle altogether.

"I could have sworn this was the way I just came," he whispered to himself. Slowly backing out he once again found himself facing the reception desk and after a moment of pure bewilderment, he shook his head and walked over to the counter.

Reception was unattended and as Jason was about to ring the service bell, a figure appeared from behind the counter. The library assistant was a short stocky woman aged somewhere between 50 and 100 years, black tribal tattoos adorning her face. Despite her age, nothing about her appeared soft or feeble, her dark weathered face and hands looking as if they were carved from wood, her dark grey hair was thick and arranged in corn rows. Her name tag read, 'Ms A. Jax'. She eyed Jason suspiciously.

"How can I help you?" she crowed in a voice barely human.

"Can I check these books out please?" Jason asked. The old woman stretched her mouth wide in a crude caricature of a smile, exposing a mouth full of square teeth that look more like the grill of an old car.

"Of course you can," she replied, her voice like the grinding of a truck's gears. "That's why I'm here after all"

Chapter 5

JASON ARRIVED HOME late in the afternoon, walking through the front door, he headed straight for the kitchen.

"Hey mum, I'm home," Jason called out, "I'm here," Helen called back. Jason entered to find that his mother had been busy since his departure; all the boxes had been cleared away, now displaying a beautiful gourmet kitchen, timber and polished granite. Helen was preparing dinner, her knife a blur as she sliced vegetables on an antique cutting board.

"How was your excursion," she enquired.

"Great. This town is crazy beautiful, if not a little strange," he replied.

"Strange?" Helen questioned as she placed the vegetables into the steamer.

"Yeah, Twin Peaks strange," Jason answered as he pulled up a stool. "Don't get me wrong, the people have been friendly enough, it's the surroundings, they remind me of a Tim Burton film. The park and library need to be seen to be believed." Helen had now stopped what she was doing and was watching her son with concern.

"This isn't a bad thing, is it?" she asked.

"No, no, of course not," Jason added quickly. "Besides, I'm not exactly Mr normal, maybe I've found a place where I fit in," he joked.

Helen visibly relaxed. "Tell me more about the library, did you find the books you were after?"

"The library resembles a Mayan temple, most of it built underground, and inside the shelves are arranged like a labyrinth. They have some of the most amazing art you've ever seen," Jason said excitedly. Helen watched her son become more animated as he described his afternoon. "And the librarian is this massive pro wrestler looking dude who dresses like a geek in a bow tie and reading glasses. I wouldn't be surprised if he's a hit man for the mob who's under witness protection or something," Jason chuckled. "He was helpful though, and I did get some books on Perigord. You'd be surprised at the selections there."

"I'll have to check out the romance section," Helen beamed. The last thing Jason wanted to do was talk about romance with his mother.

"How far away is dinner?" he asked.

"About half an hour," Helen replied.

"Good, I'll go and clean up," Jason said as he departed, leaving his mother to continue with dinner.

Jason pushed the empty plate away with a fulfilled sigh.

"I'm completely stuffed."

"Me too, that fish was divine," Helen replied "Apparently it's caught locally. Fiona stopped by after you left, she had some forms she wanted to leave with me." Jason sat up in his chair.

"Is it official?" he queried. Helen watched her son, apprehension evident on her face.

"I know I have been tight lipped about the move and the reasons behind it all, but I have had mixed feelings inheriting this estate from my uncle and the events behind his death. It's been hard." Helen took a sip of wine.

"You won't hear me complain" Jason replied.

Helen was quick to change the subject. "As I was saying earlier, when Fiona stopped by we had a coffee and she filled me in on what Perigord has to offer, for example, did you know that almost all fresh food is produced locally."

"No, I did not know that," Jason said feigning a shocked look of surprise.

"And that honey, dairy, and other produce have won awards in both district and state fairs," she added.

"You don't say!" Jason said mockingly.

"And that Perigord is a multiple winner of the tidiest town, and has record numbers of school literacy programs," Helen continued.

"She does realise that it's a done deal and that we're staying here," Jason said with a smirk "I think it's admiral that she has so much passion for this town," Helen replied.

"Yeah you definitely can't fault the woman there. So it's official then, we're Perigordians," Jason stated. "That's right sweetheart, this calls for a toast," Helen raced over to the fridge and retrieved a large bottle, undoing the cork as she walked back to the table.

"Alright the good stuff!"

"You wish, this is sparkling apple juice, it was part of

the welcome basket that Fiona left," Helen said, pouring two glasses.

"Here's to Perigord, I hope we can give something back to the community that has welcomed us in," Helen toasted.

"Here, here," Jason replied.

Chapter 6

JASON SAT ON his bed reading one of the library books by lamplight. He was absorbed in a chapter detailing how Heinrich Perigord had moved to the valley to avoid the religious persecution he had found in the big cities. His congregation was made up mostly of young women, many of whom were his wives.

"Lucky bastard," he whispered. Once Perigord had established his presence in the valley he dedicated his life to three things. First, the building of his church which later became the Perigord library; second mining; and third, the planting of the black Sequoia trees that were now found in the valley a tree purported to possess magical healing properties. Heinrich and his congregation were said to have used the sap from the tree in their religious ceremonies, but it was unclear exactly how or why.

The last thing in the book Jason saw was a picture detailing the church's holy symbol. A naked man and woman intertwined and forming the trunk of a tree, the branches reaching out and down and re-joining into the root system-much like the Celtic tree of life. Everything about the image was black apart from the leaves, which were silver. The couple bore an expression of agony, as if they were being absorbed into the tree. The symbolism was both beautiful and grotesque.

Jason noticed the next book was on the secrets of the SS and its inner circle. He frowned there must of been some mix up, as he didn't remember that particular book being included on his loan-out. Confused, he put the book back and turned the light off. He lay awake for a short while thinking about Heinrich and wondering what drove him and his obsession with the church and trees.

The following morning he regaled the story of Perigord to his mother, who was impressed with his interest and research, but less so with the bizarre story of the man himself.

"What a kook," Helen said. "Yeah I agree, but even so, it's impressive in what he accomplished," Jason said.

"They say it's a fine line between genius and insanity," Helen commented.

"Especially when we're talking about having all those wives," Jason said, smirking.

"Charming," Helen said, shaking her head.

"What's on our agenda for the day?" Jason asked changing the subject.

"Well I'm going to need to spend some time at the surgery over the weekend getting it ready for Monday's opening, I was kind of hoping that you could do a little unpacking for us here," Helen said hopefully.

"Of course, in fact leave the cooking to me tonight too," Jason said.

"You're the best. I don't expect you to finish it, I

realise you have school as well on Monday, so take it easy," Helen said.

"No probs," Jason said, "I'm actually looking forward to going through the house and checking out its nooks and crannies".

Starting in Plato's study, the first thing he noticed was a small brass plaque, eight centimetres squared, inserted into the frame of the doorway. Engraved on the plaque was an image of a wolf's head in profile, intertwined by the limbs of a thorn bush. He ran his fingers over the image, feeling the delicate indentations of the picture. He decided it was either the signature of the craftsman's work or just another interesting talking piece from the original owner. Either way he realised that he had better start working.

He entered the study. The large room was completely round, eight meters in diameter and apart from the archway, the walls were lined with built-in bookshelves constructed of dark walnut timber reaching from the floor to the ceiling-over twelve foot in height. Gaining access to the shelves via a timber ladder with fixed brass wheels attached to either end and mounted to a rail, system allowing it to roll along the front of the shelves.

Jason stood atop the ladder with a handful of books, carefully placing them onto the shelves. Despite the vast amount of books his mother owned and the books from his late uncle there was still plenty of space available. After a couple of hours of climbing the ladder he decided to take a break. Plato had amassed an impressive array of books, everything from carpentry to origami. What really grabbed his attention was an area that contained a collection of books dedicated to the strange and the supernatural. All were leather-bound and extremely old. One of the books in particular stood out. It was larger than the others, black, soft leather with runes and symbols printed on the spine and cover.

Removing the book from the shelf, Jason read the front cover, 'Transmorphagation'.

"Is that even a word?" he whispered. He carefully opened the old book, turning the pages gently. There were sketches of strange looking creatures and symbols. The pages were all beautifully hand written, but the text was in another language. After scanning one of the passages, Jason recognised a word, 'Achtung'. He remembered the word from the old commando comics he used to read. It was German for 'attention'.

Flipping back to the front page of the book, there appeared to be an inscription made out to someone, followed by a simple squiggle-the number 8, but drawn on its side. Jason closed the book and walked over to the table in the centre of the room. As he put the book down something shiny fell out. As he bent over to retrieve it, he discovered it was an iron cross, two inches long and an inch and a half wide. The ends of the cross were bulbous, like that of a bolt. At the top of the cross, a wolf's head facing out and biting down on a leather lanyard. Jason turned the cross over. There were small runes etched into the metal, much like the ones in the book. He now thought the cross looked more like a war hammer the Vikings used to use. Jason smiled as he placed the leather thong over his neck, 'not bad' he admired, tucking the cross under his collar as he continued with the unpacking.

Helen returned home late in the afternoon to find Jason preparing dinner.

"Thank you sweetheart," she said, falling into the seat opposite.

"How did it go today?" Jason enquired.

"Really good, the previous fellow had good bookkeeping skills, and I was able to familiarize myself with his system easily enough." "That's great, did you want a glass of wine?" Helen nodded thankfully. He plucked a glass from the overhead cabinet and opened a bottle of red from under the counter, he placed the half full glass in front of his mum.

"Thank you", Helen said, taking a sip, followed by a sigh. "So how was your day?" she asked.

"Fairly uneventful I finished unpacking the family room and study. Uncle Plato had quite a collection of books."

"I remember when I was a little girl staying here on holidays, he would spend hours reading in the study. His tastes were eclectic and unusual. In fact I remember there were certain shelves that were off limits to me, so mysterious," she recalled fondly.

"Yeah I had a good look at some of them, in particular his books on the supernatural. I found this in one of them," Jason said as he pulled the iron cross out from his collar and displayed it to his mother.

Helen examined the cross closely.

"That's a hell of a bookmark," she exclaimed. She then gave Jason an appraising eye, "It suits you, makes you look cool. Do kids still say that?" she asked honestly. Jason smirked and shook his head.

"Thank you, and yes we still use the word cool," he said in an exasperated voice, then gave her a condescending thumbs up, Helen smiled back, oblivious to his sarcasm.

Chapter 7

THE INSTITUTION THAT was Perigord High School at first glance appeared more like an ancient monastery than a modern learning facility. The main building was built from stone with high, narrow windows that looked like the eyes of a disapproving aunt peering down at something distasteful. Perched on the top corners of the roof were stone gargoyles, each one lionesque in appearance, both noble and powerful. Surrounding the building were ornate topiary trees and hedges sculpted with obsessive perfection, and leading inside were large stone steps toward the entrance.

Walking the path leading into the school's grounds, his back pack slung over one shoulder, Jason kept his head down as he passed groups of students. Kids mingling within their assorted cliques, laughing, talking and generally do nothing in particular. Some stopped and watched him pass. A few whispered and pointed in his direction. Ignoring the stares he made his way up and through the double doors.

The interior was a mass of activity as both teachers

and students moved about, either coming or going to classes. For a brief moment he was caught up in the swell of movement, not knowing what to do first. Two girls pushed past him as they made their way to class. This seemed to snap Jason from his reverie and looking around, he saw a sign, 'Administration Office'. Jason followed the arrows in its direction. Making his way along the corridor, he stopped as he passed the school's trophy display case. A black and yellow striped tape was draped across reading, 'Do not cross line', preventing anyone from getting too close. The cabinet had been smashed up, bits of glass and timber littered the ground and the trophies and plaques within were busted as well. The timber stand located at its centre was empty. Jason could only guess what it was supposed to hold.

After giving his details to the office staff, he was instructed to sit and wait for an interview with the Vice Principal. Jason sat outside the office fiddling impatiently with the cord on his hoodie. After a while a female voice from within the office ordered him in. Inside the office was decorated in simple decor, framed degrees and letters of thanks adorning the walls. Behind the desk, a small potted plant sat in the far corner of the room and a placard on the desk read, 'Ms Stonewall'.

The Vice Principal was a pleasant surprise. 5"9 and weighing 110 pounds of lean muscle, she was a stunning vision of perfection. Honey blonde hair flowed down her slender neck, cascading over her shoulders. Ms Stonewall's eyes were a clear blue that possessed a hint of silver in the right light. Her lips glistened, full and alluring. Jason found himself staring, entranced by her beauty.

He flushed red with embarrassment. She appeared not to notice Jason's reaction as she flicked through a large manila folder bearing his name.

"Mr Page, please take a seat" she said curtly. Jason moved quickly across the room and took a seat opposite her desk. "It says here you're a B average student who excelled in history and was on your school's boxing team," Ms Stonewall read.

"Yes Ma'am," Jason replied.

"It also says you have been suspended thirteen times, all for fighting," she continued. Jason remained calm.

"Not a very lucky number for me," he said, trying his best to be charming, then upon seeing her no nonsense icy stare, added lamely, "that's a lot, isn't it."

"I'm afraid that's not going to be an option for you here, despite your extracurricular activities at your previous school. We have a zero tolerance towards physical confrontations and bullying, do you understand?" Ms Stonewall asked.

"Yes ma'am, I have no plans of causing any trouble here," he replied giving her his most angelic smile, Ms Stonewall smiled back.

"I'm glad to hear that Mr Page. You'll find we pride ourselves on our academic achievements as well as our sporting accomplishments at Perigord High. I'm afraid that our boxing team hasn't fared well in the past few years but maybe with your experience and help we can rectify that problem." Ms Stonewall's smile was like that of a predator who knew when it had its prey cornered. Jason swallowed thickly.

"I'm always ready for a challenge," he said, although he didn't feel like it at that moment.

"Good, if there's nothing you wish to ask me, I'll let you be on your way. See Gretchen at the front office and she'll give you your timetable and a note explaining your tardiness for your first class. Thank you, Mr Page," Jason stood up just as the phone rang, Ms Stonewall answered. He was about to reply but Ms Stonewall dismissed him with a wave of her hand. He walked out looking back at the beautiful Ms Stonewall and thought what a cold bitch she was. He carefully closed the door behind him.

After getting his timetable and note from the front office he spent the next fifteen minutes attempting to navigate his way to his first class. English with Mr Rosenberg. A highly animated individual who greeted Jason warmly on arrival. Standing around 5"6 and weighing a portly 220 lb, he had receding, frizzing hair which an old friend of Jason's would have described as a Jewfro. He wore black rimmed glasses and an even blacker goatee beard. Jason was invited to introduce himself to the class, which he reluctantly agreed to, with a forced smile. After giving a brief history about himself and his mother. He made his way to an empty seat. Just before he sat down he noticed a girl seated at the back of the classroom, watching him closely. The girl seemed larger than life, dressed in dark clothing, most notably a large oversized army trench coat. Sitting-cross legged, Jason could see the toe of a black combat boot sticking up. She wore her long, jet black hair braided and her pale complexion made her dark eyeliner even more prominent. Large grey eyes regarded him frankly, making Jason almost feel naked. The moment was brief, but intense. He sat down and faced the front.

The class had been discussing the book, 'The Outsiders' by S.E Hinton. Mr Rosenberg made a lame joke that Jason might have some input, as he was currently an outsider as well. This was greeted with a large audible groan from the class, however this kind of endeared him to Jason, and having already read the book he felt comfortable with the subject matter. Without rising, Jason addressed Mr Rosenberg.

"*The Outsiders* is the story about an adolescent boy, Pony boy Curtis, and the way he deals with right and wrong in a world that he thinks makes him an outsider. He deals with this by writing an essay about the events of his past two weeks," Jason said.

"Very good, I'm glad someone here has read the novel. Would anyone else care to add anything to Mr Page's synopsis?" Mr Rosenberg asked. The class was silent and Jason could feel all eyes in the room upon him. Luckily the school bell rang, ending the uncomfortable silence. As kids scrambled to depart, Mr Rosenberg struggled to be heard over the chaos.

"Remember you only have one week left to write your report on this book. Have it on my desk by next Monday, end of play, no excuses!" The class appeared to ignore his diatribe as they exited.

Jason packed his bag and readied to leave when a figure shouldered past him making him drop his books. He looked up to see the girl in the trench coat. She turned and regarded him, her eyes boring into his. Jason was wrong earlier. Her eyes weren't grey, but a sparkling silver. A smile appeared on her face.

"Sorry about that, didn't see you there," she said arrogantly, and before Jason could respond, she strode away. He was left standing there, his books at his feet, the image of her dazzling eyes imprinted on his brain.

Mr Rosenberg snapped him from his trance.

"I'm very pleased to have you in my class young man," he said enthusiastically, shaking Jason's hand. "I don't expect you do the essay, due to your obvious knowledge of the subject and the fact that you have only just arrived, but next week we'll be studying 'Great Expectations', have you read it?" Jason shook his head in reply. "Excellent, I hope you have a good first day," Mr Rosenberg said with a smile before turning back to his desk. Jason threw his bag over his shoulder and headed for the door thinking, 'I hope so too'.

Jason's day only got worse from that moment on. Following English he had algebra with Mr Flannigan, a tall skinny man in his early forties wearing a pinched face and a hawk like nose. He seemed to derive enjoyment from the suffering of his students. Jason could literally hear the minute hand on the classroom's clock tick slowly by. After algebra was a double period of biology. Jason wasn't sure if it was the dissecting of the frog or something he had eaten, but he had started to feel queasy and warm, sweat beads stood out on his forehead as he struggled to focus on the scalpel and the amphibian. He had to take deep breaths as his heart raced. His senses seemed somehow amplified. The smell of the preserving agent and the other chemicals was intense even the stainless steel benches gave off a strong aroma. His vision seemed sharper as every detail of the frog appeared so vivid and clear. It was overwhelming. He was about to make the first incision on the frog when a nauseous lump formed in his stomach. He lurched, excusing himself to go to the bathroom, praying he wouldn't vomit in front of everyone.

His walk down the hallway became a race against time. He barely made it as he kicked open the first toilet stall and dropped to his knees, violently throwing up into the bowl until there was nothing but dry heaving. Jason leaned back against the door, getting his breath. After several minutes he was able to get to his feet. Wobbly at first, he had to steady himself against the wall before staggering on rubbery legs towards the sink. He was startled to see his pale, weary reflection staring back. He washed his face and rinsed his mouth, struggling to concentrate through a splitting headache Jason decided against going home, wanting to see his first day through. Thankfully his teacher hadn't taken much notice of his timely absence and reappearance. Jason felt weak and nauseous during the remainder of the lesson. Having decided to skip lunch, he opted to sit outside and try to enjoy the fresh air and sunshine. He was almost feeling a hundred percent by the end of lunch.

Last period of the day was gym class. The teacher, Mr Fields, was a huskily built man in his early thirties with sandy coloured hair and a ruddy complexion, giving him the appearance of having the flu. There were rumours that Jack, Jim and Gilby had contributed to his flushed skin. Mr Fields gave the class laps of the court, his booming voice never stopping as he berated everyone on their apparent lack of enthusiasm, stamina and general poor conditioning. After laps they conducted a beep test with Jason outlasting everyone, even with the persisting throb in his head. His performance didn't impress the teacher though, who chided the whole class on their weak performance.

Mr Fields nominated two boys from the class to be team captains for a game of basketball. Each captain selected one of two piles of coloured bibs, then taking turns, the captains picked their teams. The selection process seemed to take forever with Jason being picked last on team blue. The red team captain, a large muscular boy, appeared to be the teacher's favourite. Jason didn't like the way he smugly strutted around as Mr Fields joked with him about taking it easy on the blue team. Both teacher and student laughed. Looking about, Jason had an uneasy feeling about this match as it was evident that the more athletic kids were on the red team. Jason sighed and thought the sooner they started, the sooner they would finish.

Mr Fields blew the whistle and the game began. Jason was surprised to find that despite his team's apparent lack of muscle, they had solid skills and were the first to have points on the board, much to the annoyance of the red team. This wasn't helped by Jason scoring three more baskets in quick succession. The red team's captain had lost his smugness and was visibly pissed. Jason watched him confiding with another player from his team, a skinny boy with dirty blonde hair and acne scarring. They both smiled slyly and bumped their fists together in some secret understanding as they returned into position.

As Mr Fields put the ball, up it was apparent that the red team were now going to employ less than sportsman-like methods. Within minutes the red team's captain had tripped one of Jason's team mates, causing him to roll his ankle. The boy was carried from the court and taken to the nurse's station. This was only the beginning. The game had now became full contact, with Mr Fields seemingly turning a blind eye to any illegal activity caused by the red team. The next incident occurred minutes before the half time break, with the acne-riddled boy throwing an elbow into the face of a chubby boy who went down with a cry of pain and a bloody nose. He was taken to the side and given an ice pack; it was obvious he wouldn't be returning in the next half.

The two teams went their separate ways during half time. Jason's team mates were breathing hard, having worked up a decent sweat. They all gulped greedily on their water bottles, attempting to rehydrate before the second act kicked off. Jason was clearly pissed with the events in the first half and asked one of his team mates, a tall nervous looking boy, why the gym teacher wasn't doing anything about the other team's disregard of the rules.

The nervous boy spoke quietly so only Jason could hear.

"Mr Fields isn't big on creating trouble for himself, especially where those two are concerned," he pointed covertly in the direction of the other team's captain and the boy with the acne scarring.

"The big fella is Hector, Sherriff Rope's son. The one with the pizza face is Tiberius, Judge Slate's grandson. Kinda big wheels around here. I'm Rory," he said, extending his hand toward Jason, who took it, shaking it twice.

"I'm Jason," he said.

"Pleased to meet you, don't let it get you down. It's just the way things go," Rory said.

"I'm not a big one for rules myself," Jason said grimly.

"It's not worth it, Jason," Rory replied exasperated. The rest of the blue team had moved in closer around the two as they nodded their agreement. Jason slowly looked them all in the eyes, a wry smile spreading across his face.

"Hey, accidents happen," Jason said as Mr Fields blew his whistle and both teams made their way back onto the court for the second half.

The game began without incident until Rory got off a brilliant three point shot, then Hector and Tiberius continued on with their brazen lack of good conduct. Jason's head had really started to throb again and he decided to put plan A into action. Despite the red team's dirty tactics, Jason's team were quick and able, easily handing the ball from teammate to teammate, eventually finding itself in Jason's hands. Tiberius was on him in defence, physically jostling him and attempting to steal the ball, exactly what Jason hoped he would do.

Jason attempted to dribble pass Tiberius unsuccessfully, who covered him on each pass. Knowing that he wouldn't get a better opportunity, he kept his back to Tiberius and when he made his next attempt, Jason pivoted, pretending to pass the ball and brought his elbow into the face of the oncoming Tiberius. There was an audible cracking sound and Tiberius hit the ground, his nose a bloody mess.

A frightened looking Mr Fields helped him from the court where he took a seat next to the other boy nursing an ice pack. Mr Fields reminded everyone about safety on the court, glaring the whole time at Jason. The game recommenced. Both teams were conscious of the tension building between Jason and Hector. As players on both sides tried to distance themselves from any confrontation, Jason and Hector looked for an opening to get even with each other.

With minutes left on the clock, Jason was left holding the ball with Hector defending.

"Come on faggot," Hector taunted. Jason tried to get past without luck, as Hector was on him like glue.

"Think you're pretty special, don't ya," Hector spat, a mean grin plastered on his face. Jason decided at that moment to give Hector the same medicine he had given Tiberius. The move was going to plan except in the last instance, Hector ducked, avoiding the blow. He lashed out, grasping the ball and the two of them were locked in a tug of war.

"Nice try knob jockey, but you'll have to move faster than that," Hector growled, his confidence growing. Jason stared Hector down, refusing to release his hold on the ball, both boys straining for purchase.

The court had gone quiet. Everyone, including Mr Fields, was watching the battle for dominance. Jason's head was throbbing and his vision had begun to blur. Even Hector's taunts seemed to be coming from far off in the distance. The whole incident had been going for a few seconds but it felt more like hours. His strength was beginning to ebb. 'I refuse to be beaten by this imbecile',

Jason thought. Then as if a switch had been flicked, it all stopped. The headache, the blurred vision and fatigue was now replaced with rage. A hot sensation began to flow through his body, starting in his chest and working its way out to his limbs. Like an electric pulse, it reached his fingers and toes and then it was gone. Jason could now feel power coursing through his veins an almost bestial strength.

He strained, pulling on the ball and Hector, whipping them around in a hundred and eighty degree turn, like a hammer thrower at the Olympics. Jason performed the task with ease and much to everyone's amazement, Hector was able to maintain his grip on the ball until the very last moment, when he was launched across the floor, landing several meters away from Jason, sliding to a halt near the feet of Mr Fields. The teacher stood there, mouth agape, looking first at Hector, then Jason, then back towards Hector. Then as if on cue, the final bell buzzed. No one moved. Then a boy's voice broke the silence.

"Did you see that," the voice squeaked. This seemed to shake Mr Fields from his stupor. He attempted to regain his authority within the class.

"Nothing to see boys, go and hit the showers, we're done for the day," The teachers voice was a croak, then gruff. No one moved. Everyone seemed rooted to the floor. "NOW" Mr Fields barked and all the boys on the court jumped in surprise and bolted for the door. All except Hector, who was still lying on the court floor, unhurt, but stunned, and Jason, who was looking down at his own hands, wide-eyed and shaken. Mr Fields helped Hector to his feet and escorted him from the gym floor, casting a quick glance at Jason, his eyes still wide. They left, leaving Jason there alone.

By the time Jason had made his way to the locker room it was deserted. He sat down and looked up to see a message scrawled on his locker, 'You're dead'. Jason didn't look too concerned, but sighed none the less.

"Great, mum will be thrilled. Making friends staying out of trouble," he thought, as he went to clean up, remaining under the shower for a very long time.

Chapter 8

JASON ARRIVED HOME with what felt like an insatiable hunger, it was almost nauseating. The moment he stepped through the door his senses were assaulted by the aroma of his mother's cooking. He started salivating as he made his way to the kitchen. Helen was in the process of serving dinner when Jason appeared through the door. He stared, ravenous, at the food brought to him.

"Sit down love dinner's ready," Helen said. Jason didn't need to be told twice. He practically leapt into his seat, viewing the meal before him. Smoky ribs, corn on the cob, sweet potato and snow peas, his favourite meal.

"What's the occasion?" Jason asked as he tucked into his meal. Helen regarded her son fondly.

"Just thought you might appreciate it after your first day at school."

"Oh I do, I do," Jason said through a mouthful of food.

Jason pushed his plate away, licking the sticky

marinade from his fingers, not caring about the grubby image he was projecting.

"Glad you enjoyed the meal."

"It was beautiful, mum. I can't believe how hungry I was," he replied. Helen looked at him.

"Hey if you're still hungry, there's chocolate mud cake in the fridge, I picked it up today," Helen said. No sooner had she uttered those words, Jason was out of his chair and moving toward the fridge, returning with a small cardboard box and plates in his hands. Sitting back down opposite Helen, Jason worked intently serving up two slices and pushed one toward his mother, who shook her head.

"Trying to watch my figure," she said. Jason shrugged and took the other larger slice and all but inhaled it. Once it was gone, he reached out for the piece intended for Helen and devoured it as well. Helen watched on in fascination.

"Well you are a growing boy, just as long as you don't grow horizontally," she commented sarcastically.

That night in bed Jason tossed and turned, dreams of wolves and fire, stars like beacons and a blood red moon. By the time he awoke he could only remember flashes of the dream, nothing specific. Sitting up, he stretched and flexed his sore muscles. It was at that moment he noticed the large black book, 'Transmorphagation', lying at the foot of his bed. He frowned, wondering how the book had gotten there. A horrible, black feeling began to spread through his stomach, filling him with dread. He shook the thoughts from his head as he sprung from the bed snatching the book and tucking it away in his school bag, vowing to find out more about it. By the time Jason made his way downstairs there was a note and money on the kitchen bench, 'Had to see a man about a horse, didn't want to wake you. Use the money for lunch. Love mum'. Jason smiled warmly and pocketed the money.

When he walked into the school grounds it was evident that news of yesterday's scuffle with Hector had spread like wildfire. Ignoring the stares and whispers, he walked past the throng of students and entered the front doors. Jason's first few periods were relatively quiet, computer technology with Mr Chambers, an overweight, harried looking man who watched the clock more than his students. This was followed by media studies, which Jason really enjoyed. The class discussed Stanley Kubrick films and his influence on modern pop culture. The teacher, Mr Brown, a flamboyant young man, obviously enjoyed his subject matter, keeping his class engaged throughout the lesson.

After media studies Jason was on a bit of a high. Having forgotten the previous day's troubles, he made his way to the cafeteria for lunch. After collecting his tray he shuffled along the meal line, his stomach grumbling in anticipation.

"What do you want?" The lunch lady's voice came out in a raspy croak, she was obviously a two pack a day woman. He studied the selection on offer, a pale grey, watery looking dish that could have been a stew; the other was something that looked vaguely deep fried, possibly three weeks ago. Jason's stomach did a greasy back flip.

"Hurry up, others are waiting," the lunch lady said impatiently. Jason sighed.

“I think I’ll stick with the fruit” he replied.

“Whatever,” the lunch lady said, shrugging, already looking toward her next customer. Jason continued down the line grabbing a milk to go with his fruit, paying the cashier at the end. He looked around the dining hall for an available seat. Most tables were already full. After a moment of scanning, he spotted an empty table near the centre of the room. It took him a minute of weaving past people and tables before he flopped into the spare seat and started his lunch.

Half way through his meal a familiar voice spoke to Jason from behind. “All on your lonesome,” the voice said. Without turning he knew that it was Hector. And if past experience had taught him anything about this type, he knew he wouldn’t be alone. Jason kept his cool, refusing to react or turn, instead he picked up his milk and took a sip. A confused Hector looked about at his friends. Jason’s reaction wasn’t the usual response he received.

“Hey, I’m talking to you,” he barked. The dining hall went silent. All eyes in the room were now fixed on Jason. ‘So much for keeping a low profile and a promise to mum and the ice queen’, Jason thought solemnly.

Jason continued to sip his milk, keeping a bored expression on his face, he waited for Hector to make the first move, which he did, grabbing Jason roughly by the shoulder and turning him in his seat.

“Don’t ignore me pissant,” Hector growled. Jason looked up, feigning a look of surprise.

“Oh, hey Hector,” he said calmly, then pointing to the kid with the acne scarring and plastered nose to Hector’s right, “Tiberius isn’t it? How about I call you Tib? I don’t know you other three, but if you're friends of Hec and Tib's I'm sure you're good dudes," Jason gave them a sarcastic thumbs up. The five boys didn't look impressed at all.

Tiberius stepped forward.

"You think you're pretty funny, don't you, but I know you're just stalling," a predatory smile appearing on his face. At that moment, Jason decided he'd had enough of these jokers.

"No, if I were stalling, I would have made a joke about the domino's pizza complexion you have, but teenage acne is a little obvious. Don't you think? Maybe your lack of height would have been a good one, but I'd like to think I can be the bigger person," Jason remarked.

Tiberius's smile had faded, the eyes on all five boys narrowed. 'This is it', Jason thought, as he slowly got to his feet. He had a good five inches on any of the boys standing before him and as he stood to full height, Jason let them know it, pushing his broad shoulders out to maximise the effect. He could see it in their eyes, they were unsure. A primal voice growled in his head.

"But if you bottom feeders think you can intimidate me with those pipe cleaner arms, you're crazy." Jason shrugged his hoodie off, and raised his hands. The sound of his knuckles popping as his hands formed into fists was heard clearly throughout the silent hall. His muscles looked pumped, the veins standing out visibly. Jason wasn't aware of the image he was projecting, but to everyone in the dining room, he looked the epitome of dangerous.

All five boys just stood and stared. 'The best defence is

a good offence,' Jason thought, lashing out with a jab into the chin of Tiberius, whose eyes rolled back in his head as he dropped where he stood. Jason didn't hesitate, stepping over the unconscious form of Tiberius and striking Hector with a right, that sent him reeling, but not down.

The other three boys rushed Jason who was able to bring his left knee up into one of the boys, knocking the wind out of him, the other two collided with Jason, their momentum taking all three to the ground. One of the boys had Jason's right arm pinned but it was taking all his might to keep him restrained. The other had both hands around Jason's throat. He could feel the boy's nails digging into his flesh. Jason, who had been studying mixed martial arts for the past two years, knew it was important not to panic and useless to try and pry the hands from his throat. Instead he brought his free hand in close and drove his elbow hard and fast into the boy's face. He felt the sickening crunch of the boy's nose under the impact. The boy went back, the fight now out of him. He just wanted to distance himself from Jason. With his arm now free he reached across to the other boy, grabbed his ear and started to pull. The shrill scream that eminated from the boy let Jason know he was doing the right thing. Unlike Jason, the boy released his hold and tried to stop the intense pain on the side of his head, which was the worst thing he could have done. With both arms now free, Jason was able to manoeuvre himself, facing the boy's back, he positioned the blade of his forearm across the boy's throat, reinforcing it with his other arm, effectively cutting off his air supply. As soon as he felt the boy's struggles weaken, he released his hold, pushing the boy's body aside.

Jason was panting heavily. He attempted to get to his feet, when he caught movement out of the corner of his eye. He tried to roll away but was too slow, as Hector's foot connected with the side of his head. The force of the blow sent Jason rolling to one side, despite the ringing in his ears and disoriented vision, he slowly got to his knees, his arms raised in a defensive posture, blood running from his nose and the corner of his right eye.

Jason prepared himself for more when a woman's voice rang out through the dining hall.

"Stop this instant!" Everyone turned to see Ms Stonewall striding toward the brawling pair, her face devoid of sympathy.

"What the hell is going on here?" Hector was the first to respond.

"The new kid started it Ms," Hector said, sincerely.

"Really," Ms Stonewall replied, "Mr Page just decided to attack the five of you, for no good reason." She eyed him dubiously. Hector was straightening his shirt.

"Who can say Ms, from what I've heard, he has a history of this sort of thing," Hector said smugly. "Have a look at my boys here," he said, pointing to Tiberius, who was moaning and the other boy, coughing and rubbing his throat.

It was apparent that Ms Stonewall was now looking at the situation with a 'Is the school liable?' look in her eyes.

"Is what Mr Rope saying true?" she questioned Jason, now looking uncertain, not knowing how to respond.

"Hector's full of shit," a voice called out from the crowd. Everyone turned to see who had spoken up, including Ms Stonewall, Jason and Hector. A petite figure stepped from the crowd. Jason recognised her as the goth girl from his English class. Dressed pretty much the same as when he had seen her the day before, her grey army trench coat opened at the front revealing long slender legs in charcoal stockings, black shorts and combat boots. She stood with her hands on her hips, defiantly daring anyone to question her.

"Who threw the first punch?" Ms Stonewall shot back. The goth girl didn't reply. Another girl dressed in pigtails and long rainbow coloured socks spoke up.

"It was the new boy, but he…." Ms Stonewall cut her off with a steely glare.

"That's all I need to know Ms Piper". She turned to Hector, "take your friends to the nurse's station and get checked out".

"Yes Ms," Hector replied, firing a malicious glance at Jason. Jason's jaw tensed. Ms Stonewall turned her attention toward him.

"You can take yourself to the Principal's office, I'll be with you shortly," Ms Stonewall said.

"What a crock," the goth girl exclaimed. Ms Stonewall spun to face her. "And you young lady can take that filthy mouth of yours to afternoon detention. I'm sure I don't need to tell you the time and place," she said sarcastically.

Ms Stonewall raised her voice so everyone could hear.

"If there is nothing else, move away and continue with your lunch," she said and with that, turned and departed the dining hall. Jason looked around, but found the goth girl gone. His face was grim with the realisation that his day had gone from bad to worse.

Chapter 9

JASON SAT OUTSIDE the principal's office. He had been waiting about fifteen minutes and hadn't heard a peep since he arrived. He hoped that was a good sign. A door slammed and Ms Stonewall strode down the hallway toward Jason, an angry expression on her face.

"You're a lucky young man, Mr Page. It seems no permanent damage has been inflicted on the boys you attacked, our esteemed Principal, Mr Florentine has a lot on his plate due to some recent vandalism and theft, not to mention a soft spot for your mother. So you've dodged the suspension bullet." Her words were thick with venom. Jason sighed in relief. "However I've been instructed to punish you using my own discretion," she said. Jason opened his mouth to respond and was silenced with a wave of her hand.

"I'm not interested in excuses, you made a promise to me and broke it. I don't forget that sort of thing." Jason tensed, awaiting his judgement. "Two weeks detention. You'll report to the school library five minutes after the final bell, not a minute later. You will remain there until five o'clock." A wicked smile crossed her face and she leaned in close, her lips inches from his ear.

Jason could smell the faint scent of her perfume, a mixture of vanilla and cinnamon. Despite her direct bluntness and the fact that she evidently disliked him he couldn't help but feel a strong sexual attraction towards her. Her breath near his ear was driving him crazy. She lingered a little longer.

"Don't ever screw with me again," Ms Stonewall whispered. This jolted Jason, who struggled to control his reaction, apparently not well enough, as her smile spread wide, she drew back regarding Jason with her piercing eyes.

"I'm glad we understand each other, you can head back to class now." Jason watched her leave, aroused and concerned all at the same time.

The final bell sounded and he made his way quickly to the library, eager not to create any further trouble for himself. He found the area that had been set up for after school-detention. There were other students already seated some alone, others together chatting. Taking a seat near the back, he waited for the lecture he knew would be coming. The librarian emerged from her office. She was in her early sixties, her grey hair in a bun. She was wearing a light blue dress that was probably deemed conservative forties years ago and her half-moon reading glasses were perched on the end of her nose. Jason thought there must be an assembly line somewhere producing women to her exact specifications, because she reminded him of every other librarian he had come across over the years.

The librarian introduced herself as Ms Brewster.

"For those that haven't been here before," Ms Brewster finished mid-sentence as the door was flung open and the goth girl sauntered in. The librarian regarded her coolly.

"How nice of you to join us Selene, please take a seat," Ms Brewster said, Selene ignored the librarian's instruction, leisurely surveying the seating arrangements, her gaze stopping on Jason. The corners of her mouth twitched up slightly into a smile. Selene casually made her way towards Jason, her coat brushing past his chair as she sat down next to him. She leaned back and placed her feet on the chair to her front. She turned her head toward Jason and performed a kissing gesture in his direction followed by a wink of her eye. Jason's face flushed red as he turned away, evidently embarrassed by her bravado.

Ms Brewster kept her calm, clearly annoyed, but not surprised by Selene's behaviour.

"As I was saying, for those that haven't been here before, I don't care what you do as long as it's quiet and you remain in your seats. I'll be at the desk catching up on work. Place your hand up if you require my attention. Is that clear?" She took the rooms silence as acknowledgement, turned and went about her business.

As soon as Ms Brewster was out of earshot, Selene turned to Jason.

"As you already heard from old Brewster there, I'm Selene, so how are you enjoying Perigord so far?" Selene asked with a chuckle. Jason smiled, despite himself.

"I've made better first impressions that's for sure," he quipped. This was followed by more laughter from Selene.

"Those were some pretty slick moves today," Selene said, matter of fact. "Where did you learn them?"

"I have been taking boxing and a bit of MMA for the past three years, mainly for fitness, but for self-defence as well," he replied.

"Well I'd say those lessons were fairly successful," she joked.

"And I'd like to say that was my first time," he replied.

"Ew, a bad boy," Selene crooned.

"Hey could we change the subject please, I'm going to be hearing enough of this when I get home," Jason replied tiredly.

"Fair enough. Hey I like your cross," Selene said, pointing to the pendant around his neck. Jason smiled, holding it up for Selene to take a closer look.

"It belonged to my great uncle I think," Jason said.

"You're not sure?" Selene replied. Jason shrugged and explained the circumstances behind its discovery.

"In fact I have the book here if you're interested" Jason asked.

Selene nodded and rubbed her hands together.

"I'm intrigued," she replied, sitting up in her seat. Jason retrieved the book from his school bag and placed it on the table with a heavy thud.

"Whoa, you weren't kidding were you," Selene said, eyeing the large tome.

"I'm not one for exaggeration," he stated honestly as he opened the book and turned to the first page. Selene looked around as if something should be happening.

"Oh, was that it? I was half expecting some kind of demonic chanting to emanate from the netherworld, but this is a bit of a letdown," she said flatly. Jason went to close the book.

"Well if you're not interested," he replied dryly. Selene slapped her hand over the top of his, looking him seriously in the eyes.

"Hey I was just kidding, you need to get a sense of humour, Rocky," she said, slapping his hand out of the way. After a brief glance inside she turned to Jason.

"You weren't completely wrong, some of this writing is definitely in German. I can make out some of the words but nothing that would prove useful." Jason looked a little deflated as well. He didn't know why but he had hoped Selene might be able to shed some light on the book's content. Selene could read his reaction and interjected, "My grandmother is full on German. If you're interested, we could take the book around one day and let her have a look," Selene offered.

"I'd appreciate that," Jason said sincerely, giving her a warm smile. Selene returned his smile, displaying a cute pair of dimples, her silver eyes glittering. Then the moment was over, the two of them looked down both a little embarrassed at how easily they had let their guards down,

Jason flipped through some of the pages in the book and cleared his throat.

"So, what do you do for fun around here?" he asked keen to change the subject.

"If you're one of the walking dead, not too much. Hunting, fishing, getting drunk," she said bitterly, then noticing his reaction, "Oh, It's not all that bad I suppose. The Parthenon theatre shows classic horror movies Friday nights, and old Sci Fi movies on Saturday nights, the cheesier the better is their motto."

"Really?" Jason asked.

"No, but it should be," Selene joked and they both laughed.

"There's also Crow FM the local radio station, every night between ten and four the DJ plays his own selection of tunes so if you're into something a little different."

"What are you like at the moment?" Jason asked. Selene thought it over.

"I'm kinda into Darkwave, you know, Diary of Dreams, Johnny Hollow." She watched Jason closely, gauging his reaction.

"I don't mind Johnny Hollow," Jason replied.

"Really, what's your favourite song?" Clearly not believing him, Jason thought it over for a second.

"I'm kinda fond of Stone Throwers," he admitted. Selene looked impressed.

"Yeah I like that one too," she replied.

Jason yawned and Selene took it as a sign of boredom. "The DJ's a friend of mine, calls himself Beetle," Selene blurted out.

"Beetle," Jason repeated dubiously.

"I don't know his real name, he's a cool old dude, used to be a roadie back in the day for the Stones, the Who, and about a dozen other classic bands. He's got some great stories to tell if you're ever interested," Selene said.

"Sounds interesting," Jason nodded.

"Detention is over, come and sign your name in the book and you're free to go," Ms Brewster announced to the group.

"That's us," Selene said, the pair grabbing their bags and waiting for their turn to sign out.

"Can I walk you home?" Jason asked sheepishly.

"As much as I appreciate your chivalry, I'll have to sadly decline," Selene said with a smile. "I'm meeting my grandmother out front. Maybe next time."

"Okay, next time," Jason replied lamely. Selene was the first to leave the library and by the time Jason got outside there was no sign of her. He checked his watch and realised he was going to be late getting home. Jason Zipped up his hoodie and took off home at a fast sprint.

Chapter 10

BY THE TIME Jason arrived home the sun was almost gone and only its faint glow could be seen on the valley horizon. He slowed to a jog as he made his way up the driveway, already dreading the discussion he was sure to have with his mother. Entering the house Jason noted how quiet it was. He expected a cold greeting but not this absolute silence. Eventually he found a note on the kitchen message board. 'Had a last minute emergency, dinner is in the fridge, we will talk when I get home'. Jason sighed wearily.

"What did you expect," he said aloud, as he made his way to the fridge.

After dinner and a shower, he was reading Great Expectations on his bed when he heard the kombi pulling into the driveway. Jason decided not to greet his mother downstairs, instead waiting expectantly for her to appear at his door. Ten minutes later she didn't disappoint, interrupting him with a clearing of her throat.

Helen was standing in Jason's doorway, her arms crossed and looking far from happy.

“You know that man I had to see this morning, well it turns out he’s the Principal of your school, Mr Florentine, lovely man by the way. Well there I was in the middle of delivering a foal when he received a phone call from the school telling him that there had been a major fight”, Helen said calmly. She paced into his room.

“You can imagine my surprise and embarrassment to discover that not only is my son involved, but he’s the catalyst behind the entire thing,” Helen exhaled sharply. Jason tossed the book to one side as he climbed off his bed.

“It wasn’t like that at all, and if you’ll give me a second to explain my side of the story,” Jason pleaded. Helen threw her hands up.

“Two days you’ve been at school. Two days and now this. You promised me,” Helen’s voice trailed off as her eyes began to tear up.

“Mum I’m sorry,” Jason said.

“So am I,” Helen replied, wiping her eyes with the back of her hand, “I’m tired. I suggest we both turn in before we say something we’ll regret.” Jason didn’t respond as Helen turned and walked out.

The following morning he awoke early and quietly let himself out of the house, jogging slowly towards town. Running in the same direction as he had the previous day, he entered Perigords central park, the darkness illuminated by the street lights. After several minutes he picked up his pace, now running at a near sprint, his breathing coming easy as he passed several bronze statues and stopping briefly before each. One was the trunk of a large tree with a young boy and girl tying a ribbon at its base, titled The Disappearance of the Remus Twins. Another, an abnormally tall and gaunt man dressed in a tattered three piece suit and bowler hat, his feet bare and arms outstretched a hideous smile on his lips looking toward the sky titled The Resurrection of Pollux. And finally, a trio of clowns standing under an umbrella, two with their heads bowed and the one to the front holding his hat in his hands, an obvious sad expression on his face, titled The Exile of the Chiodo Brothers. Jason thought the park's creepiness factor was a definite 9.5 out of ten, but it was also kinda cool.

He reached the library and stopped to look up at the building. He noticed a light on, 'That's dedication for you' he thought, before deciding to turn back. He arrived back home, sprinting hard all the way up the drive way, barely breathing hard or sweating as he reached the front door. He entered through the rear of the house into a room he had converted into a home gym. Without stopping for a break he donned his grappling gloves. Selecting a playlist on his iphone, he closed his eyes for a second as the music flowed out. He opened his eyes and adopted a fighter's stance. Facing a suspended punching bag, Jason started striking the bag slowly at first concentrating on his technique, and as the song continued, so too did his intensity. He started throwing elbows and knees into the bag, his footwork was a blur as he moved in and out. His strikes coming hard and fast. Everywhere the bag moved Jason was on it, he never let up, giving the bag everything he had. Growling with anger, he pictured Hector and his friends on the end of every strike.

After thirty minutes he gave the bag a break and discarded his gloves, he started doing burpees. Once he reached fifty he jumped up on to the chin-up bar, keeping his legs straight and raising them horizontally so they were parallel with the ground. He started doing chin ups, holding them in that position throughout. After he got to thirty he dropped off the bar and turned to find his mother watching him, her eyes wide.

"Oh my God. I heard you leave for your run well over an hour ago and I'm pretty certain you haven't taken a break. I could feel the vibrations of your punching all through the house." Concern was evident in Helen's voice.

Jason towelled a light sheen of sweat from his face.

"I didn't mean to wake you, I just needed a quick workout," he replied, grabbing a drink from his sports bottle.

"You're not breathing hard and barely sweating," Helen said, her voice sounding alarmed. "I'd swear you even look bigger. Are you using steroids?" Jason's eyes widened.

"I have one fight and now I'm some roid monster" his voice raised in exasperation.

"It's not just one fight and you know it," she shot back.

"That's not fair , I'm never going to be one of those types that sits back and takes shit, but I don't go looking for it either," he replied, a little angrily.

"I know, and that's why I love you, but it doesn't stop me worrying," Helen said, her voice ragged with emotion. The pair stared at each other, both realising the futility of the argument.

"And just for the record, I'm not doing drugs, I'm just naturally buff," he said light hearted, Helen burst out laughing despite herself, and after a moment she looked at her son tiredly.

"I know in my heart you're not doing drugs, I'm just

concerned. What you just did would be punishing for most people, but you just cruised through it literally without breaking a sweat, promise me you'll be careful and not push yourself too hard."

"You know they gave me two week's detention, so you really don't have to punish me too," Jason said trying his best to look adorable.

"I think a week of cooking dinner will suffice," Helen sighed, then moved over to give her son a hug. Jason kissed her cheek.

"I love you mum," he said warmly.

"I love you, too," Helen replied, then added "Go and clean up, then you can make us both some breakfast."

"For you, anything," Jason replied.

Chapter 11

AS JASON ENTERED the school grounds his infamy had reached legendary proportions. He half expected another day of whispering and pointing. What he received was totally unexpected. Walking by, people said hello, some waved, some smiled, one even patted him on the shoulder. Jason wandered on, a little bewildered by the attention. Reaching the stairs he felt a tap on the shoulder and turned to find Selene standing there dressed in black jeans, union jack T-shirt, combat boots and trench coat. Her make-up was the same as before, except her eyes bore a touch of blue eyeliner.

"Morning bruiser," she said, holding her fists up mockingly with a smile.

"Hey, you were gone pretty quick yesterday," Jason replied, forgetting everything else around him. There was uncertainty in her eyes for a brief second, then replaced with an even bigger smile.

"What can I say, when I can get out of here I'm gone," she replied nonchalantly, making a forward sweeping gesture with her hands.

Selene leaned casually against the stair rail.

"How did things go at home last night?" she asked. Jason sighed.

"What I expected, but it was better this morning," he said thoughtfully. Selene looked at Jason, suddenly serious.

"Did you bring that book in today?"

"Yeah, why?" Jason asked.

"I spoke to my grandmother about it and she's very keen to have a look," Selene said. "That sounds great, but…," Jason started.

"But what?"

"But I have detention this afternoon and I have to cook dinner tonight for mum and I," Jason said. Selene smiled slyly.

"If I can clear your schedule, are we on?" Selene asked, Jason looked sceptical, but shrugged.

"Sure, you bet, but I don't like your chances." Selene's grin took on a devilish quality.

"The impossible is my specialty," Selene stated and without another word, took off.

Jason's day went by without a hitch. The students were friendly and the teachers polite, but they all watched him warily. Lunch time came and Jason was prepared, deciding not to go to the cafeteria both for the food and the unwanted attention, instead opting for a spot under a tree, overlooking the sports oval. Halfway through his tuna salad sandwich, Selene popped down next to him.

"So this is where you've been hiding, I've been looking for you everywhere," she said a little breathlessly. Jason took another bite of his sandwich.

"Yeah I thought I might prefer the fresh air and

seclusion out here," he replied through a mouthful of tuna. Just then a trio of younger girls walked by.

"Hi Jason," one of the girls called out.

"Hello," Jason replied on reflex. The girl who spoke blushed and the other two giggled. All three quickly walked by. Jason appeared to blush a little as well. Selene was clearly enjoying his discomfort.

"So that's the reason you're out here alone, to receive hero worship from young girls who clearly don't know any better," she commented sarcastically. Jason shook his head his blush deepening.

"No, no, of course not," he said in a rush.

"Relax bruiser, I'm just messing with you. Sheesh, you're such a boy scout," Selene said. Jason took another bite of his sandwich, his cheeks still flushed red.

Selene clapped her hands together and rubbed them.

"Anyhoo, the reason I hunted you down was to inform you that it's done," she said, flicking her hands up in the same manner a magician would at the end of performing a trick. Jason raised an eye brow.

"What's done?"

"Well for starters you're not required to attend detention this afternoon," she stated, a satisfied expression appearing on her face. Jason sat up. "Why, what did you do?"

"Well for starters, a thank you would be nice," Selene said.

Jason placed his sandwich down.

"Thank you. Hey it's not like I'm not grateful, but

how the hell did you pull that off?" Selene exhaled, laying on her back, staring up at the sky, her hands behind her head.

"If I didn't know any better, one would think you assumed nefarious intent on my part," Selene said with a sigh.

"My second surprise is both you and your mother are coming over to my grandmother's place for dinner, tonight," Selene said. Jason looked sceptical.

"Hey, I'm all for it, but I have to see if mum's on board with that idea first," Jason replied

"I said it's all sorted," Selene cut in. Jason looked perplexed.

"My grandmother has a lot of pull in Perigord, hence the detention and the fact your mother couldn't refuse an offer to experience the best home cooking in town," Selene said sitting up. "I'll see you tonight," and without another word she was gone. Jason shook his head smiling and continuing with his lunch. He thought to himself she was the pushiest damn girl he had ever met.

The rest of Jason's day went by easily enough; there was no sign of Hector or Tiberius in any of his classes and the other kids were beginning to relax in his presence. During his last period, his English class was interrupted by one of the administration heads. The young woman quietly excused herself, handing Mr Rosenberg a piece of paper and quickly departed. Mr Rosenberg called Jason to his desk, passing the paper on and instructing him to return to his seat, his usual jovial nature replaced with an obvious air of disapproval, aimed squarely at him.

Jason opened the paper it read.

'Mr Page you are exempt from attending detention as from today's date. Report to the library after school and present this letter to Ms Brewster. She will acquit you from her roster'.

Regards,

Leonard Florentine.

Principal.

Perigord High School.

Jason looked around and caught Selene's gaze. She gave him a slight wave with her fingertips and mouthed the words, 'you're welcome'. He folded the note and placed it in his pocket. He wasn't sure how Selene had done it, but he wasn't going to complain. The rest of English went quickly. On two occasions Jason placed his hand in the air to respond to Mr Rosenberg's questions and was clearly ignored, despite being the only volunteer in class. He thought it strange, but shrugged it off. The final bell rang and as Jason packed his bag, Selene sidled up next to him.

"I'll see you tonight." Before he could respond she was gone again. After delivering his note to Ms Brewster at the library, he returned home.

He arrived to find his mother already home. Greeting him in the kitchen, she wore a bemused expression on her face.

"I had an interesting conversation in my surgery today with a lovely old lady, Mrs Jaeger. Her granddaughter, Selene, is your age. She came in just before lunch bearing an apple pie the size of a tractor tyre, stating it was a belated welcome gift". Helen pointed to the kitchen bench where a huge deep dish apple pie was sitting, a sizeable piece missing. Helen smiled sheepishly, 'It was heavenly" she added. Jason reached over to cut himself a slice, Helen slapped his hand.

"I was only going to have a small slice," Jason protested.

"You'll spoil your appetite," Helen scolded. "As I was saying, Mrs Jaeger insisted that you and I attend dinner at her house tonight, and that she wouldn't take no for an answer. She really was quite adamant," Helen added. That must be where Selene gets it from, Jason thought to himself.

"I don't know how she did it, but Mrs Jaeger also got me out of my detention. Selene said she has a lot of pull in town," Jason replied thoughtfully.

"Well you better get stuck into your homework since your afternoon is now free of cooking duties. We're not due there for another two hours." Jason nodded dejectedly as he slowly made his way up stairs. Helen watched him go, then turned her attention to the pie sitting on the bench, a naughty smile appearing on her face.

"One small slice can't hurt," Helen whispered to herself.

Chapter 12

HELEN'S VAN PULLED onto the darkened street. Both Jason and Helen peered out through the window of the kombi. They could see a small Tudor cottage quaintly built with a thatch roof, and a cobblestone path that wound its way from the road to the cottage door. Either side of the path was lit with fairy lights strung up on trees and hedges giving the yard an ethereal glow.

"It's purty," Jason drawled in imitation of a country redneck. Helen gave him a playful elbow in the ribs.

"Behave," Helen replied. Jason placed his right hand over his heart.

"I solemnly swear to uphold the name of Page and not cause undue discomfort toward my mother drearest," he pledged. Helen shook her head with a smile.

"Let's go smartypants".

Jason rang the brass bell which was intricately engraved with images of a mounted hunt. The men on horseback had drawn bows and hounds running to their front. A large stag could be seen in the distance. Jason studied the image of the stag. Strapped to its back was a scabbard containing a sword. He thought to himself that it must be a flaw or mistake on the part of the artist. He was about to say as much to his mother when the front door opened. Jason's eyes went wide. Standing before him was Selene, wearing a beautiful blue dress, stockings and shoes. Her hair was carefully braided, her normally Goth-themed makeup was gone, replaced with a cleanly scrubbed face. Behind Selene stood an old woman, her white hair tied up in a bun. She wore a pale grey dress and black shoes. Selene's grandmother exuded a healthy pallor and a twinkle in her eye that suggested she still had a lot of good years left in her. Selene's smile was wide and friendly, but her brow was slightly creased.

"Don't just stand there, invite them in," the old woman scolded."Forgive me, this is my grandmother, Ursula," Selene said then curtsied. The action was brief and obviously forced and the look on Selene's face was one of embarrassment. Jason couldn't help himself, a smile creeping onto his face.

"Thank you for having us," Jason replied in dramatic prose, then remaining in character he leaned forward and grasped Selene's hand and gently kissed the back of it. Jason peered up from her hand with a devilish grin. Selene's face had gone crimson, her eyes wide in surprise.

"Jason," Helen exclaimed.

"Its fine Helen," Ursula said with a cackle. "I didn't think anyone could make my Selene blush. She must be a little bit sweet on your son." Now it was Jason's turn to blush.

"Now that the young ones are suitably embarrassed, please come in," Ursula invited.

The inside of the house was crammed with assorted German bric-a-brac. Old clocks adorned the walls as well as figurines and steins littering the shelves. The furniture was old and quaint with needle point pillows nestled on the sofas. Jason and Helen walked slowly around marvelling at everything Ursula had to show them, and genuinely interested in the stories each piece held.

"I love your house Ursula," Helen said.

"Why thank you, dear."

"It's exactly what you would think a turn of the century German hamlet would look like," Jason added. Ursula looked about the room with both pride and love.

"Everything you see has been in my family for generations. This will all be Selene's when I'm gone," she said fondly, indicating her granddaughter who looked extremely uncomfortable.

"That won't be for some time yet," Selene replied. Jason noted the change in her demeanour and decided to change the subject.

"I have to admit I'm really looking forward to eating some authentic German cuisine," Jason said.

"Then I hope you brought your appetite young man," Ursula said with a grin as they retired to the dining room.

After Helen and Jason felt positively stuffed, they were sitting opposite each other, both wearing the same expression of fatigue and bloating. Selene and Ursula were out of sight but familiar sounds could be heard eminating from the kitchen. Light beads of sweat had broken out on

Helen's brow as she fidgeted in her chair. Jason leaned forward, careful not to be heard by their hosts.

"That was without a doubt the best and largest meal I have ever eaten in my life," he whispered, Helen feigned mock hurt.

"The best meal you've ever had?" Jason was about to reply but Helen waved him off.

"I'm joking, Ursula is an amazing cook," she said.

"What was that roll with the bacon and onion?"

"Rouladen, what about the Sauerbraten?" Helen said but Jason shook his head, "It was the pot roast with vinegar and seasoning," Helen added.

"I remember now, who would of thought vinegar in pot roast," Jason smiled, then muffled a burp through a closed hand.

"I'll have to get the recipe for that one," Helen said. Just then Selene and Ursula entered the dining room each carrying a plate of dessert. Selene was holding a chocolate layered cake and Ursula was holding a pastry dusted with icing sugar.

"Whoa they look good," Jason said. Ursula looked pleased.

"This is a Viennese apple strudel and Selene has a Donauwellen, a chocolate and vanilla layered cake with sour cherries and cream."

"The Donauwellen is to die for," Selene interjected.

"I think I will," Helen said with a groan.

"Good, you can sample both," Ursula replied with a chuckle. Selene unstacked four small plates as Ursula cut four generous servings of each dessert, serving first Helen and Jason then Selene and herself.

"Its official, I'm not eating anything for at least a month," Helen said taking a sip of her coffee.

"Yeah Mrs Jaeger, you can have us over any time," Jason added.

"You are too kind, these are simple dishes my mother taught me and I have taught Selene. She helped cook tonight as well," Ursula said. Jason and his mother looked impressed.

"I'm afraid that's a dying practice in this day and age," Helen replied.

"I don't know whether it's the young not caring to learn or my generation not having the patience to teach, but I think it's important to pass on our lessons or they will become lost forever," Ursula said plainly.

"I totally agree" Helen said.

"I knew your Uncle, Helen" Ursula said changing the subject suddenly. "You knew Uncle Plato?"

"He was a warm, intelligent man your uncle. We both shared a passion for reading and history, in particular this town's" Ursula said, Helen smiled fondly.

"I remember as a little girl Uncle Plato telling me fairy tales. They were always so vivid and detailed, some were scary, but I didn't care. He always made me feel safe," Helen said. Jason regarded his mother as she divulged this story from her youth.

"When was the last time you saw him?" Ursula asked. Helen looked embarrassed at the question. "It's been years, more than I can count, I'm afraid."

"That's alright, life gets in the way of things. Plato knew this all too well. What was important was the time you had together. He never forgot you, he liked to talk about you after he had received one of your letters," Ursula said. Helen's eyes had darkened at this turn of discussion.

"When Selene told me of Jason's book I remembered sitting in his library having one of many discussions with him. It brought back a lot of good memories. Did you bring it with you, Jason?" Ursula asked. Jason nodded and retrieved the book from his bag.

"Here you are Mrs Jaeger," he said, handing her the book. She studied it, then looked at Jason.

"My eyes are tired tonight, would you mind if I keep it for a little bit? Selene could return it to you later," she offered.

"Of course ma'am, take as much time as you need" Jason replied.

"Grandmother have a look at this pendant Jason found in the book," Selene said quickly.

"Pendant?"

"Oh yeah, this fell out when I first found it. I thought it may have been a book mark, but I decided to wear it," Jason said as he pulled it from the collar of his shirt. Ursula moved quickly from her chair, reaching across the table, her eyes fixed on the silver cross.

"It's beautiful, and looks old like me," she laughed. "Would you mind if I kept it too? I might have some books with information about it," she continued. Before Jason could respond, Selene jumped in.

"No need, I'll take a picture of it instead," Selene said, Ursula nodded with a smile, except her eyes remained narrowed on the pendant around Jason's neck.

Later that night Jason and Helen stood outside the Jaeger front door. They thanked Ursula and Selene for dinner and a wonderful night, before waving farewell. Ursula stood watching long after the van had departed, casting the occasional glance towards the stars. She shivered and threw the scarf she wore around her neck before turning off the lights and closing the front door.

Chapter 13

HELEN WAS DRESSED in grey slacks and a white blouse, heading off for work. She was juggling a mug of coffee, keys, paperwork and a piece of toast clenched between her teeth as she opened the front door. Selene was on the other side, her fist raised ready to knock.

"Whoa, you startled me," Helen said breathlessly.

"Sorry Ms Page," Selene replied.

"Please, call me Helen," she said with a smile.

"Is Jason about?" Selene asked looking over Helen's shoulder.

"I don't think so. Being Saturday morning and the fact that he's nursing one hell of a food hangover, he'll still be in bed," Helen said laughing. "You'll have to thank your grandmother again for me, and next time it's our turn."

"That would be great," Selene replied.

"Listen I hate to be rude but I'm running late for the clinic," Helen said, then yelled out Jason's name. Jason's voice echoed groggily back in response. "He should be down in a minute, help yourself to anything in the kitchen," Helen said as she walked out the door.

Jason sat up in bed his sheets tangled around him, one of which had been ripped. He'd had another weird dream where he had been running through the forest, climbing trees and scaling mountains. The dream had appeared so vivid and real, even his muscles were aching. He rubbed his face and ran his fingers through his hair. He was just about to get up when Selene walked into the room carrying two mugs of steaming coffee. Jason was too shocked to speak as he pulled the sheets across his waist. "Thought you might need a pick me up," Selene said as she handed one of the cups to Jason. He took it sheepishly from her.

"Thanks," he said taking a big sip. Selene sat down on the end of the bed. "I was thinking if you wanted, we could go to the town library and do some research ourselves on the pendant," Selene suggested taking a sip of her coffee.

"Sounds like a good idea," Jason replied a little stiffly, attempted to act casual.

"When you get ready we'll go," Selene said.

"Right," Jason replied, as he hesitantly got up from his bed. It was painfully obvious to Selene that he was embarrassed, dressed only in boxers, he walked over to the other side of the room to retrieve some clothes. Selene was enjoying the view of Jason's muscular physique, her eyes lingered on his upper torso watching his body flex while he dressed. Jason had his back to her and when he finished, Selene turned her head away pretending not to have noticed his dressing and discomfort. Now that he was clothed, Jason was almost acting normal.

"Have you had breakfast yet? If not I can whip us up some eggs," Jason offered.

"That would be nice," Selene replied as they headed downstairs.

After breakfast they walked leisurely through Perigord Park, sharing a comfortable silence, enjoying the beautiful clear day and each other's company. They had just reached the steps to the library when they heard a loud voice call out.

"I thought the library had a no skank policy!" Jason and Selene's heads whipped around to see a small group of teens crowded by a park bench. It was Hector, Tiberius and some of their friends. They were all chuckling.

"What did you say?" Jason growled, taking a step toward the boys. Selene placed a hand on his arm. Jason stopped in his tracks. "I'll ask again, what did you say?"

"You're priceless, you get lucky, that one time and now you think you're the Wolverine," Hector said, his entourage continuing to laugh. Jason took a deep breath.

"I must have given you concussion, because you're making absolutely no sense," Jason said calmly. "But if you want a rematch I'll be glad to oblige you," he said placing his back pack on the ground and gently nudging Selene to the side. Jason advanced on the group with his fists clenched.

Jason closed in on Hector when a voice stopping him in his tracks.

"What's going on here?" It was Hector's father the Sheriff. He strode over to the group of teenagers. He was tall and lean with a square jaw, a boxers pug nose and an ugly slash for a mouth. He was dressed in a tan police uniform, black spit polished shoes and mirrored aviator sunglasses. His face was one that didn't smile much, Jason guessed. Hector and Tiberius smirked at the Sheriff's approach.

"I said what the hell is going on here?" Before Jason could answer, Hector spoke up.

"This is the kid from school dad, he was just...," Sheriff Rope silenced him with a wave of his hand as he regarded Jason.

"So you're the punk that gave my son a touch up," Sheriff Rope said.

"It wasn't like that," Selene said, but Sheriff Rope cut her off with a glare. "That was a rhetorical question, Ms Jaeger," Sheriff Rope said, placing heavy emphasis on her name.

Sheriff Rope stared intently at Jason. "I'm very interested in Mr Page at the moment. I've seen your file. Aggravated assault on numerous occasions, and you've barely been in Perigord a week and you're fighting again," Sheriff Rope said his constant gaze behind the sunglasses was unnerving. Jason met it though, his jaw clenched. He realised no matter what he said, it would be pointless to this man.

"If I had my way you would have been up on charges from the other day, do you understand?" Sheriff Rope said. Menacingly he placed a hand on Jason's shoulder, his grip digging into the muscle.

"A little early in the day for jackboots, isn't it?" Sheriff Rope and Jason turned to see Mr Walker walking purposely down the library steps, dressed the same as when

Jason had first seen him the other day; tweed suit, bow tie, and glasses.

"Mind your business Ulysses, I'm dealing with this," Sheriff Rope replied. "Dealing with what? All I saw was your son and his friends antagonizing the lad here and insulting the young lady," Mr Walker said as he continued down the steps. He nodded at Selene who gave him a grateful smile.

"I said butt out Ulysses, this is police business. Go and read a book or something," Sheriff Rope replied, clearly annoyed at Walker's interference. Walker stopped near the Sheriff who released his hand from Jason, giving the librarian his full attention.

"Go read a book. Ouch, I'm cut by your sharp wit! Maybe if you read more and acted less, you'd realise that the boy hasn't done anything, and your hand on a minor who is not committing a crime or interfering with your duties is a clear violation of his rights, as well as assault," Walker said. Both men were now standing face to face. Sheriff Rope was a couple of inches shorter than Mr Walker and a good fifty pounds lighter as well. "But if you like, I can pull the video footage from the library's CCTV system," Mr Walker said smugly.

"You're an asshole Ulysses," Sheriff Rope whispered, loud enough so that only Walker and Jason could hear.

"You better believe it, and its Mr Walker to you, you ignorant, self- important little man," Walker said. Sheriff Rope's face went ashen. He clenched his fists.

"Hold it right there, before you make the biggest mistake of your career and I embarrass you in front of your kin," Walker said quietly, a smile on his face. Sheriff Rope checked himself then glanced at the front of the library, clearly trying to spot the cameras, then shifting his gaze at Jason.

"Keep your nose clean and stay away from my boy," he growled. He then glared at Hector and his friends.

"All of you get going. I'll see you at home later," he said pointing to his son. Sheriff Rope turned back to Walker.

"This ain't finished," Sheriff Rope growled, turning and walking away.

"You mean, this ISN'T finished, don't you?" Walker called back. Sheriff Rope paused mid stride, then continued on. Hector and his friends were also hastily leaving the area.

"I love a change in my daily routine. Would you two care for some tea?" Walker exclaimed happily. Jason and Selene nodded dumbly back

Chapter 14

SELENE AND JASON sat on matching leather seats in Walker's office; they both looked in awe at their surroundings. The walls were decorated in unusual artefacts African shaman masks, Mayan weapons and a Tibetan prayer cloth. Various swords and pistols could be seen as well as a Conquistador's helmet perched on a timber bust. There were framed photos and art works from Russia, Indonesia and Antarctica, just to name a few. On one side of the room was a large engraved timber shelf, laden with strange sculptures, antique puzzle boxes, jars containing weird looking specimens and a large silver furred monkey paw. Everywhere they looked there was something weird and unusual.

"Can you believe this stuff? Selene whispered.

"It's like the Twilight Zone, Warehouse 13, and The Outer Limits all rolled into one," Jason replied. Just then Walker stepped into the office carrying a silver tray containing a fine china tea set. Placing the tray onto the small table he proceeded to pour the hot beverage into cups. He looked up at Selene and Jason.

“Milk?” They both nodded. Walker delicately poured the milk then handed them their cups.

“Thanks,” they replied in unison. Walker dropped a couple of cubes of sugar into his cup and stirred, finally taking a sip with a sigh. Jason and Selene took their cue and drank also. Walker picked up a shortbread biscuit from the tray and dunked it in his tea before popping the soggy remains into his mouth.

“I love these things,” he said with a grin.

Walker sat back in his chair and regarded both teenagers.

“Well Jason, since I’d seen you last you’ve nearly been expelled for fighting, befriended Ursula Jaeger and made an enemy of the local Sheriff and his son.”

“Two of those things are not my fault,” Jason replied.

“And you’ve also gotten yourself a girlfriend. Well done,” he said, giving Jason a slow clap.

“Selene and I are just friends,” Jason said quickly. Selene glared at Jason before returning her gaze to Walker.

“We both appreciate your help with Sheriff Rope, even though you’re on his radar now too,” Selene said. Walker let out a deep, grumbling laugh.

“Sheriff Rope and I are old acquaintances. He’s like a jackal preying on the weak, but don’t underestimate him just because he’s a bully,” Walker said soberly.

“He was scared of you though,” Jason replied.

“That’s because he knows he’s on a lower pecking order in this jungle.”

“Thanks again Mr Walker for your help and the tea,” Selene said, a little uneasily. “We should get going.” Selene started to get up.

"He called you Ulysses. Is that your name?" Jason asked candidly. Walker regarded Jason for a moment.

"Yes, but only my close friends use it, not just anyone and especially not my employees," Walker stated. Selene sat back down.

"I beg your pardon, you've lost me," Jason replied, confused.

"I thought it pretty straight forward, I'm offering you a job," Walker stated, Selene and Jason stared at each other.

"Why me, why now?"

"Why not?" Walker replied.

"A job? Is this meant to be an interview or something?" Selene said, getting to her feet again. Walker sighed.

"Yes and no, the screening process has been happening for the past couple of days," he said, a note of irritation creeping into his voice.

"Listen, I need a part time worker, grunt work, pay is minimum," Walker said.

"But," Jason replied.

"But, you'll have access to the library whenever is practical and some of its sections that are off limits to the regular public," Walker said.

"You never answered my question. Why me?"

"Like I said, grunt work, minimum wage and it's in a library. Besides it's a prerequisite that you have to have at least a middle school entry reading level for the job. That's something that's lacking around these parts. I did a little bit of poking around and I think you may be suited to the job, plus you're feisty. I like that in a minion. Are you interested?"

"That depends," Jason answered.

"On?" Walker asked.

"On the hours and some of those fringe benefits being extended to Selene here," Jason said, thinking that Walker would say no.

"Your hours would be four to six, Monday to Friday and nine to midday Sunday. I don't have a problem with Selene sharing the benefits of the library, as long as she is accompanied by you," Walker stated.

Jason got to his feet.

"It's a deal," he said, placing his hand out, which Walker took and shook. "Great, you'll start tomorrow. You'll need to report to Ms Jax at the front reception and she will get you started on your orientation. We'll discuss the finer details later. You're free to go, unless you have any other questions?"

"No I'm good," Jason replied. Selene also got up from her chair.

"Thanks for the tea and biscuits," she replied.

"You're welcome. Be sure to thank Ms Jax on your way out. She was the one who baked them after all," Walker said.

Jason and Selene had been wandering the aisles of the library for the past hour and were hopelessly lost within its labyrinth.

"This is impossible. How does anyone find anything here?" Jason said in frustration. Selene nodded in response, looking up and down the aisle.

"I'm not even sure where we are anymore, I swear it's like a maze in here," she replied. Jason was scanning a shelf close by, then shook his head.

"A maze that keeps moving," he growled, the pair rounded a corner only to find Ms Jax carrying a timber crate that was nearly as tall as she was. Jason and Selene were relieved to see her.

"Ms Jax," Jason called out. She turned toward them, placing the crate down effortlessly. When she saw it was Jason and Selene, she smiled that big car grill smile of hers.

"How can I help Mr Page," she asked in a deep, gravelly voice.

"We're having trouble finding a particular book," Selene said.

"Yeah, it's impossible to find anything in here when there are no numbers or index markers on the shelves or books. How do you do it?" Jason enquired. "I know where every book goes," Ms Jax replied simply.

"Every book?" Jason asked sceptically. She nodded.

"Every book," she repeated. Selene gave Ms Jax one of those smiles you give a child who is having trouble grappling with adult concepts.

"How long have you worked here Ms Jax?" She took her time thinking the question over, her attention focused solely on Selene. Jason pushed his toe against the box Ms Jax was carrying and found to his astonishment that he couldn't budge it at all.

"Feels like at least two hundred, no maybe two hundred and fifty years," Ms Jax said with a sigh. Jason and Selene laughed nervously.

"What book would you like to acquire?" Ms Jax asked.

Jason pulled his pendant from out of his shirt.

"I'm trying to find information on this," Jason asked, showing Ms Jax the pendant. She leaned forward, holding it up to the light, studying it intently before releasing it and regarding the pair.

"The books you require can be found two aisles over, down the south end, top shelf," Ms Jax said. Jason and Selene looked relieved at her straight forward answer and directions.

"Thanks," Jason said.

"And thank you for the biscuits as well," Selene added. Ms Jax smiled a big, toothy smile that was both hideous and kind of endearing.

"You're welcome Ms Jaeger. If there is nothing else, I best get this into the store room," Ms Jax replied, hefting the giant box into her arms and continued on.

"Well that was surprisingly helpful," Jason said as he started to make his way in the direction Ms Jax had given them.

"I think she's quite sweet," Selene said. "Love those tribal tattoos."

"Why am I not surprised," Jason said, shaking his head with a smile.

They walked slowly home, Jason's backpack full of books. They were both sipping iced coffees they had purchased along the way.

"I nearly forgot to tell you, but when Ms Jax was giving us directions earlier, I had a quick look at the box she was carrying," Jason said.

"It was bigger than her," Selene said giggling.

"Yeah and heavier as well. I couldn't budge it at all with my foot," Jason added. Selene stopped and regarded him.

"What are you saying?"

“I’m saying that even if that box was empty, it probably weighed as much as you,” he replied.

“That’s weird, maybe she’s a mutant, like the hulk,” Selene commented raising an eyebrow.

“The Hulk’s not a mutant, he was doused in gamma radiation,” Jason said. “But that’s not the point,” he added.

“What is your point?” Selene asked.

“The point is, doesn’t she strike you as a little strange?” Selene shook her head.

“We’ve all got something in us that makes us a bit of a freak. I think that the box may seem a little bit bigger to you in retrospect,” Selene said.

“Maybe,” Jason replied, not really convinced.

“Maybe you feel intimidated by a strong woman?” Selene said, amused.

“Ha ha, really funny,” Jason replied, frowning. “Hey, just too completely change the subject, may I ask you a question?” he said, suddenly serious. Selene casually took a sip of her drink.

“Sure,” she replied happily.

“I’m a little confused. Do you live with your Grandmother? If so, what about your Mum and Dad?” Selene choked on her drink and stopped in her tracks.

“That’s rather personal, don’t you think?” Selene’s cheeks started to redden. Jason looked taken aback.

“Hey I didn’t mean to pry, I was just curious. I mean I know what its like,” he said, now regretting he had decided to open his mouth.

“Really. You do, do you?” Selene’s voice was tinged with anger.

"Hey relax," Jason said calmly before being cut off by Selene.

"Don't tell me to relax!"

"All I meant was, I never knew my father and I know what it's like not to have him around," Jason said. Selene pushed him in the chest, tears beginning to run down her face.

"You're an asshole and you don't know anything," she said shrilly, before turning and running off.

"Selene, wait!" Jason called out.

"Leave me alone," She yelled back. Jason stood and watched her disappear from view.

Chapter 15

JASON LAY ON his bed, his headphones on, listening to Radiohead. A pile of books lay at his side. So far everything he had read had turned up empty. Admittedly his heart wasn't in it tonight, all he could think of was Selene's face, both furious and sad. Jason decided to take a break from his solitude and grab a snack down stairs. He slumped into a recliner clutching a bowl of cereal. His mum was curled up on the couch reading a cheesy romance novel. The TV was on but the volume turned down. Jason was slurping noisily on his cereal unaware his mother had put down her book and was now observing him, a frown creasing her brow. After a moment Helen cleared her throat.

"As much as I enjoy spending time with my favourite son, could you be any louder, it's quite distracting," Helen said slightly annoyed. Jason smiled sheepishly.

"I'm your favourite," he replied. Helen groaned and threw a pillow at him which he easily swatted mid-air.

"If you keep up that noise I may have to reconsider that choice," Helen said with a smirk.

"Harsh but fair," Jason replied.

Just then something caught Jason's eye on the TV.

"Mum, can you turn up the volume?" Helen flipped the remote and the sound came to life. A pretty brunette newsreader was standing outside the Perigord Museum, illuminated by the camera crew and a flashing red light in the distance. The bottom of the screen read, 'Late Breaking News'.

"This is Athena Roberts reporting outside Perigord Museum where local police and security are investigating the break in of one of its exhibits, the works of its Founding Father, Heinrich Perigord. The works are made up of dozens of painted canvases that have been donated by various residents to coincide with Perigord's upcoming Harvest Festival in two weeks' time. As far as sources have confirmed, nothing has been taken, but many of the canvases have been roughly cut from their frames and littered throughout the exhibit".

Just then Sheriff Rope exited the building with one of his deputies, the reporter Athena Roberts trotted over to him in her high heels.

"Sheriff, Sheriff Rope, can you tell us what leads you might have in this destructive crime tonight?" Sheriff Rope put on his best media face but it was clear he was highly uncomfortable in front of the camera.

"At the moment we have no identity into the perpetrators of this crime or their intentions" he said woodenly. Athena nodded.

"Is it true only Heinrich's works were vandalised?"

"Yes at present it appears only his paintings were the target," the Sheriff said.

"Will this impact on the Harvest festival?" Athena added, the Sheriff shook his head. "Absolutely not, now if you'll excuse me Ms Roberts, I have a long night ahead" Sheriff Rope disappeared off camera.

"Well as you can see this has been a dark night in our great town's history. I'm Athena Roberts keeping you informed as events transpire"

Helen switched off the TV.

"Who would have thought it?" Helen said surprised.

"Totally. A population of just over three thousand and they have their own news crew!" Jason replied gob-smacked. Helen threw another pillow at him. This time it connected.

"I meant the vandalism, smart ass," Helen said. Jason tossed the pillow aside.

"It's hardly breaking news," he conceded.

"For a small town it is. Besides, it looks as if the Sheriff has a handle on it," Helen said optimistically.

"He's a dick," Jason muttered to himself, rolling his eyes.

"What was that?" Helen asked.

"Oh nothing," Jason shot back. "Listen, can I get some advice?"

"Sure sweetheart," Helen replied, giving Jason her full attention. He sat up suddenly all serious.

"I had an argument with Selene today," he said regretfully.

"What did you do?"

"I didn't do anything, well at least not intentionally," Jason said as Helen looked on dubiously.

Jason relayed the events of the afternoon, everything

except the run in with the Sheriff and his son; he figured she didn't need to worry, at least not yet anyway. When he was done he stood up and looked at her thoughtfully.

"Well what do you think?" He asked tentatively. Helen sat there a moment mulling it over before responding.

"I think first up you should of minded your own business," Helen said frankly. Jason exhaled sharply. "But I don't think you've done any permanent damage, once she calms down she'll see that too," Helen said. "You think?" Jason asked. Helen nodded.

"You just have to give her time and space, and if she's half the young woman I think she is, she'll come around, you'll see," Helen said gently.

"Thanks mum" Jason replied, leaning over and giving her a kiss on the cheek. "I think I'll turn in now, night," he said, relief now evident on his face.

"Goodnight I'll see you in the morning," Helen said as Jason left the room. Helen returned to her book.

Jason awoke with a start, another bad dream waking him from his slumber. He looked about his room slightly disorientated in the darkness, his breathing hard and fast. Once he realised where he was, he relaxed with a sigh, slumping back to his pillow. He looked across at the night stand. His alarm clock's florescent face flashed 12:03. Jason stared at the ceiling for a while realising two things, sleep wasn't going to happen any time soon and his stomach wasn't going to stop grumbling either.

Jason pushed the fridge door shut with his foot, his arms laden with food. He carefully balanced everything over to the kitchen bench and started preparing an epic sized sandwich. Slicing the leftover meat on the cutting board he heard a banging sound coming from down the hall. Carefully placing the knife down, he suddenly heard further commotion and reconsidered picking the knife back up. He ventured quietly down to investigate the disturbance. Jason stealthily made his way through the dark, the sounds of books being thrown clearly coming from the study. As he approached, he could just make out the muffled voices of at least two individuals and the strafing light of a torch bouncing off the walls.

Jason stopped and propped near the entrance to the study, his eyesight becoming attuned to the darkness. He strained to hear any information he might glean from inside the room, unsure of how many might currently be in the house. He was afraid of others that might do his mum harm. Just then a gruff voice spoke up, one with an accent.

"Goddamn it, that door must be here somewhere." This was followed by a second voice, low and predatory.

"Shut up brother and keep looking." More smashing sounds were made by the dark figures within. Creeping forward he attempted to gain a better view of the situation when one of the floor boards beneath him creaked. Any other time the noise would have been ignored as nothing, but tonight it might as well have been a gunshot, the sound carrying through the house. 'Shit Jason thought', as movement and noise inside the study ceased. He stood flat against the wall, then decided he better act on it.

"I can hear you in there, I'm gunna give you thirty seconds to leave, then I'm gunna take that option from the table," Jason growled. He was starting to shake with fear, hoping like hell they took his threat seriously, afraid of what they might do if they didn't. There was no movement from within the study. "One, two, three," Jason called out and was greeted with silence. "Four, I've called the cops, they are on their way, five, six," Jason was struggling to keep his voice from wavering. He forced himself to take a step forward. "Seven, eight, nine, I'm armed and will use it if I have to," Jason took another step, the silence crystal clear.

"Ten, eleven, twelve, I'm not messing around," Jason took another step, then felt a presence from behind. He whirled around, too late, as a crushing blow clipped him just above his temple. He crumpled to the ground, barely clinging to consciousness. He struggled in the dark to see whom his assailant was, but it was all a blur. Two figures emerged from the study and joined the third standing above Jason.

"It's just a boy," one of the figures said.

"Do you think he called the police?" The other figure let out a low laugh.

"I'm pretty sure the cops aren't coming," he replied.

"Yeah of course," the second figure said.

"Did you find it?" The third figure asked.

"No, there's nothing here," the first figure said.

"Are you sure?" the third asked with full authority.

"Of course, we looked everywhere," the first figure replied quickly.

"Hello. Jason," A voice called from the top of the stairs. All three figures froze. "Jason is that you?" the voice called again, a tinge of fear creeping into it.

"It's the kid's mum," the second figure said.

"Mum, don't come down," Jason called out weakly. The third figure knelt above Jason.

"Tonight's your lucky night kid," the third figure said quietly in what Jason now realised was a Russian accent. The figure raised a small baton then brought it down in one quick movement, knocking him out cold.

Chapter 16

THE FIRST THING Jason thought as he tried unsuccessfully to sit up was, 'My head is going to explode' he closed his eyes and settled back. He felt a hand on his chest.

"Sweetheart, don't try to move, the doctor said you should rest," Helen said quietly. Jason opened his eyes and tried to focus. After several further attempts he could see his mother sitting next to him as he lay in bed, only this wasn't his bed or his room. The pale green walls and white bed sheets could only belong in a hospital.

"What happened?" Jason croaked. Helen's face was pale and her eyes red. "There was an intruder," she said, "and you must have stumbled across him," Helen continued, her voice cracking with emotion. It all started coming back to Jason. The midnight snack, the intruders, the pain, his mum, Jason sat up, wincing at the pain in his head.

"Are you alright?" Jason asked his mum. She smiled and nodded.

"I'm fine," Helen replied, as a nurse walked in.

"Ah you're awake," the nurse commented, making her way to Jason's side. "My name is April. I just need to conduct a couple of quick checks," she said with a smile.

"Do whatever you need to," Helen said quickly. April pulled a small pen light from her pocket.

"Look straight ahead please," she instructed, then took turns shining it into each eye, checking his pupil response.

"Fantastic," April commented. She attached the sphygometer to Jason's arm, checking his blood pressure.

"How are you feeling?" April asked.

"Apart from a splitting headache, good" Jason replied. April readjusted the meter then rechecked his blood pressure.

"Strange," she muttered.

"Is everything okay?" Helen asked looking concerned. April snatched the chart from the end of Jason's bed flipping through previous notes then updating it herself. April turned and faced Helen.

"It's nothing but a simple machine malfunction. Jason's blood pressure is high. I wouldn't be concerned though, I'm sure he's fine, it's just procedure anyway," April said reassuringly. Helen looked relieved.

"The doctor will want to see you both later in the morning, get some rest, the both of you," April smiled, then departed.

Jason slumped back in his bed.

"So how did I get here?" Jason asked. Helen let out a deep breath.

"I heard a commotion downstairs, I tried calling out to you and after a minute I heard running footsteps, then the front door open and slam shut," Helen said, her face ashen as she recalled the events.

"Did you see them?" Jason replied. Helen shook her head.

"Them, no, the Sheriff said there was only one," Helen said.

"What would the Sheriff know?" Jason said, clearly annoyed at the mention of Perigord's chief law enforcer.

"Well after I found you lying there I was hysterical. Before I could even call, the Sheriff arrived, apparently one of our neighbours had heard something and called the police. He was patrolling the area and he saw a figure running across our yard. It was blind luck he had said. On investigation he found us and called for an ambulance, I don't know what I would have done," Helen replied, clearly shaken. Jason attempted to sit up, his cheeks flushed red.

"He's wrong, there were at least three of them, two in the study and the one that knocked me out," Jason replied.

"Honey I don't doubt what you think you saw, but it was dark and you were under stress, not to mention the blow to your head. Any of these things could cloud your judgement," Helen said.

"No," Jason barked, "some things are still pretty clear, for example I could hear them talking," he said heatedly.

"What did they say" Helen asked.

"They were looking for something," Jason said, his brow furrowed.

"What do you think they were looking for sweetheart?" Helen replied perplexed.

"I don't know mum," Jason said, frustration in his voice. Helen rubbed his arm reassuringly.

"Try and get some rest like the nurse suggested," Helen said quietly. Jason sighed and slumped back into his bed.

Helen walked into Jason's room carrying a tray of food.

"Give the books a rest for a while," Helen said. Jason glanced up from the top of his book upon seeing her enter the room.

"Mum I'm feeling fine, really," Jason said, slightly embarrassed by the fuss. Helen neatly placed the tray on his lap.

"The doctor said you should take it easy," she replied, planting a kiss on the top of his head.

"Mum you shouldn't have," Jason drawled as he looked at the feast his mother had laid out before him.

"It's the least I can do for my little hero," Helen said proudly.

"Aw mum," Jason replied blushing. Just then the front doorbell sounded. "Eat up and I'll go see who it is," Helen said as she walked from the room.

Tucking into his lunch, he couldn't believe how hungry he felt. Halfway through his mother reappeared, a huge smile plastered across her face.

"You have a visitor," Helen said. Before he could respond, Selene edged into the room. She stood a little awkwardly at the end of Jason's bed, a coy smile on her face.

"I have to head down stairs, I'll leave you two alone," Helen announced, then departed without another word.

"Hey," Jason said.

"Hey," Selene replied back as she tucked a lock of her hair behind her ear and took a seat on Jason's bed. Jason moved his food tray to the side, and looked long and hard at Selene.

"I'm really sorry for what I said the other day, I had no right to butt in." He was halfway through his apology when Selene started to giggle. He looked confused by her response.

"Did I just say something funny?" he said a little indignant. Selene smiled "No, you just have a milk moustache is all." Jason blushed and wiped his lip with the back of his hand.

"So much for trying to be all cool and heartfelt," Jason said with mock regret.

"You didn't do anything wrong Jason, you touched a nerve and I overreacted. I felt terrible last night, and worse this morning when I heard what had happened," Selene said, exhaling loudly. There was a tangible silence in the room for a few seconds, then Jason cleared his throat.

"So we're good now, right," he asked, Selene laughed and threw her arms around his neck.

"Yes of course you loon," she said. Jason was a little surprised for a moment, then he returned her hug, a huge smile plastered on his face.

Jason and Selene sat at the end of Uncle Plato's huge timber table; a large sprawl of books lay before them.

"So you have no idea what they were looking for?" Selene asked.

"No, whatever it was they seemed adamant that it was in the study," Jason replied.

"Didn't you have a good look in there when you were unpacking?"

"I had a bit of a look, yes. A good look would have taken a month. It's quite big and packed with books," Jason said. Selene pointed to the cross around Jason's neck.

"From what you've already told me finding that cross was a bit of a fluke, but maybe there's other treasures hidden away in there too," Selene stated.

Jason leaned across the table and started to flick through the books, eventually finding the one he sought, holding it up for Selene to see. "Keys an Encyclopaedia, you've lost me,' Selene said puzzled. Jason placed the book down.

"Ms Jax dropped this in with the books we got out yesterday, she knew when she saw my cross," Jason said. Selene's eyes went wide in understanding.

"You think the cross is a key?" Jason touched the tip of his nose.

"Bingo".

Jason and Selene quickly made their way to the study.

"Where do we begin?" Selene asked.

"I have no idea," Jason replied looking around the room.

"Where did you find the cross?" Selene asked. Jason thought for a second then pointed to a section of books on a shelf.

"There, I suppose we have to start somewhere," he replied.

Piles of literature lay upon the ground as Selene and Jason worked tirelessly, removing more books and inspecting the shelves behind. They had been working solid for hours and had only managed a small section of the study, when Helen appeared at the study door. She looked about perplexed.

"What exactly are you two doing?" she asked. Both Jason and Selene stopped and gave Helen a guilty look.

"It's um… well, we…" Jason looked at Selene for help.

"We're doing some research Ms Page," Selene said. Helen looked about then let out a sigh.

"Well that makes it as clear as mud. Look I don't care as long as you clean up after your selves," Helen said.

"We will," Jason and Selene replied in unison. Helen was about to leave when she suddenly remembered something.

"Jason, Mr Walker rang. He was concerned when you hadn't turned up for work today," Helen said. Jason looked alarmed.

"Crap, I forgot all about it!" he exclaimed.

"Its fine, he heard about what had happened here and just wanted to make sure we were both okay," Helen said.

"He also said anytime you're ready, just come in and he would sort out your orientation," she added.

"That's quite considerate of him," Selene said. Jason nodded thoughtfully.

"On a completely different subject, Selene and I are going to be here a while, is there any chance she can stay for dinner?" Helen nodded.

"We're having tacos if that's okay," Helen said.

"Sounds great," Selene replied.

"Good, I'll give Ursula a call and let her know," Helen said.

Jason looked about the room.

"I'm starting to think this was a waste of time," he said with a sigh, Selene sat down on a nearby pile of books.

"You want to give up?" Jason ran his fingers through his hair, frustrated.

"Yes, no, oh I don't know! Obviously this key opens something but it could be anything or anywhere," he replied.

"I think we're close, real close, like the answer is staring us in the face," Selene said her voice trailing off.

"What are you thinking?" Jason asked, but Selene ignored him, deep in thought.

"My Grandmother sometimes says to me when you're faced with a problem you can't solve, view it from a different angle," Selene said, brightening to the idea, Jason looked sceptical.

"Is this where we stand on our heads and use our inner eye or something?" He replied. Selene rolled her eyes.

"Humour me, will you?" Selene asked as she walked over to the entrance to the study. Standing in the doorway she turned and looked back motioning for Jason to join her. He rolled his eyes but did as she requested.

The pair of them were easily able to stand shoulder to shoulder in the doorway with room to spare. Selene was scrutinizing the room while Jason stood in the archway looking bored.

"What exactly are we looking for?" He asked.

"I'm not sure," Selene said. Jason smirked.

"That narrows it down a bit," he muttered.

"If what my Grandmother has told me about your Uncle Plato is correct, I think if he was hiding something he would do it in plain sight," Selene said with mild annoyance.

"Maybe," Jason replied.

"The first time you came here, what was the first thing that caught your eye?" Selene asked, watching his reaction closely. Jason mulled the question over in his mind before responding.

"The first thing I noticed wasn't even technically in the room," Jason said. Selene raised an eyebrow, Jason shrugged his shoulders.

"It was the brass plaque to your left," he said. Selene cocked her head and looked at the plaque bearing the wolf's head engraving recessed into the timber of the door frame.

"I thought it might be a craftsman signature," Jason said. Selene studied the plaque intensely, first running a finger across the image then along the edge itself, attempting to pry it open with a fingernail, with no success.

"It's on their good!" she exclaimed.

"Be careful, those thorns actually look sharp," Jason said as he reached out and touched the engraving, jerking his hand back as he pricked his finger on the indentation.

"Sharp as a razor," he said, sucking on his cut forefinger.

"May I?" Selene interjected. Jason nodded and swept his hand in a grand gesture.

"Knock yourself out," he said. Selene placed her finger upon the wolf head and pressed. Nothing happened. She proceeded to push other parts of the plaque, each time with the same result.

“Maybe,” Selene whispered, then pressed against the thorns.

“Wait, don’t!” Jason said as the plaque made an audible click. They both watched in quiet fascination. Selene released her finger and the plaque swung open, revealing a brass inlaid keyhole.

They both stared, dumbstruck.

“Holy shit!” Jason said.

“Indeed,” Selene replied.

“How did you know?” Jason asked curiously.

“I didn’t, I guessed is all,” she said.

“Really?” Jason said.

“Really. Think about it, sometimes you have to experience a little pain in order to gain knowledge,” she said with a smile.

“You’re pretty pleased with yourself aren’t you?” he replied with a smirk. “Just a bit. Now are we going to try that key or what?” she added.

“You betcha,” Jason nodded with a smile.

Chapter 17

JASON HELD THE key out to Selene.

"Would you like the honour, after all this was your discovery?"

"Why thank you," she said daintily, Jason stepped to the side watching closely as Selene raised the key and carefully inserted it into the brass hole. It slid into place perfectly. She chewed anxiously on her lower lip.

"I can't believe how nervous I feel," she said. Jason nodded in agreement. "I wonder if this is how an archaeologist feels on the dawn of a new discovery?" Jason asked.

"Well I suppose we're not going to find out just standing here," Selene said with finality and turned the key. It moved smoothly in the lock despite its obvious age. Selene removed the key and looked at Jason apprehensively. They waited quietly as the seconds ticked by. Nothing happened.

"Well that was a bust," Jason said, the disappointment thick in his voice.

Selene was just about to reply when a faint clicking sounded from within the wall. This was followed by more mechanical sounds emanating from behind the book shelves. They followed the noise along to the other side of the room. They looked at each other expectantly. The shelf to their front started to edge forward from the wall. The sound of cogs, hydraulics and air escaping was clearly heard. Jason and Selene carefully stepped back, watching as the shelf completely shifted from the wall and came to rest on the brass railing encircling the room with a metallic click. The section of shelf then began to roll along the railing around the room, finishing neatly at the entrance of the study, completely blocking any chance of exit from the room.

Where the shelf had been now stood an entrance into a secret passage, one that was completely obscured by darkness, Jason tentatively stepped forward, followed closely by Selene. Slowly they entered the passageway. Jason groped his way along the wall until his eyes grew accústomed to the dark.

"See if you can find a light switch," Jason instructed. They both felt along the walls clumsily.

"I think I've got it," Jason muttered, barely uttering the words as the room was illuminated.

"Whoa," Selene muttered. They looked around their location. It was easiest the smallest room in the house, narrow but long. Down the far end was a plain timber door. The room was sparsely decorated with only a table and a pair of chairs inside Spartan in their presentation. One wall had been dedicated to all manner of news clippings, photos, drawings, scribbles and other varieties of weird trivia concerning the town of Perigord. Jason's first thought was of a crime drama where the detective has all his information pertaining to a case pinned up for easy recollection.

Both Jason and Selene walked toward the wall. As they moved something shifted underneath. Before either one of them could react the shelf that had revealed the secret chamber rolled back to its original position, subsequently preventing them from leaving. Jason looked at his feet, then up at Selene, sheepishly.

"I think it was a pressure plate, sorry," Jason said.

"Wasn't your fault, besides hopefully that door at the end leads somewhere, preferably out," Selene muttered. They continued to investigate their surroundings. On the other side of the room were shelves containing books and a variety of strange artefacts and items?

"What do you think of all this?" Selene asked puzzled.

"I'm not sure," Jason replied, studying the information on the wall. He tapped a picture roughly, centre of the wall with his index finger.

"See this picture here, it's of Heinrich Perigord," Jason said.

"I am from Perigord you know," Selene replied dryly.

"Well, all these other things clippings, photos and scribbles all have lines drawn toward his picture," Jason explained.

"What, you think they're somehow connected?" Selene asked.

"Exactly," Jason said excitedly. Selene looked at some of the clippings and notes.

"It can't be, look at this one," she motioned for Jason to look. "It's a headline about a missing person dated 1981. That's only thirty two years ago. Heinrich died well over two hundred. One missing person from the early eighties and this town's founding father could hardly have any relevant connection," Selene argued.

Selene left Jason who had started to take pictures of the wall using his cell phone and walked over to the shelves on the opposite side, she began hunting amongst the items laying there, eventually picking up a large brown leather ledger. Flipping through the pages she came upon something of interest.

"Listen to this. Your uncle has marked a passage in this book concerning the harvest festival," Selene said.

"What have you got there?" he asked curiously. Selene held up the ledger and showed the cover to him.

"It just says Perigord and it has that image of the wolf stamped on it," she replied.

"What does it say about the harvest festival?" Jason said, taking a deep breath.

"What doesn't it say about the festival? I mean it goes on and on," she said flipping through its pages for emphasis.

Jason looked at his watch.

"I hate to put a damper on this, but it's nearly dinner time. We better get out of here before mum suspects something's up," Jason said. Selene threw him a look of shock.

"You're telling me that you have no intention of informing your mum about your very own bat cave?" she said in a mocking tone. Jason grimaced. "Kind of. Does that make me a bad son?"

"The worst," Selene nodded. "I think it's time we try that door now," she added.

The door at the far end of the room led down a long

flight of steps and through a narrow passageway. Jason led the way using the light from his phone to illuminate their footing.

"That light would have been useful earlier," Selene commented.

"Hindsight's a great thing, isn't it," Jason replied. They continued on, eventually arriving at a wall with a steel ladder leading up.

"I'm dying to see where this leads out," Selene whispered. The ladder led up a tight square shaft, which was closed at the top. He pushed against the opening and after a few seconds of straining, the cover cracked and light flooded the shaft. Jason scrambled out and then assisted Selene from the hatch. Once clear they looked at their surroundings. They were in a room, about six foot square and three foot high, small windows and a tiny door.

"This is some serious Alice in wonderland shit. Where the hell are we?" Selene questioned. Jason was silent as he looked at the hatch from which they exited.

"I know exactly where we are. It's my tree house," Jason said with a smile.

Selene watched Jason climb carefully down from the outside of the tree house.

"Your house rocks," she stated.

"I've lived in worse, that's for sure," Jason joked as they both dusted themselves off and made their way up towards the house.

"What are you planning on telling your mum?" Selene enquired.

"Nothing yet, until we can piece together exactly what my uncle was up too," he replied.

Helen was in the process of serving dinner when Jason and Selene walked in, the kitchen heavy with the scent of Mexican cuisine.

"I'm famished," Selene whispered to Jason. Helen looked as they entered. "Ah good timing I was just about to call you both for dinner" she remarked, as they all sat down to eat.

"So what exactly have you two been doing all this time?" Helen asked, Jason looked quickly at Selene and then his mum.

"Not much. Selene, and I have been sorting through Uncle Plato's books, that's all," Jason stated, a little too hastily.

Chapter 18

SELENE AND JASON lay on his bed, discussing what they had seen in Plato's hidden chamber. The detailed notes, pictures on the walls concerning cosmic radiation, lunar calendars, chemical analysis, mineral compositions and finally, about the continued existence of Heinrich Perigord.

"I can't believe how complex and in depth your uncle's research was" Selene said in amazement.

"I can't believe my uncle still believed Perigord was alive," Jason replied. "All this complex information, what was he hoping to accomplish?" Selene asked shaking her head.

"I don't know but maybe the answers lay in that journal," Jason added. "By the way how is your grandmother going with the translation of the other book?" he asked.

"It's funny you should bring it up. I asked her about it this morning, hoping I could bring it over with me," Selene said.

"But?"

"But, she was still working on it. She said that not all

of the passages were in German, some were in other dialects as well," she relayed

"Well I'm in no rush," Jason replied.

"Ahem." Both Jason and Selene looked up to find Helen standing in the doorway. "Jason, I think it's time you take Selene, home it's getting late," she stated.

"Good idea, we can finish this at school tomorrow," Selene said.

They walked along the path up toward her house.

"Thank your mum again for dinner," Selene said politely.

"No problem," Jason replied. "I'm going to the library after school, do you want to come with me?" Selene gave him a thousand watt smile.

"You betcha," she replied. They were now standing on her doorstep when the front porch light suddenly flicked on.

"I'm glad you're okay," Selene said earnestly, and then before Jason could respond, she gently kissed him on the cheek.

"Goodnight," Selene whispered and disappeared through the door. Jason stood there a moment, stunned by her actions. The kiss had been warm against his cheek, her hair had brushed against his neck, smelling faintly of vanilla and spices. He closed his eyes and exhaled with a smile, before turning and walking away, a light spring in his step.

As Jason exited from class, Selene snuck up behind and threw her hands around his face covering his eyes.

"Guess who?" she asked. Jason froze in his tracks, a smile appearing under her hands.

"Um, Hector. No wait, Tiberius," he replied deadpan. Selene burst out laughing, releasing her grip and spinning him around.

"Wouldn't that be a funny sight?" she giggled, and after a moment Jason chuckled as well.

"What are you doing for lunch?" she asked. Jason thought it over.

"My usual spot," he replied.

"Good, we can continue with the journal, if you have it on you," Selene said.

"Dammit I left it at home," he said in frustration.

"That's alright, we can do it after school," Selene replied.

"After I dropped you off last night I went back down into Plato's library and tried to piece together the information on the walls."

"Did you come up with anything?" Selene asked, her interest piqued.

"As a matter of fact what I was able to dig up will blow your mind," he said with a grin.

During lunch they sat under a large tree overlooking the school's sports oval, eating sandwiches and pouring over Jason's notes. Selene pointed to a passage he had written down.

"Is this correct? You've written that during the first Hunter's Moon of the new millennium a cosmic event will unfold at the edge of our solar system that will awaken an unstoppable army," Selene stated. "That's some heavy shit. How does he propose it would happen?" Selene queried.

"From what I could surmise, Uncle Plato predicted that a supernova would occur within the next two weeks, it's subsequent radiation playing a pivotal part during a ceremony conducted at that precise moment, allowing that person to raise an unstoppable army," Jason said breathlessly.

"Oh is that all," Selene quipped.

"My big query is how he would know that it would happen during the festival?" Jason said.

"Well this is probably news to you, but here in Perigord everyone knows that the Harvest festival is held every thirteen years during the Hunter's moon," Selene replied matter of fact.

"And what makes this moon so special?" Jason asked.

"Well it's when the sun, moon and earth are all aligned causing a lunar eclipse," Selene said.

"And the moon turns red, how does that work?" Jason asked. Selene thought it over a few seconds.

"We discussed it in class once. It's caused by the suns radiation passing through the earth's atmospheric gases. They are more prevalent this time of year," Selene said.

"And this only occurs every thirteen years, right?" Jason asked, Selene nodded.

"Then maybe the mixture of the sun's radiation and that from the supernova will influence this ceremony my uncle was talking about, creating an army of super soldiers," Jason concluded.

"Do you think we could find out any more info on this ceremony or the supernova?" Selene shrugged.

"I don't know but we are in a school," Selene stated. And without further explanation, Selene grabbed Jason and dragged him off.

Chapter 19

MS GAIA THE science teacher was sitting in her classroom alone and eating her lunch, in-between mouthfuls humming an odd tune. She was just in the process of taking a bite when Jason and Selene burst in.

"Sorry to bother you Miss, are you busy at the moment?" Selene asked sweetly. Ms Gaia smiled back.

"Of course not dear, how can I help?" she replied, putting her lunch to one side.

"Before I ask what was that tune you were humming?" Selene asked, the question was obvious to all, including Ms Gaia a not too subtle tactic to get on her good side.

"A Norwegian folk tune, but that's not the reason that's brought you here Selene," Ms Gaia replied.

"We have a question which maybe only you can answer," Jason replied. Ms Gaia regarded him for a moment.

"Ah, you must be the famous Mr Page everyone is talking about," Ms Gaia stated with a grin. Jason nodded a little bashfully. Selene gave him a playful slap on the shoulder.

"It's him alright," Selene answered cheekily. Ms Gaia got up from her chair and walked around the table toward the pair. Jason noted to himself how quickly and fluidly she moved. Ms Gaia was in her early thirties, 5"4 and very slim. She wore her long dark brown hair in a braid that hung over her left shoulder. As she approached, Jason noticed how fair her skin was. Ms Gaia held out her hand to Jason. At the exact moment when their eyes met, Jason flinched.

"I'm sorry, I just, your eyes!" he stammered. He stared almost hypnotically at the most amazing pair of eyes he had ever seen. They were a vibrant shade of violet and practically glowed. He was completely red with embarrassment. Before he could say another word she gave him a reassuring smile.

"It's okay I get this reaction a lot from first timers. I have a condition known as Alexandria Genesis," Ms Gaia explained.

"I'm so sorry to hear that Ma'am," Jason replied apologetically. Both Ms Gaia and Selene chuckled.

"It's not fatal or anything, doofus," Selene said.

"Oh," Jason replied lamely.

"People with the disorder have fair skin a fast metabolism, no facial or body hair and purple eyes," Ms Gaia said as she pointed to her own.

"You forgot to mention heat vision," Jason replied wistfully. Selene and Ms Gaia looked at each other before bursting out in laughter, followed tentatively by Jason. Ms Gaia pointed a finger at Jason while looking at Selene.

"I like this one," she stated.

"Yeah he's weird but kinda cool," Selene replied.

All three of them sat around Ms Gaia's desk and watched as she continued to eat her lunch.

"So what is this question you want to ask Selene?" Ms Gaia said through a mouthful of food.

"It's nothing big. We just wanted to know if there was a supernova set to occur within our solar system anytime soon?" Jason asked. Ms Gaia looked at them both, a quizzical expression on her face.

"First up, is this a school thing and if so, why don't I know anything about it; and secondly, as a matter of fact yes, yes there is," she said curiously.

"It's not for school, just general interest," Selene replied.

"Yeah we heard about it and wanted to know more," Jason interjected. "Wait just a second," Ms Gaia instructed hopping up from her chair and walking briskly across the room to a locked cupboard. After a minute of fumbling with the lock she rummaged through the cupboard's contents, as they waited Jason took a look around the classroom, littering the walls were flyers for various eco charities and posters depicting warnings about climate change and pollution concerns, Jason thought to himself that she must be some hard core hippie. Ms Gaia returned with a long cardboard cylinder under her arm.

"What's that?" Jason asked as Ms Gaia sat back down in her chair and removed the cylinders contents, unrolled a large celestial map onto the table.

"Look here," Ms Gaia said pointing to a spot on the map. "This star is known as Sirius, or the dog star. These other two smaller stars are its companions, Sirius B and Sirius C, also known as the pups," she explained.

"Look how far they are from the earth!" Jason commented.

"They're about eight point six light years from the earth" Ms Gaia replied,

"I don't know what that is but it sounds impressive," Jason replied. Ms Gaia leaned back in her chair.

"Well one of the pups, Sirius C, went in to Supernova about eight and a half years ago, its light will reach us in about two weeks," Ms Gaia concluded.

"I've heard that a supernova transmits radiation, is it harmful to us?" Selene enquired,

"The residual radiation that will pass the earth is completely harmless to life on earth," Ms Gaia replied.

"Well that's a relief," Jason said.

"Not that I'm complaining about helping a student on this subject, but I am puzzled about the origin of your interest," Ms Gaia said, Both Selene and Jason looked at each other, then at Ms Gaia.

"Just curious is all. Thanks for your help but we better get going" Selene said quickly, then dragging Jason, they departed, not wanting to arouse any more suspicion.

Both Selene and Jason walked quickly down the corridor.

"That was a bit rude," Jason said.

"Sorry, she was asking too many questions and to be quite frank I'm enjoying this whole secrecy thing," Selene replied with a wry smile. "Women, who can understand them?" Jason muttered to himself. Just then the bell rang. "Better get to class, I'll meet you after school," Jason said taking off down the corridor, leaving Selene to find her own way to class.

The final bell rang signalling the end of school. Selene was waiting for Jason at the front gates, leaning casually against one of its stone pillars, twirling a lock of her hair with one hand and wearing a bored expression on her face. She instantly brightened when she saw him amidst the throng of other students eagerly departing their daily grind.

"About time," Selene said pushing away from the pillar with one foot. Jason walked briskly toward her.

"I got here as soon as I could," Jason remarked a little testily.

"Relax, I just thought you'd be in a hurry for your first day on the job," she said sweetly.

They made their way down the staircase toward the library's front reception desk. Selene grabbed his hand and gave it a gentle squeeze. "You'll be right," she said sensing his trepidation.

"Thanks," he said and squeezed her hand back. "I'm going to need it," he muttered.

"I'll be around if you need me," Selene said, leaving Jason to wait alone. Ms Jax had her back to Jason as he patiently waited for her to finish loading returned books onto a push cart. Once finished, she turned and regarded him for a moment, her face a stony mask of neutrality.

"It's good to see you up and about Mr Page," she said in her gravelly voice. "Thank you" Jason said. "Oh and please call me Jason".

Ms Jax smiled her big toothy smile.

"How is your mother?" Ms Jax enquired.

"She's good," Jason said.

"Mr Walker and I were concerned when we heard about your unwanted visitor, but now you're here and well, which is good," Ms Jax stated plainly. Jason returned her smile.

"Yeah, um, where do you want me to start?" Jason asked eagerly. Ms Jax bent down behind the desk and produced a broom, brush, and dustpan.

"At the top," she said, pointing to the top of the staircase. Jason followed her gaze up to the entrance way, mentally counting the stairs in his head, losing count somewhere around the two hundred mark. His smile faltered as he inwardly groaned.

"Great, let me at it," Jason said. Taking the cleaning tools from Ms Jax, he trudging his way up the staircase.

He had been sweeping solidly for an hour when he finally reached the bottom. Grabbing his cleaning equipment he took a final look at his handy work before making his way back to the desk. When he returned, Ms Jax gave him furniture polish, cleaning cloths and a ladder, instructing him to start in the north wing cleaning shelves. Jason grimaced but went off without a word of complaint.

Stopping at the first shelf he came to Jason unfolded the ladder. Removing the books from the top shelf he commenced by wiping the shelf free of dust, then using the polish he buffed the shelf to a high shine before replacing the books. He continued on like this for several hours working steady and methodically. Jason had just finished replacing the books on one of the shelves when he heard a set of footsteps from behind. He turned to see Ms Jax approaching.

"You work well, I think you can call it a day," she said regarding his handy work.

"Thanks, I'll just grab Selene and head home," Jason replied as he dusted his hands on his pants.

"She's already gone. I told her not to wait as I knew you would be a while. I hope I didn't overstep my authority," Ms Jax said.

"No, no, of course not, I'm glad she didn't wait around for me," Jason said. "Good, then I'll see you again Wednesday, same time," Ms Jax instructed, flashing her toothy smile.

Arriving home stiff and sore he was half regretting his decision in accepting his job. As he entered the kitchen, his mother gave him a sympathetic smile as she laid his meal on the table.

"You poor dear, Selene stopped by on her way home and said you might be a bit tired," Helen said. Jason nodded wearily.

"Yeah, I think they're getting their pound of flesh from me," he replied. Helen patted the seat by the table.

"Well, have something to eat and you can tell me all about it," Helen commiserated. During their meal Jason explained the ordeals he had faced at work while Helen patiently listened to her son's detailed descriptions of his first day; knowing only too well what long hours and hard physical labour was all about.

After dinner Jason went up into his room, showered and completed his homework. Despite his busy day he no longer felt tired but actually quite energised. He decided to continue with his detective work. Having been through the books on Heinrich Perigord, most of them said the same things. Not much was known of his early childhood, he had multiple wives and his church had been persecuted in the major cities. But the information he really sought concerning the harvest festival eluded him. Jason decided to gather some more information from his uncle's journal, but upon further investigation he couldn't locate it amongst the large pile of books amassed on his bed.

"Where the hell could it be?" he muttered to himself as he turned his room upside down without any luck.

He eventually gave up on his search and collapsed on his bed in frustration. Looking at the pile of books still sitting there, he carefully tossed them onto the floor when he noticed the book on the secrets of the SS and its inner circle. He shrugged and picked it up. The book had detailed chapters on the Unit's politics, its high ranking officers and the part the Unit played during World War II. One of the chapters that caught his eye concerned the medical experimentation of prisoners within the camps. Jason had heard the horror stories about the Third Reich. The chapter detailed the events from camps such as Auschwitz and Mauthausen where inmates were subjected to various experiments designed to help the military in combat situations, create new weapons and aid in the recovery of military personnel that had been injured. More often than not, these scientists just conducted experimentation on the innocent for their own perverse reasons.

As Jason read through it there was a sub-chapter on Hitler's super soldiers which told of the Fuhrer's obsession with the perfect Arian subject. There was a picture of one of the scientists that was leading the research into creating his perfect warriors, a middle aged officer dressed in a SS ceremonial uniform. Beneath the picture it read Colonel Heinrich Perigord. Jason did a double take.

"What the hell, it couldn't be," Jason whispered, but there was no mistaking the face and those piercing eyes. "Sonofabitch!" Jason grabbed one of the other books from the floor and flicked through it until he found what he was looking for, a picture of Perigord's founding father, Heinrich Perigord. Jason placed the pictures from both books side by side. Apart from some grooming differences it was definitely the same man, including the three inch scar running vertically down from the right eye. Two pictures of the same man separated by a hundred and twenty years and he hadn't aged a day. Jason couldn't believe what he was seeing but the evidence was right in front of him. He marked each page in the books and slipped them into his school bag. 'Wait till Selene see's this,' Jason thought as he turned off the light. Thoughts of Heinrich stayed with him until sleep came.

Selene was sitting in their usual lunch time spot on the grass overlooking the oval, casually eating when Jason arrived.

"Hey, where have you been?" Selene asked.

"Got held up with an assignment. Why, did you miss me?" Jason replied, batting his eyes daintily.

"No," Selene said coyly. "I'm just keeping an eye out for you is all".

"You won't believe what I discovered last night," Jason said changing the subject. He placed the book about Heinrich Perigord on the grass beside her. It was opened displaying a clear image of the man.

"Take a look at that," Jason said. Selene peered down and studied the photo, then turned back to Jason.

"It's Perigord, so what?" She replied, nonplussed. Without saying a word Jason placed another book down next to it and pointed to the picture of Perigord the Nazi scientist. Again she glanced at the picture, then at Jason. "You've lost me," Selene said again. Jason smiled patiently.

"Look at the pictures closely, then look at the dates," he replied. He watched as Selene studied the books, her gaze going from one then to the other. After a couple of seconds, realisation dawned on her. Again Jason smiled at her reaction.

"This can't be right," Selene whispered.

"Oh it is," Jason replied, "Somehow, Heinrich Perigord, priest and pioneer settler, was also a scientist working for Adolph Hitler." Selene was speechless. "Doesn't it just blow your mind?" Jason said with a grin.

Chapter 20

SELENE AND JASON sat hunched over a pile of books at the Perigord Town Library reviewing what they had discovered so far.

"It has to be some kind of mistake, I mean, come on it has to be a fake," Selene said. Jason shook his head.

"I know it's not, this book is over thirty years old," Jason replied. Selene gave him a blank look. "It might be common place nowadays to photo shop a picture, but thirty years ago not such an easy feat," Jason added. Selene didn't look too convinced.

"It wouldn't be easy, but not impossible," Selene said sceptically.

"But why go to the trouble?" Jason interjected.

"Who knows, but if it's legit, it raises more questions than answers," Selene said solemnly.

Jason mulled over Selene's question.

"The first thing that comes to mind apart from the obvious, is does this have anything to do with the upcoming Harvest Festival?" Jason queried.

"That's a big leap," Selene questioned. Jason sighed but continued.

"Not really, think about it. From what we've learned so far about the Nazis' quest to produce the perfect race and the prophecy concerning the raising of a super Army, in the middle we have this scientist that can't die," he said.

"Hey, we don't know that for certain," Selene replied.

"But what if he isn't dead? What if he's still alive and here in Perigord?" Jason replied with finality. Selene looked at Jason with concern.

"We have to get to the bottom of this, we need to study your Uncle's journal," she said urgently, then noticed his agitation. "What's the matter?"

"I don't know where it is," Jason said.

"You don't know, or you're not sure?" Selene urged gently.

"I honestly don't know, I could have sworn I placed it in my room," he said. But?" Selene interrupted.

"But I've looked everywhere. It's like it just vanished," Jason said, clearly upset. Selene gave him a consoling look.

"Don't worry I'm sure it'll turn up, but in the meantime we need to find the information through other means," Selene said.

"And how do we do that?"

"Well for starters we need more information on the ceremony, what exactly is needed and where it needs to be conducted," Selene said. Jason thought for a minute before answering.

"Has anything strange happened here in in the past couple of months?" Jason asked. Selene shrugged.

"I don't know, I have to admit that I don't really take

that much notice about the day to day events that happen here," Selene said truthfully. "But I'm sure if we checked through the town's old newspapers we might find exactly what you're looking for, whatever that may be".

"I'm not sure, anything out of the ordinary, something not explained, weird, strange, who knows?" Jason said perplexed.

"Let's go see Ms Jax, I'm sure the library keeps a hold of all the old newspapers," Selene suggested. And without another word they took off in search of the assistant librarian.

Jason and Selene found Ms Jax in one of the aisles in the west wing of the library unloading her book cart. She greeted them warmly when she saw them approach.

"How can I help?" Ms Jax asked.

"I was wondering do we keep copies Perigord's old newspapers, and if so could we get access to them?" Selene replied.

"Yes we do, and yes you can. Here take this," Ms Jax said as she removed a large metal key from a ring on her belt and handed it to Jason "Down the end of the east wing you'll find a door. Inside is a storage area. The shelves on the left hand side have the old papers. Good luck with your investigation," she said.

"Thanks Ms Jax," Jason replied as they turned to leave.

"Wait-how did you know we...," Selene hadn't finished her sentence when she turned back only to find the enigmatic librarian gone. Selene's eyes went wide.

"Where the hell did she go?" she asked. Jason shrugged.

"I'm actually starting to get used to that," Jason said as he grabbed Selene by the arm and led her away.

The door had a brass number one inlaid upon it and Jason slid the key into the lock and turned the handle. Darkness greeted them as Jason fumbled for the switch. Light flooded the area as they both let out a gasp. They stood on a steel catwalk staring down at an area the size of a football field.

"How can they have something so big in here?" Selene said shocked.

"And if this is door number one, how many others are there, and are they all as big as this?" Jason replied.

"Impossible, right?" Selene said dubiously.

"That's a question for another day. Right now we have some papers to track down," Jason said. Selene looked around and pointed to the left.

"I think we should start there," she said.

Jason and Selene were sitting on the floor with three opened boxes and piles of old newspapers before them.

"I feel like we're in that warehouse at the end of 'Raiders of the Lost Ark'. I wonder what else they have in here?" Selene said. Jason looked up from the paper he was reading.

"Yeah it does have that feeling to it. Hey, you do realise we can come here whenever we want?" he said as Selene grabbed another paper.

"We are definitely going to have some fun in here," she replied and Jason blushed thinking of something else entirely.

"Hey I remember this," Selene exclaimed pointing to the front page of her paper. It was an article on kids using dynamite at the quarry. "Yeah some kids were setting off explosions there. They did some minor damage to one of the shafts. The police never found out who did it," Selene said matter of fact.

"I think we can put that on the weird and strange pile," Jason replied.

After a couple of hours of trolling through the newspapers Jason and Selene had amassed a decent pile of articles.

"I think that's about it. What have we got in total?" Selene asked. Jason started to flip through the articles.

"Let's see, we have missing pets, the vandalism of the Perigord art exhibit, the quarry explosions, the school's missing sceptre, a drop in numbers of spawning trout, and of course the Harvest Festival. Have I forgotten anything?" Jason said.

"You forgot the disappearance of your uncle," Selene replied. Jason raised an eyebrow.

"Missing? He's dead," Jason queried.

"Well, he's assumed dead but the reality is they never found the body. He went hiking in the hills and was never seen again," Selene said. Jason looked quite shocked by this revelation. "You didn't know?" Selene questioned.

"I never knew the man. Mum didn't say and I didn't ask. He was an old man, I just thought it was a natural death," Jason said with a shrug, then added, "How do you know so much anyway".

"Your uncle was kind of a big deal in this town. He was well travelled and educated, he raised money for local charities and probably best known to any kid in this town for being the second weirdest man in it," Selene said. "Oh yeah, who's the weirdest?" Jason asked.

"That's easy, your new boss," Selene replied.

Jason walked in through the front door of the veterinary surgery and up to the reception desk. Seated behind the desk sat an older woman in her late fifties, pleasant faced with grey hair, dressed neatly. Her name tag read Andraste. She was talking to someone on the phone as Jason approached. He waited patiently until she had finished with her call.

"How can I help you young man?" Andraste asked politely. Jason smiled back.

"I'm here to see my mum, Mrs Page," Jason replied.

"Oh you're the special man in her life," Andraste said, offering her hand to Jason.

"Pleased to meet you ma'am," Jason replied.

"Such manners. Your mum talks about you all the time," Andraste replied. Jason blushed. "And for once I think the doting mother wasn't exaggerating. I'll let Helen know you're here," she added.

Helen was in her office typing away on her computer when Jason strolled in.

"Hey hun be with you in a second," Helen said without looking up. Jason grabbed a seat behind her and waited. After a minute of clacking keys Helen spun in her swivel chair and faced her son.

"Sorry to keep you waiting," Helen said happily, her smile fading when she noticed Jason's serious demeanour. "What's up?" she asked.

"Is it true that Uncle Plato's not dead?" Jason blurted out. Helen looked stunned at his statement.

"Well honey, he was presumed deceased after being missing for two months. All the search parties could find was his backpack and jacket, both were bloody and torn up," Helen said.

"But there could still be a chance he's alive? I mean they didn't find a body?" Helen put a reassuring hand on his leg.

"Jason he was an old man stuck out in the elements. The chances that he's still alive are nearly impossible. What's this all about, really?" Helen said. Jason shook his head.

"I don't know, after living in his house I kinda feel connected to him. When Selene showed me the article in the paper, I felt, I don't know, I felt like we're freeloading, using his stuff, and that we're glad he's gone so we can live in his wonderful house. But I promise I honestly feel terrible for Uncle Plato, and I'd be happy for him to still be alive, even if it meant that we'd be out on the street," Jason replied, struggling to find the words.

Helen looked at her son with admiration

"I'm so proud of you. If I thought for a second there was maybe a sliver of hope that Uncle Plato was alive, I'd be out there looking myself," Helen said calmly. "Between your assault, your training, a new school, job, and girl," Helen said.

"Mum," Jason said, looking embarrassed. "All I'm saying is, don't put yourself under any unnecessary stress," Helen added. Jason nodded. "Was there anything else" Helen asked. "No, that was about it," Jason replied. "Good, because I'm kind of swamped. I hate to shoo you off, but…," Helen was cut off mid-sentence. "Consider myself shooed," Jason replied.

Chapter 21

JASON WAS AT work cleaning shelves when Selene snuck up and pinched him from behind. He jumped with surprise.

"Hey you," Jason said his manly feelings hurt.

"Hey yourself," Selene replied. She eyed the pile of books on the ground and the empty shelves. "I see they still have you on cleaning detail," she added.

"Yeah, I guess I'm still a probationary till I prove myself," Jason said.

"Have you come to watch me in action, or have you an ulterior motive?" "As much as the idea of watching you slave for the man has merit, I was thinking we jump start the mystery machine and crack this case," Selene said enthusiastically. "Crack this case," Jason said, poorly imitating Scooby Doo. Selene shook her head. "And I know exactly where we should start. Remember the article on the art exhibit?" Jason nodded as he continued to wipe the book shelves down. "Yeah I remember

"Well it reminded me of something I saw on the

discovery channel about texts and writings sometimes being on the back of old paintings," Selene noted.

"And you think that may be the case here?" Jason said, his interest piqued. "Just like you're uncle. What better way to hide something than in plain sight?"

"Yeah by all accounts that would be Perigord's style, arrogant all the way. However that doesn't help us. All his paintings were cut out, but not taken. Any ideas?" Jason said.

"Obviously those from the exhibit weren't the ones because none were missing, now if we knew of any other ones in the area then we might have a break in the case," Selene replied gloomily, Jason gave her a rueful smile.

"I just might be able to help you there," he said.

Selene and Jason were sitting in the library's staff room. It was small and quaint with antique timber and leather furniture. The kitchen was granite and stone, simple, but elegant.

"Don't keep me waiting any longer, where is this other painting?" Selene asked forcefully.

"It was the day I first arrived at Black River Realty. Ms Appleby had one on display in her sitting room," Jason replied.

"I doubt she'll just give it to us and allow us to inspect the back of the canvas," Selene said.

"You never know," Jason said thoughtfully.

"Fat chance of that," Selene replied.

"Then we'll just have to liberate it," Jason said.

"You can't be serious!" Selene shot back, she saw the resolute set of his jaw. "You are! You're suggesting we break in and steal it?"

"Yes and no. Maybe we don't have to take it. We are living in the technology age after all" Jason replied.

"I'm not a big fan of technology myself," Mr Walker said.

Jason and Selene spun in their seats to find Mr Walker at the kitchen area making himself a cup of tea.

"Where did you come from?" Jason asked. Mr Walker smiled as he stirred his tea.

"Through the door." He pointed to the plain timber door off to the side of the room. Selene and Jason did a double take.

"I could have sworn that door wasn't there before," Selene muttered. Mr Walker laughed.

"It must be, because I just walked through it," he replied nonchalantly.

"I hope you don't mind I'm taking a break," Jason asked.

"Of course not, you've been doing a stellar job, Ms Jax is very impressed," Mr Walker replied, taking another sip of his tea.

"Yeah what's the go with her? I watched her hulk out the other day," Selene commented. Mr Walker slurped his tea, but regained his composure immediately.

"Hulk out? I'm not familiar with the term," Mr Walker quizzed.

"She was hefting a box the other day with ease that Jason couldn't budge at all," Selene asked.

"Ms Jax was a power lifter in her youth and as you've seen, she's still quite strong," Mr Walker interjected with a smile. "So what have you two been doing?" Mr Walker added, changing the subject quickly. Both Jason and

Selene were stricken with the knowledge that they didn't know exactly how long Mr Walker had been in the room as they were hatching their plan.

"Nothing much," they replied in unison. Mr Walker watched them oddly as he finished his tea.

"Oh well, I better get back to work. You kids have fun," he said before disappearing through the small timber door.

"What an unusual man," Selene commented, then turning her attention back to Jason, "So tell me more about this idea of yours," she asked.

Jason and Selene walked down Perigord Main Street carrying a gift wrapped basket.

"What did you say to your mum?" Selene asked.

"I didn't have to sell her the idea, she was keen straight away," Jason replied.

"So we go in, get a conversation going, create a diversion," Selene said.

"And then case the joint," Jason replied.

"Case the joint, what are you, a 1920s gangster?" she said.

"Stick with me doll face," Jason attempted a poor James Cagney impression. Selene laughed out loud.

"What the hell was that supposed to be?" she said.

"Er, nothing," Jason replied embarrassed as they continued on.

The door to Black River Realty opened and a harried looking Mrs Appleby peered up from the reception desk to see Jason and Selene walk in.

"Well, hello Jason, so good to see you, and who's your friend?" Mrs Appleby asked.

"This is Selene," Jason introduced.

"Pleased to meet you Selene. Do I know your mum?" Mrs Appleby asked.

"You probably know my grandmother, Ms Jaeger," Selene replied. Mrs Appleby smiled immediately.

"Of course I see it now, you have her eyes. How is she dear?" Mrs Appleby enquired.

"Great! Sharp as a whip and twice as lethal," Selene replied.

"That's definitely her alright," Mrs Appleby said with a laugh. Jason stepped forward and placed the basket he had been carrying on her desk.

"What's this?" Mrs Appleby asked curiously, her eyes eagerly taking in the assortment of goodies on display.

"Oh how kind," she beamed.

"Just a small gesture from Mum and I," he replied.

Mrs Appleby gave out a little squeal of delight as she tore into the basket which had mixed gourmet items from cheese and pâté to chocolate and biscuits sitting on top of it was a can of diet soft drink.

"You and your mum are such sweethearts," Mrs Appleby said, holding the can of soda. She cracked the top and foaming liquid erupted over her.

"Oh no, my blouse," she cried, juggling the can and racing into the back room.

"Don't worry, we'll clean up out here," Selene called out. Without waiting they both ran over to Perigord's painting and attempted to move it from the wall. It wouldn't budge.

"Shit, it won't move, it's been screwed to the wall," Jason grunted.

"What now?" Selene asked.

"I'll have to find a way in for later. Can you clean and distract?" Jason instructed.

"Leave it to me," Selene nodded and went about wiping the spill with paper towelling. "Mrs Appleby do you need any help?" Selene called out.

"I'm fine dear, I'll be out in a minute," Mrs Appleby replied. Selene looked around at Jason who was frantically scouring the office windows and doors. Their eyes met and Jason shook his head.

"No luck. This place is locked up tighter than a drum," Jason whispered. The sound of running water could be heard from the rear office.

"As soon as that water stops we're done," Selene whispered, Jason nodded. Running his hands through his hair, he looked up and froze, a smile spreading across his face. Located directly above Jason, recessed into the high ceiling was a pull out folding ladder leading up to a skylight. Jason pointed up.

"I need to get up there, any ideas?" he asked. Selene thought for a moment.

"A hook. She would have to have a tool to pull the ladder down," Selene replied as she looked behind the desk, then rummaging through the drawers. Just then the sound of running water stopped. Both Selene and Jason froze for what seemed an eternity, then the sound of a hair dryer started up. They both let out a collective breath. Selene continued to look through the desk drawers. She let out a little squeak of excitement. Jason turned to find Selene holding a short rod with a hook attached triumphantly above her head. "I don't think that'll reach," Jason said as

Selene pulled on either end of the rod. It slid open nearly tripling in length.

"No but this should do," Selene whispered sarcastically. Jason bit his tongue and instead grabbed the rod from her and used it to pull the ladder down. Quickly scaling the ladder he climbed up to the skylight, however once there the latch refused to move.

"Crap, it won't budge," Jason muttered.

"Keep trying, it probably hasn't been opened for quite a while," Selene said. Jason was struggling, when he felt a hot sensation course through him. "Hurry," Selene coaxed. Suddenly the hair dryer stopped. Both Selene's and Jason's eyes went wide.

"Come on you little," Jason whispered through gritted teeth. The latch creaked and slowly turned in his grip. They could hear sounds of movement from the rear. Jason leapt from the ladder landing quietly like a cat, something Selene noted with a frown. He tucked the ladder back up and threw the hook to Selene, who tucked it away, racing back to Jason's side just as Mrs Appleby returned.

"I'm sorry about the mess," Jason said apologetically. Mrs Appleby waved it off.

"Please, accidents happen, besides nothing was damaged or hurt."

"Well we better get going," Jason said.

"Please, thank your mum for the basket," Mrs Appleby replied sincerely.

"No worries, bye," Jason said hurriedly, wanting to get out.

"And a pleasure to meet you as well Selene. Say hello to Ursula for me." The pair practically fled from her office. Selene glanced back, her face a mixture of regret and worry.

"I love the excitement, but I feel guilty as hell for doing this to such a nice lady," she said.

"Me too, but if all goes well, no one will be any the wiser," Jason replied.

"Yeah, if all goes well," Selene sighed.

Chapter 22

JASON LAY ON his bed his homework was sprawled around him, listening to music on his headphones when Helen walked in.

"Jason," Helen said, then after receiving no response, tapped him gently on the foot. Jason sat up with a start, pulling his headphones off.

"Whoa you startled me,"

"Sorry honey, but I'm not surprised though, what with that music blaring," Helen queried.

"You get used to it, what's up?" Jason asked.

"I'm just letting you know that I'm turning in now, I have an early start tomorrow," Helen said.

"That's cool I've got this homework I need to hammer through. I'll try to keep the noise to a minimum," he said.

"Thanks luv, night," Helen replied.

"Night mum," Jason said, watching her leave, listening as her footfalls disappeared down the hall. As soon as he was sure she had turned in, he jumped up from his bed and locked his door. Quickly changing into a dark t-shirt and jeans, he had just finished dressing when

Selene climbed in through the window. She was dressed in a heavy black jacket and back pack.

"Have we got a green light?" Selene enquired as she took a seat on his bed. Jason gave her the thumbs up.

"We're good to go, Mum's turned in early. She thinks I'm doing my homework."

"Aw, aren't you a good widdle boy." Selene coddled.

"Steady on, what excuse did you give?" Jason asked.

"I'm my own woman, a lone she wolf, I make my own rules," Selene stated triumphantly.

"Whatever. What's in the backpack?"

"Have you ever heard of the seven Ps?"

"Can't say that I have," Jason said shaking his head. Selene held up her hands and counted them off on her fingers.

"Prior preparation and planning prevents a piss poor performance," Selene said tapping her back pack "this is my seven Ps"

"Well since you're done bragging, how about we get this show on the road?" Jason said.

They quietly left through the window and climbed down the side gabling, then made their way through town. Sticking to the shadows, carefully avoiding the few people who were out walking dogs or returning home from work. They cut through Perigord Park hoping it would be deserted. It was, except for a group of teenagers who were congregated by a fountain drinking and laughing. Jason led Selene around them using the trees as cover. Luckily the teens were too caught up in themselves to notice the shadowy figures slip past.

"That was easy," Selene whispered as they crouched at

the edge of the tree-line directly across the road from the Realty. The stretch of offices was well lit by street lights.

"Any ideas?" Jason asked.

"I have one," Selene replied. Selene pointed to an area near their position, obscured by a park bench and bushes.

"There's a storm drain there that intersects under most of the town," Selene said. Jason looked dubious

"One of the tunnels comes up behind those offices," she stated.

"Are they big enough to fit us?" Jason asked.

"It'll be tight but yes, we'll fit, I used to do a little exploring when I was younger, so relax, we'll be fine" Selene said putting a reassuring hand on his, then snatching it back.

"Shit, you're hot," Selene said.

"I know," Jason said with a grin. She placed a hand on his forehead.

"No, Your burning up," Selene said looking worried. Jason pushed her hand away.

"Are you kidding, I feel great," Jason declared.

"You sure?"

"Hey are you going to keep stalling or are we doing this?"

"I was just being concerned," Selene replied stiffly.

"And it's appreciated."

"Don't be a smartass, you've made your point okay."

"Good then let's do this," Jason said, and without a further word they descended into the drain. Once inside Selene produced two small black flashlights from her bag and handed one to Jason. With a little manoeuvring they were able to squeeze through a tight section of drain and into a larger tunnel. Once there Selene turned on her torch and a red beam lit the compact tunnel.

"Hey that's pretty cool," Jason whispered.

"It's tactical, preserves your night vision."

Jason nodded mildly impressed. He flicked his on as well. Ahead their tunnel split into three junctions.

"Which one Indie?" Jason whispered.

"The left takes us across the road and should come up into an alley behind the offices."

"Lead on," Jason said, indicating with his hand for Selene to take the point. Their movement was slow as the tunnel was small.

"Bloody hell this is cramped," Jason muttered.

"Yeah it's a little smaller than I remember," Selene replied ruefully. After twenty minutes of crawling they came to a rise with a steel ladder leading up. Jason led the way, quietly pushing the manhole cover off, being careful not to make any noise. Once clear he helped Selene out. She attempted to push the cover back over the manhole but it wouldn't budge. Jason gently eased past her and with no visible effort replaced the cover over the hole. They both remained crouched listening to the silence, making sure they were alone. Selene removed something from her back pack.

"Hey that looks like some kind of ninja grappling hook?" Jason said.

"It certainly does, doesn't it?" Selene smirked, uncoiling the rope.

"After tonight, we're going to talk" Jason said. Selene surveyed the roof, her eyes fixating on one particular spot. She started to swing the grappling hook by the rope in a circular motion. Once it reached maximum velocity she released the hook. It shot up and over the roof making a small metallic ping. Selene tugged on the rope and it went taunt. Gripping the rope with both hands, she lifted her feet up and let the rope take her weight. It held. Satisfied, she was about to start climbing when Jason put a hand on her shoulder.

"Let me go, but first I have an idea I want to try," he said enigmatically. Without waiting for a reply he dashed off towards the end of the alley, up to a large industrial dumpster. After briefly looking in, Jason pushed it back towards a now highly curious Selene.

"Are you nuts? What's with the dumpster?" Selene asked.

"Have a look in" Jason instructed. Selene slowly pulled herself up and peered in.

"Boxes, so?" Selene asked nonplussed.

"So, it'll make getting down easier and we won't have to leave the rope behind."

"Good thinking."

"I didn't get the memo on the seven Ps so I have to bring something to the party," Jason quipped, then grasping the rope, started to climb. Once on the roof edge he motioned for Selene to grab the rope as well.

"Hold on tight," Jason rasped, as he pulled the rope and Selene up to the roof. They moved quickly and once they had located the skylight they descended into the Realty.

The pair made their way through the Realty, flashlights held at the ready. Jason was the first to locate the painting. After close inspection, Selene produced an electronic screw driver from her pack and proceeded to unfasten it from the wall.

"Be gentle," Jason whispered as they removed the canvas and inspected the back only to find it blank. The disappointment was written all over Jason's face.

"Well we kind of knew it wasn't going to be that easy," Selene stated.

"I kind of hoped it would," Jason sighed.

"Don't fret, I've got a couple of tricks up my sleeve," Selene said with a grin, producing yet another torch.

"What's that torch do?" Jason asked, but his question was completely ignored by Selene as she flicked it on, a dim purplish glow emitting as she scanned it back and forth across the canvas.

"Black light produces an ultraviolet light which will pick up any fluorescent ink used," she said. After a thorough scan with no results, Selene put the torch away. "Well that was a bust, but let's see what else may work." she reached back into her bag.

"What is that, the Tardis?" Jason asked as Selene pulled a variety of items out.

"Hand me the hairdryer," Selene said. Jason passed her a small battery-powered dryer which she proceeded to wave back and forward over the canvas.

"What's that going to do?" Jason asked wearily.

"If there's a heat activated ink, it will react to a sodium carbonate-based solution," Selene replied. They waited and watched, again no result.

"Maybe there is nothing there," Jason said. Selene sat silent clearly weighing her options, when an idea came to her. Picking up a small spray bottle, she gently sprayed a section of canvas.

"There are so many different types of chemical reaction inks and I only have a few solutions," Selene started to explain when words began to appear in blue on the canvas.

"Oh my god, what did you do?" Jason whispered in awe, as Selene smiled.

"As I was saying, there are so many chemical types, however what would Perigord have used back in his day?" Selene asked rhetorically. Jason shook his head.

"I just sprayed a solution of red cabbage, which means he must of used plain old vinegar," she said triumphantly. She continued to spray the red cabbage solution until the entire canvas was covered in faint blue letters.

"It looks like it's in German," Selene whispered, studying the writing intently. Jason pulled his phone from his pocket and proceeded to take photos.

"We can translate it later," he said as he prepared to put the canvas back in the frame.

"Wait," Selene said. Jason stopped as Selene pulled another spray from her pack.

"What are you doing now?" Jason asked.

"We can't let this information fall into the wrong hands. This is bleach, it will wipe the previous writing away so no one else can read it," Selene said. After a moment's hesitation, Jason nodded. Selene sprayed a liberal amount of bleach on and used a sponge to mop up the excess fluid.

"That should do it," Selene said.

"It won't wreck the painting on the other side, will it?" Jason asked.

"No I used the bleach sparingly, not to mention those old canvases are pretty thick," Selene said. Jason seemed happy with her assessment as he replaced the picture back to the wall. After packing up her equipment they climbed back out through the skylight, careful to leave everything as it was.

Jason led Selene to the edge of the roof where they prepared to leap off into the previously placed dumpster.

"One, two, three," Jason counted before jumping and pulling Selene with him, their flight was brief, but exhilarating, the cardboard boxes absorbing the impact.

"Nothing is ever dull with you around," Selene stated, her buoyancy hard to suppress. Jason climbed out first, then assisted Selene who slipped and fell into his arms. They both hesitated, neither of them wanting to pull away. Her eyes shimmering in the night, she gazed down at Jason, both of them breathing hard from the adrenaline. He could feel her heart racing as he lowered his face to hers, their lips lightly touching. He could feel himself being swept away on a torrent of emotion, when he sensed movement from behind.

Still holding Selene, Jason pulled her back and turned just in time to see a hulking figure close in on them both. Pulling her down, Selene let out a terrified scream. The dark figure missed them by inches, instead colliding with the dumpster, knocking it on its side. It slid toward the brick wall in a shower of sparks.

"Are you okay?" Jason demanded. Selene nodded, a little dazed.

"What the hell was that?" Selene asked, as a roar emanated from the fallen dumpster.

"No time to explain, let's get the hell out of here," Jason said as he helped Selene to her feet. Both of them stood transfixed as the dumpster slowly began to rise from the ground.

"What the?" Jason blurted.

"Hell," Selene finished.

"You want to play? Good!" an iron-like voice announced.

"Run!" Jason yelled, pushing Selene ahead of him. The dark figure tensed muscles like steel cables and hurled the dumpster in their direction. Jason glanced over his shoulder at the oncoming juggernaut. 'Shit,' he thought as he dived at Selene, both of them hitting the ground in a roll. The dumpster sailed narrowly over their heads before colliding with a parked car on the main street. Without missing a beat, Jason jumped to his feet, dragging Selene with him. They ran for their lives into the park.

The dark figure stood to his full height, well over seven foot, then shrugging its massive shoulders, dusted itself off. A smaller figure landed beside it from seemingly nowhere.

"Where are they Onyx?" a static charged feminine voice asked.

"They're heading for the park. Do your thing Strix," Onyx replied. Gleaming white teeth formed a predatory smile on the smaller female figure.

Jason and Selene ran frantically into the park. The teenagers they had avoided earlier were now gone. They sprinted toward a large elm and hid behind its trunk.

"Oh my God, what was that freak?" Selene whispered.

"WHAT is right, it definitely wasn't human," Jason confirmed.

"Did you see what it did to the dumpster?"

"See it, we almost wore it. SSShhh, I can hear something," Jason whispered. A static charged laugh echoed through the park. It set his nerves on edge.

"I'm pretty sure whoever that is, they are not here to help," Jason said, as he continued to scan the area.

"Let's go," Selene whispered her voice shaky with fear.

"Ssshh, not yet," Jason said straining to hear, when a thud in the distance broke the silence. "Did you hear that?"

Selene shook her head. A female stepped out into the clearing near them. The pair froze, trying desperately to slow their breathing as if this figure might sense their presence. The female appeared to be dressed in black military clothing, her hair ragged and sharp. She was squatting like a perched hawk and appeared to be sniffing at the air. Her body never moved except for her head, which twitched from side to side.

"Great, another freak," Jason whispered.

The woman whipped her head around in their direction and for a split second Jason swore her eyes glowed an emerald green before disappearing like a dying ember. She then looked away and disappeared in a blur of motion.

"Where did she go?" Selene hissed.

"I think she's gone. I hope she's gone," Jason said. Selene nodded, hoping to God he was right, when they heard the faint sound of footsteps from behind, followed by a woman's voice.

"You think to hide from me," Strix questioned. Jason and Selene gasped and spun around. Jason had been correct about her attire. The figure was dressed in black combat pants and boots with a matching black thermal top that hugged her lean, muscular figure. What made the pair stare in shock were her features. Jet black eyes set in a beautiful, but cold face and a head full of thick grey feathers that spilled over her shoulders and down her back.

"Give me Perigord's secret, and...," Strix instructed.

"And you'll let us go?" Selene replied. Strix gave them a smile that would make a shark proud.

"And, I'll make your death relatively painless," Strix said matter of fact.

From his crouched position Jason covertly scooped up a handful of dirt and held it tight in his fist.

"That's a real tempting offer but we'll have to decline. Thanks though," he said, jumping to his feet and throwing the handful of dirt into the creature's eyes. It struck with unerring accuracy. Strix let out an inhuman shriek of pain and fury. Not wasting any time, Jason grabbed Selene by the arm and ran into the darkness, straight into what seemed like a wall, but was actually the giant named Onyx. Jason was able to roll with the impact but Selene wasn't as lucky, her head colliding with the brute, knocking her out cold. Jason desperately tried to revive her with no success

"C'mon Selene, get up," he cried urgently. He heard the laughter then the movement, narrowly ducking under the huge right that was thrown at him. Rolling to the side of the attack, Jason scrambled to his feet and adopted a fighter's stance. His opponent, Onyx, was big, but slow.

The punch he had thrown had sent him off balance and was only now approaching the teenager. Onyx moved like the terminator, huge arms hanging at his sides attached to wrecking ball sized fists. He moved as if nothing could or would, slow him down. Not wanting to abandon Selene, he had no choice but to fight. Feigning a punch at his opponent, he then drove a front kick at the behemoth's right knee. It was like connecting with a telephone pole. The giant stopped and started to laugh, despite the faint glow from the parks lights, Jason couldn't make out any of the big man's facial features, only a square, hairless head. Feeling a burning rage start to build within him at the sound of the beast's laughter, a red hot ball of hate began to glow in the depths of his stomach.

"Are you trying to fight us?" Onyx asked incredulously.

"Us? Shit," Jason muttered, as he realised with dawning horror he'd forgotten all about the other creature. Searing pain raked his back. He turned to see Strix standing behind him, her talon-like hands red with his blood. She started to lick it from her fingers, the expression of ecstasy on her face. Jason reached behind and winced at the pain, jerking his hand back. It too was covered in blood. Strix began to laugh. There was no warmth in the sound, just inhuman pain and suffering. The burning ember in his stomach ignited into a flame spreading throughout his body. He could now feel that heat Selene had talked about earlier, only now it was turning supernova. The laughter had died in both Onyx and Strix as they now watched him closely.

"Hey Strix, I think the boy's mad," Onyx said, Jason roared in fury, he could feel power building up within him then exploding from his body like hot magma, pouring out from his core to his extremities. He spun and kicked out at Strix, clipping her in the head with his foot. She flew back as if kicked by a car, spinning in mid-air, then hitting the ground with a heavy thud.

"The hell," Onyx spat. Jason turned and shoulder-charged the massive man, striking low at his midsection. Onyx grunted and grasped one of Jason's arms in its giant hand with a grip that could have crushed a tow ball. Jason steeled himself against the brutal strength exerted by Onyx. Refusing to cry out, instead utilising his free arm, Jason brought his fist down onto the giant's forearm, striking the radial nerve. The blow caused Onyx to release his grip. Jason stepped forward and slammed a brutal uppercut into the behemoth's jaw. The noise of the blow and Onyx's teeth slamming together sounded like a thunderclap. Onyx staggered back and Jason slammed both fists as hard as he could into the giant's midsection, sending Onyx into the air and on his back.

There was a deathly silence broken only by Jason's ragged breathing. He looked down at his hands and was shocked to instead find a pair of large metallic grey hands in their place. Jason opened and closed his hands. They felt the same, but looked completely alien. Clapping them together they produced a spark and loud metallic ring. The transformation of his hands appeared to cover his entire body as he studied the skin on his arms and face.

"What's happening to me?" he asked aloud. His voice now had a deeper, resonate quality to it. Totally consumed with his current condition, Jason was completely unaware that Strix had recovered and was closing in silently from behind. She launched herself with an animal ferocity, her foot connecting with the back of his neck. The attack caught him totally unawares. He stumbled forward, landing into the crushing right fist of Onyx who had been playing possum, waiting for Strix's attack. The blow sent Jason reeling as the two combatants took turns attacking the stunned Jason. Unable to recover, he was knocked, kicked and thrown by their unrelenting assault. Despite his current armoured form, their combined attacks were wearing him down.

While going blow for blow with Onyx, Strix struck Jason from behind, knocking him to his knees. Onyx then brought both fists down onto the back of Jason's head. Lying semi-conscious he was defenceless as Onyx picked him up by the neck with one arm. Holding him aloft, Onyx stared at Jason's face.

"Seems the boy ain't human," Onyx stated.

"What is he then?" Strix asked.

"Not sure, but he's a tough one. Kid hurt my fists," Onyx said.

"For real?" Strix said surprised.

"Yeah, that's not easy for me to admit either," Onyx said.

"Good thing I was here then," Strix replied.

"I would have finished him. Just would have taken me a bit longer is all," Onyx elaborated. This made Strix laugh as she walked over to inert figure of Selene.

"I'm sure you would of," Strix said casually.

"Don't make fun of me girl," Onyx growled.

"Relax Onyx, I wouldn't dream of pissing you off. Do you think the girl's special too?"

Onyx glanced over at Strix and then the still figure of Selene at her feet.

"Nah, she smells human. We'll have to kill her though," he commented.

"Of course, wouldn't have it any other way," Strix smiled.

"I'll handle the boy," Onyx stated.

The black giant placed both hands on Jason's neck and was about to wring them when a figure bounded out of the tree line and into the back of Onyx.

Onyx cried out, dropping Jason as they both fell to the ground. A startled Strix whirled to face her unknown assailant but was too slow, as the figure struck her with blinding speed, sending the female assassin crashing into the trunk of a tree, then falling face first onto the grass. She remained still. The figure stepped into the light. It was Ulysses, dressed only in sweat pants. The cold was apparently having no effect on him. Ulysses quickly checked the vitals on Selene, then turned to face Onyx who was slowly getting to his feet.

"Ulysses, I should have guessed," Onyx growled.

"You should of, but you've never been terribly bright, Onyx," Ulysses replied.

"This is none of your business changeling," Onyx stated.

"You come to my town, attack its citizens and expect me to do nothing? I ought to slay you and your partner as a warning to others, however I'm turning over a new leaf. A kinder, gentler me," Ulysses said. Onyx smiled, displaying his black glistening teeth.

"The rumours are true then, you have gotten weak over the past millennia," Onyx said.

"Some say rumours, I say wishful thinking. I'll give you the chance to take Strix and get the hell out of Perigord though," Ulysses said.

"Not leaving without that bag," Onyx stated, pointing to Selene's back pack.

"These two are under my protection, so no, you can't have the bag," Ulysses said.

"It's not a request," Onyx roared and charged the librarian. Ulysses stood his ground calmly and cocked his fist as Onyx bore down on him like a rampaging rhino. Ulysses smiled and transformed, his limbs seemed to lengthen and his muscles thickened into solid slabs. The colour and texture of his skin changed becoming rougher and turning a deep blue. His face stretched, becoming slightly elongated. Feet and hands grew becoming blunt and powerful in proportion to his new muscularity. Veins popped and throbbed and ran along the muscles of his arms and legs. Thick black horns grew from the top of his head curving back and following the contours of his skull under his ears, finally pointing out from his cheeks like a ram. The transformation took mere seconds and with Onyx nearly upon him, Ulysses released his cocked fist into a wrecking-ball powered punch that sounded like an explosion when it connected with Onyx's jaw. The punch stopped the giant black thug in his tracks.

"Tag you're it," Ulysses grunted and followed up his attack on Onyx with a series of punishing blows to his neck and head. Onyx tried desperately to ward Ulysses off, but it was obvious his battle with Jason had weakened him, something which the transformed librarian was taking full advantage of. Ulysses grabbed Onyx around the back of his head and proceeded to fire knees into his sides. The giant groaned under each blow. Finally Ulysses grabbed the sagging form of Onyx and delivered a crushing head butt to his face, sending Onyx back to the ground where he laid still.

Jason had watched the entire fight through groggy eyes, not certain of what he was seeing. Attempting to get to his feet he slipped face first to the ground. He was barely aware of powerful arms scooping him up from the ground. The last thing Jason remembered was the still figure of Selene on the ground before the darkness took him.

Chapter 23

JASON GASPED AND tried to sit up, but his body felt like one giant bruise. He was lying atop a leather chase lounge with a blanket draped over him. The room was dimly lit and his eyes were blurry. He was having trouble making out where he was. Every movement he made sent waves of pain throughout his body. He was so caught up in his own misery that he didn't even sense the figure as it entered the room.

"Ah, you're awake." The voice sounded familiar, but it took him a moment to place it. Before he could respond, the figure stepped closer, bearing a tray of china. It was Ms Jax.

"Where am I?" Jason rasped.

"The library of course," Ms Jax replied with a toothy grin.

"What am I?" Jason asked, but before Ms Jax could respond, another voice chimed in.

"The same as me," Ulysses stated, walking casually into the room. He was now dressed as he usually was, in a tweed three-piece suit. Jason's face was a map of confusion.

"And what's that?" Jason asked.

"Not human," Ulysses replied casually as he sat down opposite Jason and poured himself a cup of hot tea.

"Are you being funny, because the last thing I remember were two freaks pounding the shit out of me, and Selene," Jason's eyes went wide. "Shit, Selene, where is she?" he yelled as he attempted to climb off the lounge. Ulysses waved him down.

"Relax slugger, she's asleep in the next room," Ulysses said.

"I don't understand Mr Walker, or is that a fake name too?" Jason said, slumping back.

"Ulysses is a name I've acquired since my time here,"

"Here? What does that mean?" Jason demanded.

"It means that the people from planet earth aren't alone in the universe," Ulysses replied.

"What?" All three of them turned to see Selene standing in the doorway.

"Selene, I'm so pleased you could join us. Take a seat, this concerns you as well," Ulysses invited.

"Have you lost your mind? Jason, tell me you're not buying what he's selling," Selene replied with frank disbelief.

"You didn't see what I saw," Jason shot back.

"I don't know what you think you saw, but," Selene didn't finish her sentence as Ulysses' face changed before her eyes, in both colour and shape. Reptilian scales pushed forth from his skin, which changed a pale green. His mouth widened and eyes sunk into his head and blinked a yellow caste. Ulysses' frame seemed to shrink within his suit and long slender arms grew forth from the cuffs of his sleeves. The hands were talons with small nodules protruding from the palms.

The process took mere seconds and the metamorphosis had the desired reaction on Selene who, with the guiding hand of Ms Jax, slumped into the seat placed behind her. Selene's eyes never left Ulysses who, despite his new form, continued to sip his tea. A sharp blue tongue darted out from his mouth every few seconds. Ulysses even appeared to be smiling.

"Ms Jax please pour Selene a tea. I do believe she's still feeling a little faint".

After filling Selene in on the events that had transpired after her blackout, the room fell quiet. Letting the information sink in, Selene seemed to take it rather well.

"Who are they and what did they want?" Selene asked Ulysses, who had changed back into his human form.

"They, the two you refer to are hired goons. The large one is Onyx, a nasty Runine, his race are mineral composites. Strix is a Syrin, her biology is similar to earth's avian wild life. They nearly always work together. As for the why, I'm sure it has something to do with Perigord," Ulysses said.

"Heinrich, that's who you're talking about, right? Heinrich Perigord?" Jason asked.

"That's correct," Ulysses said.

"But he's been dead for centuries," Selene replied.

"Did you see him die? No. And as for age, I'm well over a thousand years myself, give or take a decade. Ms Jax is older still," Ulysses said off hand.

"So what about you, Mr Walker, are you from a planet

of lizard men?" Selene asked haughtily. Ulysses burst out laughing and Ms Jax issued a chuckle as well.

"That reptilian transformation I performed earlier for your benefit is just a teaser. I'm a Therian, we can pretty much change into whatever we want. This is limited to size and imagination," Ulysses said. Selene nodded, then pointed to Ms Jax.

"What about her?" Selene questioned.

"Ms Jax is from a planet with a heavy gravity and atmospheric pressure, like what you'd find at the bottom of the Ocean. Her people have an amazing body density and strength. You mentioned the Hulk the other day. Well Ms Jax would destroy him," Ulysses said with a grin. Selene and Jason looked highly impressed by this revelation. Jason suddenly went quiet. Selene seemed to sense the change in his demeanour.

"What's the matter?" she asked.

"What am I, and how did this happen to me? Does that mean my mum's an Alien too?" Jason said to Selene. Although the question was aimed at Ulysses.

"Your mum's human. I wasn't sure about you at first, but after watching you the past week and seeing your actions against Onyx and Strix, I'm positive that you're part Therian too," Ulysses said.

"Like you."

"Like me."

"How is that possible? Who's my father?" Jason demanded.

"I don't know the answer to that, but I think that's a conversation for another day," Ulysses said solemnly, Jason sighed then nodded.

"I agree, but we will continue this discussion," Jason said.

"Fair enough," Ulysses replied.

"How can there be aliens running around, yet no one knows?" Selene interjected.

"Humanity has known for most of its history," Ms Jax said.

"She's correct you know. In every civilisation there are tales of beings with great powers. Gods, Demons, myths, legends, creatures that could fly and swim, boogiemen and monsters," Ulysses said.

"You're telling me our religions, fairy tales and myths are based on alien beings living on earth?" Selene replied incredulously.

"In a nutshell, yes," Ulysses nodded.

"How many?" Selene asked. Ulysses thought for a second before answering.

"A few thousand at a guess and that's not including half breeds," Ulysses replied. Both Selene and Jason looked at him quizzically.

"Those like Jason that are half human," Ulysses added.

"How many half breeds?" Jason asked.

"How long is a piece of string? You're asking how many thousand alien beings have mated with humans over a few thousand years," Ulysses let the question remain open.

"How come there aren't more super powered people running around? Nothing on the news, or internet?" Selene asked.

"We are all very careful not to expose ourselves. None of us want to end up on a steel gurney being dissected by the military, and not every alien has special abilities.

Sometimes traits aren't passed on to children; just like the child of a great musician doesn't necessarily have their parent's musical talent. Sometimes over generations, abilities are lessoned or lost. You might find certain people with extra sensory perceptions."

"You mean like telekinesis or telepathy?" Jason cut in.

"To name but a few."

"What about my abilities and how did you sense them?" Jason asked.

"Believe it or not, it was when you first came in. Do you remember?" Ulysses prompted. Jason mulled it over.

"When I first met you?"

"No, before that. What was your first impression on arrival?" Ulysses asked.

"I came in walked down the stairs, touched one of the gargoyles, then met you," Jason recalled.

"That was the reason I approached you."

"I don't understand, because I touched the gargoyle?" Jason said, confused.

"No, because you saw the gargoyle,"

"You've lost me," Jason said, puzzled.

"Too nearly everyone the library looks like, well a regular run of the mill library, boring, plain, ordinary. The fact that you could see it in its true form means you are different. Humans see what they want to see. Only those with special attributes tend to see the library as something truly special," Ulysses said.

"Then why can Selene see it as well?" Jason asked.

"I don't know, maybe it's because of you, Jason. Maybe she was able to see because you opened it up to her."

"How can you control who sees and who doesn't?" Selene questioned.

"I can't, she does," Ulysses said.

"Ms Jax? How?" Jason asked.

"Ha, no, no, not I," Ms Jax replied.

"I don't understand," Selene said.

"I think I do. This place is alive, isn't it?" Jason asked. Ulysses touched his finger to his nose. "Very clever. How did you guess?"

"The place gives off a vibe, it kinda makes sense. The library is always changing isn't it, moving," Jason said.

"I thought Perigord built it," Selene said.

"That's hard to explain. Jason, do you remember me telling you, don't believe everything you read or hear concerning Heinrich? This is one of those times. Heinrich discovered her, added to and enslaved her for a time. But times change," Ulysses said, a hardness to his tone. Ms Jax interrupted them with a polite clearing of her throat as she pointed to the clock on the wall. Ulysses checked his wrist watch and nodded.

"You're right, it's getting late and we have to get you home. Jason, do you mind leaving the information you liberated with us tonight? I would like to look through it. I promise we'll share anything we find," Ulysses said.

"No problem," Jason replied.

"What about us? What if they attack us at home?" Selene interrupted.

"Trust me, tonight you'll be safe. That pair are off licking their wounds and tomorrow I'll set up something a little more permanent," Ulysses replied. Both Jason and Selene looked slightly comforted by his words.

"Selene, your Grandmother is aware of where you currently are, so you don't have to try and sneak in. However Jason, I believe you can climb back in through your window without assistance," Ulysses said. The two teenagers looked taken aback, but before either one could answer, Ulysses cut them off.

"Save your questions for later. Ms Jax will drive you home and I'll see you both tomorrow," Ulysses replied.

After ensuring Selene arrived home safely, Jason thanked Ms Jax and quietly let himself back into the house. Checking on his mum who was sleeping soundly, Jason decided to have a quick shower and hit the sheets. Despite the late hour and the exhausting events of the night, it took him awhile to close his eyes. Thoughts of Gods and monsters ran through his head. Jason wondered if anything would ever be the same again.

Chapter 24

JASON AWOKE AND his first thought was, 'What bloody day is it?' Then it dawned on him. "Shit, school!" He glanced at his watch and cursed. Jumping from his bed, Jason changed quickly and raced downstairs. Stopping briefly in the kitchen for a piece of fruit, he flew out the door and ran toward school.

"I'm gonna be late," he mumbled, picking up his pace as he weaved through the streets. Letting his mind drift Jason's subconscious took over and his body began to change subtlety. Limbs lengthened, his feet spread within the confines of his footwear and muscle fibres grew. Jason's gait widened, strengthened tendons and ligaments worked alongside powerful muscles propelling him along at a breakneck speed. Not even aware it was happening at first, Jason leapt over a fire hydrant, clearing it easily and landing a couple of metres past it. He smiled with a joyful exuberance and thought to himself how fantastic this felt. His efforts were putting him under no strain, it was if he were taking a leisurely stroll.

Jason passed a young boy playing in his front yard.

The boy stopped and stared, his mouth hung open as Jason whistled past. Jason caught the boy's reaction, then he saw his reflection in the window of a parked car. His physical form had changed dramatically. An elongated face with sharp teeth lined his mouth, black eyes stared back unblinking. Long pointed ears and a light tan skin finished his wild appearance. Without breaking his stride, Jason focused his will and attempted to force his change back. Slowing his breathing, he concentrated and imagined himself transforming back. It took a bit of his will but Jason was able to morph back to his original form by the time he reached the school gates, which luckily, were empty of witnesses. However from across the street a hooded figure watched as Jason entered the school grounds.

Sprinting the length of the corridor, Jason checked his watch.

"Thank God, I still have a few minutes," he muttered as he burst through the class room door, just as Mr Rosenberg was calling roll.

"Ah Mr Page, thank you for gracing us with your presence. Please take a seat," Mr Rosenberg said wearily. Jason scanned the room and found Selene nestled up the back. She was patting the empty seat next to her. He made his way to her as Mr Rosenberg finished calling the roll.

"Hey, how are you feeling this morning? I kind of half expected you to stay home," Jason whispered.

"I'm a little sore, but otherwise I'll live," Selene replied.

"I'm feeling great, there was no way I was staying home today," Jason said.

"Me too, I would of gone stir crazy," Selene said. A

book was slammed down hard on Jason's desk, making them both jump in their seats. Mr Rosenberg was looking down at them with a look of disdain on his face.

"Am I interrupting you two?" Mr Rosenberg asked sarcastically.

"I'm sorry Sir, I didn't mean to," Jason began.

"Don't even bother. Just do your work and keep quiet," Mr Rosenberg said as he walked back to his desk.

"What was that about?" whispered Selene.

"I don't know, he's been like this for the past week towards me," Jason replied.

"Well it's probably in your best interest if we keep our talking to a minimum." Jason nodded and pulled out his work book.

As soon as school was finished Jason met Selene at the front gate.

"Hey, what kept you?" he asked.

"Oh, you know, the usual."

"And what would that be?"

"Talking my way out of a detention," Selene said with a grin.

"Again?"

"Hey it wasn't my fault," she said.

"It never is," Jason said with a chuckle. "Are you right to head over to the library with me?" Jason asked, Selene looked a little uncomfortable.

"What's the matter?"

"We have to make a stop first," she said.

"Where?" Jason asked.

"My Grandmother's," Selene said ominously.

Jason and Selene sat at Ursula's table as the old woman

silently poured them all tea. The only noise was the ticking of the old grandfather clock in the corner of the room. After serving them each a cup she sat back in her chair and took a dainty sip of her own.

"So, Jason, what species are you exactly?" Ursula asked matter of fact. Jason coughed, nearly spilling his tea. Selene simply looked at her Grandmother with her mouth open.

"I beg your pardon ma'am, I didn't quite get that," Jason spluttered.

"Oh you heard me young man, the real question you should be asking yourself is how and why is she asking me in the first place?" Ursula replied with a wry smile. Before either Jason or Selene could respond, Ursula placed a circular silver pendant on the table. The pair studied it closely. There was an image of a wolf surrounded by thorns, the same as the plaque in Plato's library. Selene picked it up and held it out to her Grandmother.

"What's this supposed to mean and where did you get it?" She demanded.

"I take it you've seen this image before," Ursula said.

"At my house. I mean my Uncle Plato's, there's a plaque that bears the same image, leading…," Jason was unable to finish his sentence as Selene kicked him from under the table. Ursula saw this but didn't pursue.

"Your uncle and I were members of a select organisation, one that bore that emblem," Ursula stated.

"And what organisation would that be?" Jason asked.

"The Guild of Wolves," Ursula replied.

"The Guild of Wolves?" Selene and Jason repeated in unison.

"That's right dear, our charter is to protect Perigord from the unknown and dangerous," Ursula said taking a sip of her tea. Selene got up from her chair and stalked to the end of the room and back, her face a mask of mixed emotion. Jason and Ursula watched her expectantly.

"So you're telling me you've been a member of a secret society here in Perigord," Selene said.

"Yes," Ursula replied.

"And you don't feel bad for not telling me this?" Selene asked.

"I'm telling you now, dear."

"Only because somehow I'm involved and you have no other choice."

"I'll admit the time of this conversation is not of my choosing, but I had full intentions of telling you after," Ursula sighed.

"After, after what?" Selene demanded.

"After your training of course."

"Training?" Selene replied confused.

"That's right, there's no way you're taking over from me without properly being prepared."

"I don't understand."

"I'm not going to be around forever and it's only logical that my only heir take up the mantle of sentry for Perigord. Why do you think I keep you busy with unusual tasks and hobbies?"

"You've been training me all this time?" Selene asked.

"Ever since your mother died. That's exactly what we've been doing." Ursula turned to Jason. "And if your Uncle hadn't passed away and your physiology changed so drastically, you would have been recruited as well," Ursula added.

"Like your plans for Selene," Jason said.

"That's right, but I'm afraid since the emergence of your birthright, I'm sure Ulysses has other plans set for you now."

"How do you know about Ulysses, and myself, for that matter?"

"I wouldn't be worth my salt if I didn't know about everything and anything here in Perigord, not to mention Ulysses, and I have an understanding," Ursula said.

"And what would that be?" Jason asked.

"Let's just say our interests and motivations cross and intersect, but the protection of Perigord is paramount to us all."

"So you know all about Jason and Ulysses and what they are?" Selene asked.

"I know Ulysses is not from earth and Jason also carries a special pedigree, but no, not the particulars of their heritage. I am aware there are others out there, I've seen them on occasion. The good, the bad and the hideous," Ursula said with a chuckle.

"Do you know we were attacked last night?" Selene asked.

"I do, as I know that brazen attack is only the start of something that has the potential to destroy Perigord."

"What about the book Selene gave you to translate, is it of any help?" Jason asked.

"I'm afraid most of the texts within are beyond my level of expertise. I'm hoping Ulysses can make out its ramblings," Ursula said, frustrated.

"Well with the information we were able to get last night, hopefully we can start to make sense of exactly what's coming." Jason said. Ursula nodded and stood up from the table.

"I hope you're right young man, but for now I think you two should be on your way. I know Ulysses is waiting on you. Good luck Jason," Ursula said cryptically.

Jason and Selene arrived at the library shortly after; Ulysses was waiting patiently for them both.

"How was your afternoon tea with Mrs Jaeger?" Ulysses enquired.

"Not what I was expecting and to be honest, it still raises more questions than answers," Selene replied.

"Well to be fair on Mrs Jaeger's part, she has a lot to impart on you and a short time to do it."

"Why do I feel Jason and I are well and truly behind the eight ball?" Selene muttered.

"I don't know Selene, you two seem to have a knack of catching on real quick," Ulysses said with a smile.

"What now?" Jason asked anxiously.

"Road trip," Ulysses said pointedly at Jason.

"What about Selene?"

"She's going to be busy with Ms Jax. Besides, this only concerns you," Ulysses said. Jason looked nervously at Selene, who gave him an encouraging nod.

"I'm ready," Jason exclaimed.

Jason sat nervously in the passenger seat of the jeep wrangler as it bounced and jostled along the dirt trail. Ulysses kept a steady speed, expertly steering the vehicle through the forest.

"Where exactly are we going?" Jason asked.

"You'll know when we get there," Ulysses replied, and that was the last thing he said during the drive. Jason gave up on conversation, realising it was just his nerves wanting to break the tension. It was obvious Ulysses was off in his own head as well. Slumping back in his seat, Jason tried to enjoy the scenery. The rhythmic passing of the trees was definitely having a hypnotic effect on Jason. He could feel himself drifting off to sleep when all of a sudden the jeep came to a screeching halt. He sat up with a jerk and looked around.

"Grab your bongos kid, we're here," Ulysses announced.

"Bongos" Jason repeated, but climbed out of the jeep to check out this mysterious destination. They were parked in a small clearing of wild grass surrounded by a thick tree line. It was quiet and secluded, but otherwise unremarkable.

"I don't get it what's so important about this place," Jason stated, unimpressed.

"It's not the place but rather its location," Ulysses remarked. Jason shook his head.

"We're away from prying eyes, noise and distraction. A good spot to begin your training," Ulysses continued.

"I get it, like Spiderman. With great power comes great responsibility. This should be a snap," Jason said smugly. Ulysses didn't look too impressed with Jason's flippancy

"I'll admit I was mildly impressed with the way you handled yourself last night,"

"Mildly impressed? I kicked ass!" Jason said.

"You were lucky, lucky that Onyx and Strix were careless, but you better believe that won't happen again. Not to mention there other dangers and threats that are waiting for us out there," Ulysses stressed.

"You make it sound like there are legions of bad guys preparing to attack," Jason replied dubiously.

"Not legions, but if enough decided to work together and take the library by force, then I shudder to think of the implications."

"Why would they want the library?" Jason asked, clearly puzzled. Ulysses sighed leaning against the bonnet of the jeep.

"The library is more than just a storage depot for books. She is capable of so much more than that and in the wrong hands, well I think that's better left for another discussion. Besides, we're here today because of you." Jason clearly didn't like the change in direction of their conversation and decided they were going to continue with it at a later time.

"Okay Yoda where do we start?" Jason asked.

"Who the hell is Yoda?" Ulysses scoffed and turned his back on Jason.

"You're kidding right? You've never heard of Yoda from Star…," Jason didn't finish the sentence as Ulysses spun around and jumped at him. Long slender arms and hideous thin talon-like hands reached for him. Ulysses' facial features had changed horribly too. His nose had receded and was almost gone, the corners of his mouth had widened almost to the sides of the head, exposing dozens of long needle-like teeth. The skin was cracked and had a yellowish hue to it, but the worst thing were the eyes. They were too large and were as black as midnight.

"Holy shit!" Jason shrieked as he threw himself back,

landing on his backside, his arms held up defensively. The horrific looking figure that had, previously been Ulysses stopped in its tracks and began to chuckle his body heaving as the laughter ripped through him. Jason slowly got to his feet, staring at Ulysses who was now transforming back to his regular appearance, laughter still erupting from him. Jason's face had turned red with anger.

'You asshole!" Jason exploded

"I'm sorry," Ulysses responded, even though it was evident he wasn't.

"Why did you do that?"

"Because you were acting cocky and frankly it was pissing me off," Ulysses said plainly wiping a tear from his eye. Jason was looking embarrassed, both from his mentor's words and his reaction to the scare he'd received.

"I still don't appreciate being made to look like a fool," Jason said as he dusted the dirt from the back of his jeans.

"That wasn't my intention Jason, but in my-our-line of work, it pays to expect the unexpected." Ulysses walked away from the jeep and motioned Jason to follow. "Our race is pretty unique within the cosmos, even compared with other alien species. The ability to transform is part of it but I like to think it's more than that. We're like the Marines, we improvise, we adapt and we overcome," Ulysses said.

"Like how I transformed into steel?" Jason replied.

"Partly. Our bodies sense our surroundings and can adjust accordingly, no matter the circumstances, whether it's water, jungle, desert, hot or cold. No matter the atmospheric content, our bodies' genetic makeup changes to cope with differences. Sometimes we make drastic alterations in response to eminent danger."

"And I can do all this?"

"I don't know, but that's why we're out here to find out," Ulysses said, transforming in front of Jason, his frame growing in size, broad shoulders and thick chest. The arms extended to the ground under the weight of a pair of massive, coarse hands that closed and formed into fists the size of microwave ovens. The skin had turned a dirty mottled brown with clumps of hair growing randomly all over. Ulysses' head remained the same size making it look tiny, however the features were blunt and hard and a single row of stiff black fur ran down the centre of the head from the brow, much like a Mohawk. Ulysses smiled, showing a row of grey, ugly teeth. Jason stood transfixed in front of the bestial presence of Ulysses. He was shaken from his stupor when the creature spoke, a single sentence in a deep guttural voice.

"Let's see what you got?"

Jason was barely able to dodge the punch that was fired at him. The cannon ball of a fist sailed mere inches over his head, the length of the beast's arms making it easy to reach him. Leaping back, Jason transformed as well, taking the same form he had adopted when battling Onyx. He stood his ground as the gigantic fists were propelled in his direction. He attempted to halt the second assault from Ulysses with his hands raised in defence. They struck with the force of a runaway juggernaut and despite the fact that Jason was armoured and ready, he was knocked from his feet and thrown into the trunk of a waiting tree. Struggling to get to his feet, Jason looked around for

Ulysses who had changed his form yet again. This time into something smaller and sleeker, a cross between a leopard and a baboon. Taloned arms and a long face sporting dagger-like teeth. Sprinting at Jason with blinding speed, the fur on Ulysses' body bore a camouflage pattern of silver and grey that shimmered as it moved. Jason had only just gotten to his feet when Ulysses leapt and slammed into him feet first, the impact knocking Jason back down. Ulysses used this momentum to backflip and land catlike on his feet.

Jason sat up and looked around a little groggily at the approaching Ulysses. He formed a time out sign with his hands until Ulysses had changed his form back to his regular human appearance.

"Give me a second," Jason blurted out.

"Maybe this wasn't the best way to go about this," Ulysses replied.

"I'll be right, I just need a moment," Jason said breathlessly as he too reverted back to his human form.

"You might not get that opportunity from an adversary," Ulysses chided.

"That's not entirely fair."

"Again fair doesn't come into the equation. I noticed you choose the steel form again. Is it the only one you can do?"

"No, I can do others," Jason said defensively.

"Well let's see then," Ulysses requested. Jason nodded then stood back. Closing his eyes he held his arms out from his side and nothing happened. He opened his eyes, looked at his hands and swore under his breath.

"Relax," Ulysses soothed. Jason clenched his fists and shut his eyes, again trying to force the change.

"What were you thinking the first time you changed?" Ulysses asked. Jason kept his eyes shut, trying to remain focused.

"I wasn't really thinking anything, I was angry," Jason answered.

"That's good use that emotion. Don't think, feel what you want to do as opposed to trying to become something specific," Ulysses said.

"I'll try," Jason whispered, as the effort drained from his face and the tension ebbed from his body.

"What do you want to do?" Ulysses asked.

"Fly," Jason whispered and with that he changed. Golden fur ran from his neck down to his extremities, limbs transformed in shape and size. His body grew, ripping through his clothing and turning it to rags which fell from him. Jason wasn't aware of what was occurring as he dropped to all fours, a long tail sprouting from his lower back, his human form changing to that of a regal lion. Dark brown feathers seeped from the skin on Jason's head as his eyes grew large and his mouth and nose elongated together, forming a beak. Finally two majestic silver wings erupted from his back. The wings opened in a wide arc and began to beat in a slow, rhythmic motion, lifting Jason from the ground.

"Holy shit, a griffin, I don't believe it," Ulysses muttered. Upon hearing these words, Jason opened his eyes and was startled to see that he was hovering metres from the ground. He glanced down at Ulysses who was grinning broadly.

"Well done Jason," Ulysses called out, he then motioned for Jason to come down. Jason let out a screech and shook his head. Without waiting for a response he launched himself into the sky.

"Jason, wait!" Ulysses yelled, but Jason was well out of earshot, spiralling directly up into the open sky. Jason felt total exhilaration as the wind rushed past him, his newly acquired eyes seem to take in everything. Despite the distance he could easily make out Ulysses on the ground. Jason spun then dived towards the tree tops, his paws brushing them as he passed. The feeling was almost indescribable and he yelled out in pure joy, only the sound came out a loud screech. He rose high into the sky, gliding on the thermal shifts in the air as he took in the beautiful scenery. Jason's eyes caught a shimmering reflection in the distance and without further thought flew in its direction.

Ulysses watched as Jason in his newly acquired form was flying further and further away. Without waiting another second Ulysses transformed as well, adopting a similar form as Jason. His griffin however was different in both size and design, slightly smaller in stature. The body was a camouflaged leopard, the wings jet black and the head was that of a pure white bald eagle. Ulysses let out a piercing screech, took a giant bound then leapt into the sky, flying directly after his young protégé.

Jason flew on towards the shimmering image of Greymeade Lake that lay beyond Perigord. Climbing and diving through the cloud coverage his attention was completely focused on the pure joy of the flight, until Ulysses pulled up alongside him.

"Jason, return to the car right now," Ulysses screeched.

"Oh my god, Ulysses, can you believe we're flying? This is incredible"

"Jason, listen to me we can't afford to be spotted."

"Relax, we're too far up, nobody can possibly see us,"

"I'm not asking, I'm telling you. Get your ass back to the car Jason."

"I just want to swoop over the lake. One swoop, I promise," and without waiting for permission, Jason streaked ahead.

"Jason!" Ulysses yelled, but it was useless.

"Bloody kids," Ulysses muttered and with that he took off after him.

Jason had dived down toward the water and was gliding inches above it when Ulysses collided with him from above, their momentum propelling them into the water with a loud splash. A family that had been hiking near the lake didn't see the two griffins, but saw the erupting water from their entry. They stopped to see what had caused the commotion. As Ulysses and Jason tumbled into the depths of Greymeade Lake, they were separated by the force of the impact. Ulysses quickly transformed, ditching the guise of the griffin and adopted a form better suited to the water. Jason flipped and spun in the dark water, his lungs bursting for air. Completely disorientated, he couldn't work out which way it was to the surface. The wings that made him soar through the sky were now a hindrance. Panicking from the lack oxygen, Jason reverted back to his human form. The exertion of the change and his reduced lung capacity had taken its toll. His vision began to fade and just before he blacked out, he caught a glimpse of a figure darting through the water toward him, a vaguely human torso and octopus tentacles where the legs should have been.

Ulysses grabbed the now unconscious Jason and took off toward the far bank like a torpedo. As he tore through the water he checked Jason's pulse and was happy to find the inert figure had now grown gills that were running along his jaw line. They reached the bank but remained below the water line. Ulysses knew about the family near the lake and decided to stay low until he was sure they were gone. As he waited, Jason came to and began to thrash about in his grip.

"Hold still, your fine," Ulysses said gripping Jason firmly until he felt the boy relax in his grip.

"Where are we?" Jason attempted to say, only his words were garbled by the water.

"You only partially changed, your body went into survival mode when you passed out. Look at me and try to copy. The combination of your will and our skin touching should be enough to complete the change. Jason stared hard at Ulysses, then taking a deep breath he transformed, his body replicating the librarian right down to a cellular level.

Jason moved the tentacles that were his legs and was amazed at what he was seeing, his eyesight clearly able to see through the murky water. Apart from Ulysses he could see everything under the lake, weeds, fish and an old car, the only thing he couldn't see was the lakes bottom. After a moment the gravity of the situation hit Jason and he looked at Ulysses.

"I'm so sorry Ulysses," Jason pleaded.

"And so you should be. You ignored my instructions and nearly revealed us both."

"I know."

"No you don't. I brought you out so we could see the extent of your abilities without human eyes watching. But instead you disobeyed my words and consequently we were nearly discovered by a nearby family. Not to mention you nearly drowned," Ulysses growled.

"I don't know what to say,"

"How about I'll never do that again Ulysses. From now on I'll only do as you say Ulysses. I'm a complete turd and I'll try harder Ulysses." Jason looked completely ashamed.

"You're right there's no excuse for my behaviour and I promise...," Jason was cut off mid-sentence.

"Hold it there, don't make promises you can't keep. Besides you're not entirely to blame, I should have laid down some boundaries before we started. So let's put this down to shit happens and move on," Ulysses said.

"Works for me," Jason said, happy that they weren't going to dwell on his mistake.

"I want you to wait here while I conduct a quick recce topside, okay?" Ulysses asked. Jason nodded in agreement as his mentor departed for the surface. Ulysses returned a short time later.

"The coast is clear, are you ready to go?"

"I am, but I have to admit I've started to feel very comfortable down here under the lake," Jason said.

"That's one of the benefits of who we are. Once our kind inhabit a form, the longer we remain in it, the more it feels completely natural to us."

"Any form?"

"That's right," Ulysses replied. The pair swum to the surface then climbed onto the bank, both of them adopting their human forms. Jason was shocked to discover he was naked, then he remembered his transformation into the griffin earlier had destroyed the clothing he had worn. However Ulysses was dressed in the clothes he had worn from before. Jason attempted to cover himself, feeling completely embarrassed about his appearance.

"How come you're clothed?" Jason asked.

"Well that's because I'm wearing cloth made from unstable molecules, an item that can change into anything I want and adapt to any form I become. Otherwise, well, it would get very expensive," Ulysses replied.

"Handy thing to have," Jason stated with interest.

"I agree, in the meantime why don't we shift and we can continue our discussion on the way back to the jeep."

"Any ideas?" Jason asked with a grin.

"How about this?" Ulysses said as he fell to his knees. Hands on the ground, he turned into a dog, long limbed, lean and healthy. The dog regarded Jason as it sat on its haunches.

"A German Short Haired Pointer. Unusual choice, but what the hey," Jason said. Stepping forward, he touched the dog on the head, concentrated, and then transformed himself. Jason turned three times sharply, then sat down and faced Ulysses.

"Why did you do that for?" Ulysses asked.

"That's what dogs do when they sit down isn't it?"

"Idiot. When they lay down, and not always," Ulysses said with a sigh as he stood up and began to walk off toward an open trail. Jason let out a bark and chased after him.

The two dogs trotted down the trail, the padding of their paws breaking the silence in the forest.

"So why a dog? Why not a wolf, or a werewolf, that would be cool!" Jason said.

"Kids," Ulysses said shaking his head. "Something like a dog isn't going to be noticed by other people, not to mention leaving behind unusual paw prints will raise suspicion. Besides, you're still receiving essential training."

"Am I?" Jason asked.

"Too right you are. Concentrate and smell your surroundings," Ulysses instructed. Jason inhaled deeply then sneezed suddenly. After shaking his head he tried again and was amazed at what he could smell.

"Oh my god, is this for real."

"Tell me Jason, tell me what you smell?"

"I can smell everything, birds, animals, you," Jason laughed. "I can even smell the water."

"Good now do the same with your hearing," Ulysses replied. Jason closed his eyes and let the surrounding sound wash over him. He turned his head from side, to side picking up the chirping of a bird, a climbing squirrel, the wind rustling through the leaves.

"Impressive isn't it? Something as simple as a dog can have abilities and uses other animals or creatures can't. This guise you're wearing can do things brute strength and ferocity can't," Ulysses said. Jason was silent as he pondered this.

"Imagine an ant the size of a human and you would have a being that could lift five tonne, be able to run 70 miles per hour and smell food from miles away. Now that's what I call impressive," Ulysses added.

"Why is the transformation easier when we touch something we want to change into?" Jason asked.

"Good question. Now you're starting to think. That touch gives us access to it on a molecular level. Without it we're just guessing."

"But I was able to turn into a griffin," Jason replied.

"No not really, you became your idea of what a griffin is but not the real thing," Ulysses said. Jason looked a little dejected and confused.

"I don't think I understand," he said.

"Imagine a simple scenery, then take a dozen artists and tell them to each paint the same scene. Do you think you would have twelve identical paintings?"

"No of course not, each painting would be subject to the artists own interpretation."

"And it's no different with us. Without the physical touch of what we want to become, we have to improvise. However…"

"However what?" Jason asked.

"However once you have an intimate knowledge of a subject its then with you forever. Our people call it cataloguing," Ulysses said with what Jason thought was a grin.

"So whenever I want I can become this form now?"

"Correct."

"That's pretty bloody cool."

"Whenever you have the opportunity, practice and learn your body's abilities."

"Will do. Hey Ulysses, let's see who's faster," Jason replied as he waited for a response from his mentor, only to be pushed aside as the older man charged past him and bounded up the trail.

"Last one back buys the coffees" Ulysses barked.

"You're going to need that head start old man," Jason replied as he took off in pursuit.

Ulysses had reverted back to his human appearance and was leaning against the bonnet of the jeep when Jason finally made his way into the clearing. He was panting heavily as he trotted over and around the other side of the jeep changing back to his regular form.

"You wouldn't have a towel or something I could cover up with?" Jason asked.

"As a matter of fact I have just the thing you need," Ulysses replied and produced a small bundle wrapped in plain brown paper. Jason took it with a nod of thanks and unwrapped its contents. Inside he found a grey pair of coveralls. He looked slightly disappointed at his discovery, which was painfully obvious to Ulysses.

"Gee thanks, you shouldn't have," Jason said.

"You're welcome, try it on," Ulysses replied with an enthusiasm the boy couldn't understand. However he thought to himself it was better than riding back into town stark naked and at least his mentor had the foresight to bring something in the first place. He dressed quickly, donning the coveralls behind the jeep. Once dressed he walked around to Ulysses. Jason's outfit was a little baggy and covered him from the neck to his feet, and as he zipped up the front the most amazing thing happened. The coverall started to tighten around his body, conforming to his length and girth until it fit snugly. On inspection, Jason could see no loose areas of material.

"It feels so comfortable," Jason marvelled.

"It gets better. Try to imagine something you would like to wear."

"Really?"

"Yes really. Concentrate, picture the clothing in your head."

Jason thought for a moment then his face lit up.

"I've got it." Suddenly the cloth started to change colour and shape, conforming to the idea in his head. One minute he was wearing the tight grey jumpsuit and the next he was wearing a black tuxedo and matching dress shoes. Jason attempted to adopt a sophisticated pose against the jeep.

"The name's Page, Jason Page," he said with a poor Scottish accent. Ulysses shook his head in confusion.

"I don't get it."

"You know, like the secret agent?" Jason threw his hands up in disgust. "Bloody hopeless," he added. Jason's tuxedo melted away and was replaced with camouflaged pants singlet and combat boots. He immediately flexed his muscles.

"I'll be back," Jason drawled.

"I get it you're Clint Eastwood," Ulysses said, evidently proud of deduction.

"It's Schwarzenegger. How the hell did you get Eastwood?" Jason said disgusted.

"Give me a break, they're very similar."

"Similar? One's got huge muscles and speaks with an Austrian accent and the other is a lean, tough guy with a gravelly voice. What's the point?" Jason said shaking his head.

"Well apart from my massive faux pas concerning two famous sporting heroes, how do you like the gift?" Ulysses asked. Jason let out a sigh concerning Ulysses comment and decided to let it go.

"It's fantastic. It doesn't even feel heavy. Wait a minute, did you say gift? You mean it's mine to keep?" Jason asked stunned.

"That's what a gift usually means and I take your reaction for happiness and gratitude."

"Yes, yes, thank you Ulysses, this is amazing."

"You'll never have to remove it ever again. The clothing does not require washing and neither will you as it consumes the waste and bacteria from your body," Ulysses stated, Jason looked a little nervous at this comment, which his mentor picked up on.

"However if you so desire, the clothing will retract in on itself to the size of an atom so that it's completely invisible to you and anyone else, awaiting for you to summon it," Ulysses instructed. Jason looked suitably impressed as his clothing changed into jeans hoodie and sneakers. He rubbed his hand along the fabric.

"It feels like the real thing."

"It is, no one on earth would ever know the difference. Let's head back," Ulysses said. The pair climbed into the jeep and departed for the library.

Chapter 25

THEY ARRIVED BACK at the library on dusk and found Ms Jax and Selene drinking tea in the staff lounge. Much to their surprise they were laughing and appeared to be getting along quite well. They stopped when Jason and Ulysses entered the room.

"What are you two talking about?" Jason asked suspiciously. Ms Jax and Selene gave each other a knowing glance as they sipped their tea.

"Oh you know, girl stuff," Selene answered and Ms Jax let out a little giggle, much to the surprise of everyone in the room.

"Okay. I think you two better get home, it's getting late," Ulysses said.

"Yeah, I won't argue, I'm buggered," Jason agreed.

They walked slowly home through the park. Jason regaled Selene with what had happened in the forest and how Ulysses had shared information on his ancestry, abilities and his new clothes.

"New clothes?" Selene said eyebrows raised. "That's, um, nice."

"Try not to be too condescending will you?" Jason replied with a smirk. "They're special."

"I can see that, "Selene giggled. Without trying to explain it further, Jason thought for a second. Smiling, his clothes melted and reformed into a complete set of samurai armour. The whole transformation took seconds. Selene's jaw dropped open as she stared gobsmacked at his newly acquired outfit. After a few moments of silence she reached out and tapped his shoulder with her fist and felt the hard steel plates through the soft silk.

"That's freaking awesome!" Selene squealed as she jumped on the spot and clapped her hands together. This brought a huge smile to Jason's face.

"I wasn't sure I could do it, but there you go, pretty impressive, isn't it?"

"I'll say, what else can you make it do?"

"How about this?" Jason said and the armour melted away, replaced with a batman costume. He placed his hands on his hips, threw his shoulder forward and raised his head.

"I'm Batman!"

"Corny, but cool."

Without waiting for further prompting, he changed his clothing again. This time he stood before her dressed like the lead guitarist from KISS. Jason started to play air guitar in imitation.

"You have no shame," Selene laughed.

"No shame, hey?" Jason muttered with a sly grin. This time the clothes changed into a revealing Tarzan style loin cloth. Selene blushed a little as her eyes roamed his muscular body. Jason was unaware of her heated stare and started to thump his chest, letting out the trademark lord of the ape's call, which echoed in the abandoned park.

"Keep it down, idiot!" a distant voice yelled back. This made Jason blush and he quickly changed back to his hoodie and jeans.

"Since you're finished with your impromptu catwalk romp, maybe we should get going," Selene said wistfully.

"I think that's a good idea," Jason replied, still a little red in the face.

Jason stopped outside Selene's house and leaned against the gate.

"Do you think Ulysses could get me one of those?" Selene asked hopefully.

"I don't see why not, you're part of the team too," Jason replied.

"Hey, don't forget we have to be at school early tomorrow," Selene said. Jason raised an eyebrow.

"Did you forget about the school excursion to the Black River Brewery?"

"Um, yeah kinda."

"I suppose with everything that's been going on in your life lately. You're to be forgiven with these momentary lapses" Selene said.

"Why are we going to a brewery anyway? Doesn't that just promote teenage drinking?" Jason asked.

"I suppose, but one in four adults work there and the town itself depends on its success. Not to mention the brewery pumps a lot of money back into the school. Well I guess you can see where I'm coming from."

"Yeah, I am kinda interested to see the inside, might be fun."

"That's the spirit. We'll make a yokel out of you yet," Selene said as she unlocked the front door. "Goodnight Jason."

"Night Selene, I'll see you tomorrow," Jason replied as he walked off into the night.

Chapter 26

HELEN AWOKE THE following morning to find Jason entering her room with a tray bearing freshly brewed coffee, toast and marmalade. She sat up and gave him a warm smile as he placed the tray on her lap.

"I'm pretty sure it's not my birthday and Mother's day has been and gone, so what's the occasion?" Helen asked suspiciously.

"Hey, am I that much of a butthead that when I do something nice there's an angle?"

"Well," Helen replied. Jason pretended mock hurt.

"I'm kidding!"

"I just thought brekkie in bed for my poor, hardworking mum would be my good deed for the day."

"I appreciate the sentiment" Helen said as she took a bite of her toast. "So what's on the agenda today?"

"School excursion to the brewing company. A couple of ciders before math should get me through the day," Jason stated.

"Hilarious, however I think you'll enjoy your trip. The

Brewery is important to the town and they supply a world class product from all accounts."

"Yeah, Selene gave me the rundown," Jason replied. Helen shifted her attention to her son.

"So, what's the go with you two anyway?" Helen asked enjoying Jason's unease.

"I'm not sure. I mean I like her, and…"

"And?"

"And I'd rather not talk about this with my mum," Jason said uncomfortably.

"Fair enough," Helen said as she took a sip of her coffee."

"I better get ready for school, early start," Jason replied, keen to change the subject.

"Okay sweetheart, don't forget to say goodbye before you leave."

"Will do mum," Jason said, leaving her to finish breakfast.

He arrived at the front gate of the school. A bus was parked out front and Mr Flannigan was standing near the passenger door, a clip board in hand, ticking off the names of the students as they entered the bus. As Jason approached, Selene stuck her head out of a window and waved to him.

"Hurry up I've saved you a seat," she called. Jason nodded and after Mr Flannigan recorded his name he entered the bus as well. He squeezed his way past the cramped and noisy students and dropped down into the vacant seat next to Selene.

"Cutting it kind of close aren't you?" Selene said with a smirk. As if on cue, Mr Flannigan stepped onto the bus.

"Now that everyone's here," Mr Flannigan said, giving Jason a cold glare. "We can get going."

The bus ride only lasted ten minutes but the noise within was so loud it seemed longer. The bus drove slowly up the brewery's entrance which was lined with tall lustrous pine trees that opened into a large circular keyway with an immaculately maintained garden in its centre. The Black River Brewery was an imposing building built from old limestone that had been carefully maintained. The bus parked near the front entrance and all students remained seated while Mr Flannigan read them all the riot act prior to disembarking. However no one really paid him any attention as they were more interested in starting the tour and possibly sampling the brewery's merchandise.

The students slowly exited the bus and waited as Mr Flannigan conducted a quick headcount by which time the brewery manager had arrived to greet them. The manager was a big burly man with a course beard, dressed in jeans, shirt and tie. The image was comical as he looked like someone had attempted to dress a bear and make it civilised. The manager cleared his throat and addressed the class.

"Good morning kids. Some of you may already know me, but for those that don't, my name is Mr Sucell and I'm the general manager here at Black River Brewery."

"Can I have a job?" a voice yelled out from the group in jest. Everyone laughed including Mr Sucell. Everyone except Mr Flannigan who scanned the class with a withered scowl.

"Yes, you can have a job but you'll have to finish

school first," Mr Sucell said with a chuckle. "Now if you'll all follow me, we can start the tour.

Mr Sucell started the tour in the company's briefing room with a short documentary movie on the history of beer and cider, an animated beer bottle conducted the narrating and spoke with the most annoying voice. Jason thought it sounded like a cross between the Count from Sesame Street and Roger Rabbit. Despite the students' eagerness to begin the tour, they were struggling to keep their eyes open. Everyone all but cheered when the lights were turned on and Mr Sucell announced they would begin.

Everyone was given a hard hat to wear due to the company's safety regulations. They started with the cooperage where the brewery constructed their own oak barrels which Mr Sucell explained only a few breweries still did. As they moved on he also explained what ingredients were required in brewing and about the key differences between beer and cider. Jason was amazed at the science behind it all, not to mention the quality ingredients that went into its makeup.

"I'm actually really enjoying myself today," he whispered to Selene, who nodded back.

"I thought you might," she replied. The group made their way around the facility and were introduced to supervisors and key position holders, who explained their function with obvious pride and knowledge. The tour had been going for some time and was nearing its end. The class had been attentive and quiet whenever the manager spoke and explained how something worked or was prepared. They passed an area where the prepared fluid was stored in giant stainless steel vats and where they bottled and stored the beverages while awaiting transport to consumers. The students followed Mr Sucell in a single file along steep, steel catwalks overlooking the vast enterprise. They watched as dozens of men worked diligently at their respected stations. Now and again an employee waved to the class. This was always returned by an embarrassed looking student.

"As you can see it takes a town to run a large company such as this which is why we employ a large percentage of Perigord to work here," Mr Sucell said as they continued along the cat walk, eventually making their way back to the briefing room.

"I'm afraid we've come to the end of the tour. Do any of you have questions you would like to ask me?" Mr Sucell asked. Everyone was quiet and just when it appeared no one would answer, a small girl named Wendy stood up. She wore large black glasses and her hair was pulled back and tied in a sensible fashion.

"Could you please tell us about the story behind the stone goblin cider?" Wendy asked fascinated. Once she realised everyone was watching her she blushed and sat back down, her eyes down cast as she attempted to hide her obscurity.

"Ah, the story on our famous cider," Mr Sucell said with a grin on his face, and a twinkle in his eye. "Would the rest of the class like to hear it too?" he added. Everyone nodded including Selene and Jason as they waited for the manager to tell his tale.

"Well, we have a watered down version which we have printed on the back of every label, but the original story that was told to me by my grandfather is a lot stranger," Mr Sucell said as he pulled up a stool and sat facing the class, his face becoming serious. "It all began about a hundred and fifty years ago. The man who discovered the recipe was my great, great, great, great, grandfather Dion Sucell. Back then he was like a lot of other Perigorians who had come here for the mining of silver. He had a small claim over the west side of the valley and the word on him was that he was a bit of a loner and drinker. Dion had been here roughly 2 years and eight months and his meagre budget had been stretched extremely thin. In fact he was on the verge of packing it in and heading back east when something peculiar happened one night," Mr Sucell said.

"What happened?" a voice called out. This was met with a universal ssshhhh from the class.

"I was just getting to that," he said patiently, Mr Sucell was a gifted storyteller and it was obvious he had told the tale dozens of times, he spoke with only minimal pause playing on dramatic effect. The class hung off his every word.

"As I was saying, something peculiar happened? By his own account he was camped near his mine and had settled by the fire when he heard a sound in the dark. The sound was like nothing he had ever heard before. A primal fear gripped him as he snatched his gun in both hands and was about to back into his tent when he realised the sound was coming in the direction of his mine. Now his fear had turned to anger and greed. A thought crept into his head that someone was trying to steal from his claim. Why he was concerned with his claim when it hadn't produced an earning was anyone's guess. So Dion took a belt of whiskey for courage, and headed slowly down the trail towards his claim."

Mr Sucell paused to take a sip of water and let the story settle into the heads of the audience.

"Dion's progress was slow in the dark, despite the full moon and his kerosene lantern. He had half hoped that whoever was down there would be gone by the time he arrived. Just before he reached the mine Dion turned off the lantern and crouched at the end of the trail, trying desperately to see anything out of the ordinary. At first all seemed quiet and Dion was about to turn back when the noise he had heard earlier started up this time it was emanating from deep within the mine. The sound was a hissing laughter that echoed through the tunnel adding a haunted quality to it. Dion took another shot of his whiskey and walked towards the mouth of the mine, his gun raised, the muzzle pointed ready for business. I don't know whether it was fear, the whiskey, or blind luck but Dion never said a word or made a sound. A light eminated from inside the tunnel which helped him navigate the narrow corridors towards the inhuman laughter. Dion had almost travelled the length of the chasm when he stumbled across something that at first made him question his sobriety then his sanity.

"What was it?" another voice from the class blurted out. This put a smile on Mr Sucell's face as if he had been expecting the interruption.

"What my great grandfather saw was, well he called it a stone goblin. Standing only a foot tall with pale leathery grey skin and sinewy arms and legs, it was wearing plain leather pants. A crude iron band sat high on its naked head, its long pointed ears jutting out like wings. The goblin's face was rough and aggressive in appearance. A large hawkish nose and wide green unblinking eyes seemed to study him with a predator's detachment. But what really caught Dion's eye was the wide mouth filled with dozens of razor sharp teeth. The goblin had been holding a small pick but had dropped it when Dion had come upon it. He stood transfixed by the tiny beast, his gun trained on it. However he clearly did not know what to do next when suddenly the creature spoke.

"What do you plan to do now?" it's voice deep and issued with a hiss.

Dion was shocked, although it was dressed in rudimentary clothes, he clearly did not expect it to speak.

"You can talk!" Dion said astonished.

"Yes, of course I can talk, you stupid man," The goblin spat. "I'll only ask again. What do you plan to do now?"

"I have no idea. You are the last thing I expected to find here," Dion said. The Goblin laughed, although the sound was not something one would associate with mirth. It was more like a vile substance bubbling forth from the bowels of the earth. "And now you have me cornered with your boom stick," the goblin let his question remain open. Dion's mind ticked over with the implications of his current situation.

"I'm betting nobody has ever seen anything like you before?" Dion pondered aloud. The goblin snarled and stood its ground.

"You plan to show me in public like some oddity for profit? You filthy human, you have no idea who I am," the goblin growled, a deep hatred glowing in its eyes. Dion shifted uncomfortably as he contemplated the logistics of trying to capture the vengeful beast in the middle of the night with no provisions and no help. Dion explained his financial woes and the creature's eyes twinkled at the mention of his predicament.

"So it is wealth you seek. If so, maybe we can come to an agreement," The goblin replied.

"I'm listening beast."

"If you were to release me, I could give you something that would earn you all the money that you desire."

"What could you give me? Diamonds, gold, gems?"

"Knowledge."

Dion looked sceptical.

"What sort of knowledge?"

"Well for starters, I could tell you where to dig to find those elements you humans hold important, things that shine and sparkle," the goblin chuckled.

"And?"

"And, what more do you want?" the goblin said, anger creeping into its voice.

"I don't know. Digging information in return for your freedom seems a little one sided."

"One sided indeed, but if you think the deal's unfair, I'll gladly sweeten the pot."

"I'm listening."

"I have noticed a certain aroma upon you, one that suggests you have a liking for a certain type of beverage," the goblin said with certainty. Dion tried to maintain a neutrality but a blush had begun to creep up his neck.

"I'm not judging you, merely trying to ascertain the

pleasures with which you like to engage in," the goblin said. Dion was a simple man and for some reason the ugly creature before him was starting to make him anxious.

"I have in my possession a recipe."

"Recipe?" Dion said, looking perplexed.

"Not just any recipe, but one that produces the most amazing cider any human has tasted in over a thousand years. This cider will make men fight for it and women compliant after it," the goblin said with a sneer. "Any man that knows how to make this cider has a license to print money." Dion had started to sweat over the thought of so much money, his mind dancing at the prospect of untold wealth.

"How do I know that I can trust you?" Dion asked warily. It was obvious that the goblin was angered by the accusation. It breathed deeply and ignored the jibe.

"I'll give you my word that you shall have everything I've promised or my life is forfeit," the goblin touched two fingers to his forehead, then to the centre of his chest, then held them high to the sky. "Do we have a deal?"

Dion thought it over then nodded.

"We do."

"And that kids, is the legend of how Dion Sucell acquired the Stone Goblin Cider and started the Black River Brewing Company," Mr Sucell concluded. The class had sat quietly throughout the entire story, however this was short lived.

"What a crock of shit!" a voice said from the back of the class. Everyone turned around, but Jason already knew who it was.

"Hector, watch your mouth young man!" Mr

Flannigan barked, but looked extremely uncomfortable chastising the influential student.

"That's okay, I find the tale completely absurd, considering what a drunk my great grandfather was, but the story has always been good for sales," Mr Sucell said frankly. Wendy, who had originally asked Mr Sucell about the story looked disappointed.

"You really don't believe the tale sir?" she asked, like a child that's been told that Santa Clause isn't real. Mr Sucell shrugged.

"I suppose nothing in life is certain and for those that have an active imagination there is a life size stone statue of the goblin standing in the lobby. My great grandfather had it made I suspect to enhance the story," Mr Sucell said.

"Well it was a fine story," Mr Flannigan said. "The class and I would like to thank you for allowing us to come and visit your company and giving us your valuable time. Class," Mr Flannigan gave the class a sharp look and they all thanked Mr Sucell in a monotone chorus.

"Oh and one last thing," Mr Sucell said excitedly. "As you are all aware our brewery is supplying refreshments for the Harvest Festival. We are planning on unveiling our new cider, a non-alcoholic one, as well as our alcoholic ones. The new brew is something that hasn't been done in the history of the company, I'll personally guarantee it'll change this town." Mr Sucell said.

After the manager's closing speech, the class filed out through the lobby. Everyone including Hector stopped and looked at the goblin statue located at its centre. Lingering last, Jason and Selene studied the statue closely.

"That story Mr Sucell told us probably has some truth to it," Selene whispered.

"What do you think happened to the goblin?" Jason asked.

"You heard the story, Dion Sucell let it go and got his reward."

"I suppose," Jason said with a shrug as he cast one last glance at the statue. As they walked away, Wendy stepped out from behind the statue and watched them leave, having heard their whole conversation.

'How interesting,' Wendy thought.

The bus arrived back at school after lunch and the students were allowed to go home early. Most of them disappeared quickly off the grounds, not wanting to be there if the teacher were to suddenly change his mind. Jason and Selene took their time walking out and were met surprisingly by Hector at the front gate. Jason appeared aloof, not wanting to goad the boy, but not really acknowledging him either. Hector saw this and waved an imaginary white flag comically.

"I don't want to fight," Hector said peaceably. Jason now gave him his full attention and raised an eyebrow.

"What do you want then?" Jason asked tersely.

"I suppose I deserve this reaction from you," Hector replied sheepishly. "I realise that we didn't quite start off on the right foot."

"Ya think?" Selene interjected. Hector's face darkened, but it was gone almost immediately, replaced with an apologetic look.

"You're right, I've been a huge douche bag recently and I know it's not an excuse, but things at home haven't been great lately with my dad and I might have taken it out on you at the time."

Jason was still not completely sure of Hectors true intentions but he was beginning to think he had been hasty in completely condemning the boy.

"I'm not too sure what you want from me though?" Jason stated.

"Nothing from you, I just thought that maybe we could not do the whole enemies for life schtick. After all, it's a small town and I'm sure you don't want to be glancing over your shoulder all the time and I don't need the heartache from the school, my mum and anyone else for that matter. Look this doesn't make us BFF's, but maybe it means we can say hello instead of punching on, what do you say?" Hector said earnestly, holding out his hand in offering. Jason was quiet for a long moment and both Selene and Hector were thinking that he was going to tell him to take a hike. Finally he reached out and shook his hand.

"Why not, life's too short to bear a grudge," Jason replied.

"I'm glad to hear it. Listen why don't you two come out to the lake this Saturday, a few of us are going out to fish, swim and just chill if you're interested." Hector said. Jason mulled it over for a brief moment.

"Sure."

"Great, I'll pick you up from Selene's place at midday."

"No prob," Jason replied.

"Just bring a towel," Hector said, then checked his watch. "Well, I better get going, I'll see you both tomorrow," Hector added with a grin and gave them the pistol click with his thumb and finger pointed before walking off down the street.

"Well that was totally unexpected," Jason said, watching Hector disappear in the distance. Selene looked dubious as she too watched Hector.

"Yeah, when something seems too good to be true, it's because it usually is," Selene replied.

Chapter 27

JASON AND SELENE arrived at the library and were surprised to find it closed.

"That's unusual, I wonder what's up?" Selene said.

"This could be serious," Jason replied, concern etched upon his face. He pulled a key from his pocket and let them in through the front door. They made their way quickly down the stairs and in to the staff room where they found Ulysses and Ms Jax engaged in a heated conversation with Ursula Jaeger, their tone deadly serious.

"It's time for you both to sit down, we have a lot to discuss," Ursula said bluntly. The pair took their seats without comment and waited for an explanation.

"We're running out of time and with the new information your grandmother has brought to us, the situation is worse than we imagined," Ulysses stated.

"You were able to translate the book?" Selene asked.

"Books?" Ursula corrected. Selene and Jason both gave her a puzzled look.

"Have you acquired another piece of the puzzle?" Jason asked.

"No, but you did," Ursula replied, looking embarrassed.

"I'm afraid you've lost me."

"You have to remember that I still didn't know you that well."

"Grandmother what are talking about?" Selene interrupted. Ursula ignored her as she pleaded her case to Jason.

"The guild comes first, it has to," Ursula continued.

"What did you do?" Selene insisted. Ursula looked uncomfortable, but matched her stare.

"Your uncle's journal, you never misplaced it. I, I took it," Ursula said.

"You what?" Selene yelled in outrage. Ursula stood her ground, but the obvious red blush that had crept up her neck was clear to all that she was ashamed of her actions.

"Your uncle was my Captain, the items he has in his possession are Guild property. All I can say is I'm sorry for my deception," Ursula said emotion cracking her voice, her eyes brimming red.

"I can't believe you would do this under our noses," Selene fumed. Jason put a hand on her shoulder, but she shrugged it off.

"Selene its okay," Jason tried to placate her. Selene looked at him in confused anger.

"How can you defend her?"

"Hey, I'm not entirely happy with this situation, but I'm sure she had her reasons," Jason said.

"No, it's not good enough. She probably did it while you were sleeping, sneaking in like a thief in the night. It's creepy and cowardly and just plain wrong," Selene ranted.

"We don't have time for this," Ulysses said exasperated. He was completely ignored by the pair.

"Who are you anyway?" Selene said, looking at her grandmother with disgust. Ulysses stepped forward with raised hands between the two women.

"Ursula, Selene, you need to put aside your family issues for the moment so we can get to the heart of the real issue," Ulysses said bluntly. This seemed to snap the two from their standoff.

"You're right Ulysses, this is something we can discuss later at home in private," Selene snapped, glaring at her grandmother.

"The procurement of my uncle's journal aside, what have you found that's so urgent Ms Jaeger?" Jason asked. Ursula looked toward Ulysses who gave her a curt nod to continue.

"First up, Jason, let me apologise," Ursula said. He was about to wave her off but she shook her head. "I did what I did out of necessity, nothing more. But the more I have gotten to know you and the influence you have had over my granddaughter, I have found you to be a rather upstanding young man. So maybe over time you can forgive me," Ursula added. Jason nodded. He was still annoyed by her actions but also pleased by her praises.

"I understand we all have information, patchy as it may be, concerning the Harvest Festival. The information I have been able to gleam from Jason's books indicates Perigord is attempting to perform a ceremony he started two hundred years ago," Ursula said.

"Yeah, we kinda figured that part out. He wants to turn his devotees into superhuman beasts that only he can control," Selene said defiantly, Ursula ignored the outburst.

"No, not entirely. It's not his plan to turn his devotees. No Perigord will be conducting the ceremony with plans of turning the entire town," Ursula stated.

"You can't be serious?" Jason asked shocked

"I'd believe it Jason. Perigord was a sick man, he's capable of anything," Ulysses added.

"So I've been told. Imagine thousands of creatures, virtually immune to disease and injury, with strength speed and endurance a hundred times greater than any human swarming over the planet," Ursula replied. Jason and Selene looked on in shock

"With Heinrich controlling them, it would be a massacre on a global scale," Jason whispered.

"Global genocide," Ulysses agreed.

"How can we stop him?" Selene asked.

"We first need to know how he intends to conduct the ceremony and what elements he may require," Ursula said.

"I think I can help in that department, or rather Jason already has," Ulysses answered. Jason gave him a quizzical look in return.

"The photographic evidence you both took from the realty the other night details the ceremony," Ulysses said.

"Why do I feel like a but is coming?"

"Well for starters there is one key component that would be impossible for Perigord to procure."

"What would that be?" Ursula asked urgently.

"The Gjallarhorn," Ulysses said.

"Impossible, it's only a myth," Ursula shot back flatly.

"Just like goblins, shape shifters, and vampires," Ulysses said patiently.

"Touché."

"Wait, hold it, vampires are real?" Jason said astonished.

"Not now Jason," Ulysses admonished. Jason appeared embarrassed by his outburst and looked sheepishly at Selene who ignored him, her attention on the conversation between Ulysses and Ursula.

"The horn was given its current name by the Vikings who believed that Heimdall would blow the horn signifying Ragnarok, the end of the world. But the horn predates this by tens of thousands of years when it was first brought to this planet," Ulysses said to the group.

"Who brought it?" Jason said totally consumed by the tale.

"I don't know, but I'm sure the answer of the horn and the being who brought it is in here somewhere," Ulysses said as he pointed to the library's walls.

"What else do we need, to know?" Selene asked.

"The information I'm really lacking are the chemicals and elements Perigord needed for his potion" Ulysses said frustrated.

"Plato's book, Transmorphagation, details the ingredients required for the ceremony," Ursula interrupted.

"What are they?" Ulysses asked.

"One is an element in fairly high abundance within this region, the sap from the black sequoia," Ursula said.

"And the other ingredient?" Jason asked eagerly.

"The other is a mineral called Ambroxilene, usually only found deep within the earth, however I don't know what it's used for," Ursula commented.

"Well that's a starting point for us. Can you two find any information on Ambroxilene, where it's found and what it's used for?"

"We'll see what we can do," Jason replied.

"Don't see, do. This is important Jason," Ulysses scolded. Jason nodded. "Selene, along with helping Jason, we need to know of anyone new in town, people Perigord may want here, people here to assist him somehow in the ceremony," Ulysses continued.

"What about Onyx and Strix?" Selene replied.

"They're the muscle. Mind you, Heinrich needs them and they won't be too far away, so be careful. I can't stress this enough," Ulysses added.

"Time is running out, we have only ten days till the Harvest moon," Ursula said.

"I think it's crucial that we all meet here after closing each day so we can pool our information together. Agreed?" Ulysses asked, and everyone nodded, the realisation of the events that were unfolding around them and the gravity of the situation hitting home.

Jason and Selene arrived back at his house. His mother was half way through preparing dinner when they entered the kitchen.

"Hey you two how are things?" Helen said warmly.

"Fine," Selene and Jason replied in unison.

"You don't mind if Selene stays for dinner, do you?" Jason asked sweetly.

"No of course not, you know she's always welcome," Helen replied.

"Don't worry my grandmother knows where I am," Selene cut in bitterly. Jason gave her a small tap with his elbow and Selene put on her best smile, which didn't go unnoticed by Helen who decided not to say anything, but lock it in the memory bank for latter.

After dinner Jason and Selene sat in the study pouring over Plato's books on chemistry.

"I can't believe there's only a small amount of information on Ambroxilene on the net," Selene said over the top of her book.

"Oh I don't know, we have a brief description and what it's used for that's a start," Jason replied.

"How strange that something used as a preserving compound is a key ingredient in creating a super race."

"Speaking of super races, aren't we supposed to go to the lake with Hector tomorrow?" Jason said smugly, Selene laughed out loud.

"Do we have to?" She whined.

"I think it might be good to get out and mingle, maybe this time I won't drown."

"That's not funny," Selene said seriously and threw a pillow at his face, which he caught it in mid-air.

"I wasn't trying to be," Jason said seriously, the memory of that moment with Ulysses still fresh in his mind. Selene noticed his sudden change in mood and she got up and put a hand on his.

"Are you okay?"

"I'm fine," Jason forced a smile to his face and Selene's eyes twinkled as she caressed his hand with her fingertips.

"What are you doing?" he asked quietly. Selene furrowed her brow slightly.

"Oh I thought it was obvious, ya big lug."

"Not that obvious."

"I don't believe it, a big tough guy and you're afraid of little old me," Selene said, a note of frustration creeping into her voice. She started to get to her feet. Jason tugged gently on her arm and pulled her into his lap. Looking into her beautiful silver grey eyes he lent forward to kiss her.

"Oh, I'm sorry," a voice said, startled. Jason jumped out from his seat and Selene fell to the floor as they both looked around to find Helen leaving the room. Jason was about to call out to her when he finally noticed Selene at his feet.

"Shit, I'm so sorry, she kind of startled me," he said apologetically, as he helped her to her feet. Selene rubbed her backside.

"You think?" she said candidly and then seeing Jason's unhappy expression, "don't worry about it."

"Maybe we should call it a night, after all we have a big day tomorrow," Jason said, attempting to change the subject.

"You're right, do you think your mum will mind if I don't say goodbye?"

"Under the circumstances I'm sure she'll understand," Jason said with a grin.

Later that night Helen stopped by Jason's room to say goodnight.

"Are you awake?" Helen said. Jason flicked on his bedside light and peered at the doorway through bleary eyes.

"What's up mum?"

"I just wanted to say goodnight and that I'm sorry for spoiling your moment with Selene." Jason was quiet a moment before he answered.

"It's fine, no harm done. But promise me you won't be acting all funny the next time you see her okay?"

"I promise," Helen seemed to waiver at the door.

"Is there anything else you wanted to say mum?"

"Jason, Selene is a great girl, but promise me you'll take it easy, okay?"

"Is this the sex thing you're worried about?"

"Yes and no, I don't won't to see either of you hurt. Remember you don't have to rush things."

"I wish," Jason muttered.

"What was that?"

"Nothing, point taken. I promise to take things nice and slow. Happy?"

"Yes, now get some sleep," and without another word Helen switched the light off and closed the door.

Chapter 28

DESPITE THE FACT it was a Saturday, Jason had set his alarm early and crawled out of bed. The mornings had been getting colder but Jason found the weather no longer bothered him as his body regulated his temperature automatically. The alien clothing that Ulysses had given him also worked to protect him from the elements. It also freaked him out a little, the way it responded to his thoughts, however this morning he was glad he had it. Sneaking downstairs, Jason let himself out through the back door and ducked into the shadows. After looking around and ensuring he was alone, Jason concentrated and transformed his body into that of a dog. The changes were occurring easier each time and as Jason practiced, he found he was getting better at cataloguing the process, taking nothing more than concentrating on a memory.

He bolted through the streets in his dog form wearing a small backpack. The freedom of anonymity in this simple guise was exhilarating. The still of the early morning allowed him to stretch his senses. His hearing and smell picked up the wildlife around him. His vision allowed him to see in the dark. Jason ran for a while jumping through shrubs and over bushes, chasing cats and peeing on the occasional car. He then remembered why he had come out in the first place.

Selene stirred in her sleep then sat upright in her bed as she heard a noise from outside her window. She made her way over with a torch from her bedside. Whisking the curtain aside she brandished the beam to the ground below. Dressed in jeans and hoodie stood Jason his hand raised to shield his eyes from her torch light. She quietly opened the window.

"Hey, I thought you might like to come for a ride," Jason said with a grin. "But before you come, put this on," Jason added. Before she could respond, he tossed a small parcel in through the open window.

"What's this?" Selene said puzzled.

"Do you even have to ask?" Jason replied. Selene thought it over for a second then let out a little squeal. Quickly slapping a hand over her mouth to muffle the noise.

"Oh my God, you didn't? You did! This is so cool!" Selene rambled.

"Hurry up and get changed," Jason said, waving her away. Selene disappeared out of sight into her room.

Jason paced outside, waiting anxiously for Selene to appear. He was just about to call out to her when a dark figure leapt from the window and landed like a cat in a crouched position a few feet from him. Selene slowly got to her feet. She was now dressed in tight black leather pants, matching knee high boots and a long flowing black leather jacket

"Whoa," was all Jason could get out. Selene smiled in response.

"Damn straight, so where's this ride you promised me?"

"Stand back, this is about to get spectacular," Jason announced. Selene took a couple of paces back just as Jason transformed before her. A large black shape at first, the dark of the early morning partly obscuring his form, until he got to his feet, all four of them. Selene looked on with wide eyes at the beast before her, a magnificent black stallion complete with giant black feathered wings.

Selene climbed onto the stallions back and without thinking, leaned forward and ran her fingers through his thick mane. Jason blew a raspberry and flared his nostrils. Selene snatched back her hand and blushed, realising the intimate action she had performed on him. The stallion beat its wings and began to climb towards the sky. Selene was thrown forward from the sudden movement as she clung desperately to the stallion's neck. Jason gave a mighty flap of his wings and the stallion exploded upward to the heavens. Selene let out a gasp of excitement as they took off. Jason's flight path took them directly up into the cloud-filled sky, the air felt damp and cool. Selene's new clothing changed subtly in response to the cooler air. The leather thickened providing her with more warmth and greater protection from the elements. Once they had reached an altitude where Jason was fairly certain they could no longer be visible to the town's residents, he levelled out and hovered within the cloud. They were still able to view the valley below but were given ample camouflage at the same time.

"This is freakin' awesome," Selene screamed out. Jason neighed in response. "If only we could talk…," Selene was interrupted as the collar on her jacket grew, creeping up and spreading over her ears. She panicked and attempted to pull the alien material from her head when she heard Jason's voice.

"Don't fight it, I'm sure it's not trying to hurt you," Jason soothed.

"Hey I can hear you."

"That's what the jacket's doing on your ears, it's acting as a universal translator"

"This is so cool," Selene gushed.

"You haven't seen anything yet. Hold on" Jason replied. Selene gripped the stallion's mane tight just as they went into a steep nosedive. Despite the fact that she had been expecting something, her eyes went wide and she squealed in exhilaration and fear. They plummeted down sharply. The view of the valley in the morning dawn was like a dark blur. Selene could see the ground approaching, getting closer and closer. Her heart was beating rapidly as they continued to fall. She started to see the tops of the trees as her grip tightened on the stallion's mane.

"Jason, pull up, pull up now!" Selene screamed frantically. At the very last minute Jason pulled up and skimmed across the tops of the trees. Selene let out deep breath and relaxed her grip slightly with one hand and slapped the stallion's neck with the other.

"That was too close, I nearly wet myself."

"Ew, that would have been gross."

"You would have deserved it too, scaring me like that."

"Hey, I was in full control the entire time," Jason shot back.

"I know, but it was still pretty scary."

"I'm sorry, I just thought a little fright and you might hug a little tighter," Jason said candidly. Selene smiled, despite herself.

"Hey if that's what you want, all you have to do is ask."

"Maybe I will," Jason whispered. The pair flew near the lake but detoured away when they could see lights coming from the east side.

"What do you think that is?" Jason asked.

"I don't know, probably just some locals going fishing."

"You don't think they saw us do you?"

"Nah, it's still pretty dark and we were fairly quiet."

"I think so too. I promised Ulysses that I would act responsibly and remain out of sight," Jason said soberly.

"Yeah, I'd imagine he wouldn't be too impressed if there were regular sightings of mythical creatures soaring across the skies," Selene replied.

"It does go against the whole idea of being covert, doesn't it," Jason said as they started to descend to the outskirts of the forest.

"Is everything alright?" Selene asked, concerned.

"Yeah fine, I just thought we'd land somewhere without the possibility of prying eyes catching us."

"Good idea, we're not too far from town and we can walk the rest of the way in. I was thinking I could take you to breakfast if you want and I know the perfect place," Selene said wryly.

Jason and Selene followed a winding trail through the forest. They passed a clearing and stopped to take in the view before them. The sun was just coming over the range, the light catching the clouds and casting a beautiful array of purple and orange hues. Jason was struck dumb by its beauty.

"I don't know what to say," Jason whispered.

"Then don't say anything," Selene replied, taking a hold of his hand. They eventually cleared the forest, both now dressed casually in jeans, hiking boots and hoodies. Selene dragged him along the road.

"Hey, what's the hurry?" Jason growled good naturedly.

"Trust me, after you eat, you'll wonder why we weren't running instead of walking," Selene replied. Jason rolled his eyes and let himself be led on.

They entered a small diner that was located on the outskirts of town. The interior was plain but neat, vinyl trimmed stools lined a stainless steel bench that ran the length of the eatery. There were no customers seated, but noises could be heard from within the kitchen, as well as a cacophony of delightful aromas.

"That smell is to die for. Grab a seat and I'll see if I can get us some service," Selene said. Jason sat down at the first available seat.

"Hey, hello? Anybody there. Selene called out.

"Be right there," a gruff voice called back, Selene pulled up a stool next to Jason.

"So what do you think?" Selene asked.

"It's alright I suppose."

"You suppose? Take a good look around, feel the atmosphere."

"I mean, sure, the retro look is pretty cool, but I haven't eaten yet, so I'll reserve my judgement till then."

"And I expect nothing else from any of my patrons," a voice said sharply. Jason and Selene looked up to find the owner and head chef walking out from the kitchen. Something didn't quite appear right with the way he moved. Jason tried to peer over the counter without appearing too obvious. He saw was a series of ramps and ledges running within the kitchen workspace. The owner was walking along one of the ledges. He was extremely short, standing a mere three foot tall and sporting a bald head and grey goatee. He had the most remarkable broad shoulders on his stunted body.

"Ash how are you?" Selene exclaimed with delight.

"Selene, I've been good, how about yourself" Ash replied with a wry grin. "And who have you brought in on this fine morning?"

"This is Jason. He's new to Perigord but with old ties to the community, and a dear friend so please look after him."

Ash regarded him a moment, his weathered features lined. He squinted his eyes, looked Jason up and down, then nodded and held out an abnormally large hand.

"Well any friend of the spitfire here is a friend of mine," Ash said. Jason took his hand which seemed dwarfed in his and shook.

"Pleased to meet you too. Sir, Selene has been raving about your food."

"Ah, she's too kind. Compared to her grandmother's culinary expertise I'm afraid my simple cuisine might pale in comparison," Ash said humbly.

"Don't sell yourself short, you're the best cook in town," Selene added. Ash gave a chuckle but was clearly chuffed by her words of praise.

"So who is your kin here in Perigord?" Ash said, changing the subject.

"My uncle was Plato Wyngard," Jason replied. Ash's features softened and he looked genuinely saddened by this information.

"I'm sorry for your loss. Your uncle was a decent gentleman, something lacking in these parts."

"Thank you. I didn't get to meet him but I feel I've gotten to know him better since I moved here."

"Yes I've heard all about you." Ash said with a grin.

"Oh don't believe everything you hear."

"I'm not gullible, but I do believe that where there's smoke there's fire, plus there's nothing wrong with a decent campfire," Ash said.

"So what's on the menu this morning?" Selene asked, her eyes glinting in anticipation.

"Oh you're in for a treat. I'm cooking Swedish rye blueberry pancakes with cinnamon twists," Ash said, kissing his fingers.

"Sounds heavenly," Selene said. Jason nodded in agreement.

"Well why don't you put some tunes on and I'll get your meals ready. They're just about done, I personally guarantee you'll love it," Ash said. Without another word he disappeared into the kitchen nimbly, moving along the runs built behind the counters like a mountain goat.

Selene hopped down from her stool and walked over to the jukebox. It was an old 1947 Wurlitzer, beautifully lit with coloured lights. It looked as if it had been recently cleaned as the glass sparkled and surfaces shined. After a short deliberation Selene fed some change into the coin slot, then pressed in her selection. The machine clicked and clunked as the interior mechanics picked up the vinyl record and placed it onto the turnstile where the needle delicately moved into position. Selene walked back over to Jason as the textured sound of the needle on vinyl filtered through the speakers, followed by the earthy sound of a guitar. Selene climbed back onto her stool and faced Jason.

"This is different, what's it called?" Jason asked.

"It's called kind hearted woman blues by Robert Johnson."

"Why do I know that name," Jason asked.

"He's probably one of the most famous names in blues. You probably heard of the musician who went to a crossroad and sold his soul to the devil?" Selene explained.

"That's him!"

"Yep, that's him"

Just then Ash returned bearing a large tray containing two plates of blueberry pancakes and a side order of cinnamon twists. It was both visually and aromatically arresting. Jason could feel his hunger double instantly.

"Would you like some coffee as well? It's a Rwandan blend, very nice. Both Selene and Jason nodded.

"Great," Ash said and poured them each a steamy cup of the dark roasted coffee.

"We'll I've got to start organising lunch, please enjoy," Ash said and disappeared back into the kitchen.

"Thank you," Jason called out and was met with the sounds of a whisk on a metal bowl.

"Very efficient, isn't he?" Jason remarked.

"Yeah, he's in the zone when he's here. You might not believe this but he's a very talented dancer and quite popular with the ladies around here."

"I wouldn't doubt it at all. A man who owns his own business, can cook and dance, what's not to love?" Jason said with a grin.

"That's what I love about you, I don't need to spell it out," Selene replied before placing a forkful of pancake into her mouth with a moan.

Chapter 29

AFTER BREAKFAST THEY went their separate ways, each wanting to chase up information for Ulysses before their afternoon at the lake. Jason arrived at Selene's house around eleven and after being greeted at the door by Selene, he tentatively entered.

"So is it safe to come in?" Jason asked.

"Of course, we've done nothing wrong," Selene snapped, then seeing Jason's reaction, softened.

"I'm sorry, I guess I'm still a little sensitive about what happened."

"I know it's not my place to say, but try and take it easy on her, after all she was only doing what she thought was right."

"On one level I know what you're saying is right, but it still hurts to know that she had been skulking around behind our backs. I'll forgive her, but its gonna take time and a huge amount of sucking up on her part," Selene said with a wicked smile.

"That's my girl."

"Oh, I'm your girl, am I?" Selene said with her hands

on her hips and a defiant look on her face. Jason was just about to retract his last statement when Selene added.

"Relax tiger," she leant over and grasped his hand in hers, giving it a gentle squeeze, followed by a kiss on the cheek.

"Have you had lunch yet?" Selene asked.

"No, I wasn't sure what you were doing."

"Great, I made something light and there's more than enough for both of us," Selene replied. She led Jason out onto the back terrace where she had a platter of fruit and cheese and a jug of iced tea waiting.

After eating lunch they sat on the timber bench seat in a comfortable silence enjoying the sunshine and view. Ursula's backyard consisted of beautiful sprawling wild flowers and garden herbs meticulously arranged in a way that allowed for easy upkeep, but also looked natural and abundant.

"I think I could easily sit here for the rest of the day," Jason observed. Selene moved closer to Jason on the seat and rested her head on his shoulder, sliding an arm around his waist.

"Yeah, I could do the same," she replied. Jason wrapped an arm around her shoulder and let out a satisfied sigh in response. Just then a car horn sounded out by the street, followed by a young man's voice calling out. Selene grumbled and pushed herself off Jason.

"Great, I'm pretty sure that's Hector out front," Selene muttered.

"Yeah, I was kind of wondering when he was going to turn up."

"I guess we better go and have some fun then," Selene said miserably.

Hector was sitting alone in his beat-up convertible four wheel drive directly out front of Selene's house. The engine was running and hip hop music flooded out into the street. He hadn't noticed Jason and Selene approach, his face was set in an irritated scowl.

"Hey sorry to keep you waiting," Jason called out, Hector spun around in his seat, his brow furrowed in thought. Almost immediately he turned on a thousand watt smile.

"Hey, I was beginning to think I might have to come and get you two," Hector replied good naturedly.

"Are we good to go?" Selene said, as she tossed her bag into the back seat, Hector appeared a little annoyed by her comment but threw it off straight away, keeping his attention primarily focused on Jason.

"Grab a seat and we'll get going," Hector said. Jason and Selene climbed into the vehicle. They had barely sat down when Hector floored the accelerator as his car took off down the street like a rocket.

The three of them sped through town. Hector was very adept behind the wheel and knew his way around, finding the shortcuts and missing most of the small town traffic. He also proved equally skilled on the dirt roads that lay through the forest. They made it to the far side of the lake in a short time. Jason and Selene gripped the undersides of their seats and tried to remain calm and indifferent to Hector's wild driving. The four wheel drive eventually came to a skidding halt in a small clearing where a handful of similar styled vehicles were awaiting them.

“This is our stop,” Hector said with a grin. Jason and Selene looked around at their destination. It was one of many small inlets that made up the vast Greymeade Lake. Jason was taken aback by the beauty of the spot. A couple of large trees stood on the edge of the bank, their vast branches reaching out over the dark and shimmering water. Rope swings were suspended from the branches and all were in use by girls and boys Jason's age. The kids were climbing tall rope ladders high into the tree tops then swinging down and out across the lake, letting go at the last second as they were flung out above the water's surface, then landing with a gleeful scream and splash. A few of the boys called out to Hector as the three of them approached the bank's edge. Jason noted one of them was Tiberius.

“This is quite a setup?” Jason said, impressed.

“Yeah, kids have been coming out to this spot for years,” Hector replied.

“Have you ever been here before?” Jason asked Selene. She shook her head quickly.

“It's usually only couples that come out, right Selene?” Hector interjected smugly. This made Selene blush but she covered it carefully, pretending to brush the hair from her face. Some of the other kids had noticed their arrival and were making their way over to them.

“You guys remember Jason and Selene?” Hector announced to the group, some of whom nodded in response. Others gave a wave or said their greetings. Hector picked up on the nervous anxiety of his friends.

“It's alright, we've had our problems in the past, but we've buried the hatchet now, so it's all cool,” Hector added, Tiberius had joined the group and wore a dirty grin on his face now.

"Hey, enough of all this touchy feely shit, let's have some fun!" Hector called out. This was met with laughter and cheering. The group broke, some racing for the trees. A few hung around to make small talk with the new arrivals.

"I don't know about you two but I feel like getting wet," Hector remarked.

Jason and Selene ducked behind a couple of trees and engaged their alien suits. Jason was the first to emerge, wearing a simple pair of red and black swimming trunks. He strolled over to Hector who was still in the process of retrieving his clothing from the boot of his car. Hector looked up as Jason approached, a look of surprise on his face.

"Hey buddy you didn't waste any time did ya?" Hector commented. Jason shrugged and realised that he shouldn't have rushed the change, lest he aroused suspicion. Jason was about to say something when he noticed Hector staring at something behind him. Jason turned to see Selene walking over to them, dressed in a revealing floral two piece swim suit. Her hair was down and it flowed over her strong lean shoulders. It was obvious to both boys that she took her exercising seriously as her exposed flesh was taunt and athletic.

"Is something wrong? You two look a little flushed," Selene commented oblivious to the effect she was having on Jason and Hector.

"No I'm, I mean we're good, right?" Jason said, flustered.

"Right," Hector agreed readily, then muttered under his breath so only Jason could hear. "You lucky bastard."

The three of them joined the others at the lake side, both Selene and Jason getting their share of approving glances.

"I feel like a piece of meat in this," Selene muttered. Jason laughed.

"Well that costume of yours leaves nothing to the imagination, but obviously yours is pretty resourceful," Jason whispered back. The three of them climbed into the trees and grabbed a rope each.

"Here goes," Jason called out. He swung down, yelling out in imitation to Tarzan. He released at the last moment. His momentum lifted him into the air, then gravity pulled him back down as he entered the water with a mighty splash. The water was cool, but refreshing. As he surfaced Selene and Hector were mere seconds behind him, making dual impacts in the water near him. Selene was the first to surface, her now wet hair slicked back and a huge smile spread wide.

"That was awesome, let's go again," Selene said excitedly. Just then Hector broke the surface and let out a huge whopping sound.

"I love this place," Hector yelled out. This was met by laughter and cheers of equal agreement.

"Yeah I think this place could grow on me," Jason said ruefully. Selene playfully slapped water in his direction.

After spending the afternoon in and out of the water, Jason and Selene lay side by side on the grassy bank staring up at the sky.

"You know I think this might be the most relaxing day

that I've had so far in Perigord," Jason said, then stretched out as if to prove the point.

"Yeah I'd have to agree, I've always thought these guys were real douche bags, but they've proven me wrong today," Selene replied. As if on cue, Hector called out to them.

"Hey you two come here I have something to show you," he said.

"What is it?" Jason replied, not wanting to get up.

"I mean it, you've really got to check this out man," Hector insisted. Jason looked at Selene, then shrugged.

"You want to check it out?" Jason asked.

"Nah, you go on, I think I'll just lay here and enjoy the sun."

"Fair enough," Jason replied as he slowly got to his feet. "Your loss." He made his way over to Hector who was with Tiberius and a couple of the other girls Jason had met during the afternoon. Mandy, a tall willowy blonde who started every sentence with "Oh my God" and Jade, a petite redhead who giggled every time she made eye contact with Jason. The four of them were standing at the back of Tiberius's van.

"What's going on?" Jason asked Hector, who gave him a knowing grin.

"Hey bud, we've been having a pretty good time today, right?" Hector asked cryptically.

"Yeah sure, it's been a blast," Jason replied.

"It's been okay, but it's missing one thing," Tiberius added cryptically.

"Oh yeah, what's that?" Jason asked.

"I'm glad you asked," Hector said and flung open the back of the van revealing cartons of Black River Cider.

"Oh my God," Mandy cried, which drew the attention of the others who were sitting on the edge of the bank. The group started to cheer and clap when they saw the payload awaiting them. One of Tiberius's friends, a short skinny kid with a half grown mohawk whom everyone called Halo, started to chant "drink, drink," and soon everyone else was chanting as well. Everyone except for Jason.

"Okay, okay hold it down," Hector said, addressing the crowd, a huge grin on his face. Selene was now joining the group and she saw the bottles of booze that lined the back of the van.

"Holy shit," Selene said, surprised at what she saw. Hector was instructing the other boys in the group to unload the van and within a short time there was a couple of chests sitting by the lake filled with ice and cider. Before long they were sitting in deck chairs and drinking liberally. Jason and Selene hung back from the group and it was now noticeable that they were the only ones not indulging.

"You're not drinking Jason?" Hector enquired dubiously.

"Ah nah, I'm not really in the mood," Jason replied, attempting to be disinterested. "One or two drinks aren't gonna kill you."

"We know," Selene said coldly. Hector walked over to the ice chest and retrieved two bottles. Cracking the tops off them, he handed them to the pair. Selene grabbed hers and took a long swallow from it.

"There, that wasn't so hard was it?" Hector said,

watching Jason closely until he too took a gulp from his bottle.

"Whoo hoo, now it's a party," Hector exclaimed, clapping his hands together and making his way over to the ice chest for another beverage.

"He's right you know, a couple of these won't kill us. Hell, even the label says that they use all natural ingredients," Jason said with a grin.

"So what you're saying is having a couple of brews is actually beneficial?" Selene replied.

"Bingo," Jason said and they both burst out laughing.

Dusk had crept up on them as they sat around a campfire. Most of the kids had paired off and were making out in the flickering light. The ground around them was littered with empty bottles. Jason was lying on his back, his head resting on Selene's lap as she gently combed her fingers through his hair. A light sheen of sweat had formed on his brow and Selene noticed his temperature was a little warmer. She was not sure whether this was due to the close proximity to the fire or the ciders Jason had consumed. Selene looked across the fire towards Tiberius who was telling a dirty joke to Jade, who had obviously drunk way too much and was laughing hysterically in all the wrong places.

"So how were you able to get the alcohol?" Selene asked pointedly. Tiberius turned from his conversation with Jade and smiled, the glow from the fire giving him a creepy aura.

"Let's just say that our dads have a bit of pull with the local merchants," Tiberius said smugly, indicating himself and Hector.

"Yeah you'd be amazed what we can get or hands on," Hector added, completely full of himself. "How's the big fella there?" he added, clearly not concerned with Jason's wellbeing.

"Oh he's fine, just resting. He was up pretty early this morning training," Selene replied. This comment clearly annoyed Hector who barely tried to conceal his emotions. Jason sat up at the mention of his name and peered over at the two boys opposite.

"Someone say my name?" Jason asked. This was met with laughter from everyone but Selene.

"Yeah, we were just saying that you're looking a little out of sorts," Tiberius replied. This was also met with cruel laughter.

"No I'm fine, just a little tired, been a big day," Jason said. His pale sweaty face indicated that he was more than just fatigued.

"So we've been told," Hector admonished. "I hope you've got a little energy left for the surprise later on," Hector added with a laugh. This time only Tiberius joined in. Jason wiped the sweat from his brow and tried to get to his feet.

"What surprise?" Selene asked, her eyes narrowing in concern.

"Well we were going to show you later, but I think we're about to wrap things up here," Hector said. This was met by groans from the group.

"Don't worry we're going to continue at my place. Dad's out of town for the night, so we can kick on there" Hector added. The group cheered and got to their feet. They went about packing their vehicles, their industriousness driven only by their desire to continue drinking.

After the campsite was packed, people climbed into their cars.

"Mandy, head on to my place with the others. Tib and I will be along shortly we just want to show Jason and Selene something first," Hector instructed Mandy and threw her his keys.

"Don't be long," Mandy said sweetly, then blew him a kiss.

"I won't," he said with a grin and a wink.

"Selene was watching this with trepidation, thinking that Hector had made it clear only he and Tiberius would be going back to the party. She looked at Jason who was having trouble standing, his features were pale and slicked with sweat. Even his eyes looked slightly glazed.

"I don't know if Jason's up to it," Selene said, concerned.

"Nonsense, he'll be fine, it won't take long then we'll drop you both off," Tiberius replied.

"Okay," Selene said, though she didn't believe him, but thought with Jason not well, her options were limited. The four of them got into Tiberius's van and he drove them down a track that ran parallel with the edge of the lake. It was completely dark now and the van's headlights cast thin beams through the vegetation, covering the seldom used track.

"So, um, how long is this going to take?" Selene asked an urgent edge to her voice. Both Hector and Tiberius looked at each other and chuckled.

"What's your rush?" Tiberius replied cockily.

"I'm just concerned about Jason," Selene responded. Jason had his head resting against the passenger side window his breathing was coming in deep rasps.

"He's not going to spew is he?" Tiberius asked, a look of disgust on his face.

"He can't handle his booze, can he?" Hector added, slightly amused by Tiberius's reaction to possible vomiting and the fact that alcohol had` proved to be Jason's Achilles heel.

"It's not the cider, I think he's sick, like food poisoning or something," Selene said hotly. Just then the van came to a halt.

"We're here," Hector announced. Selene looked out her window but couldn't see anything in the darkness.

"What the hell am I supposed to be looking at?" Selene demanded.

"You can't see it from here, plus we'll need this," Tiberius replied and produced a large torch.

"Well let's get this over with," Selene sighed.

"That's the spirit," Hector said laughing.

The four of them walked down a narrow path toward the lake. Both Hector and Tiberius were on either side of Jason, gripping his arms to prevent him from falling over. Jason was deathly pale now and Selene was pretty sure he had no idea where he was. As they got closer to the lake Selene could make out a large shape ahead of them which she assumed was an old shack of some kind.

"What's that supposed to be?" Selene questioned.

"It's the water plant for the Black River Brewing Company, where they conduct the initial purification," Tiberius explained.

"And you thought we'd like this because?"

"Well It's hard to explain, but easier to show," Hector replied. They led Selene and Jason through a hole in the security fence and towards the small brick utility which appeared to be locked up tight.

"It's a locked building," Selene said, agitated.

"And I have the key," Hector said and produced a screwdriver.

"Are you planning on breaking in?" Selene said shocked.

"Relax, I'm not going to vandalise or steal anything." Without waiting for Selene to respond, Tiberius helped Hector scale the wall and reach a small, closed window. After a moment, perched on the window sill, Hector was able to pry the window open with his screwdriver and crawl in. Selene could see the beam of the torch bouncing around inside and after a few minutes the back door opened and Hector emerged, the torch directly perched under his chin, giving him a rather ghoulish appearance.

"Walk this way," Hector said in a bad English accent. Tiberius and Selene helped Jason through the door as they followed Hector with the torch. Machinery and pumps were running inside and a faint glow of display lights cast the surroundings in an eerie green glow.

"This is it!" Hector exclaimed and pointed to a large pit with a steel grill covering the top. Hector and Tiberius went right away, flipping some nearby switches. The steel grate started to lift, hoisted up by thick steel chains. The noise was deafening. Hector shined his torch into the pit. A strange blue glow could be seen coming from the bottom.

"Have a closer look," Hector urged. Selene, who was holding Jason, looked uneasy.

"Take a look, I've got him," Tiberius repeated and grabbed a hold of Jason's shoulder. Selene reluctantly released her hold and stepped forward, peering into the dark abyss. What she saw in the pit was water slowly flowing in through a large pipe, obviously being fed from Greymeade Lake and through a large steel sleeve that filtered any mud and muck, preventing it from getting into the pumps. What really caught Selene's attention was the blue glow which emanated from hundreds of blue luminescent rocks lining the bottom of the pit.

"What are those rocks, they're beautiful," she whispered.

"Ah girls and their sparkly things," Tiberius chuckled.

"They're a mineral that apparently helps with the purification process. Hard to get anywhere else but can be found in abundance this side of the lake. Oh yeah, in the absence of UV light, it emits a blue glow. Pretty cool hey?"

"Actually it is pretty cool, however I'm sure seeing this could of waited for another time," Selene said, pointing at Jason.

"Yeah I suppose, but that's not the reason we brought you," Hector said cryptically. Selene gave him a puzzled look. Hector nodded to Tiberius who was holding Jason up, then without provocation, pushed him into the pit. When Jason hit the water he proceeded to sink like a stone.

"No!" Selene screamed and struck Hector with a right cross. She dove into the pit after Jason. Selene was able to find him easily at the bottom due to the strong blue glow. Jason was floating, his body moving back and forward to the rhythmic pulsing of the pumps. She grabbed him by the t-shirt and dragged him to the surface. She was gasping for air but Jason was unconscious and not breathing.

"Thanks for jumping, saved us pushing you in as well," Tiberius called out. They both broke into more laughter.

"You bastards get us out of here, right now!" Selene screamed angrily. This was met with more laughter from above. Selene ignored them as she struggled to keep herself and Jason afloat. She cradled his head in the crook of her arm and proceeded with a great deal of difficulty to start giving him CPR. Hector and Tiberius watched passively from the top. After several tense minutes of performing mouth to mouth, Jason convulsed and spewed up a gutful of water and alcohol, his eyes slowly opening.

"Hey beautiful anything for a kiss, eh?" Jason spluttered weakly. Selene gave him a weak smile back, then hugged him fiercely.

"You asshole, you had me so worried, I thought I was going to lose you," she said, her eyes full of tears.

"Well I'm still here, wherever that is. The last thing I remember was getting into Tiberius's van," Jason said, the strain evident in his voice. Selene pointed to the top of the pit.

"Those shitheads up there planned this, but if they don't get us out right now they're gonna get their asses kicked," Selene yelled.

"Please, spare us the feisty girl speech Selene. You two aren't going anywhere, ever again," Hector said coldly.

"Hey enough's enough. You've had your joke. This is no longer funny, get us out now," Jason rasped.

"That's not happening. You know I haven't stopped

thinking about that beating you dished out. Nobody could have done what you did, both on the basketball court or the cafeteria. I've been following you around lately, things don't appear right and I've come to a conclusion," Hector stated calmly.

"And what's that?" Jason asked, exhaustion and concern on his face.

"Why, you're not human, that's what."

"What?" Jason and Selene exclaimed incredulously. Even Tiberius looked uncomfortable.

"You heard me, I know your secret. My dad told me about that freak Ulysses and all the strange stuff that happens around him, and then you show up and become his number one disciple. You, him and that library are all evil. And it's about time somebody did something about it," Hector concluded righteously.

"Are you out of your mind?" Selene screamed.

"And let's not forget about you, the goth girl who's shacking up with that abomination," Hector spat.

"Hector, whatever you think your problem is, it's with me, not her."

"I saw you change," Hector said frankly. Jason and Selene went quiet. "No, nothing to add? Your silence says it all" Hector continued.

"I don't know what you think you saw," Jason said hastily.

"Don't even try to deny it, I know it's true."

"You're crazy," Jason whispered.

"I thought so too the first time. You brazenly changed shape running to school," Hector replied. Jason remained silent which made Hector smile. "That's what I thought," Hector added.

"Hector, don't do this," Selene said angrily.

"I was late for school too that day, algebra test," Hector continued with his story in a robotic tone. Everyone was watching him strangely, including Tiberius. "I saw this blur in the distance. You. I didn't know it at first, but I stopped and tried to get a better view at what it was. Then BAM, you came rocketing past. It was you but it wasn't. You're arms and legs were longer and your face, my God your face was distorted, longer, streamlined. But it was definitely you. You were jumping and running and landing like a cat, it was incredible," his voice trailed off. Tiberius put his arm on his shoulder. This seemed to shake Hector from his trance, a furious look appearing on his face.

"But it was wrong. WRONG!" Hector screamed. Everyone flinched except for Jason who was too tired and exhausted to react. His self-preservation meter was going into the red.

"Okay I'm willing to concede that since coming to Perigord I have undergone some changes, but I'm human and definitely not evil. Now you have to listen to reason," Jason said calmly, trying in vain to reason with Hector.

"I don't want to hear your lies and I don't want to have your presence, your infection around anymore. This ends tonight. You end tonight," Hector said with finality and walked back over to the switchboard.

"Whatever you're thinking, don't do it," Jason pleaded. Without warning the machinery started up and the large steel grate that had been covering the pit was hoisted into the air once again. As it appeared over the pit Selene screamed in realisation, watching helplessly as it slowly lowered into position.

"No!" Jason and Selene screamed in unison as the grate clanged into position, sitting atop the pit. Hector and Tiberius looked down one last time, smiling coldly, their eyes black and lifeless in the darkness. Jason felt total despair for their situation. Then they were gone, the sound of their footsteps echoing as they left the building. The last thing they heard was the door slamming shut behind them. Selene gripped Jason tight, her eyes we're wide with fear and the dawning knowledge of where they were.

"OhmyGod," Selene said, panic stricken.

"Relax, we're going to be fine," Jason said, trying to sooth her, despite the fact that he was feeling weaker than ever.

"Don't you understand, nobody knows that we're here," Selene said shrilly.

"There's bound to be someone that comes out to check on this place,"

"On the weekend?"

"I know, this seems pretty screwed up, but we can't give up can we?" Jason said strained. "I don't know why I feel so goddamn useless," he added. His last comment proved to be the mental slap Selene needed to get a hold of her emotions. Her jaw set in grim determination.

"Can you tread water on your own for a minute?" Selene asked. Jason nodded. She released her grip on him and padded her way to the side of the pit. Jason watched her closely, his head barely above the water line, his movements slow and laboured. Selene ran her hand up the concrete wall trying to find an edge or imperfection allowing for a grip or a handhold. She tried several times to scale the side of the pit. Each attempt failed and resulted in a yell of frustration and a loud splash.

"Shit, shit, shit!" Selene cursed as she swam back over to Jason.

"This pit was definitely not designed to be climbed out of," Selene added as she grabbed a hold of Jason's arm.

"I don't mean to ask a stupid question, but why don't you just turn into a giant eagle and fly us out of here?" Selene said deadpan, Jason let out a sigh.

"Well for starters there's that grate above our head," he replied.

"It doesn't have to be an eagle, I'd be pretty much happy for a flying squirrel that shoots lasers from its eyes if that helps," Selene quipped.

"I've been trying to change, from the moment that you revived me, but I can't," Jason replied exasperated.

"You can't, or you're having trouble changing?"

"I can't, as in at all. Maybe my powers are gone for good. I am half human after all," Jason said miserably.

"I don't know about any of that, we can sort it out later, but right now we need to find another way out and the only other way is down," Selene said determined.

"So what's your plan then?" Jason asked.

"Recon" and without another word, she let go of Jason and plunged under the water. She swam directly down near the glowing rocks that littered the bottom, allowing her to clearly see her surroundings. After frantically checking from side to side, Selene eventually spotted an opening, a circular port one meter in diameter with a steel mesh sleeve slotted over the opening. She silently cursed their bad luck as she swam over to it for a better look. She slid her hand around the edges of the sleeve inspecting it for a means of removal. She couldn't see or feel any screws or bolts holding it in place as she continued to search the rim. Selene's lungs were burning for air and her throat was raw. Nearly at the point of giving up, her hands felt something promising. A draw bolt latch snapped noiselessly open under her fingers. She mentally cheered as she pushed off from the bottom towards the surface. Jason's patience had grown thin waiting and he was just preparing to go and look for her when she exploded through the surface next to him.

"Thank God you're okay!" Jason exclaimed with an anxious smile.

"I did it, we have a way out through the intake valve," Selene replied breathlessly.

"That's great!" Jason rasped. Selene could hear the exhaustion in his voice and then it dawned on her. Jason saw her reaction and nodded solemnly.

"I'm not leaving you here," Selene growled angrily.

"It's the only way. The pipe leading out must be fifty, sixty meters long and I'm too weak," he gasped.

"Screw that, both of us go or neither. They're the only two options on the table," Selene thundered.

"Once you're out," Jason said logically.

"I mean it, SHUT UP!" Selene replied, but Jason continued.

"Once you're clear come back and pull me out."

"What if I can't get into the building? What if I

can't work the machinery? What if I can't pull you out? What if…"

"That's a lot of what ifs," Jason interjected. If all else fails you run and get help, I'll be fine."

"No, no, no, and that's final," Selene replied. "We're getting out together and that's all there is to it."

Jason was about to respond when Selene gave him a scathing glare.

"What's the plan then?" Jason asked with a sigh.

"Simple, we swim to the bottom, I pull off the steel sleeve and we swim through the length of the pipe."

"Then?"

"Then we find those dweebs and kick their asses."

"That's the one part of the plan I actually like," Jason said ruefully.

"Good, then let's get started."

The pair readied themselves by taking long deep breaths, saturating their lungs with oxygen. They both knew they had one shot at this and they knew they had to make it count. Selene counted down on her hand, three, two, one. They both took a huge breath and dived below. Moving together they reached the bottom and as they approached the blue glowing rocks, Jason began to convulse. Selene's eyes went wide but instead of grabbing him she made the painful decision to continue on with her plan. With minimal effort she was able to ease the steel sleeve, without deliberation She scooped up a handful of the glowing rock. With her other free hand she grabbed Jason and proceeded to drag him through the pipeline.

Using the blue rocks Selene was able to illuminate the tight passage way, however her progress was painfully slow.

After twenty meters of movement Selene's progress came to a sudden halt. Looking back, she was horrified to find that Jason had become snagged on something. Releasing her grip, she slowly worked her way back, squeezing past Jason until she was in line with his feet. With the rocks in hand she could see that the laces of his left shoe had become tangled on the metal lip of a pipe. Without wasting time Selene frantically ripped the shoe from his foot and dropped it without another thought. The shoe almost immediately reverted into a grey gloop that then dissolved into nothing. Shocked at first, she then remembered the alien clothing they were wearing as she pulled herself past the still form of Jason.

By now Selene's lungs were burning worse than ever as she attempted to grab Jason's arm only to discover her hand wouldn't work. She tried again with the same result, her vision was also starting to blur. 'Oh no, please God don't let us die here underground in the dark, Selene pleaded silently, then blacked out.

Chapter 30

JASON AWOKE WITH a start and gasped as if struggling for air. It took him a few seconds before he realised that he wasn't in the pit but lying on his bed at home safe. He looked around at the sunlight flooding in through the bedroom window, he watched as it caught the stained glass, the multi-coloured spectrum casting an ethereal quality around him. Mixed emotions played with his mind.

"Selene!" Jason yelled. "How the hell did I get here?" he muttered out loud as his head fell back onto his pillow.

"Am I going mad?" Jason yelled out.

"No, you're not," a voice answered back. Jason jumped in surprise.

"Who's there?" Jason demanded as he jumped up from his bed, looking around the room. A figure stepped forward from the far side of the room. Despite the fact the room was bathed in light, it was surprising that Jason hadn't noticed the figure until now. He adopted a fighter's stance.

"You've got five seconds to tell me who you are or so

help me I'm gonna go total beast mode on your ass," Jason said, confusion giving way to anger. With everything that had happened to him recently he now had a target to let it all out on.

"Relax Jason, I mean you no harm, in fact the opposite," The figure said. Jason looked the individual up and down. A tall, lean, middle aged man dressed casually in jeans, plain cotton shirt and boots. He wore dark brown hair and a beard that appeared well trimmed and immaculately groomed. The skin on his face was tanned with crows' feet etched at the corner of his eyes which were a deep crystal blue. The figure was smiling but Jason thought it looked kind of sad at the same time.

"Where's Selene?" Jason asked, still wary of the stranger and how he suddenly appeared.

"I'm here to help you and your friend," the stranger replied.

"Where's Selene?"

"She's in trouble and she needs your help."

"What? How? We have to help her," Jason insisted.

"And you will, but first I have something to tell you," the stranger said calmly.

"No, we have to help her first," Jason said agitation in his voice.

"We have time Jason, have patience and listen to what I have to tell you." Jason screwed his fists up to his face and growled.

"Ugh, I am so sick to death of people telling me what to do," he snarled, transforming into stone, He brought both hands down onto his bed shattering it completely.

Jason then turned to face the stranger. "Great, look what you made me do."

"Relax Jason, its fine," the stranger said pleasantly. Jason fell to his knees in frustration staring at the grey slabs that were now his hands. The anger fled from him as he transformed back into his human form.

"No it's not. I wreck everything and when it's truly important, I can't even save the people I love."

"You haven't wrecked anything, look," the stranger indicated.

Jason turned his head with a sigh only to find his bed as it was before, unbroken and intact. He turned back to the stranger, a puzzled expression on his face.

"This isn't real is it?" Jason asked.

"Yes and no," the stranger replied quizzically. "Please trust me for the moment," the stranger added. Taking a step forward, he placed his hand on Jason's forearm and closed his eyes.

"Is this necessary?" Jason started to comment, when a searing surge of heat coursed through his arm where the stranger was holding him. Jason cried out and tried to pull his arm away, but the grip was too strong. Then as fast as the pain appeared it was gone, replaced with a soothing cool. The stranger released his grip on Jason who snatched it away, rubbing the spot that the stranger had held. The pain was already a distant memory.

"What the hell did you do that for?" Jason grumbled.

"It was your legacy Jason, but I have one more thing for you," the stranger added. Jason took a careful step back, keeping his arms a respectful distance from the stranger, who laughed at his reaction. The laughter was honest and for some reason, he knew at that moment that he could trust him.

"Just some simple words of advice," the stranger said. Jason nodded for him to continue. "No man or woman born, coward or brave, can shun his destiny," the stranger said.

"I don't understand," Jason stated.

"You'll know when the time is right," the stranger said.

"Really, you're gonna lay that old chestnut on me? I want to know how to save Selene," he cursed.

"Then you need to wake up," the stranger said simply and touched Jason on the forehead.

"What are you talking about?" he asked. The room seemed to shimmer and blur and Jason felt what he could only describe as a vacuum effect pulling him in all directions. The room began to darken.

"Who are you?" Jason called out.

"My name is Be…," the stranger said and was cut off in mid-sentence as Jason's world pitched into black.

Jason slowly opened his eyes and discovered a darkness of a different kind. Claustrophobic, grimy and wet he realised with an unsettling certainty that he was underwater. His body's defences had kicked in to cope with its new environment, altering to the form that Ulysses and he bore when swimming deep within the lake earlier in the week. His eyes adapted to the dark and the water allowed him to view his surroundings easily. Remembering Selene, he twisted and turned in the tight confines until he saw her body floating lifelessly ahead of him in the pipeline.

"Selene!" he screamed, as his lower torso which was now made up of thick tentacles contracted and propelled him through the pipe towards her. Slowing his momentum he approached her and delicately took her into his arms. Turning her face towards his he was shocked to see the pale and vacant expression on her face. Jason hugged her, despair gripping his heart. He shook the feelings from his head, a fierce determination taking hold as he propelled himself like a torpedo through the pipeline, carefully shielding her body from anything obstructing their path.

The surface of the lake was tranquil and still, the cool weather having deterred any one from town venturing out at this late hour. Only the sounds of forest wildlife could be heard. This was short lived as Jason and Selene erupted from the black surface in an explosive shower of water, his speed propelling them high into the air. For a brief moment Jason's aquatic form and Selene's limp figure seemed to hang in the night sky, neither falling nor climbing. Inevitably gravity took over and the pair began their descent. Jason transformed again, this time into the guise of a huge eagle. The change took a split second, his large, powerful talons delicately gripping Selene's still form. Without hesitation Jason flew off into the night sky, the loud, rhythmic beating of his wings clearly audible through the forest.

In his newly acquired form he circled over the town of Perigord before coming in for a landing directly at the front of the library. Jason carefully placed Selene on the front steps then reverted back to his human form, his clothes automatically changing. He scooped Selene up in his arms and raced for the front doors. Kicking them open he ran through and stood at the top of the internal stairs looking frantically down into the dark interior.

"Ulysses! Jax! I need help!" Jason screamed as he charged down the stairs. About half way down lights started to flicker on, illuminating Jason's progress. As he reached the bottom he was met by Ms Jax dressed in a nightgown, slippers and hair net. Under any other situation Jason would have found her appearance comical but under the current circumstances he was just glad to see her.

"Thank God, I need help, it's Selene," Jason gasped as he presented her body. Ms Jax looked shocked and then determined.

"With me," she said with authority. Jason nodded and followed quickly through the double doors and into the staff area, then through yet another door, one he had never seen before. They entered a large, empty room with a single stone bench located in the centre. Jason looked around, clearly bewildered by his surroundings.

"Place her down," Ms Jax instructed briskly. Jason just stared at the stone bench. "Now!" Ms Jax barked. Jason nodded dumbly then stumbled forward and placed Selene's still form gently on the bench.

"Step back," Ms Jax instructed and motioned Jason to step away from the bench. "Greymeade, initiate nightingale protocol," Ms Jax spoke aloud to the empty room and grabbed Jason's arm, pulling them both back away from the bench. A large, empty echoing sound reverberated through the room, then quite expectantly, a circular opening appeared above them in the ceiling.

"What the hell is that?" Jason breathed as dozens of

thick tendrils poured from the opening. He thought they looked exactly like tree roots. The tendrils rippled and quivered and slowly descended towards the still form of Selene. Jason took a step toward her but was held firm by the vice like grip of Ms Jax.

"Don't interfere," Ms Jax said in her gravelly voice. "Please, trust me, okay?"

Jason watched with apprehension as the roots flowed down like running water toward Selene. The tendrils curled and twisted, slowly enveloping her. Jason found the scene almost impossible to watch as the roots started to form a crude, egg-like shape around Selene's body. Hundreds of tiny shoots began to sprout forth all over the egg, then slowly each shoot unfurled into a vibrant, green leaf.

The leaves proceeded to flatten against the surface, eventually covering every inch of the egg shape beneath. It reminded Jason of the sack certain types of ants make by excreting a sticky substance that bonds leaves together in a soft ball sized shape. The leaf-covered egg remained perched upon the stone bench, then as if things weren't strange enough, it began to hum. A pale electric light within started to pulse. Jason covered his eyes with his hand, trying to watch the process. He could just make out the still figure of Selene illuminated within during each burst of light. The humming noise grew louder and the light pulses increased in both speed and brightness. It elevated to such a level that Jason had to cover his ears and shield his eyes completely. The room was enveloped with the strobe light pulses emanating from the egg. Ms Jax leant over and whispered something in Jason's ear, but he couldn't hear. He watched as she too covered her eyes. The pulsing light stopped for a split second and then one pure nova burst of light seared through the room. Even with his eyes covered it wasn't enough. As quickly as it had started, it suddenly stopped. The light and the humming were replaced with a haunting silence. Jason struggled to make out anything in the room, his vision blurred from the light exposure. He rubbed his eyes and was able to catch a glimpse of the roots retracting into the ceiling, leaving the egg shape on the bench. The shapes' leaves were now dry and brown.

"Selene!" Jason exclaimed as he raced over to the bench. He knelt beside the eggs and slowly extended his hand, gently brushing the surface. The dried leaves turned to fine ash under his touch, creating a shockwave effect as the entire surface became consumed by ash. It eventually disappeared revealing Selene underneath. Jason carefully stroked her cheek and was overwhelmed to find it warm to the touch. He checked her pulse and found it steady. He could see she was breathing and colour had returned to her pale features.

"Thank God," Jason whispered, his eyes wet with tears. Ms Jax came up behind him and placed her hand on his shoulder. In a moment of pure abandon Jason turned and swept Ms Jax into his arms hugging her fiercely.

"Thank you Ms Jax, I don't know what to say," Jason said his voice cracking with emotion. She looked a little taken aback and then smiled warmly and returned his hug.

"She's going to be okay," Ms Jax replied. Jason stepped back and wiped his eyes on the back of his hand.

"Let's move her into the staff room," Ms Jax instructed.

Lifting Selene gently Jason carried her through the doors and laid her down upon the lounge opposite the fire place. He was now starting to feel the effects of his fatigue and slumped down beside her.

"I don't understand, what just happened?" Jason asked.

"I need to make some phone calls, stay with her," Ms Jax replied, then departed quickly, leaving Jason to ponder the miracle he had just witnessed.

He must have dozed off, for how long he had no idea, but when he awoke he was still on the lounge with Selene's head resting on his lap, her body covered with a blanket. She was breathing peacefully and despite everything that had happened, looked quite well. Stroking her hair, Jason thought to himself how beautiful she looked and that even though they had only known each other for a short time, how horrible life would be without her. His thoughts then turned to how they had found themselves in this predicament. Hector and Tiberius, those murderous sacks of crap, he would make them pay for what they nearly accomplished. Lost in thought he jumped as Ulysses burst through the door, followed closely by Ursula and Ms Jax.

"Are you okay?" Ulysses asked, concerned. Jason gently slid from under Selene, careful not to move or waken her.

"I'm fine, and so is Selene I think?" Jason answered. Ursula went straight to her granddaughter's side. Kneeling by the lounge she placed her head on Selene's stomach and began to cry tears of relief and happiness at seeing her granddaughter alive.

"I'm so sorry," Ursula cried, her body shaking with

emotion. Selene stirred and everyone went quiet, watching with anticipation as she slowly opened her eyes.

"What's going on? Where am I?" Selene asked, groggily as the group converged around her.

Everyone listened as Jason told them the events of the night, with Selene filling in some of the details. When Jason was finished they looked on in disbelief.

"That's outrageous!" Ulysses snarled.

"I knew those two were rotten, but murder! I can't fathom what was going through their minds" Ursula said.

"I can, they think I'm evil," Jason replied, but Selene shook her head.

"No, I mean yes, Hector does, but not Tiberius. Did you see his face when Hector was ranting? He was giving him this queer, uncomfortable look the entire time. Up until then Tiberius looked excited," Selene said.

"Either way they planned on killing you both," Ulysses commented.

"What do we do?" Selene asked weakly.

"We go to the police," Ursula said.

"And say what? Those two boys were trying to kill us because they think I'm the spawn of Satan? Who are people going to believe, us or them? Not to mention when it comes to the law in Perigord they have that sown up too," Jason said as he slumped down next to Selene.

"He's right you know," Ulysses replied. Ursula looked shocked at his statement.

"No, he's not. It's not right and the town needs to know what it's harbouring. They can't get away with what they've done, they just can't," Ursula said indignantly; but her voice had begun to falter and her eyes had started to fill with tears again. Selene grabbed her hand and gave it a squeeze.

"I've got it!" Jason exclaimed. Everyone looked at him expectantly.

"I go to their houses, invite them to come and talk then I fly them a mile into the sky and drop them," Jason added. Selene and Ms Jax burst out laughing. Ursula looked as if she was seriously contemplating the idea. Ulysses looked less than impressed.

"Be serious Jason," Ulysses lectured.

"I am," Jason argued.

"They have it coming Ulysses," Ursula said coolly.

"How about we do nothing," Selene announced to the group. Everyone looked at her as if she had gone mad.

"Selene, sweetheart, you've had a terrible night and I think…," Ursula started to say.

"I have more reason than anyone here to want revenge but to be honest there's not much we can do, and either can they," Selene let her statement hang in the air a moment then added. "You're all forgetting the biggest issue at hand."

"And that is?" Ursula asked.

"The Harvest Festival. We have a potentially end of the world scenario about to take place and anything else just pales in comparison."

"She's right," Ulysses agreed reluctantly. Ursula also nodded but didn't look happy about the notion.

"Fine, for now we continue our efforts, but the sooner we're done, the sooner we can come back and tidy this other little mess up," Ursula said defiantly.

"Agreed," everyone replied in unison.

"One last thing. How exactly were you able to free yourself from the purification plant? From what Selene said, you were as weak as a baby," Ulysses asked. Jason remembered the man from his dream and he started to rub his arm absent minded. He didn't want to tell anyone about this for now, so he decided to keep that detail to himself.

"I'm not too sure, but I woke up in the pipe where I found Selene floating," Jason shuddered at the memory. "I changed my form and set us free, the rest you know," Jason said quietly. Ulysses watched him closely, in particular the way he was rubbing his arm and realised that Jason was holding something back. He decided not to pursue it for now, instead turning his gaze on Selene.

"And how did you find your way in the darkness to the bottom of the pit and through the pipe?" Ulysses asked.

"That was the easy part. The bottom of the pit was lit up with these glowing blue rocks," Selene replied.

"Glowing rocks," Ursula repeated.

"Yeah, with the rocks I was able to clearly see the entire time, in fact...," Selene said as she dug one of her hands into her pocket. "Ms Jax, can you get the light please?"

Ms Jax nodded moved to the door and flicked the switch off. Except for the flickering of the fire in the far corner, the room was shrouded in darkness. Now that Selene had everyone's attention she pulled her closed hand from her pocket and opened it for everyone to see. In the palm of her hand were four small blue glowing pebbles. Groaning loudly, Ulysses staggered back from Selene. Jason also shied from the rocks as if they were hot embers.

Dropping to his knees, Ulysses slumped forward and into the arms of Ms Jax.

"Selene, quick, put those rocks away!" Ursula ordered. Selene jammed the rocks back into her pocket, the effect was instantaneous. Ulysses shook his head as his eyes lost that glazed appearance and the colour returned to his face.

"It feels like I've been riding a rollercoaster," Jason said weakly. "For a week," he added. Ulysses nodded in agreement as Ms Jax helped him to his feet.

"I don't know what those rocks are, but I want to find out ASAP," Ulysses said, a look of controlled rage upon his face.

"I could possibly find out from one of my teachers," Selene replied.

"Well at least we now know what caused Jason's mysterious illness," Ursula said.

"Oh my God, what time is it? Mum's probably going ape shit wondering where I am!" Jason blurted out as he got to his feet.

"Give her a call and tell her you're at my place," Ursula replied. As Jason made the call, Selene interrupted Ulysses and Ms Jax who were talking privately.

"Have you made any progress in regards to the description of The Gjallarhorn?" Selene asked. Ulysses looked a little unprepared for her question.

"We found a couple of images of what the horn supposedly looks like," Ms Jax interjected. "I'll be right back," Ms Jax added and left the room.

"We're not entirely sure how accurate they are though," Ulysses said. Jason finished talking.

"Well that's one thing that's gone off without a hitch

tonight," Jason said, as Ms Jax re-entered the room carrying a handful of books.

"This is all the library could find on the subject," Ms Jax said as Jason, Ursula and Selene took one each from her.

"I've bookmarked the appropriate pages," Ms Jax added. The trio thumbed through them until Ulysses cleared his throat loudly. Everyone turned to look at him.

"I've got a better idea, come with me," Ulysses said cryptically. Without so much as a word from anyone they followed him to a heavy set timber and steel door at the far end of the room.

They passed through a large, mostly empty room. In its centre was a short stone pillar three foot in height and intricately carved with beautiful jungle scenery. The top of the pillar was inlaid with a cloudy green crystal. Everyone except Ms Jax and Ulysses looked around the room, which was dark and damp.

"Can I have one of the books please?" Ulysses asked in a polite tone. Ursula gave him her book without comment. Opening it up, Ulysses then placed it gently on the pillar and then looked toward the ceiling.

"If I could ask everyone, when you're in this room, please keep all noise to a minimum," Ulysses said. "Greymeade, can you display this book, please?" Ulysses asked respectfully. The crystal began to glow, then a strong emerald light enveloped the book. To Jason's amazement it projected a large, three dimensional image into the air. The contents of the pages were displayed with crystal clarity for everyone to see.

"Whoa," Jason and Selene breathed. Ursula remained

silent but was clearly impressed with the technology being utilised. The group scrutinised the image from the book which was of a crudely drawn Gjallarhorn. The picture was useless, but the description was a little more detailed - 'long and twisted in appearance, gold rimmed and jewel adornments, engraved upon the wooden surface images of a serpent a wolf and winter.' Ulysses tried the other books in their possession but nothing else came close to the first book.

"Maybe if we tried something a little more comprehensive and up to date than texts, like, um, the internet?" Selene asked sarcastically. Ulysses gave her a deadpan look.

"Greymeade, find any pictures or descriptions of the Gjallarhorn on earth's internet," Ulysses asked in a neutral tone. Hundreds of listed texts filed in view, projected into the air.

"Greymeade can you list them numerically in file size. Those with images and information from scholarly references, eliminate those with fiction based locations and social media sites and the misuse of the origin's name and properties?" Ulysses asked again. He stared at Selene with a bored expression on his face. Immediately the list was shortened to that of sixteen items.

"Show off," Selene hissed.

"Greymeade, can you open the last file please?" Jason asked politely. The file opened and displayed its contents in the air. Ulysses and Ms Jax looked at Jason, eyebrows raised.

"How did you do that?" Ulysses asked.

"Just like you did, duh," Jason said matter of fact.

"Because only those chosen can commune with

Greymeade" Ulysses replied, then looked at the display without further explanation. The file showed little other than what they had already seen in the books.

"Greymeade, can you show us the next file please?" Selene asked. This time nothing happened. "I guess I'm not one of the chosen then," Selene added a tone of annoyance in her voice. They continued through the list with Jason navigating. Nothing new was discovered until they viewed the third last file, a report written by a Scandinavian professor on the events of Ragnarok. One passage in particular detailed the Gjallarhorn and gave a clear detailed image.

"Greymeade, display picture Gjallarhorn?" Ulysses asked urgently. The image was enlarged immediately before their eyes, ten times its size and crystal clear.

"Wow, that is pretty impressive," Selene said and everyone nodded in agreement.

"Is that just an artist's interpretation or a detailed picture of the actual horn?" Jason asked.

"It doesn't say, but I think it's our best lead so far," Ursula replied.

"You might think I'm crazy, but the horn looks familiar, but I can't think why," Selene said.

"The likelihood that you've come across the horn is statistically impossible," Ulysses replied.

"You're probably right, but I can't seem to shake the feeling that I've seen it before," Selene said as she stared at the image of the horn.

"Hey, is it possible Greymeade could find us the information we want on the rocks Selene has in her pocket?" Jason asked. Ulysses nodded,

"I was going to suggest that before, thanks for reminding me." "Selene could you place one of the rocks on the crystal display?" Ulysses asked.

"What about you and Jason?" Selene said. This time Ulysses smiled knowingly.

"Greymeade, place a containment field around rock sample and evaluate its content and origin," Ulysses asked. "We should be okay," he said, turning to Selene.

Selene retrieved one of the rocks from her pocket and carefully placed it upon the pillar. A faint green glow could be seen surrounding the rock and Selene. Ms Jax and Ursula watched Jason and Ulysses for any sign or reaction. Everyone let out a breath of relief when nothing occurred. After waiting for one long drawn out minute, Ulysses looked at Ms Jax with a raised eyebrow and a shrug of his shoulders.

"Greymeade, analyse mineral content and origin," Ulysses repeated. Again they waited and again nothing happened. They were just about to give up when five words appeared in the air above them. 'Unknown mineral, alien in origin'.

"What does that mean?" Jason asked.

"It means there is nothing in Greymeade's data base concerning those rocks," Ulysses replied.

"Should we be concerned?" Ursula asked.

"Not for the moment anyway. I'm tempted to let Selene ask one of her teachers. Seeing as how these rocks are in this region, maybe one of your teachers has knowledge about it," Ulysses said. Selene quickly removed the rock from the pillar and placed it back into her pocket.

"We can only try, right?" Selene said.

"Well I think we should call it a night. You two kids need rest after the day you both have had," Ulysses said.

"I agree. Jason, you'll be staying the night at my place," Ursula said, then gave Jason a shrewd look. "No hanky panky, you'll have your own room," Ursula added. Selene went red, protesting loudly and Ulysses let out a loud belly laugh. Ms Jax walked them all out but Jason hung back and grabbed Ulysses by the arm.

"Where were you tonight? You look kinda dressed up," Jason asked with interest. Ulysses looked taken aback by the question then gave Jason a smirk.

"Not that it's any of your business, but I was out on a date," Ulysses said pointedly.

"Date? You? Really?" Jason blurted out in surprise.

"What, you don't think a good looking rooster like me can land a date?" Ulysses replied with a raised eyebrow.

"Hey, that's not what I said, of course you can. Do what you want, but I mean, you know, you're not human. How does that work?" Jason spluttered.

"How does what work?" Ulysses said playing dumb.

"You know, yours and her anatomy?"

"Who said it was a woman?" Ulysses replied, amused.

"I, I, didn't mean anything. I was just curious that's all."

"Relax Jason, I'm just messing with you. I'm in human form on earth, most of the time and I do appreciate a bit of company from time to time, especially the female kind."

"Fair enough, I better get going. I'll see you tomorrow," Jason replied and turned to catch up with the others.

"Jason," Ulysses called out, stopping him in his tracks.

"I'm glad you two are all right, good work," Ulysses added. Jason nodded then ran off to catch up with the others.

He met the others at the front door where he found Ursula giving Ms Jax a big hug.

"I can't thank you enough Amelia, I'm indebted. Anything you need, please don't hesitate to ask," Ursula said warmly.

"It was my pleasure. I'm just glad no one was hurt," Ms Jax replied.

"I don't mean to interrupt Ms Jaeger, but I promised to help Ulysses with something and Ms Jax could drop me off at your house after? It won't take long if that's okay with you?" Jason asked. Ursula nodded.

"I don't mind dropping him off later," Ms Jax said.

"Fine Jason, but not much longer. I promised your mother and I don't take that lightly," Ursula said.

"Do you want me to stay as well?" Selene asked, but Jason shook his head.

"Oh I don't think so young lady, you're coming home with me and getting some rest," Ursula said.

"I'll be there soon," Jason added with a smile. Selene still looked fatigued and didn't put up a fight.

"Don't be long okay," Selene said.

"I'll be right behind you," Jason replied. Ursula and Selene departed down the library front stairs and into the night.

"What has Ulysses got you doing?" Ms Jax queried. Jason turned to her with an expression of guilt on his face.

"Ulysses doesn't need me tonight," Jason said.

"I don't understand, why did you lie?" Ms Jax asked.

"Because I need to run an errand."

"At this time of the night? What's so important?"

"I can't say, please don't tell Ulysses," Jason pleaded. Ms Jax appeared torn at the request and after a brief moment of hesitation nodded.

"Okay I promise, but you have to promise me as well. No one else is going to get hurt tonight, least of all yourself," Ms Jax said sternly.

"I promise, you won't regret it," Jason replied and kissed her on the cheek.

"I regret it already, just go and be safe," Ms Jax muttered.

"Will do," Jason said and transformed before her into an eagle. With a massive beat of his wings, he took off into the night sky.

Chapter 31

THE PARTY AT Hector's had been going strong for the past few hours. Everyone inside was heavily inebriated and were either making out or consuming more alcohol. Hector walked through the house as if he were the Lord of the manor. The noise emanating from the party was deafening but the neighbouring houses all feared Sheriff Rope, so they remained silent. This fact was not lost on Hector, who tended to treat them with disdain.

"Is everyone having a good time or what?" Hector called out, a huge shit-eating grin on his face. This was met with drunken cheering from the group. Hector continued to strut around drinking liberally from a bottle of cider. He strolled over to Halo who was sitting on a lounge, trying unsuccessfully to cop a feel from a young brunette who was glad to be at Hector's party, but not happy to be the object of Halo's affections.

"Halo my man, have you seen Tib?" Hector asked casually. Halo shook his head, barely taking his eyes or hands off the young girl.

"I think he's upstairs, with Mandy," Halo replied, a

dirty grin on his face. Hector nodded, images of his own time with Mandy still fresh in his mind.

"Cool, I'm going for a piss," Hector commented as he walked toward the back balcony and quietly let himself out. He leaned against the railing and looked out into the night, the cool breeze having a slightly sobering effect on his senses. He could faintly hear the sounds of the party happening from inside the house. This brought a smile to his face.

"Whoo hoo!" Hector screamed into the night.

"That's all you have to say for yourself? Whoo hoo?" a deep, gravelling voice replied. Hector jumped at the unexpected sound.

"Who's there? Do you think you're funny?" Hector yelled, angry at being caught off guard.

"You're right, it's not funny, in fact it's deadly serious," the voice growled back through the darkness. Hector continued to peer into the night but his courage was faltering. Something wasn't right. The hairs stood up on the back of his neck. Before he could move a large, dark figure swooped down in front of him. All Hector could make out were two enormous bat-like wings, a pair of red glowing eyes that stared with murderous hate and white canines that no human could possibly possess. Hector stood paralysed with fear. He took a huge breath and prepared to scream when the figure grabbed him by the shoulders with its large taloned hands and ripped him up into the sky, before He could make a sound.

The first hundred metres they flew directly skyward. Hector remained limp, his heart in his throat. The second hundred he regained some sense and tried vainly to see who or what, his assailant was. Now in the moonlight he caught nightmare glimpses. Hooved feet, a flowing reptilian tail, leathery skin, finally a bestial face straight from Dante's inferno that peered at him, its mouth open, displaying white razor sharp teeth arranged in what seemed to be a grin.

"Will you stop squirming or I might accidently drop you?" The creature said casually. This time Hector did scream long and loud, ending in a high pitched wail as they continued their flight up. By now Hector had screamed himself to the point of exhaustion. The demonic looking creature breached the cloud cover that hung over Perigord. Bathed in the silvery reflection of the moon, the creature hovered there slowly flapping its wings. It held Hector out with one hand at arm's length, appearing to just study him. Hector whimpered under the beast's glare.

"What do you want with me?" Hector blubbered.

"Do you know who I am?" the creature thundered.

"No, please don't eat me!"

"Eat you? How splendid! I must admit the idea never even crossed my mind, til now," the creature growled as it pulled Hector close and opened its mouth wide.

"No. No please stop! I didn't mean, don't, I'll do anything, stop!" Hector screamed with every fibre of his being. The creature paused, Hector's head inches from its opened mouth. It seemed to ponder his fate thoughtfully. After a few moments that felt like an eternity to Hector, the creature sighed, then held Hector out again.

"You'll do anything, I love that phrase," the creature said, waiting patiently for Hector to answer. The silence that followed along with his shaking proved that none would be forthcoming.

"I've been watching you," the creature said letting the words hang in the air. Hector looked terrified and started to sob.

"Quiet!" the creature roared and tossed Hector away with ease, like someone throwing a ball. Hector went sailing through the air tumbling head over foot, then disappearing entirely into the cloud canopy. Hector's vision was a blur. The night sky and his spinning form made it impossible to get his bearings. He shut his eyes tightly and waited for death. His limp and silent body hurtled toward the earth. The trees below appeared to be reaching out for his still form. Then at the very last second, the demonic creature swooped in from nowhere and snatched him mere moments from impact. When Hector finally opened his eyes, he was again staring at the creature. This time however he was being held by his ankle and viewing the nightmare upside down.

"I know what you did tonight," the creature breathed.

"I don't know what you're talking about," Hector said, shaking uncontrollably. The creature let out a huge laugh that sounded like thunder.

"That's the spirit. A murderer and a liar, just like your father," the creature added.

"You've mistaken me for someone else," Hector whined and squirmed.

"I'll look forward to seeing you both in the pit," the creature chuckled then without further warning, dropped Hector into the black void below. There was no scream this time as Hector passed out and plummeted toward the earth.

Jason knocked on Ursula's front door and was met by Selene, moments later.

"Hey, what took you?" Selene said smiling, clearly happy to see him. Her voice still heavy with fatigue.

"I just needed to stop and pick up this," Jason said and pulled out a colourful bouquet of wild flowers from behind his back, holding them out in offering. Selene took the flowers from him and let him through the door.

"I'm not really the flowers and chocolates type of girl but I appreciate the thought. They are very pretty though," Selene replied. Ursula met them in the front landing, in her arms a large blanket.

"What beautiful flowers," Ursula observed. "I've made up a bed, but you might need this to take the chill off," Ursula said. Jason took the blanket.

"Thanks, you shouldn't have gone to so much trouble on my behalf," Jason replied. Ursula waved it off.

"Tish tosh, it's the very least I could do for a guest in my home. Selene will show you to your room. It's been a big day for everyone. Do try and get some sleep, in your own beds, okay?" Ursula added. The pair blushed.

"Gee, that wasn't embarrassing, was it?" Selene said with a sigh and a small grin.

"I'm too old to waste time mincing my words, besides I've said my peace and that's that, goodnight," Ursula said, as she departed down the hallway to her own bedroom.

"And on that awkward note, I'll take you to your room," Selene said. They stopped at the kitchen along the way and made a small snack of milk and cookies which they nibbled on slowly. They talked about things that teenagers their age find interesting- movies, music and school gossip. They avoided all references to Heinrich and the Harvest Festival and despite his fatigue, Jason enjoyed his time with Selene. He stretched and let out a long yawn.

"I'm sorry," Jason said sheepishly

"It's okay, I'm tired too," Selene replied. "My grandmother's right though, we've had a big day and an even bigger one tomorrow," Selene added as she climbed out of her chair and held out her hand to Jason, who took it as she pulled him to his feet with a groan.

"I suppose you're right, we only have one more day until the festival starts," Jason replied.

"Come on then," Selene said reluctantly. Still holding his hand, she pulled him along down the corridor toward his room.

"This is your stop, if you do need anything I'm just down the corridor, first door on the left," Selene said without a hint of innuendo.

"Thanks, will do," Jason mumbled shyly.

"Goodnight," Selene replied as she started to leave. Jason felt frustrated by his lack of confidence in regards to their budding relationship. Frustration turned to impulse as he took a deep breath and grabbed her by the shoulders, spinning her around to face him. Selene's eyes went wide in surprise as Jason lent in and kissed her deeply on the lips, his hands moving from her shoulders to her waist as he pulled her in close. Selene's body began to relax as she pressed herself against him and returned his kiss with a renewed passion. They could both feel each other's heat. Their sexual tension had been building for the past week and now their kiss felt pure, sweet and a little awkward, all at once. After what seemed an eternity, their lips parted. Both of them took a deep breath before opening their eyes. After a brief moment Jason blushed and averted his eyes.

"I hope you don't...," Jason stammered, but was silenced by a ssshhh from Selene.

"Don't say another word," Selene breathed with a relaxed and sensual smile, and without another word she turned and walked away to her room, turning once before she disappeared to smile and blow him a kiss. Jason watched her then he too retired to bed.

Chapter 32

THE NEXT MORNING Jason awoke and for the first time in ages felt truly rested. He laid there for a long while enjoying the tranquillity and quiet that can only be found on a Sunday morning. After a while he could hear familiar noises coming from the kitchen and decided he should get up. After quietly showering, getting dressed and making his bed he wandered out to greet his hosts. Much to his disappointment he arrived in the kitchen only to find Ursula preparing coffee and toast. She greeted him warmly with a smile.

"I hope I didn't wake you Jason," Ursula said in a quiet tone. Jason shook his head.

"No I've been awake for a little bit just lying in bed," Jason replied sheepishly.

"No need to feel guilty after the day you two had yesterday," Ursula said shaking her head. "That's why I've decided to let Selene sleep in. It's normally not like her to still be in bed at this hour, I fear that her ordeal has more than just knocked the wind from her sails," Ursula said.

"I agree, better to let her sleep and recover as much as possible," Jason replied.

"Feel free to help yourself to breakfast, you'll need to keep your energy up as well," Ursula said. Jason's eyes gleamed at the mention of food; it felt as if he hadn't eaten in weeks.

"I think I will," Jason said as Ursula poured him a cup of steaming coffee. He went about making cereal and toast.

"I'll leave you to your breakfast. I have a ton of things that I need to do this morning, thanks again for Selene," Ursula said humbly and exited the room.

After a brief stop off home, Jason made his way through town. He was surprised to find that there appeared to be a small army of volunteers working in and around the central park area, busily organising decorations, stalls and anything and everything to coincide with the Harvest Festival. He spotted kids and teachers among the helpers who were all busy assembling stages and marquees. Jason tried to be inconspicuous as he cut his way through the park towards the library. Every so often he would see someone he knew and would give them a brief wave then continue on, not wanting to get caught up in pointless, idle chatter. Arriving at the library he let out a sigh of relief. Behind its giant doors, Ms Jax was the first to see him as he entered the rear staff room.

"I really wasn't expecting you in so early," Ms Jax said surprised.

"I didn't feel like sleeping in before the end of the world," Jason replied with a shrug.

"Oh it's not that bad." A voice echoed through the room and the pair turned to see Ulysses stroll casually towards them sipping a cup of tea. He smiled as if to parlay their fears. "I've been in tighter spots before," he said coolly.

"Really?" Jason asked incredulously.

"Really. The battle for the three moons comes to mind and then there was the elemental rebellion. No wait, that didn't turn out so well," Ulysses said as he pondered this.

"What do you mean it didn't turn out so well?" Jason asked, clearly puzzled by his statement.

"Well for starters it's why I'm here," Ulysses said in an agitated voice. Jason waited for him to elaborate further but Ulysses appeared to be deep within his own thoughts. He then turned to Ms Jax for support but it was obvious she wasn't going to talk either.

"Another time maybe. Have you an overall plan of attack then?" Jason asked, trying to clear the air.

"Selene phoned just before you arrived," Ms Jax said.

"Is everything okay?" Jason replied, concerned.

"Relax, she just wanted to say that she was stopping by a friend to ask about the stones," Ms Jax said.

"Well as you can see outside, the festival is here and there's nothing we can do to stop that, but that doesn't mean were sunk. Right?" Ulysses said. Jason shrugged.

"I've been thinking about this all morning. Ms Jax is going to continue to hit all of earth's databases for more information," Ulysses said.

"I'm on it," Ms Jax replied in her usual deep gravelly voice.

"Jason I want you and Selene to stay close to the park and keep an eye on the set up and proceedings. You see anything out of the ordinary, phone it in to Ms Jax," Ulysses instructed.

"That's all? Surely my time could be better suited to something else?" Jason replied tersely. Ulysses placed a hand on Jason's shoulder and looked him square in the eye.

"I know this doesn't appear to be very important, but we desperately need your eyes on the ground today, especially considering we are severely lacking in any decent intelligence. Use your abilities, your senses. I have a bad feeling that we are going to have some out of town visitors today," Ulysses said.

"Out of town?" Jason said confused.

"Not of this earth Jason, beings like us. Find them, but don't approach. Don't do anything just report it."

"Report it, what's the point in that? I'm ready, I can handle it," Jason said a little testily.

"I mean it, there are people on earth, and I use the term loosely, that make Onyx look like a cute and cuddly squirrel. If you try and engage an unknown quantity you not only risk yourself but innocent people as well. Do not engage, am I clear on this!" Ulysses said sternly. Jason nodded reluctantly.

"Fine, fine, I just have one question though" Jason said.

"Shoot," Ulysses replied.

"What are you going to be doing today?" he asked.

"I'm going to follow a lead," Ulysses replied cryptically. Jason's curiosity was killing him.

"And that would be?" Jason asked, but Ulysses shook his head.

"I'd rather not say at this stage," Ulysses said. Ms Jax appeared taken aback by his statement but remained silent. "We all have a job to do today, let's not waste any more time."

Chapter 33

WHEN SELENE AWOKE that morning she opened her eyes and just laid there. Between everything that had happened to her in the past couple of weeks, it all seemed a little surreal. She eventually sat up which required some effort. Her body felt like one big bruise and after painfully climbing out of bed and slowly getting dressed, she joined Ursula for breakfast.

"Is Jason up yet?" Selene asked.

"Yes dear, he had breakfast and left," Ursula replied.

"Oh," Selene said and appeared to deflate.

"Don't be upset with him, he didn't want to wake you and I agree. In fact I really think you should go back to bed, you look pale and tired," Ursula said concerned, but Selene shook it off.

"I'm fine really, I'm not made of porcelain," Selene replied. Ursula clearly wanted to say more but bit her tongue on the subject. They sat quietly for a while as Selene ate her breakfast.

"Today's the day," Ursula said as she got to her feet

and started to clear the table, despite the fact Selene was still eating.

"Yes, yes it is. I'm curious what your plans are today, or should I say what are the Guild of Wolves' orders for preventing the apocalypse," Selene said casually through a mouthful of toast.

"Please don't talk like that," Ursula said uncomfortably.

"I don't understand. Is it or is it not the end of days?" Selene shot back, then immediately felt guilty for it. "I'm sorry, I'm just a little tense," she added. Ursula shook her head.

"The Guild doesn't operate like that anymore. We would try to look at things in the long term, eradicate small threats. We were never capable of handling things of this magnitude," Ursula said quietly.

"Well I'm going to see someone about those rocks and then I'll meet up with Jason at the library," Selene said as she rose from the table. "Maybe you could join us?"

"That's exactly what I plan to do, roll up my sleeves and see where Ulysses wants to use me," Ursula replied with a grin.

"Great," Selene said as she rounded the table and planted a kiss on Ursula's cheek. "I'll see you there."

Selene made her way to the west side of town toward a quiet street that backed onto the edge of the forest. She eventually reached a small cottage that was positioned second from the end. The cottage was plain, but well maintained and appeared to be inserted directly into the tree line. Selene walked up a path made of stone and moss. Large unkempt hedges lined the path which gave it a natural feel as well as provided privacy from the road. Approaching the porch steps, a female voice called out.

"Good morning Selene, what brings you around here this early in the morning?" the voice asked pleasantly. Selene's head whipped around in surprise.

"Oh, hey, I didn't see you there Ms Gaia," Selene said smiling as she climbed the steps up to the house. Ms Gaia was sitting on a large oversized chair that had been carefully crafted from twisted tree branches, and like everything else on the property, it was hand fashioned and completely natural. "I hope you don't mind me popping in unannounced," Selene added.

"Not at all. What brings you to my little corner of the world?" Ms Gaia asked warmly.

"I wanted to ask you a question," Selene said.

"School work during the festival? How dedicated," Ms Gaia replied.

"Hardly. No I found these rocks the other day and I was wondering if you could tell me anything about them" Selene asked, as she fished something from her pocket.

"I'm probably not the best one to ask as geology is not my field of expertise. Mr Marin one of the other science teachers would be a better one to consult as geology is his passion," Ms Gaia replied. Selene produced three rocks that glowed faintly under the shade of the porch roof.

"May I?" Ms Gaia asked and took one of the rocks from Selene's hand. After studying it for a few seconds, she then looked up satisfied.

"I think I can help you with this after all," she added.

"Fantastic, what is it?" Selene asked excitedly.

"It's a rock known as Ambroxilene," Ms Gaia said.

Selene who was leaning against the porch railing stood straight with a jolt.

"Ambroxilene? Are you sure?" Selene asked.

"Absolutely, it's used at the brewery for sterilisation," Ms Gaia said as she tossed the rock back to Selene. "Now for the million dollar question. What's so important about this rock that you needed to come and ask me on a public holiday, and does it have anything to do with the supernova you and Jason came and saw me about the other day?" Ms Gaia asked curiously.

"I didn't think it was until now," Selene replied. Ms Gaia's eyes seemed to dance at Selene's answer.

"Now I'm definitely intrigued," Ms Gaia said. "Please tell me more".

"I'm afraid I can't at the moment, but I promise later I'll fill you in with what I can," Selene said as she reached for something in her back pocket only to find it wasn't there. "Could I possibly use your phone? I seem to have left mine at home," Selene added.

"Of course, come inside," Ms Gaia said and led Selene in through the front door.

Inside the house was plain but neat, nothing out of place as only a single person living on their own would keep it.

"If you would like a drink, please help yourself to something cold from the fridge. I'll see if I can find my cell phone in the bedroom," Ms Gaia said.

"Thank you, I think I will," Selene replied. Ms Gaia nodded then departed down the hallway in search of her phone. Selene went over to the cupboard looking for a glass. After opening several doors with no success she went over to the pantry and peered inside. Again no glasses, but what she did find was something tall standing up against the wall and covered in a long, flowing cloth that appeared to have a primitive astronomical chart stitched clearly and painstakingly into it.

"What's this?" Selene whispered as she slowly pulled the cloth from the hidden object underneath. What she found may her gasp and drop the cloth. Leaning against the wall was a long, twisted staff covered in runes, polished stones and engraved figures. At that moment Selene realised that she was staring at the Gjallarhorn and the missing festival sceptre that had been stolen from school.

"Oh my God, it can't be" Selene muttered as she picked up the Gjallarhorn with a grunt and examined it closely. "The harvest sceptre is the Gjallarhorn" Selene said.

"Yes, yes it is," a voice behind said, Selene spun to see Ms Gaia swinging a rolling pin in her direction, then darkness overcame her.

Selene slowly opened her eyes and lifted her head which felt as if it weighed a tonne and throbbed with a blinding intensity. She tried to focus her vision on her surroundings which seemed to be an impossible task.

"Ah, you're awake already, I was right about you, you're a tough one," Ms Gaia said. Selene blinked and shook her head as she attempted to clear her vision.

"What have you done to me?" Selene groaned.

"Oh you took a nasty bump to the head," Ms Gaia replied with a chuckle. Selene's vision had started to clear but the throbbing in her head still made it hard to concentrate. She looked down to find that she had been bound to a chair in what she guessed was Ms Gaia's basement.

"Why are you doing this to me?" Selene growled. This was met with laughter.

"I think what you should be asking me is what am I doing with the Gjallarhorn?" Ms Gaia said.

"How did you know that the sceptre was the Gjallarhorn?" Selene asked coolly.

"I like to think of myself as an educated woman, one who despite her intelligence had not been given the opportunities to realise her full potential, until now," Ms Gaia stated.

"I'm afraid you've lost me," Selene replied confused.

"Of course I have dear, but you're like every other hick in this town who wouldn't know a horn from a sceptre. Me on the other hand, I like to read and I have a healthy curiosity for the unusual and unexplained. That horn sitting in plain sight for anyone to see was practically humming with untapped power. Isn't it funny how the small minded people in Perigord don't seem to notice the strange things that happen in this town?" Ms Gaia said as she paced the floor.

"What are you planning to do with it?" Selene asked.

"Let's not beat around the bush shall we. I've been keeping tabs on you and your boyfriend. You know what the Gjallarhorn is capable of, I intend to see its destiny fulfilled," Ms Gaia said.

"Are you out of your mind? You want to see the end of the world? Just so you can act out some insane power trip?" Selene yelled.

"You're no different than all the others, so small minded that you cannot behold the endless possibilities. Humanity is like a virus destroying this planet, I have spent years trying to address ecological issues and fight against greedy capitalism, but no one really cares. As long as people have their Wi-Fi and McDonalds they couldn't care less about the destruction of the rainforests or the culling of whales," Ms Gaia said vehemently.

"So what are you saying," Selene said.

"That with the power of the Gjallarhorn and its unstoppable army at my disposal I will restore the planet to its former glory and then I intend to take my army and vision to the stars," Ms Gaia roared. Selene stared hard at Ms Gaia in total disbelief, then she started to giggle quietly. This turned to a gentle chuckle and finally full gut bursting side splitting laughter. Ms Gaia's eyes narrowed with anger as she watched Selene buck under the strains of her bonds with laughter.

"Stop laughing!" Ms Gaia snarled, but this only made Selene laugh harder. "I can't," Selene cackled, tears streaming down her face.

"I said stop it, you little bitch," Ms Gaia yelled as she grabbed Selene by the shoulders and shook her.

"Listen to yourself, you sound like a comic book villain," Selene said through gales of laughter. "I intend to take my army and vision to the stars, mmmwwwhahaha. I'm surprised you weren't stroking your pussy while you were saying that. Whoops, that was a bit rude, I meant your cat," Selene said, then continued laughing hysterically.

"I said shut your mouth," Ms Gaia growled and slapped Selene full force across the face. The blow had the desired effect. It silenced Selene, rocking her head back and leaving a blazing scarlet mark on the side of her face.

"There, that seemed to shut you up," Ms Gaia said with a level of triumph. "Some educated woman you are, having to resort to violence to get your point across," Selene said calmly. "But then again you're not completely sane, are you?" Selene added.

"I'm not here to state my case, but to prevent you from informing your colleagues of my involvement in this," Ms Gaia stated, then walked towards the door.

"Wait!" Selene called out. Ms Gaia stopped mid step and turned around. "I have to know. How you are planning on distributing the potion to the town?" Selene asked. Ms Gaia paused to think this over.

"Why not, you're going to be present when it happens. I'm still not sure whether to let you join them in the transformation or be amongst their first victims," Ms Gaia said thoughtfully.

"You're a freak," Selene spat back.

"During the festival the town will be drinking free cider supplied by the Black River Brewery. Both alcoholic and non-alcoholic contain the ingredients vital to the ceremony," Ms Gaia said smugly.

"My friends will stop you," Selene said suddenly, sounding unsure.

"I have my own friends to ensure that won't happen, but you won't be there to see. I have to go dear. I'm sure you'll appreciate that I have a lot to do today," Ms Gaia said, looking at her watch then spun on her heel and walked out. "Feel free to yell and scream, no one will hear you. I've placed enchantments nullifying any interruptions," Ms Gaia called back as the lights went out, leaving Selene sitting in the dark tied to a chair with the realisation that no one knew where she was.

Chapter 34

IMMEDIATELY AFTER JASON had left the library, Ulysses went to his study looking urgently for something hidden in his desk. He ripped out each draw one at a time emptying the contents and searching until he found what he was looking for, a long roll of parchment. Ulysses wiped the desk clear with one broad stroke of his arm and untied the black ribbon that was knotted carefully around the parchment. He unrolled the parchment revealing a large detailed map of Perigord. Ulysses was leaning over studying the map when Ms Jax entered the room. She viewed the mess before her with a stern eye. Ulysses looked up then back to the map.

"Not now Amelia, I'm busy," Ulysses said tiredly, but Ms Jax stood firm.

"Is this the lead you plan on following?" Ms Jax asked. Ulysses sighed and pointed to an area on the map showing the forests in the valley.

"He's out there somewhere, I know it. I can feel it," Ulysses said.

"How can you be so sure?" Ms Jax said shaking her head.

"If not him than whom, it has to be Heinrich," Ulysses said slamming a fist down in frustration.

"It has to be, or you want it to be? I've put this behind me, why can't you?" Ms Jax replied.

"Enough," Ulysses said sharply. He then paused and his expression softened as he regarded his old friend. "I have to do this. The woods will be free of people today of all days and I will be able to roam unimpeded. I ask that you remain here and continue your task and assist Jason and Selene when required," Ulysses said.

"And when will you return?" Ms Jax asked concerned.

"I don't know, but don't worry I'll be back well before the festivities start. I promise," Ulysses said. Ms Jax nodded and departed without another word, leaving Ulysses to continue to study the map in silence.

Within the hour Ulysses was racing through the dense forest, his form that of a rezire, a large cat-like creature from the jungle planet of H'soth, the form had rough black and grey fur and long retractable claws. Its head was more like that of a hammerhead shark, broad and blunt, its eyes located on the sides constantly scanning the surroundings. Below the eyes were what looked like dozens of small puncture holes. Their purpose was olfactory perception just like earth's jungle cats, only hundreds of times keener. At the bottom of the broad head, a wide mouth full of razor sharp teeth. The cat's two prehensile tails constantly moved about detecting variations in the air, alerting it to anyone or thing in its vicinity. Ulysses moved with purpose, his head darting quickly from side to side his powerful muscular body traversing the thick terrain with ease.

After carefully making his way around the lake, he eventually found himself at the far end of the valley facing a small clearing. In the centre stood an abandoned timber shack, barely bigger than a tool shed and obviously uninhabited due to its location and state of disrepair. Ulysses kept a low profile within the tree line and carefully circled the shack, watching closely for any signs of movement.

The clouds overhead had started to amass casting the entire area in dark shadows. Ulysses stopped in his tracks. Lifting his head he scanned his surroundings. The forest had become deathly quiet. He crouched low and emitted a low steady growl. His claws popped forth from his feet as he awaited an assault. He didn't have to wait long, a crashing sound came through the brush from behind. Ulysses spun to meet his assailant - a tall dark figure moving at a superhuman speed. He barely had time to move as the figure dived at him and slashed his face with its deadly sharp talons. Before Ulysses could recover, the figure was gone. Ulysses let rip with a deafening roar out of rage and frustration. The slash marks left long deep trails in the flesh across his face. He watched the trees into which the figure had disappeared, another figure ploughed into his left side. This one was a little smaller and it too slashed his side however it was slower in its departure and Ulysses was able to see his attacker. It was humanoid in form but larger than a man, it had pointed ears and a tail like a cat, spotted camouflage covered its skin similar to a leopard.

"A bloody Were Leopard," he muttered to himself, as another figure rushed him from the tree line. Ulysses was ready this time. Crouching low he prepared to leap at his assailant when he was struck on the side by another. Ulysses howled in pain as the perpetrator raked his side, leaving a trail of open wounds in its wake. He was able to see his attacker closely this time, as it grinned at his cries of pain. Ulysses struck out clumsily. The leopard easily ducked his blow and leapt back out of Ulysses' range. The lone Were was then joined by two others of its kind, forming a semi-circle around the wounded Ulysses. All three were sporting hungry smiles that held no mirth.

Ulysses changed back to his human form. The transformation partially healed his wounds, although they were still visible, only now as raw scar tissue. Ulysses winced as he felt his side. This brought laughter from the Were-leopards, the sound more like hyenas than that of jungle cats.

"Ah the Stumpp brothers I presume, what brings you to Perigord?" Ulysses said trying to sound calm. This brought more laughter from the Weres.

"Why the famous Ulysses Walker, that's what," the tallest of the three replied casually in a strong Russian accent.

"I'm flattered really. You should have called ahead and we could have done lunch," Ulysses said, this time there was no laughter.

"His reputation is as bloated as a fat sow brothers," the smaller one said.

"I agree he's trying to stall," the tall one replied. "No matter, we're getting paid for the kill, not in the manner in which it is conducted," he added.

"I would have done this for free Peter. After all, to

claim this one's hide will only add to our rep and infamy," the short one said.

"Who's paying you?" Ulysses demanded.

"Why, are you going to double it?" the short one sneered. "I swear, they're all the same. Pathetic," he added.

"Hardly, I just needed the information so once I was done with you three I could finish this once and for all," Ulysses said boldly. This brought growls from the three brothers. "Tell me, does the other one talk?" Ulysses asked, indicating the third brother who stood silently glaring at him with one eye. The other eye was missing and covered by an ugly scar.

"He prefers to let his actions speak louder than his words," the tall one said defiantly.

"You know what I think? When I'm done with you three, the Stumpp brothers name will be synonymous with cowering like a dog," Ulysses said with a grin.

"Rip him apart brothers!" the tall one growled and all three of them rushed at Ulysses, their mouths open with exposed fangs and their eyes filled with rage and blood lust. Ulysses closed his eyes for a brief moment, his face still and devoid of any emotion. When he did open them a split second later, his mouth turned up in a small smile as his body transformed. His skin turned blood red in colour and formed into rough, hard scales. His mass increased and doubled in size. A large tail formed from his lower back, stretching and spreading out along the ground, ending in a sharp whip. His arms and legs lengthened, lean and sinewy with both talons forming on his feet and hands. Finally his head enlarged, reptilian in features, wide mouth full of small dagger like teeth and large yellow serpent eyes that took in everything. Ulysses looked like a cross between a raptor and one of Dante's demons.

The transformation took seconds to complete and when he was finished, he roared like something that was born from the pit. The three Were Leopards charged Ulysses. He leapt as well, fangs gaping and claws exposed ready to tear flesh asunder. This was a battle for survival and all the combatants were well aware of the stakes involved. The three brothers were experienced fighters who had spent lifetimes working with each other, knowing their own strengths and weaknesses explicitly. Their style had evolved over the years and it showed as they flowed as one. Ulysses on the other hand was used to working alone. Despite the fact that he was fighting three deadly assailants he was able to cut loose without fear of hurting or harming an ally or friend. His strikes and blows were efficient and precise. The short one leapt onto his back and attempted to apply a choke on him from behind. One eye darted toward Ulysses with the intention of disembowelling him with his outstretched claws. Turning suddenly, Ulysses struck one eye with his whip like tail, sending him flying into the path of a small tree.

"Hold him tight brother," the tall one said as he weaved past one of Ulysses' strikes that nearly cleaved his head from his shoulders. The tall one kicked out into Ulysses' stomach, only to find it hard and unyielding. Ulysses leaned back on his tail, balancing carefully. He kicked out with both feet, sending the tall one hurtling through the air and into the side of the shack. The short one was still attempting to choke him from behind, its hold was great and Ulysses tried but couldn't shake him.

He tried a different tactic, changing form once again. The colour of his skin turned a dark shade of blue. The arms and legs withered away to nothing, the body now that of a long serpent. The head became broad and armoured with long horns growing from the base of the skull, twisting out in a curved arc. Similar horns, smaller than these began to appear from the neck and worked their way down his spine toward the tail. The shorter Were Leopard managed to hold on the entire time during the transformation, once complete however, Ulysses coiled his powerful body around the Were Leopard and squeezed with all his might. The creature cried out and released its grip on Ulysses who only squeezed tighter. Eventually the sounds of bones cracking and breaking could easily be heard. Ulysses refused to stop though even after the Were Leopard's eyes burst from their sockets and a torrent of blood gushed from its mouth. Finally Ulysses' head poised ready to strike, his mouth open exposing two prominent fangs, which were dripping with yellow venom.

"NO!" the Were with one eye screamed as Ulysses struck the throat of the short one, his fangs digging deep, injecting lethal doses of venom into the Were Leopards blood stream. It blindly convulsed in its death throes, then went still. The great serpent released its hold as the body fell from its grip. The two remaining Weres stared dumbstruck at their fallen brother, then turned their murderous gazes onto Ulysses who remained erect like a cobra. The Weres howled in unison and prepared to attack when Ulysses whipped his head forward in a short controlled movement. His mouth opened wide and a burst of luminescent green fire billowed toward the two unprepared

Weres. At the very last moment both dived to the side barely evading the mystical green fire. The intense heat singed the fur on their bodies and they rolled behind the trees for cover.

The serpent reared back and watched for any movement, its large yellow eyes staring unblinking for signs of a counter attack. The forest had become eerily quiet except for the ragged breath of the hidden Weres.

"And then there were two. Your reputation has been grossly exaggerated," Ulysses said as he turned back into human form. "Oh where oh where have the two Weres gone?" Ulysses added in a playful sing song voice.

"You're a dead man Ulysses," the tall Were screamed out from the forest.

"That's what I want to hear. I was afraid that you'd packed up and gone home," Ulysses taunted. An angry growl back was the only reply.

"I'm glad you're pissed because so am I. You wanted to play the role of the hunter, well now you're going to find out what it's like to be the hunted. Ready or not, here I come," Ulysses called out as he transformed yet again. This time his body morphed into a large scorpion-like creature. Long black legs sprouted from his torso which grew in size and shape to accommodate the multiple appendages. A gigantic stinger sprouted from his back and rose up poised to strike. Finally his head changed and dozens of midnight black eyes looked out from a face without a nose and a mouth. Two jagged mandibles jutted out from the jaw working in a pincer style movement. The entire body was hard and armoured. The tail moved to and fro. The barbed stinger seemed poised to strike at any moment.

The creature let loose with an ear piercing shriek of excitement then scuttled into the tree line in pursuit of the two remaining brothers who were now running deeper into the forest hoping to gain a better vantage on their attacker and possibly get revenge for the murder of their brother minutes earlier. Ulysses had been right. The hunters were now the hunted.

Chapter 35

PERIGORD PARK WAS a blur of movement. Burly workmen were frantically erecting stages and stalls, a small army of women busily thread streamers and lights through tree branches and over lamp posts. The entire town square was a hub of activity and in the middle of it all sat Jason on a park bench. He watched the proceedings around him with an eagle eye. To the casual observer, Jason looked like a typical, disinterested teenager, lazy and totally consumed with one thing-himself. Every so often he would pull his phone out, pretending to text a friend. In actuality he was logging the movement of certain people and taking the occasional photo for later reference. He would move every half hour so as not to attract attention and to also change his perspective on the day's proceedings. After several hours of amateur spy work Jason had come to one conclusion. James Bond needn't worry about losing his licence to kill from him, anyway.

"I can't believe I'm wasting my time here," Jason muttered to himself when a large, firm hand landed on his shoulder from behind. He jumped in surprise and turned to see Sheriff Rope standing there dressed in his uniform, his mirrored sunglasses concealing his eyes. A smile spread widely on his face and it was anything but warm and friendly.

"Ah, Mr Page," Sherriff Rope said. "Looking forward to the festival tonight?" Jason started to get to his feet but the Sheriff motioned for him to remain seated.

"Please Jason don't get up on my account," the Sheriff said. Jason sat back down and watched Rope warily.

"Can I help you Sheriff?" Jason asked stiffly. The Sheriff's smile widened, exposing a lot of teeth.

"Me? Nah, I'm good, but thanks for asking," Rope replied, then stood there staring at Jason, who was a little unnerved.

"So, what brings you here this morning?" Jason asked, trying to make small talk.

"Well as you're probably not aware, being new to our town, this is the one time that we allow the consumption of alcohol in a public place," Rope stated. Jason shrugged his shoulders. "So as the town's duly elected law enforcement official, I'm here to oversee the delivery of tonight's refreshments and ensure they remain unmolested until the start of the festivities," Rope added. As if on cue, three large refrigeration trucks pulled up into view, the Black River Brewery company name and logo printed on their sides.

"And here they are, Rope stated as he checked his watch. "Right on time". "Wow, you've definitely got your hands full at the moment. I'll just leave you to your duties and get going," Jason said as he climbed to his feet.

"Jason," Rope said aloud, halting him in his tracks.

"You haven't seen Hector have you?" Jason's jaw clenched tight as he turned to face the Sheriff. "He told me you two have buried the hatchet and are best buds," Rope added.

"No I'm afraid not Sheriff. I haven't seen him since yesterday afternoon at the lake," Jason replied trying to keep the anger from his voice.

"You didn't go to the party afterwards?" Rope asked, watching Jason closely for a reaction.

"No I can't say that I did," Jason replied steadily.

"Interesting. You must have missed a hell of a party by all accounts. He left quite a mess. Probably thought I would be home later in the day and that he would have time to clean it up," Rope commented.

"No, sorry. As I said before Selene and I parted company with your son yesterday and I haven't seen him since," Jason said a tinge of annoyance creeping into his voice. This was apparent to the Sheriff who appeared more amused than angry.

"Ah yes, Selene. Where is she today? You two have become quite the item I've been told," Rope asked bemused.

"She's at her grandmothers," Jason replied quickly, wanting to get away.

"Well if I don't see you again before the festival, enjoy yourself. Party like there's no tomorrow," Rope said creepily before turning and making his way toward the refrigeration trucks.

"What a freak," Jason muttered as he watched him walk away.

After his weird run-in with the Sheriff, Jason decided to remain mobile. For the next hour he patrolled every inch of the park starting with the very outer perimeter. As he walked slowly through the ancient trees, Jason let his senses flow out. It required a great deal of his concentration but it was amazing what his hearing could pick up. He overhead an elderly couple discussing what they were going to have for dinner the following night. He then heard a young mum threaten her son with missing the festival if he didn't start behaving. One thing Jason had learned in his short time as an alien shape shifter was that the other alien beings had a completely different smell to humans, no matter how they tried to blend in with humanity. He hoped his ability to detect others such as him using his olfactory perception would become an invaluable asset today.

After completing one lap of the outer limits of the park, Jason decided that whatever or whomever was going to reveal themselves wouldn't be out this far from the main proceedings. He was about to start making his way in toward the central more populated areas when a scent caught his attention, stopping him dead in his tracks. The smell was definitely not of this world, but oddly strangely familiar. The air was extremely cool and his breath could be easily seen when he exhaled. This was made more noticeable as he stood poised, eyes closed, taking in big lung fulls of air through his nose. As the scent became stronger he turned in the direction of its origin. Then just as quickly as it appeared, it was gone, vanishing completely from his senses. Jason's eyes flicked open as he desperately scanned his immediate vicinity trying to locate his possible protagonist. He ran in the direction he had last held the scent and after a few minutes gave up, having seen no one remotely nearby.

"Shit, shit," he cursed to himself. He continued to look around in the hope he might spot something, but in his heart he knew it was pointless. Whoever had been nearby had been watching him and had taken off before they could be discovered. The fact that they had gotten so close with nearly no detection spooked him greatly. They were clearly experienced in this area and more than likely hadn't finished with him. Jason pulled his cell phone from his pocket and called the library to let Ms Jax know of his current situation but his phone was out of reception. He then tried Selene, with the same result. As he made his way back to the central area he tried several more times without luck. He didn't want to go running back to Ms Jax with nothing concrete confirmed, so he decided to remain outside and continue his search for the mystery visitor. Again he wondered where Selene was and what she was doing.

Chapter 36

AS JASON WAS being silently stalked in the park, Selene was battling an unseen force as well-time. The bonds that held her had been tied well. Ever since Ms Gaia had left, Selene had been straining valiantly against her ropes to no avail. She cursed herself for not picking up on Ms Gaea's subterfuge. It hurt her pride to know that the key to this entire mystery had been under their nose and being coveted by a trusted friend no less. Tears of frustration trickled down her cheeks in the knowledge that her friends may fail due to the fact that she couldn't get free.

"Damn it all!" Selene roared in anger as her head fell to her chest in resignation. She sat there for a long time, almost ready to give in as she thought of her friends and family in mortal danger. Slowly her despair gave way to defiance as she realised that the people she loved and cared for wouldn't give up on her, and neither could she. This thought filled her with hope. She realised that her only chance of escape didn't lie in futile strength, but in something she did possess-intelligence and cunning. She started to look around closely at her surroundings. Something caught her eye and a wicked grin spread across her face.

"I'm coming for you bitch," Selene whispered to the darkness as she started to slowly hop the chair along the floor.

Chapter 37

THE REMAINING STUMPP brothers had managed to elude Ulysses for the past hour, but not easily. They had been moving at a high speed, desperately trying to stay out of his reach. Although Ulysses had lead the hunt so far, the Weres weren't just randomly running for their lives through the forest. The Stumpp brothers had been in the mercenary racket for the past three hundred years, plying their expertise as soldiers, assassins and bounty hunters. They hadn't survived this long without a backup plan.

Despite the seriousness of the situation, Ulysses was enjoying himself. His latest incarnation was a predatory creature from the dead moon of Rashtar. The beast was known as a M'org. At first glance he looked like a dead tree without bark, with grey mottled skin. Tall with a thick trunk-like torso, his strong powerful legs strode with purpose along the forest floor sending sounds of crushed logs in his wake. Ulysses' four long arms appeared more like branches, his hands were wide splayd talons that easily pushed small trees from his path. The head of the M'org was a rough lump with no visible eyes or ears, but a large maw-like mouth with jagged teeth, nearly six inches in length. Ulysses made no attempt at stealth as he went in search of the Stumpp brothers. He was certain of two things as he hunted the Weres. One they wouldn't be too far ahead of him, and two, despite the brutal killing of their brother, pride would keep them in the forest, their precious reputation meaning everything to them. Ulysses was also willing to bet they would have a plan B waiting for him, so this merry little chase they were leading was obviously designed to ensnare him into a well laid trap, with them as the bait.

The Stumpp brothers had prepared weeks earlier for the assassination of Ulysses Walker. As with every hit they undertook their employer was unknown to them. The Stumpp brother's only stipulation was that they be paid in advance and they take a trophy of their kill, usually the head. This was non-negotiable. As soon as the money had been placed in their account they had started to plan the hit. Their employer wanted the hit to take place today, which suited them just fine, allowing them plenty of time to conduct surveillance on their mark whom they knew through reputation only. When Ulysses had unexpectedly taken off into the woods that morning they had been delighted, for even though it screwed up their initial plan, the idea that they could engage their target completely unnoticed and conducted in the old ways was an opportunity they couldn't pass up. When they had first arrived in Perigord they had set up a weapons cache in the woods where it wouldn't be discovered and they could quickly access it. Now after their disastrous attempt on Walker's life, they had made their way to the cache with Ulysses hot on their heels. The brothers worked quickly, adding to the booby traps they had already laid. They reinforced their ambush area with claymores and grenades set on trip wires. They were ready for the shape shifter as they themselves crawled into position, armed with modified M4 assault rifles that housed forty millimetre grenade launchers. The tall Were scanned the trees waiting for Ulysses. He could hear the sound of him approaching in the distance. The fact that Ulysses wasn't trying to keep his progress quiet meant that he felt confident. That would be his undoing, the tall Were thought.

"He will be here soon, and so will night," the tall Were whispered into his headset as he watched the setting sun.

"For Michael," the one-eyed Were breathed back. Then there was silence as they waited for Ulysses to trip their ambush.

As Ulysses crashed his way through the forest he was beginning to think that the Stumpp brothers had cleared off for good. Cowards, he thought. So used to their victims being just that. He had dealt with their type before-bullies, so used to getting their own way they truly believed there was only one way. Weren't they in for a big surprise?

Chapter 38

IT WAS NOW late in the afternoon and the people of Perigord were making their way to the centre of town. This wasn't just an annual event to be celebrated yearly, but something that you only experienced a few times in a lifetime. Everyone in the valley would be in attendance. Jason was starting to get nervous. He hadn't heard from anyone all day. Red flags were sounding in his head and he knew it was time to see Ms Jax and find out what exactly what they should do next.

As he made his way through the throng of people towards the library, all he could think about was Selene and why she hadn't called. He was nearly at the front of the library when an all too familiar voice called out to him. He stopped in his tracks and turned to see his mother who was engaged in conversation with someone that Jason couldn't quite see. Not now, he thought, as he tried his best to smile and not look worried.

"Hey mum," Jason called back with a wave, as he reluctantly made his way over to her. As he got closer he saw that his mother had been talking to Ms Stonewall the Vice Principal. When she saw Jason's reaction, a smile crossed her face.

"Hello Jason, I was just asking your mother where her son was hiding, then here you are," Ms Stonewall said, her cold calculating eyes never leaving him.

"Hello Ms Stonewall," Jason said his voice dripping in indifference. It must have been obvious because his mother gave him a reproachful look.

"Jason!" Helen exclaimed, but Ms Stonewall waved her off.

"It's okay Helen. Not many kids want to have their parents associate with teachers, or the Vice Principal no less," Ms Stonewall's amusement was evident.

"I suppose that must be true," Helen said begrudgingly.

"So what do you think of our little festival so far?" Ms Stonewall asked.

"The town seems to love it," Jason replied.

"And you don't?" Ms Stonewall asked in mock surprise.

"I'll reserve my judgement until later," Jason replied in a slightly irritated tone.

"Jason, what's got into you today?" Helen scolded.

"I like his attitude. Anyone else in his position would be saying what they think I want to hear, but not you Jason, why is that?" Ms Stonewall enquired.

"Because I'm certain you'd see through my bullshit," Jason replied. Helen looked on shocked, but Ms Stonewall laughed out loud.

"Excellent Jason, with that sort of insight you'll go far. Have fun and enjoy the festival. It was a pleasure to finally meet you Helen. We'll have to do lunch one day," Ms Stonewall added before disappearing into the crowd.

Jason watched her go then turned to find his mother glaring at him, her arms crossed.

"I don't know whether to slap you or according to Ms Stonewall, congratulate you on your honesty and integrity," Helen said bitterly.

"I'd go with the second one," Jason replied cheekily. Helen went to give him a playful slap and broke into laughter.

"I swear you'll go too far one day," Helen said shaking her head.

"I'm sorry mum, but if you'd seen the way she was with me in week one you'd understand," Jason said.

"I'm sure it wasn't that bad," Helen replied.

"I know you're best buds now, but I just don't trust that woman" Jason said. It was clear that Helen didn't buy his distrust of the Vice Principal. "Listen sweetheart, not to interrupt you, but I'm meeting up with a couple of the girls from work soon. Are you going to be alright? Where's Selene?"

"At the mention of her name Jason completely lost interest in the conversation with his mum.

"That's great mum. Have fun, I have to get going too," Jason said hurriedly and then as an afterthought gave Helen a kiss on the cheek.

"I'll see you later, bye," Jason added and took off in the direction of the library leaving Helen to watch him go. As he made his way he had a horrible thought. 'What if that was the last time I see her alive?' Jason wondered. 'What if we fail and I never got to tell her how much I admire and care about her?' This thought haunted Jason as he ran up the stairs and into the library. Sprouting wings, he flew down the length of the stairs, removing them on landing. He called out to Ms Jax as he ran to the staff area, only to have her meet him half way.

"Is Ulysses back yet?" Jason asked, only to see the worried look in her eyes. He knew the answer to his question. "Shit, the sun's starting to go down outside and I haven't heard from or seen either Selene or Ulysses," Jason added.

"What's the matter with Selene?" a voice called. Jason spun to see a concerned Ursula walking towards them.

"I haven't heard from her," Jason repeated.

"I don't understand. She was going to see a friend this morning, then meet you here," Ursula replied, fear spreading on her face like a cancer.

"Well I can tell you I haven't seen her since last night," Jason said. "The same goes for Ulysses, nothing since this morning," he added.

"I'm afraid I suspect the worst. Whoever is behind this is well aware of our intentions to stop them," Ms Jax said gravely.

"What do you mean?" Ursula asked. Secretly she already knew the answer to her own question.

"I mean these individuals might have removed them from the playing field," Ms Jax said, her normally gravelly voice going up an octave. "And any one of us may be next. The only reason that probably hasn't happened yet is because of our current location here" Ms Jax added.

"When I was out walking the park earlier I sensed someone watching me. When I tried to pinpoint them, I lost the scent. I didn't want to tell you because I had no proof," Jason said dejectedly.

"It's okay. I'm afraid it wouldn't have improved our situation," Ursula interjected.

"What do we do now?" Jason asked, a firm resolve creeping back into his voice.

"Well the news here isn't much better. We've turned up nothing," Ms Jax replied.

"What are our options?" Jason asked.

"We join the festivities," Ms Jax said.

"You're kidding, right?" Jason said incredulous.

"We spread out, keep our eyes open and remain in contact, using these," Ursula said and produced three small objects from her pocket.

"What are they?" Jason asked as he plucked one from her hand and inspected it closely. The object was a small plastic clip that was moulded to fit over a person's ear.

"First up, what is it? Second, where's the rest of it?" he enquired and Ursula smiled.

"That's a state of the art, first generation, spec ops grade communications device, made in Germany and not yet on the market," Ursula said matter-of-fact.

"And you got it how?"

"Let's just say they're friends of the family and leave it at that," Ursula replied.

"Excellent," Jason said as he fitted it to his ear. "Have you any other toys?"

"As a matter of fact I do, but nothing I fear that will add to your already impressive arsenal," Ursula said.

"What are they?" Jason asked intrigued. He stared at the small framed woman who looked more like an old world gypsy than a modern operative from an ancient order.

"I have everything I need carefully hidden from view," Ursula said with a light blush. Jason caught a glimpse of the beautiful woman she had been in her youth, a woman that looked a lot like Selene.

"Then if we're all good, I suggest we join the party," Ms Jax said with a grin.

Chapter 39

AS SOON AS Ms Gaia had left Selene had tried to engage her suit to somehow aid in her escape, but the suit refused to respond. She assumed it had something to do with the enchantments Ms Gaia had mentioned before she left. It had taken Selene well over an hour of fidgeting and wiggling to get herself and the chair over to the far side of the room where with some effort, she was able to grab hold of a straw broom that was leaning against the wall. Selene's hands had been fastened from behind, so the act of procuring the broom had been far from easy. Now that she had it firmly in her grip, she had no intention of letting it go. The hard part was still to come as she now had to get back to where she had initially started, with the broom in her hands no less.

After another two hours of grunting, shuffling and some cursing, Selene made it back to the other side of the room. She nearly lost her hold on the broom several times, but through sheer perseverance, was able to retain her prize. The basement in which she had been placed didn't contain many things. On one side there were large sacks of rice, flour and other grains. On the other side of the room where Selene was currently located was a tall single shelf mounted to the wall, high and near the ceiling. This was to be integral to Selene's plan. Atop the shelf lay a large tin can, its contents a mystery. She was hoping that whatever lay within was heavy, but not so that she couldn't carry out her plan.

Chapter 40

THE SUN HAD officially fled the town of Perigord, leaving only a dim splash of orange to line the top of the mountain range. The Harvest Festival had officially arrived. Perigord Park was littered with thousands of locals who had come to celebrate this rare holiday. As he strolled through the centre of the park Jason couldn't help but be impressed with the amount of work that had gone into the organisation and setup of everything. There were food stalls that catered everything from battered hotdogs to chak-chas a Russian delicacy. Tents of all sizes had been pitched selling craft items such as wind chimes and lucky rabbits' feet, to gag t-shirts that read 'I'm with stupid' and 'Daddy's little Princess'. Throughout the park the Black River Brewery was handing out free refreshments, both alcoholic and non-alcoholic, as well as programs of the night's festivities. Jason declined a cider with a grimace, but took a program. At the centre was a large stage where a variety of bands were entertaining the crowd. While enjoying the music he browsed the program and noted that a number of historical re-enactments were scheduled. Given the time, he would try to catch one of them.

Chapter 41

MS JAX STAYED in the shadows of the surroundings trees, her gaze more than once being drawn to the full moon in the night sky. Her own native planet had two suns and four moons but somehow this adopted world where she now lived held such beauty, especially on nights like tonight that she rarely missed the place of her birth. Ms Jax sighed and was about to step off, when a loud explosion erupted from the Park center. She spun in time to see fireworks erupt into the night sky. Colorful bursts of red, blue and green illuminated the darkness and a collective gasp escaped all who were there to watch. This went on for several minutes followed by a small pause. Just when it seemed as if they had exhausted their supply, another series of colorful explosions rocked the night, much to the delight and squeals of the patrons watching. For the first time that night, Ms Jax wished her dear friend Ulysses was there to share in the spectacle.

Chapter 42

THE STUMPP BROTHERS had been the epitome of patience. For the past thirty minutes they had been silently lying in wait with a visual on their target. They agreed that they had underestimated the shape shifter and they wouldn't make the same mistake twice. When the brothers struck again, they wanted to make certain they hit Ulysses with everything they had, leaving him dead to rights.

Ulysses had just entered their ambush kill zone when there was a sudden burst in the sky. He crouched quickly and looked up to see the dazzling fireworks from town. Climbing to his feet, a second series of explosions rocked him as hundreds of tiny ball bearings ripped into him, fired from carefully targeted claymores. The blast threw him into the path of a series of planted grenades. That blast and fragmentation threw him backwards and before he hit the ground 5.56 mm rounds tore into him. Fired in controlled bursts from two separate locations. Ulysses was able to roll at the last minute, minimizing the damage he received as minor flesh wounds. He crawled into a depression in the earth in an attempt to escape their assault. 'Clever bastards,' Ulysses thought and raised his head, straining to see through the smoke-filled underbrush and dirt that was being kicked up by the Stumpp brother's fire. After several moments he was able to pinpoint their locations. 'Shame on you two, bringing guns to a beast fight,' he thought and let loose with a berserker roar, that sounded like nothing on earth.

Both Weres had stopped to reload at the exact moment that Ulysses' roar ripped through the forest.

"He's still alive," one-eye breathed into his headset incredulously.

"Focus brother," the tall one growled back as his fingers fumbled for the spare magazine. The brothers had barely reloaded and were scanning their kill area when Ulysses came rampaging out of the smoky haze like a missile towards one-eye, who unleashed a full clip that barely stopped the juggernaut. Ulysses tore through every obstacle before him. His goal reach one-eye. Having closed the gap, Ulysses was almost upon one-eye when he tripped another wire, this one releasing a large suspended log with reinforced steel rods that jutted out like spikes. The log came swinging down in a deadly arc from a nearby tree. It collided with Ulysses, knocking him from his course. The protruding steel penetrated his tough hide.

The tall Were came racing to his brother's side. Both started reloading and readying their weapons.

"Is he dead?" the tall Were asked.

"I honestly don't know," one-eye replied, his gaze fixed on the area where Ulysses had fallen. "We've hit him with everything we have. If he's still breathing, I don't know what else we can do," he added. The tall one nodded.

"I think it's time we leave this shit hole. Money or no money, we can't spend it if we're dead," the tall one growled.

"Peter's dead and that's already too steep a price we've had to pay," one-eye replied. At that exact moment, the sound of moving timber could be heard coming from where Ulysses had fallen. The two Weres looked first in the direction of the noise then at each other, both of them with expressions of disbelief and fear.

"Grab what you can carry on the run, let's go!" the tall Were instructed as he got to his feet. His brother stuffed a couple of grenades into the pouches of his vest, then he too got to his feet.

"I'm ready, what's your play?" one-eye asked.

"We're gone, ghosts. I don't want to set foot in this valley again," the tall Were replied. One-eye nodded then without another word, the pair bolted into the darkness.

Ulysses groaned as he lay under the weight of the log that had blindsided him. Even with his beast's abilities he had been momentarily knocked out. As he came to, it took him a minute to work out where he was and what had happened.

"I need an aspirin, or ten," he muttered as he slowly pushed the log off. It took him at least five minutes to clear his head, then another five before he was able to stand. He realized that things had changed significantly since the ambush and the fact that he was still standing meant that his assailants had given up on him. He doubted they were lying in wait, as he was pretty sure their last effort had been just that. So now the only question was, where to now. It didn't take him long to realize the answer to that.

"Perigord," Ulysses whispered. He attempted to change, this time into a beast with wings, however his last escapade had wrenched his right arm and he found the ability to fly was not an option.

"Shit," he growled. "Something fast, nothing pretty," he added as he changed into a large grey wolf. Leaping into the darkness he made his way back to town.

Chapter 43

THE FIREWORKS DISPLAY lasted well over thirty minutes. The town's people were completely unaware of the life and death struggle that had been taking place nearby between Ulysses and the Stumpp brothers. Ms Jax was staring up at the light show when a dark silhouette flickered across one of the building roof tops looking over the park.

"Ursula, Jason, this is Amelia. I've just sighted something suspicious south of the park, on the roof of the Parthenon theatre," Ms Jax said over her headset.

"Amelia, this is Ursula. I copy that. Meet me in the alley that runs behind the theatre, we can use the fire escape to access the roof," Ursula replied. "Copy that," Ms Jax replied. "Jason. Jason, do you copy?" she added, but was met with static.

"Leave him, us girls can handle this one," Ursula said.

"Acknowledged. I'll meet you there in two minutes," Ms Jax said as she tried to make her way through the crowd inconspicuously. Fortunately the patrons were more interested in what was happening in the sky.

As Ms Jax approached the theatre she caught sight of Ursula ducking into the alley behind. She moved more like an athlete than someone in their twilight years, much to Ms Jax's surprise. As she too rounded, the corner Ursula was waiting, crouched with a small pistol in her hands.

"How do you want to handle this?" Ursula whispered.

"Well seeing as how you're armed, I thought you'd take the point," Ms Jax replied. Ursula reached behind and produced another pistol and offered it to Ms Jax.

"You can use this if you prefer," Ursula said, but Ms Jax shook her head.

"I prefer these," Ms Jax replied. With a savage grin she pulled something from her own handbag that clanged together as she brought them into the dim light. They were a pair of rough iron gauntlets, fashioned to fit her large powerful hands. She pulled them on each hand, one at a time. They slipped on perfectly. She finished by tapping the knuckles together like a pro boxer. "I never seem to have any complaints when I wear them," Ms Jax added.

"Where ever did you get them?" Ursula asked in awe.

"My mother. They are an old family heirloom," Ms Jax whispered back.

"I should very much like to meet her one day, she sounds like my sort of woman," Ursula said. Ms Jax remained silent, a thoughtful look upon her face.

"We'd better get going," Ms Jax said. The two women silently made their way up the fire escape.

Chapter 44

THE BASEMENT WAS almost in complete darkness. The first part of Selene's plan, although timely, had gone off without a hitch. However after making her way across the room with the broom held tight, she started phase two of her operation which although sounded simple on paper, was proving to be a bitch. The darkness had compounded the difficulty of the task. She had to knock a tin can residing on the wall shelf on its side, then send it rolling the length of the shelf into the window basement on the other side of the room. The feat required Selene to lean forward on the chair so that the back legs were off the ground, as she balanced between the two front legs and her own feet, grasping the broom by the very end of the handle. She then needed to plant her toes down hard and stretch as far as she was able, striking the other end of the broom against the bottom of the shelf directly under the tin. So far she had come close on more than a few occasions, but that was it. However despite the dwindling light, she had pressed on. Now in the pitch black her resolve and strength were starting to crumble. After another failed attempt she slumped back in the chair, panting hard.

"Goddamn it," Selene snarled as she thrashed in her chair, frustration taking hold of her. "A break wouldn't be too much to ask for would it?" Selene closed her eyes and focused herself. "Everything or nothing," she whispered and drove with all her might, striking the shelf as hard as she could, the impact smashing into the bottom of the shelf. The jarring impact also caused her to lose her grip on the broom.

"No!" Selene cried as the broom clattered to the ground. Her head slumped forward in despair. At the same time the tin on the shelf had been lifted a good couple of inches from the force of the blow. Landing on its edge, it remained balanced for a split second before tipping and landing on its side. The contents within rattled with a metallic sound, sounding like nuts and bolts or something of that nature. Selene's head jerked up at the unexpected sound as she strained to see in the darkness. The can slowly rolled along the shelf, its half-full contents giving it an egg like inertia. It increased in speed towards the basement window. Selene followed its progress by sound alone, praying with all her might for her plan to succeed.

The can stayed the course, striking the window with the desired result. The broken shards of glass rained down onto the floor below. Selene sat in the chair dumbstruck at first, then almost immediately she began hopping the chair towards the window. After thirty minutes she reached her target and with a little effort, toppled the chair over on its side. She winced from the fall and the subsequent shards beneath. She struggled with her bonds and was able to locate a piece of glass large enough with which to carefully cut through her restraints. She was a little shaky as she got to her feet. The last few hours had put a terrible strain on her both physically and mentally but despite this, she had never felt so alive. Trying the basement door she found it to be locked, which she suspected would be the case. She spent the next few minutes kicking and shoulder charging the door but too little affect.

Panting from the exertion, Selene looked up at the narrow broken basement window and debated whether she would be able to reach the window, let alone squeeze her petite frame through.

"What other choice do I have?" she muttered to herself as she placed the chair under the window and stepped up. Her first attempt required her to leap from the chair, grasp a hold on the window and heave herself up. This resulted in cut fingers from the protruding glass shards and Selene having to drop down to the floor.

"Shit, crap, bugger," Selene cursed as she gripped her hands in pain. Looking around the nearly bare room, her gaze lingered on the sacks of grains in the far corner.

"What I really need are a pair of gloves, but…," Selene finished mid-sentence. She picked up a piece of glass and walked over to the sacks.

It took more time than she wished, but by the end Selene was reasonably happy with the results. Wrapped around each hand were strips of hessian cut from the sacks using the piece of glass. She didn't waste any time with her second attempt on the window, which lasted all of ten seconds, as fatigue and bad luck caused her to lose her grip.

"If I don't do this now I'll be down here all night,"

Selene whispered as she climbed atop the chair again, determination set in her face. She steadied herself, then paused.

"Here goes everything," she said to the darkness and leapt with all her might. Her grip held strong and with a growl and groan of exertion, she slowly pulled her weight to the ledge. Using her feet to walk the wall, she was able to raise her head and shoulders and poke them through the opening of the window. In this position, she was then able to rest momentarily as she readjusted her grip and reached for a small shrub sitting a foot from the house. Testing its ability to take her weight, she was then able to slowly pull herself through the window and onto the earth outside. Laying there gasping from the exertion, she eventually rolled onto her back and stared up at the stars as she caught her breath.

Glancing at her watch she sat up with a start.

"No," she said horrified, realizing she only had half an hour till the Harvest Moon ceremony started. Selene jumped to her feet and took off in a sprint towards town. She prayed her friends had already discovered that the person behind this was Ms Gaia and that the fate of the world didn't rest on her shoulders.

Chapter 45

THE FIRE ESCAPE at the Parthenon Theatre had been upgraded two years earlier due to a non-compliance with new fire safety laws. As such, Ms Jax and Ursula had been able to climb their way to the top with barely a sound made. The pair were confident they would have the element of surprise on their side when confronting their target.

The first person to reach the top was Ursula. Staying low, she ascended the ladder onto the roof. Even with her night vision goggles she had trouble seeing any movement past the large air conditioning units and extractor fans that lay staggered across the roof top. With Ms Jax following close behind, they spread out in an attempt to cover the area quickly. Motioning for Ms Jax to stop, Ursula crept around the air conditioning unit, her silenced pistol raised at the ready her movements quick and precise.

Waiting anxiously, her fists cocked, Ms Jax watched Ursula disappear out of view, fully expecting her to reappear on the other side. A tap on the shoulder broke her concentration. She turned in time to see a large, closed fist come crashing down into her face. Attempting to roll with the blow she was thrown backward by the impact, the dark figure advancing upon her. Moving quickly to her feet, she raised her hands to defend herself, the light from the street below glinted off the gauntlets she wore.

"She wants to play," another voice spoke up. Ms Jax turned to see another figure walk into view, this one smaller, dragging the still figure of Ursula behind.

"Don't underestimate her, she took one of my strongest hits and she's still standing, not to mention she's armed," the tall dark figure advised warily.

"This one was armed too, not that it helped her any," the feminine figure said in a static charged voice.

"Let's finish this quick. I don't want any other unexpected visitors," the tall figure said.

"Will you relax? Ulysses is being taken care of as we speak," the feminine one replied.

"What did you say?" Ms Jax said, alarmed at the mention of her friend's name.

"I wouldn't worry about Ulysses," the feminine one said. Just then another series of fireworks lit up the night sky, illuminating the roof top and all its inhabitants.

"You!" Ms Jax cried and charged the unsuspecting pair, her fists raised displaying the brutal gauntlets she now wore. Strix was not ready for Ms Jax's speed and ferocity as she lunged back in surprise. Ms Jax swung her fist in a deadly arc aimed at the avian hunter's face, the only thing that was preventing the removal of her head was the intervention of Onyx. Throwing himself at his partner, he instead received the blow meant for Strix. The sound of steel on rock made a residing tang. Ms Jax followed up with a kick to Onyx's midsection, the force of which lifted him several feet from the ground.

As she prepared to deliver the final blow to the still form of Onyx, she was kicked from behind by Strix who had doubled around to Ms Jax's flank, waiting for the right time to strike. The kick itself wasn't very powerful but the angle of the blow had caught her unaware, knocking her off balance and landing atop Onyx. As she scrambled to her feet, Strix was ready. Producing a pair of titanium tipped batons, she attacked without hesitation. The batons were a blur of movement as she struck Ms Jax multiple times, hitting vital points that on an ordinary human would have incapacitated or killed, but on Ms Jax, it was just pissing her off.

The speed in which Strix moved was extraordinary. Ms Jax had centuries of combat experience fighting in battles both on earth and off, but despite this, she was completely unable to land a single blow.

"Rraaaggghhh," Ms Jax raged as she advanced forward, firing a punch forward with each step, only to be met by Strix's back flipping figure and unnerving static laughter.

"I can't believe I was concerned about you, the famous warrior Ajax," Strix sang as she danced around Ms Jax's attacks.

"I've heard about you too," Ms Jax growled back. "Assassin, mercenary, no honour, just dirty work in the dark," she added.

"Hey bitch, I'm not hiding now," Strix shouted back as she launched a flurry of strikes delivered from the ends of her batons.

The hits were blinding her vision as she raised her

gauntlets in defence. Taking a step back she tripped on an exposed vent protruding from the roof. She landed on her back, the breath knocked from her. Without missing a beat Strix jumped in the air bringing her foot down onto the exposed face of Ms Jax, who rolled at the very last second. The combat boot came down hard onto the roof, missing Ms Jax's head by mere inches. Swinging wildly, Ms Jax struck the ankle of Strix who shrieked and flipped head over tail, hitting the ground with a loud thud.

Struggling to her feet Ms Jax rushed the fallen form of Strix, grasping her by the hair with one hand and raising her other metallic clad hand in a fist ready to deliver the coup de gra. She was stopped in her tracks by a burst of sudden excruciating pain. Struggling to turn from the agonising pain, she peered through blurred vision and found Onyx standing before her, a small black device held in one hand, his thumb poised on the trigger. A blinding white energy was pouring out of the device and into her. Onyx smirked and removed his thumb from trigger. Instantly the pain stopped. Dropping to her hands and knees she gasped in relief.

"I've gotta give it to you Ajax, you've more than lived up to your rep. Neither of us is an easy mark," Onyx said casually as he indicated himself and his avian partner who was also getting to her feet, a look of anger and scorn on her face.

"Don't play with her Onyx, just put her down," Strix said.

"That's not your call. She wants them both alive," Onyx replied.

"Who wants us?" Ms Jax asked, wincing as she tried to get to her feet.

"Hold it there Ajax," Onyx ordered, his voice wary. Ms Jax froze, her gaze on his.

"Who's behind this?" Ms Jax asked again.

"You'll meet her soon enough," Onyx replied as he depressed the trigger, sending thousands of volts of electricity coursing through her. Ms Jax gritted her teeth, trying to retain consciousness. Despite her fighting spirit, both time and firepower were on her adversary's side and after what seemed an eternity of pain, she blacked out, her body slumping to the ground.

"Check her," Onyx said as he kept the black device trained on her still form. Strix moved forward warily and after a brief examination stepped away.

"She's alive, her pulse is as strong as a bull," she replied with disdain.

"Good. I know our orders are to bring them in alive, but if this didn't work I don't know what would," Onyx said indicating the black device he held in his hand. Strix had already started restraining their two fallen foes. The chains and cuffs she used were a sparkling silver in colour and appeared slender, almost fragile.

"Will these hold her?" Strix asked, referring to the chains.

"They better. If they can tether a Martian sand worm, than they should hold her," Onyx stated plainly. "Let's hurry up and get these two below, it's almost time," he added.

Chapter 46

MOST OF THE festivities had already played out, not that Jason had been able to enjoy it. He was sick with worry over Ulysses and Selene. Now he was unable to raise Ms Jax or Ursula on his comms headset. The whole town was present in the city centre awaiting the rare celestial event. With the introduction of free cider provided by the Black River Brewery, the patrons appeared jovial and happy. Children were running around playing hide and seek among the fairy light lit trees. Some of the teenage boys had managed to procure a number of bottles of the alcoholic cider and now loaded up with Dutch courage, were doing their best to impress the girls with feats of strength and bravado. Men and woman gathered in groups discussing work, kids, the wonders of the universe, and what's on TV at the moment.

On several occasions Jason had drifted into the darkness and changed shape into something small and obscure, like a cat or a dog, searching the outer lying area for anything out of the ordinary. Despite being surrounded by the entire township of Perigord, Jason had never felt so alone. Drifting through the crowd he made his way toward the library. Climbing its steps he flopped down at the top and dropped his head onto his folded arms.

"Where the hell is everyone?" he breathed.

A high piercing static sound shot through the PA system on the main stage. It made everyone jump, including Jason. The sound was followed by a heavy thump, thump of someone tapping a microphone. Everyone's attention was drawn to the stage where a large, portly figure dressed in an immaculate navy blue suit stood. The figure loudly cleared his throat before addressing the crowd.

"Ahem. First up, I'd just like to say what a pleasure it is to see such a wonderful turnout tonight and as Mayor, how proud I am that festivities have been conducted in the spirit with which they were intended. So thank you all," the Mayor said in a polished voice. His speech was met with applause and cheering from the crowd. "Especially you Lloyd," the Mayor added with a smirk. Everyone turned to a skinny dishevelled figure sitting against a tree nursing a bottle of cider, obviously drunk as a skunk. The crowd cheered again including Lloyd.

"How long till the moon changes colour?" a young voice called out from the crowd.

"A very good question young man. The lunar event I've been told starts in exactly ten minutes," the Mayor announced. This was met with more cheering. "Please enjoy the night," the Mayor added and waved to the crowd before stepping down from the dais.

He sat there stunned. The words of the Mayor sinking in.

"Ten minutes. I have ten bloody minutes," Jason whispered sitting on the top step staring into space.

"What do I do? Where is everyone? I don't know what to do," he mumbled dropping his head in his hands, despair taking over. Sitting there for several minutes, he was unable to move. Fear of the unknown, fear of failure, fear of everything. These thoughts and more sunk into his bones.

"Jason," a faint voice carried through the crowd. At first he wasn't even sure he heard it.

"Jason," the voice was a little stronger now. The noise of the crowd was loud and boisterous but the name being called was definitely there. His ears pricked. He scanned the crowd looking for whoever was calling his name.

"Jason." This time the voice was clear and concise. Still looking, he didn't have to wait as Selene burst from the swarm of people below. They both locked eyes and ran to each other. Her relief at finding each other and the stress they had both been placed under seemed not to exist as they dived into each other's arms.

"Where have you been?" Jason stammered as he hugged her tight.

"I've got so much to tell you," Selene replied as she held Jason at arm's length. This was the first time Jason had really taken a good look at her and he was shocked at what he saw.

"What the hell happened to you?" he asked as he continued to take in her ruffled and dirty appearance.

"I'll tell you later. I know who's behind this," Selene said. This statement silenced Jason as he waited to hear more.

"It's Ms Gaia. She has the Gjallerhorn and she's here somewhere getting ready to use it," Selene added.

"Ms Gaia? What, I don't understand? How is she planning to distribute the potion and conduct the ceremony?" Jason replied perplexed.

"The potion, it's in the cider," Selene said much to Jason's confusion. "The cider. The ingredients are in the free cider everyone's drinking." Jason's eyes darted over the crowd. Everyone he spied had a bottle in hand. Men, women and children were all drinking or holding one of the locally brewed beverages.

"Oh my God," Jason breathed as the full realisation sunk in.

"That's right. The whole town is gonna go Jekyll and Hyde…," Selene checked her watch and added, "In three minutes." Jason pulled a program from his pocket.

"What's this?" Selene asked as she took the program from him.

"Have a look at the bottom. I think she's planning on performing the ceremony in plain sight," Jason said. "There's several performances starting in the next few minutes, but I'm betting it's the historical re-enactment of Heinrich Perigord, on the main dais," Jason said with complete certainty.

"I agree. Where are the others?" Selene asked as they both started to push their way through the crowd toward the centre stage.

"I don't know. I lost contact with Ursula and Ms Jax half an hour ago. I haven't seen Ulysses since this morning." The pair slowly made their way through the throng of party goers.

"Are you saying the others are all MIA?" Selene asked shocked.

"Yeah I'm afraid we're on our own," Jason said grimly as he pulled Selene by the hand. They had just located the dais up ahead when a darkness fell across them. This was followed by a collective gasp from the crowd. They looked up to the sky. The sight stopped them momentarily in their tracks.

The full moon was looming abnormally large on the horizon, now a blood red in colour.

"Keep moving," Jason yelled as he continued to pull himself and Selene along. They managed to reach the stage, now under the glare of a crimson light. Several performers dressed in hooded robes were beginning their act.

"I can't see her," Selene cried as she struggled to see Ms Gaia.

"Me neither," Jason replied dubiously.

"We have to get up there now" Selene instructed as they raced to the side of the dais and up the stairs. A large tattooed security guard blocked their way at the top, raising his hand motioning for them to stop. Jason changed his size, slightly increasing his muscle mass. That coupled with his momentum, allowed him to easily push the guard from the steps and to the ground below. The pair entered the stage where the four performers stopped mid step to regard the intruders before them.

"Which one?" Jason called out. Selene had a moment of hesitation. Before she could answer the largest robed figure took a step toward Jason.

"What the hell are you two doing?" the robed figure growled. This was all the motivation Jason needed. He dived at the figure, tackling him roughly to the ground. There was a collective gasp from the crowd as they watched Jason manhandle the robed actor. With his added strength, Jason was easily able to pin the large figure and rip the hood back, revealing his identity beneath.

"Get off of my son," one of the other robed figures screamed out as it too pulled back its hood to reveal a plump middle aged woman in her fifties. She was looking at him in wide eyed horror. Jason stared at the woman then down at the figure he was sitting on. It was a kid Jason recognised from school. He was in a grade beneath him. The boy was big for his age but had a soft pudgy face. His eyes were clenched shut and his hands were raised awaiting the beating he suspected he was about to receive.

"It's not them," Selene said weakly. Jason nodded dumbly in response.

"I'm sorry," Jason said, but the kid peered up at him and refused to move. It took Jason a moment to realise that he was still sitting on him and had a fist raised above him.

"Get off of him you horrible child," the boy's mother screamed. "He's done nothing to you," she added.

"Yeah asshole." Another of the robed figures had thrown back its hood. An elder gentleman in his early sixties with a weathered face looked scornfully at Jason. "Pick on someone your own size," the older man added. The crowd had by now recovered from the initial shock and people were now angrily hurling their disgust and ridicule at Jason and Selene. Jason got to his feet and tried to help the robed boy to his feet.

"Don't touch me," the boy cried and tried to pull away. Jason realised with shame that the younger boy had begun to cry. Despite the urgency of what was about to happen, Jason felt completely worthless as he stood in front of the crowd as they yelled abuse at him.

"It's all just a misunderstanding, we didn't mean it," Selene cried out to the crowd as she tried to angle herself between Jason and them.

The crowd had started to call for the sheriff to come. The robed actors had left the stage leaving Jason and Selene to face the angry mob alone. "We've really messed up," Jason whispered to Selene who nodded in agreement.

"What do we do now?" she whispered. Jason was about to respond when the deep resonating sound of a horn erupted from nearby. Everyone stopped in their tracks and turned in the direction of the horn blast.

"What was that?" Jason said mystified.

"I don't know," Selene replied. The horn trumpeted again louder and longer this time. The crowd that had only moments earlier been berating Selene and Jason were now transfixed on the sound and the direction from which it was coming. As the horn sounded off again, everyone began to shuffle toward it. Looking on in a state of panic, Jason and Selene watched the people of Perigord stagger away from them and toward a small stage erected at the far side of the festival. Their movements were jerky spasmodic. Glazed eyes stared at the small figure sitting on a large chair made of Wicca. The figure had the Gjallerhorn rested upon the ground and was blowing it slowly and rhythmically, much like a musician on the bagpipes. As the town's people reached the figure they started to spread out subconsciously and form a perfect circle around the musician. Thousands of people all facing in, men, women and children, fell to their knees.

"No," Jason said, his face beholding a primal fear. Selene's face had turned an ashen grey.

"We're too late, that's the Gjallerhorn," Selene said hollowly.

Chapter 47

THE HORN BLEW over and over. Every person within Perigord that had sampled the cider surrounded the small stage and knelt before the figure blowing the horn. Jason and Selene leapt from the stage and raced towards Ms Gaia.

"Stop!" Jason shouted on the run but his voice was drowned out by the sound of the booming horn. They approached cautiously through the sea of kneeling people who appeared rigid and unmoving. Despite their careful movement forward, Jason nearly tripped several times over the still figures littering the ground.

They could now clearly make out Ms Gaia seated upon the chair. She paused and gave the pair a wicked smile then mouthed the words "You're too late." She continued to blow the horn, all the while keeping her eyes locked on them.

"Screw this," Jason said angrily as he strode forward. Selene reached out and grabbed his arm.

"I don't like this," Selene said warily.

"Don't worry, I'll just walk over, grab the horn and

we'll go home, trust me." His cockiness lasted all of two seconds as a scream was issued from someone within the crowd. Jason spun around to see one of the kneeling people, not ten metres away writhing on the ground in pain. This was followed by another scream, then another and another. They looked around in concern and terror as people before their eyes began to change. Not the natural seamless way in which Jason did, but in a bone crunching, muscle tearing way you'd envisaged would happen in a B grade horror movie. The screams soon gave way to growls and roars.

"Mum!" Jason yelled out as he frantically looked around for her. By now all of the town's people looked like one giant seething mass of teeth, claws and muscle. Before they could take another step toward the stage, Ms Gaia stopped blowing the horn and was standing with it raised above her head, her purple eyes ablaze with an unnatural fire.

"Feast my minions," she screamed loudly and pointed one finger in Jason and Selene's direction. There was a clear pause as all of the now fully transformed crowd turned their hungry eyes towards them. The only sound was the heavy breathing of the beasts as surveyed their prey.

Selene stood frozen to the ground, paralysed with fear, completely unsure of what to do next. A large roar was issued from one of the beasts. It sounded as if it were coming directly from the gates of hell, a cross between an elephant, a lion and a touch of otherworldly madness thrown in for good measure. It was soon joined by another, then a dozen more and finally the entire congregation of creatures, their black dead eyes regarded them unblinking.

Jason changed his form, becoming like that of a gorilla, squat and powerful but without hair. Instead the skin was grey in colour and thickened its density like hardened leather now with distinct armoured ridges. Jason's head was now broad and blunt with two small horns, one on the forehead the other on the bridge of the nose like a rhinoceros.

Now in full beast mode, Jason scooped Selene up with one of his powerful arms and with his other free hand, bounded over several beasts like a child playing leap frog. He was able to do this quickly and with relative ease, landing them temporarily out of harm's way. Their sudden movement forced the beasts around them into action. The nearest one charged the pair, swinging its massive head. It attempted to take a bite out of Selene with its gnashing jaws. Jason brought his arm down onto the head of the beast at the last moment, his heavy fist laying it down hard.

"Be careful," Selene screamed, but Jason just stared at her incredulously. "They can't help themselves," Selene added hopelessly. It was then the realisation hit him. These slavering creatures were the victims and despite the imminent danger they posed, he had to be careful not to inflict any permanent danger on any of them. As if on cue, three of them bounded towards Jason, their teeth and claws bared ready to rend flesh and bone apart.

"Run!" Jason growled, his newly acquired form barely able to spit the words out. Selene, understanding the inflection of the words and the immediate danger they meant, ran quite literally for her life toward the library entrance. Jason held his ground defending her fleeing form from the advancing beasts. She was nearly at the steps to the library when a shadowy figure streaked out of nowhere knocking her to the ground. Jason caught this movement out of the corner of his eye as he traded blows with another pair of beasts.

"Selene!" Jason screamed as he spun to face her assailant, in the process turning his back on the army of Perigord who had now stopped their assault. The beasts were now waiting passively as Ms Gaia moved forward to see what was transpiring.

Although the blow with which she had received had been intended to kill, Selene was far from dead. Her assailant was holding Selene up by her hair with one hand, the other poised at her throat.

"Strix," Jason growled angrily. Yet another added antagonist to an already one sided fight. "If you've hurt her, I'll make you pay," he added.

"Too late for that," another voice yelled out. Jason turned his gaze at the additional figure that was joining them near the steps of the library. The broad figure of Onyx strolled almost casually out of the tree line carrying the chain-bound figures of Ursula and Ms Jax over his shoulder. He stopped short and dumped his captives to the ground with a thud.

"Give up boy, you're on your own," Onyx ordered.

"I'm not alone, Ulysses is...," Jason started, but was cut off mid-sentence.

"Ulysses is dead," Onyx said smugly, clearly relishing the chance to reveal this information.

"Bullshit, you couldn't bring him down if you tried," Jason said furiously. This honest appraisal of Onyx's abilities clearly pissed off the mercenary as he struggled to keep his emotions in check.

"Ms Gaia's assassins would have finished him off hours ago. Like I said, you're all alone, pup," Onyx stated. Ms Gaia now stood at the head of her army, all of which stood motionless awaiting her next instruction.

"Where the hell have you two been?" she ordered, clearly displeased.

"We had to deal with these two before we could make our way back," Onyx replied, indicating the two figures at this feet.

"When I first hired you two I was under the impression I was gaining an exceptional pair of warriors that could get any job done. From what I've seen, this is far from the truth," Ms Gaia said bitterly.

"Now hold on a second," Onyx bristled with annoyance. "We've done everything you've asked. Without us you wouldn't have your army," he added.

"My planning, foresight and perseverance are what have got me where I am now," Ms Gaia thundered, her army of creatures growling behind her as if in agreement.

"Stupid human, don't you dare dream of reneging on your side of the bargain," Strix said. Ms Gaia shook her head and smiled.

"My vision doesn't include the likes of you two. Consider your services terminated."

"Bitch!" Strix screamed as she dropped Selene and charged Ms Gaia.

"No!" Onyx yelled. He watched in horror as the army of the Harvest Moon who had been standing motionless behind Ms Gaia stampeded from behind their new mistress, ready to protect her from harm. It happened almost too fast to see. One moment Strix was charging forward and the next she was gone, washed away in a wave of howling carnage. Without thinking, Onyx too, ran into the fray, his large wrecking ball fists smashing into the rampaging beasts. No matter how many he hit there were ten more to take its place, and the ones he hit simply shook off the beating and came back for more. Incredibly, the sound of Strix fighting could be heard somewhere within the writhing mess. Jason, not wanting to waste an opportunity, raced to where Selene lay and again scooped her up in his arms. He fought his way through the throng of beasts to the top of the library stairs, however was unable to open the front door.

"Why won't it open?" Jason grunted.

"Don't worry about it," Selene said weakly, nursing her gashed forehead. "Save gran and Ms Jax," Selene added, pointing to where the two lay bound in chains. Jason changed back to his human form, kneeing beside Selene.

"Okay, but stay up here out of sight," he ordered. Selene looked dazed, but defiant.

"I want to help," she said.

"I know you do, but I can't be worrying about your safety and at the same time trying to help them, okay?" Selene met his gaze, her expression hurt by his words. She nodded her acknowledgement then without warning leaned forward and kissed him deeply.

"Be careful," she said gently. Jason, initially stunned, smiled back, a glint in his eye.

"For you anything," he replied as he turned to granite and charged down the stairs and into battle. Selene sat there, a proud smile etched on her face. She watched him fight his way through to her grandmother and wished she could do more. Suddenly she heard the door behind her creak open. She crept forward to investigate who or what was behind it. As she peered into the darkness, she was met by a brilliant white light.

"I don't believe it," Selene whispered as she walked willingly through the door. Ever so slowly the door shut behind her.

After what seemed an eternity, Jason was finally able to reach his chained friends. Ursula was still unconscious but Ms Jax had come to. Relief flooded her face upon seeing Jason. The chains had been applied to her from behind, bounding her feet and hands much like a steer in a rodeo, allowing her no leverage.

"Am I glad to see you," Ms Jax said. "But I fear these chains may be beyond the abilities of us both."

"Let's not give up just yet shall we?" Jason replied. He set to work trying to break her restraints. When sheer strength didn't work he started to pound on the cuffed areas that held her wrists and ankles. This too proved equally fruitless.

"Shit sake," Jason growled in frustration. "Are we ever going to get a break tonight?" Out of nowhere a large silver key hit him in the chest and fell into his lap. Not realising what it was, he lifted it up for inspection.

"It's the bloody key to those chains," an angry voice called out. Jason looked around to find a bloody and bruised Strix battling it out with half a dozen creatures. Every move she made was with a blinding and self-assured speed that Jason found mesmerising. Strix stopped only momentarily to give him an impatient look.

"Would you hurry up? I can't keep this up indefinitely!" Strix said. Nodding dumbly, Jason fumbled with the key as he unlocked Ms Jax's restrains. They fell noisily to the ground. Rubbing her wrists Ms Jax climbed to her feet, crouching beside Jason. The pair joined in the battle. They were eventually joined by Strix and Onyx. The four of them formed a crude circle around the still figure of Ursula.

"Our only chance of survival is to work together," Onyx cried, struggling to be heard over the noise of battle.

"Agreed," Ms Jax replied, clearly not pleased with her options. The four continued to fight, despite the fact they were clearly not making a dent in their opposition's numbers.

Chapter 48

HAVING BEEN UNABLE to track down the two remaining Stumpp brothers Ulysses had slowly made his way back to town, hampered by the injured arm he had received in the ambush. In his wolf form he had reached the outskirts of the township and could now clearly hear sounds of destruction emanating from the town centre. He raced toward the centre of town, determined to either help or avenge his friends. His wildest thoughts however did not prepare him for the sight that greeted him. Thousands of crazed beasts bellowed and rampaged near his library, all of them attacking four lone figures. Two he knew well, the other two he wished he didn't. All four were fighting together and that was all he needed to know. Without waiting for an invitation, Ulysses dived into the battle, changing his form into solid rock.

An uneasy alliance now existed between the hired mercenaries, Jason and Ms Jax. A flash of movement to Jason's right got his attention as he prepared to face his new threat, only to find Ulysses' presence in the fray

"Ulysses!" Jason cheered. Whipping her head around, Ms Jax smiled broadly at the addition of her old friend. Ulysses had joined the group and their chances had increased by a factor of one.

"Don't you hate it when you arrive at a party only to find someone wearing the same outfit as you?" Ulysses joked as he and Jason fist bumped each other with a loud rocky thump.

"I'm glad you could make it," Ms Jax said as she grabbed a creature by the head and tossed it into the path of another five oncoming beasts.

"Wouldn't miss it," Ulysses said with a wry grin. "By the way you haven't seen two Weres making their way through town?" Ulysses asked.

"Hey shit head, pay attention!" Onyx growled angrily as he brought two fists down onto the back of a beast.

"Hey Onyx, as much as I appreciate your help here, this is our party, so shut your mouth and pull your weight," Ulysses said savagely. "Oh, remind me later, we need to have a chat about your involvement in our current predicament okay," he added as he tossed an oncoming beast high into the air. As it returned to earth, Ulysses lined it up and punched the falling figure, sending it flying into the tree tops. Onyx continued to hold his own, choosing not to reply.

"No I haven't," Jason yelled to a confused Ulysses. "I haven't seen your two Weres, have you misplaced them?" he said. Despite the dire situation, Ulysses let out a big laugh.

"No can't say that I'm missing them," Ulysses said.

"By the way can someone fill me in? I feel like I've walked in on the last half of a movie."

"Ms Gaia, a teacher from school is the mastermind behind this. She kidnapped Selene, who escaped, hired thugs to eliminate us and you, blew the Gjallerhorn starting Ragnerok and we are now in a battle for our lives," Jason said all in one breath.

"Selene," Ulysses replied.

"Safe," Jason said as he threw a quick glance at the library entrance.

"Your mum," Ulysses asked, but was answered by a worried look. "Ouch," he added. "Options?"

"I was hoping you could answer that, big dog," Jason said as he ducked the blow of a snarling beast.

"I was afraid of that," Ulysses said. "I think our only option from what you've told me is to grab the teacher and take the horn," Ulysses said bluntly.

"Easier said than done," Ms Jax said, pointing to the object of their discussion in the distance, surrounded by an impossible number of beasts ready to defend her to the death.

"Forget it, our only chance is to run," Onyx growled. Ulysses shot him a look of barely suppressed rage.

"You and your partner run and I swear by all that I hold holy, I'll spend the rest of my days hunting you down," Ulysses said. Everyone present knew it was no idle threat.

"What's your plan then shifter?" Onyx said, trying to sound calm.

"Pull back to the trees, lure them into the darkness.

Then Jason and I will flank the teacher and steal the Gjallerhorn," Ulysses said.

"That's your plan?" Strix hissed.

"Unless you have something better?" Ulysses said. His comment was met with silence. "You and Birdy go first, head east. The rest of us will hold them off. We'll join you once we've seen you clear the tree line," Ulysses snapped. Onyx was about to retort but Strix grabbed him by the arm and shook her head. This seemed to be enough for the mercenary as they pulled back, fighting the entire way.

"Can we trust them?" Jason asked suspiciously.

"I doubt it, but all I need to rely on is you two, and that is something that isn't bothering me in the slightest," Ulysses said honestly.

"They're at the tree line," Ms Jax interrupted.

"Amelia grab Ursula," Ulysses instructed. "On me, let's go," he added. The three of them with the unconscious Ursula followed in the direction of Onyx and Strix. It seemed as if there was a never ending supply of foes to fight. Once in the cover and concealment of the trees, they were able to find Strix and Onyx who were standing over a pile of beast bodies.

"Are they dead?" Jason demanded. His question was met with contempt.

"And what if they are?" Onyx replied.

"You Sonofabitch!" Jason yelled as he advanced on the large mercenary. Ms Jax held him back.

"I think they're fine," Ulysses said. "I can see the rise and fall of their chests."

"Watch your mouth kid. I might let your boss get

away with a bit of lip, but not his pup," Onyx said casually. Jason bristled at his words.

"Later Jason. Right now we need to continue to move back. There's a slight rise in the terrain and we could definitely use some high ground," Ulysses said.

"Agreed," Strix said.

"Run, little piggies, run far, far away," a voice sang out in the darkness." They all stopped to listen.

"I take it, that's your teacher friend?" Ulysses said.

"Friend is too strong a word. She sounds bat shit crazy now though," Jason replied.

"Keep moving," Ulysses ordered. The rag tag collection of aliens and humans stealthily withdrew. Occasionally having to deal with a lone beast, they were eventually able to find the rise in the ground that Ulysses had described and located in its centre a large tree. Its thick trunk and out reaching branches appeared to be the answer to their prayers.

"This is where you three are going to defend. Amelia, take Ursula, get high. From what I've seen those beasts won't be able to navigate their way up there easily," Ulysses said.

"And once we're up there, how long?" Strix asked.

"As long as it takes," Ulysses reminded her. "If we're successful you'll know."

"And if you're not?" Onyx asked.

"I'm sure you'll figure it out," Ulysses said with a grin. "Amelia, you know where to go?" Ms Jax nodded.

"It's been a pleasure, I'll see you one way or the other," Ms Jax said.

"In the halls they'll be singing songs of our battles,"

Ulysses replied. Ms Jax pulled Jason into a bear hug, followed by a kiss on the cheek.

"I haven't known you long, Jason, but I've come to admire your spirit and courage. May the Gods be witness to your exploits here today," she said. Jason appeared to be a little choked up by her words. He chose to remain silent.

"Are we done jerking each other off here?" Onyx interrupted gruffly. Ulysses spun to face the mercenary. Stepping up and into his face he poked a finger into his chest.

"I haven't forgotten your role here tonight and I'm going to enjoy hearing your side of it," Ulysses said calmly, tapping his finger each time into Onyx's chest.

"Yeah I'm looking forward to it too," Onyx replied. Ulysses ignored the jibe and turned to Jason.

"Let's go son, time's a wasting," Ulysses said as he grabbed Jason and steered him away into the darkness. Jason cast one last look over his shoulder and saw Ms Jax, laden with Ursula, leap twenty metres up and into the tree, landing softly on a large branch.

"She'll be fine," Ulysses said, seeing the concerned look upon Jason's face.

"Even with those other two with her?" Jason replied.

"Ha, they have no option but to pitch in and heaven help them if they try to screw her over," Ulysses joked. This made Jason feel a little better, but not by much. He gave them one last look before the darkness swallowed them up.

Chapter 49

ULYSSES AND JASON spent the next few minutes doubling back past Ms Jax and Ursula, then around to the extreme outer flank of Ms Gaia and her inner guard of transformed beasts. They were able to get into position without detection. They lay there awaiting the moment to attack.

"What are we waiting for?" Jason asked.

"On my command, Ms Jax is going to draw your teacher's forces and when she is at her most vulnerable, we'll attack," Ulysses replied.

"And when is that?" Jason asked.

"Now," Ulysses said and Jason noticed that he was holding one of Ursula's headsets to his mouth. "Amelia, you're up," he whispered.

Ms Jax had placed Ursula safely into the crook of a branch and was now perched below her unconscious friend. She moved through the tree top as if she was one born to it. Straining to see into the darkness for any sign of movement, she heard Ulysses' signal over her headset. Ms Jax stood tall on her branch, puffed out her chest and let loose with an inhuman scream. It sounded like the cross between an eagle's shriek and the baying of a hound.

"What the hell are you doing?" Onyx growled as he looked up at Ms Jax from a lower branch. "Is that your friend's plan, to get us killed while he sits it out?" he added. Ms Jax paused briefly to give him a scathing glance, then continued with her cries.

"Forget it, what's done is done. Prepare yourself brother, for the time for battle is upon us," Strix said.

Ms Gaia moved as if she were out taking a midnight stroll, dressed in a simple black robe with the Gjallerhorn in her hand, using it as if it were a staff. Dozens of her beasts walked beside her, constantly scanning the surroundings for threats. Now and again she would lovingly scratch behind the ear of a beast, much like someone would do a beloved pet. When the sounds of Ms Jax's screams reached Ms Gaia, she gave a benevolent smile.

"Go forth, rip and tear asunder, bring me their heads," Ms Gaia breathed quietly. The reaction of the beasts was as if she had trumpeted the call to battle. Hundreds raced forth into the darkness on her command, their blood curdling howls sending ripples of madness into the night.

They lay in the grass, hidden by foliage, watching the events play out.

"They're going," Jason whispered excitedly.

"Not all of them though," Ulysses replied sourly. Jason watched closely. Even though hundreds of beasts had taken off in pursuit, an even greater number had remained behind.

"There's still hundreds of them," Jason whispered.

"It was always going to be a long shot," Ulysses

replied, placing a reassuring hand on his arm. "But just because we're outnumbered doesn't mean we don't have a chance."

"You really think we have a chance?" Jason asked hopefully.

"Sure, but if we don't, at least we'll go down in a blaze of glory." Jason's exuberance immediately plummeted.

"Way to pump me up before the main event," he said sarcastically.

"Hey, I think it could go either way. I'm not going to sugar coat it. Things are dire, but nothing is ever certain," Ulysses said.

"Now that's what I'm talking about," Jason said. "What do we do now?" he added.

"I'll think you'll like this," Ulysses said.

Ms Jax had finished her alien call and was perched upon a branch for the beasts to arrive. She cast a glance towards Strix and Onyx who were also waiting patiently on the branches nearby. Mercenaries who were now aiding their cause. She hoped that their mettle would hold out long enough for Ulysses and Jason to accomplish their mission. Ursula, who was laying close by, stirred and groaned loudly. Kneeling beside her, Ms Jax stroked her brow.

"Sssshhh, lay still," Ms Jax instructed.

"What happened? Where are we?" Ursula asked weakly.

"We're currently sitting high in a tree awaiting the harvest beasts to attack, while Ulysses and Jason flank their main force," Ms Jax replied.

"And Selene?" Ursula asked.

"Safe at the library," Ms Jax said.

"Pay attention Ajax, we don't have time for you to molly coddle the old woman," Onyx interrupted coldly. Ursula peered around in the dark, shocked to see the two individuals who had assaulted her earlier.

"What the hell are they doing here?" Ursula asked as she struggled to sit up.

"It's a long story, but they're here to help. Since you're awake, is there anything in this that can help?" Ms Jax asked, holding up a small black bag. "Maybe a thing or two," Ursula replied as she took the bag and rummaged through its contents. Noise drew their attention to the ground below which was now crawling with dozens of snarling beasts, their glittering eyes appearing like fireflies in the darkness.

"I don't think they can climb," Onyx grunted. The first few slowly started to make their way up using their claws to dig into the massive trunk and painstakingly climb upwards to their prey.

"Nice one idiot, had to open your big mouth, didn't you?" Strix said as she crouched into a fighter's stance, waiting to attack. The beasts were able to reach the first set of lower branches and once there, they launched themselves towards Ms Jax and the others. The battle was fast and furious. The first wave attacked the group with speed and ferocity that along with their single mindedness and physical attributes, made them near perfect killing machines. Ms Jax and her colleagues also had speed, strength, weapons, a desire to remain alive and most importantly, the high ground. Almost dancing along the branches, Strix darted back and forth, striking mercilessly quick before her foes had a chance to regain their balance or grip on any given branch. Ursula had a twelve gauge shotgun with the stock removed. She fired at close range with reflexes and skill that belied her age and passive appearance, reloading and firing without pause. Both Ms Jax and Onyx took a more simple approach. Standing firm, they pounded their foes. One, two, three at a time, brutally with clenched fists, knees or elbows. The sounds of the impacts were ear shattering. Each enemy they dispatched to the ground below was simply replaced by another and the ones that fell, shook it off seemingly uninjured.

"This is insane, they just keep coming!" Onyx roared.

"Shut up and keep fighting," Ms Jax called back as she tossed another beast to the ground.

"I'm starting to run low on ammo," Ursula called out as she pulled more rounds from her black bag and carefully reloaded her shotgun.

"Do the best you can, we just have to hold our line for as long as possible," Ms Jax replied with a grim face. Strix cried out as one of the beasts blindsided her, knocking her on her back then dived in for the kill. A blast from Ursula's shotgun stopped the beast mid-air just before it was able to rip her throat out. Strix looked up, her eyes wide. Her confidence shattered, she looked around to see Ursula giving her a brazen look that said, 'I only did it because I need you alive'. Ms Jax looked down at the ground only to find none. Just the rippling movement of beasts awaiting their turn at this deadly game of king of the mountain. A chill ran through her and she hoped their coming sacrifice would be enough for Ulysses and Jason to carry out what needed to be done.

Ms Gaia stood transfixed by the sound of the battle

that lay ahead. Her confidence in her troops was complete and absolute, which was why when Ulysses and Jason charged her from the flank, it didn't register at all that she was under attack. There was nothing sophisticated about their flanking assault. Jason and Ulysses had changed their form yet again. Half man, half bull, one of Greek mythology's most formidable creatures, the Minotaur. Standing in at eight foot tall with broad powerful shoulders, they were clad in leather and bronze studded armour, similar to that worn by the ancient Greeks. Their long silver horns jutted out from their heads like raised swords glinting in the moonlight. They raced towards Ms Gaia and her inner guard. Her forces ran to meet them head on. They appeared like two giant rocks in a steady flowing river. The proverbial unstoppable force meeting the immovable object.

They clashed with ferocity, the stakes being the fate of the earth. Standing back to back, Ulysses and Jason fought like there was no tomorrow, throwing everything into every attack and block. But for all their vaunted power and skills, they were unable to advance any further due to the mass and scale of their enemy. The numbers were just too great and the events of the night had wearied them greatly. Their movements now became slow and laboured. Ms Gaia could see this too, and a wide and condescending smile spread across her face.

She continued to scream orders at her minions. She held the advantage however her army couldn't seem to bring these two warriors down. Their tenacity and resolve pushed them beyond any normal level of endurance.

"Destroy them!" Ms Gaia screamed, anger at her

inability to remove this final hurdle. She held aloft the Gjallerhorn, determined to rally her forces. She screamed bloody murder. Ms Gaia was on the verge of victory. Two opponents against her unstoppable army, time on her side, their defeat inevitable. All appeared hopeless then suddenly her eyes went wide in horror. Her smile dissolved as she slowly looked down at the tip of an arrow head protruding from her chest. It was as if someone had flipped a switch, one which resulted in every beast simply stopping dead in its tracks, completely immobile and frozen, their ragged breathing the only indication of life.

Jason and Ulysses had stopped too, now looking in disbelief at the mortally wounded figure of Ms Gaia, who had now dropped to her knees, her hands clutched to her chest, struggling to stay upright. She eventually fell face first to the ground where she remained still and unmoving. Jason looked about, his eyes scanning the horizon before finally settling upon a tiny figure in the distance.

"Selene!" Jason yelled as he grabbed Ulysses by the shoulder and pointed in her direction. Selene was standing in an archer's pose, her arm raised, holding a bow of simple but elegant design. Her other arm hung at her side. Selene's face was still. her eyes clearly anguished. She stared at the fallen figure of Ms Gaia. Jason pushed his way through the throng of living statues and ran to her side, changing back to human in the process. Ulysses didn't waste any time as he raced to Ms Gaia and retrieved the Gjallarhorn that lay at her side.

As Jason approached Selene, she dropped the bow, he swept her into his arms, tears spilling down her cheeks as she gripped him tight.

“I didn’t want to, I swear,” Selene sobbed.

“Ssshhh,” Jason whispered as he held her close. “She brought this on herself, not you. It was the only way,” Jason added. Now in his human, form Ulysses strode over to Selene and Jason, the Gjallarhorn held firmly in his grasp.

“I hate to break up this reunion but look around, we still have a huge problem.” Jason and Selene parted reluctantly and surveyed the area around them. The scene was eerily quiet, strands of moonlight filtered through the tree canopy casting an ethereal glow on their surroundings. The beasts were now completely still, their lower limbs shrouded in a mist that rolled along the park floor. “Why didn’t it work?” Jason asked Ulysses, who shrugged as he studied the Gjallarhorn.

“I’m not sure, I’m assuming that she was only the catalyst that caused the transformation to happen and without her, they can’t function. She could no more control their form than say a scientist can control the outcome of an experiment,” Ulysses theorised.

“What the hell is going on?” a voice rumbled through the still night. They looked around to find Onyx and Strix striding toward them, followed closely by Ms Jax who was supporting Ursula.

“Answer me!” Onyx instructed.

“I appreciate your help, but don’t think for a second that my quietly contemplating our current predicament is my subservience to you. Right now I’m willing to see you meet a similar fate as your previous employer,” Ulysses said calmly. Onyx remained silent, clearly seething at the librarian’s words.

"Surely someone has an idea on how to reverse the transformation?" Jason pleaded. He was met with silence. "Come on, my mum is one of these sonsofbitches," he added in frustration. Selene grabbed his hand and held it tight.

"We'll find a way," Selene whispered softly.

"What if we destroy the horn?" Strix asked.

"I don't think it'd work, besides, even if we were to try, that should be our last resort," Ulysses replied.

"Maybe it has a reverse switch or reset button?" Jason offered with a shrug.

"You're an idiot," Strix said.

"No he's not, he's brilliant," Selene interjected.

"It was just an idea," Jason replied.

"Ulysses, may I see the horn?" Selene said. He nodded and handed it over. Inspecting the inscriptions on its outer surface, Selene ran her finger along the length until she found what she was looking for.

"See this," Selene said, pointing to a picture of a ravenous wolf, a hole in the horn where the wolf's mouth was.

"It's Fenrir the beast that apparently swallows Odin alive during Ragnerok," Ursula replied.

"Exactly. Jason, give me your necklace," Selene said. Jason slipped the leather thong over his head and handed to her.

"Jason and I worked out that this pendant was also a key, one that I hope will also unlock the Gjallarhorn," Selene said. Grasping the pendant in her hand she inserted it into the opening located in Fenrir's mouth. It slid in perfectly. Everyone had crowded in, watching intently as Selene slowly turned the key which clicked into position.

The Gjallarhorn started to vibrate. Selene dropped it to the ground in surprise, then stared on as the horn started to twist and open slowly, reconfiguring itself before their eyes. The sounds it made was similar to that of a ticking clock counting down to something important.

"I don't believe it!" Jason murmured as the ticking suddenly stopped. What remained of the twisted horn with the random images was now perfectly straight. The images were arranged into a story depicting the end of the world.

"What do we do now?" Selene said as she looked at the others.

"I don't know about the rest of you but blowing the Gjallarhorn seems to be our only option," Jason said. There was a mixed murmur from the group.

"Surely it can't get any worst, Right?" Jason added.

"Famous last words," Ulysses replied.

"Jason's right. We owe it to the town, the world, to try," Ms Jax said.

"How long till the moon is back to normal?" Jason queried.

"Five minutes," Ursula replied quickly, checking her watch.

"Do it Jason and screw the consequences," Selene said.

"I don't know about the rest of you, but we're throwing away a perfectly good opportunity," Onyx said hastily. Strix looked uncertain.

"Shut your pie hole you blathering idiot," Ulysses spat. Before he could elaborate further, Ms Jax stepped forward and punched the black mercenary in the head, the blow sending him flying into the path of a tree. Onyx sat where he landed, looking dazed. Everyone else turned and stared at Strix who took a step back and shrugged her shoulders.

"We're partners, not husband and wife," Strix explained.

"We're running out of time," Jason said looking at Ulysses for confirmation. "Do it, consequences be damned," Ulysses said with a devil may care smile. Everyone nodded in agreement as Jason picked the horn from the ground.

"Well here goes everything," Jason said as he raised the Gjallarhorn to his lips and blew with everything that he had.

The sound that emanated was surprisingly high in pitch with a beautiful melodious tune. The expression on Jason's face showed that this was completely unintentional. Apart from the music emanating from the horn, there was no other result. Then the most astounding thing happened. Everywhere they looked the beasts began to drop to their sides and shake uncontrollably, as if they were having seizures, only faster and more violent. One by one the convulsing beasts stopped and reverted back to their original human form, unconscious and naked. Jason had now stopped blowing the horn and was staring closely at the bodies that littered the ground.

"Are they…," Jason was unable to finish the sentence.

"Dead? No, I can see their breathing," Ursula commented. Jason was about to reply when all around them the fallen people of Perigord started to rise to their feet.

"Look, they're getting up!" Selene exclaimed pointing to those nearest. They rose as if moving in reverse. One second they were lying on the ground and the next they were on their feet, as if they were falling up.

Waving a hand in the face of a nearby person, Selene was shocked to discover their unblinking eyes stared straight ahead, as if in a trance.

"They can't see us," Selene said. There was movement all around, people moving in reverse, like they were in a movie and the viewer was rewinding the footage. They watched in stunned silence as the town's people's speed increased, faster and faster. Every citizen of Perigord moved in the direction of the festival centre. Husbands, wives, sisters and brothers, some running alone, others carrying children. They moved with a single- minded purpose like a flock. Silent, unshakeable, the speed of their movements almost becoming a blur.

"What do we do? They're getting away from us!" Selene asked.

"We follow!" Jason yelled, dropping the horn as took off in pursuit. The rest of the group followed close behind.

They arrived at the park's centre only to find them literally frozen in time, presumably in their positions prior to the blowing of the Gjallarhorn.

"What now? Why are they just standing there?" Jason asked as he looked around, trying to locate his mother.

"I don't think any of us has the answer. This is unlike anything I've ever experienced," Ulysses replied. Jason wasn't listening to his mentor as something had caught his eye. Without explanation, Jason made his way through the frozen crowd, followed closely by Selene and Ulysses. They eventually caught up with Jason who was now standing in front of his mother. Helen was like the rest of the township, frozen in time at the moment of the ceremony. She was staring up at the sky, a peaceful expression on her face. Jason reached out to touch her shoulder then recoiled at the stone-like texture of her skin.

"She's my rock, you know," Jason said quietly. Ursula and Ms Jax arrived. "She tells everyone that I'm hers, but she's the strong one. Hardworking, caring, intelligent and honest. I'm so proud of her raising a kid on her own, especially one like me. Do you think she knows how I feel about her?" Ursula came up behind him placing a hand on his shoulder.

"As a parent who cares deeply for their child, it's easy to recognise those traits in another. She knows how you feel Jason," Ursula replied.

"How much time is left before the blood moon is gone?" Jason asked, not taking his eyes from his mother.

"Two minutes left," Selene said uncomfortably, looking at her watch.

"Why won't they change back?" Jason fumed.

"Because we're holding the horn and we want our army," a voice growled. The group spun to find Strix and Onyx who were now holding the horn.

"Ah, for shit sake, really? You're going to pull this now?" Jason raged as he took a pace towards them.

"I wouldn't if I were you, or Onyx will smash the horn and leave your mummy and the town frozen forever," Strix ordered.

"So I'm meant to just stand here and do nothing while you change them all into mindless beasts?" Jason barked.

"Oh don't worry, we'll have their minds. They won't

miss them at all," Onyx said with a smirk. Jason roared and charged the pair.

"No!" Onyx yelled and raised the Gjallarhorn above his head, preparing to smash it.

From the moment Onyx and Strix arrived with the Gjallerhorn announcing their intentions, Ursula had slunk into the darkness, slowly manoeuvring her way around behind the pair. When Jason saw the mercenaries, he completely lost control and charged the pair, murder in his eyes. Onyx made the mistake of raising the horn up high and away from the rampaging Jason, providing Ursula the opportunity to fire a grappling hook from her high powered air compression gun.

With their attention diverted, the grappling hook struck its target, coiling around it tight. Onyx barely had time to register his predicament when Ursula hit the reverse switch. A tiny motor within the gun ripped the horn from Onyx's grasp and reeled the Gjallarhorn in. At the same time Jason crossed the distance towards the mercenaries. He could see Onyx lose his grip on their prize. A smile escaped his face as he changed form into reinforced steel, leaping at his target and firing off a massive grey fist into the jaw of Onyx. The mineral comprised alien was out cold before he hit the ground. As quick as she was, by the time Strix realised what had happened, Ms Jax and Ulysses were standing either side of her pinning her arms firm. She struggled to get loose, her efforts in vain. Ms Jax raised a hand towards Strix, her index finger flexed. She then flicked her finger into the temple of the avian warrior. The power released knocked her unconscious. Ursula, now with the Gjallarhorn in hand, tossed it to Ulysses who caught it mid-air.

"We have thirty seconds left," Selene cried.

"Here, blow it one more time Jason. I have a gut feeling about this," Ulysses said, throwing the horn to Jason. He wasted no time raising the horn to his lips and gave it everything he had.

The moment the music emerged from the horn, a strong wind started to pick up in and around the park, swirling like a vortex. Jason, Selene and the others ran for cover as the wind whipped around them, threatening to snatch them all within its embrace. From the safety of the library entrance they watched as the wind swirled around the town's people, who appeared untouched and immoveable like statues. On the wind, debris was flying around, torn clothing, broken timber and canvas from the marques and stages that were destroyed during the battle. None of it appeared to be injuring the people at the centre of the vortex. The wind and debris eventually moved at such a high speed that nothing within could be seen.

"What do we do?" Jason yelled as he struggled to be heard over the top of the noise.

"There's nothing we can do, we have to let this play out," Ulysses replied sympathetically. They all watched, matching looks of apprehension on their tired faces. The fate of the town and its people literally resting on the Gods.

The centre of town was now a blur of colours, the sound of the winds like the moaning of the dead. Then at the height of its intensity, explosions of light appeared to be going off within the centre. It literally appeared as if a storm cloud was hovering in the centre of town. The bursts of light were like lightning strikes, followed by an earth shattering explosion. It was so loud that it set off shop and car alarms all through town. The wind had now stopped and was replaced with a jet black mist that was slowly dispersing into the night sky, once again lit by a normal pale moon.

Jason and the others raced from the safety of their shelter as the last of the mist evaporated. The people of Perigord appeared, unharmed and fully clothed. The stalls, marques and stages were as they were prior to the battle. An applause rippled through the crowd, followed by cheers and general good-natured enthusiasm. People praised the visual light show of the Harvest Moon. Jason led the others through the crowd as he looked for his mother. The town's people appeared to be acting normal as if nothing unusual had been happening. Ulysses mysteriously departed from the group giving Ms Jax the thumbs up signal before leaving. Jason continued on until he found Helen, grateful that she was now clothed like the rest of the town. As he approached, he broke into a run and picked her up in a bear hug. Helen seemed surprised at first, but like any mother was happily overwhelmed to have her teenage son show his affection unashamedly in a public venue.

"What was that for?" Helen asked curiously. "Not that I'm complaining," she added. Jason placed Helen down carefully.

"That was for bringing us to Perigord, and this," Jason said, leaning over and giving her a kiss on the cheek. "Is for being you," he added with a twinkle in his eye. Helen looked at him strangely.

"Did I miss something?" Helen said.

"No, not at all," Jason replied.

Epilogue

THOSE THAT HAD been pivotal in the salvation of Perigord were sitting around the table of the library staff room, talking. Ulysses, Ms Jax, Ursula and holding hands at the far end, Jason and Selene. Everyone was sipping on tea and despite the fatigue, lumps and bruisers, they wore the smiles only those that have achieved something truly special wear.

"Selene, I have to know, where did you get the bow and quiver full of arrows?" Ulysses enquired. Selene suddenly became all serious as she thought carefully over her answer, glancing at the bow and quiver at her feet.

"Do you remember when you all left me near the front door?" she said. "Yeah, it wouldn't open," Jason replied. Everyone at the table was listening carefully.

"I was crouched low near the door thinking, what am I gonna do, when the door cracked open. A brilliant pure white light spilled out," Selene said.

"What happened then?" Jason asked enthralled in her story.

"I couldn't help myself. I walked through the door, almost in a trance towards the statue," Selene said.

"What statue?" Jason asked impatiently.

"The statue of Artemis," Ulysses interrupted.

"That's right," Selene said. "How did you know?" she added. Ulysses didn't reply.

"Well, I approached Artemis. She looked beautiful, striking a pose with her bow. I was standing directly in front of her, then the next thing I remember I was back outside, the bow in my hand and the quiver of arrows on my back," Selene added.

"That's incredible!" Ursula said.

"Too right, she now has a weapon and she saves the day," Jason commented. Selene suddenly realised that Ulysses was staring at her strangely. Feeling uncomfortable, she retrieved the bow and quiver that now lay at her feet and handed them across to Ulysses.

"I'm sorry, I should have given them back to you sooner," she said. Ulysses shook his head and gave her a sad smile.

"It's yours now," he replied.

"I don't understand," Selene said.

"For whatever reason, the library has named you as its champion" Ulysses said.

"That's fantastic! What an honour!" Selene said, gushing at the news.

"Yes, yes it is," Ulysses replied, less than enthusiastic. No one noticed his attitude change except for Ms Jax who decided not to brooch the subject there.

"What about Ms Gaia?" Ursula asked. Ulysses was glad to have a change of subject.

"When I went to retrieve Ms Gaia from the woods, all I could find was this," Ulysses said as he pulled a vial from his pocket and shook the contents for everyone to see. Inside was a course black powder.

"What is it?" Jason asked.

"I don't know and neither does Greymeade," Ulysses replied. "But this was all that was there where her body had been," he added.

"And if anyone wants to know, we currently have Onyx and Strix detained within the library. One they can't possibly escape from," Ms Jax interjected. This particular news was well received from everyone.

Ulysses tapped the side of his tea cup with a spoon as he stood and faced his companions.

"Quiet please," Ulysses said only to be drowned out by their applause and cheering. Temporarily giving in to their adulation, Ulysses stood there and waited them out.

"I'd like to make a toast," Ulysses declared. "On behalf of the citizens of Perigord, thank you for your determination and unwavering fighting spirit. And from me thank you for your friendship and loyalty," Ulysses said soberly. "To the employees of earth's finest library," Ulysses added and raised his cup to the room. The other members present returned the gesture.

"Hear, hear," they replied and everyone drank.

The party only lasted a short while. Fatigue was their enemy in the wee hours of the morning. Ursula literally dragged Jason and Selene out the front door. As they made their way home. They stopped briefly at the statue of Artemis, whose pose was now of her standing with hands on hips looking ethereal and heroic. They left shortly after as Ulysses and Ms Jax watched them go.

"They're good people," Ulysses said.

"Amongst the finest I've ever met," Ms Jax replied. They made their way slowly down the staircase.

"I've think it's time we turned in as well," Ulysses said when he noticed the doorway into the library's inner sanctum was open.

"Unusual," Ulysses muttered. Upon entering, there was an image of the Perigord Park blown up with crystal clarity.

"Greymeade, where and when is this location?" Ulysses asked. Text at the bottom of the image appeared. 'S/E position Perigord Park 0330h this morning'.

"That was twenty minutes ago," Ulysses said. "Greymeade, why are you showing us this image?" Ulysses added. The image began to zoom in on a tree located at the bottom left hand side. Standing at the base of the tree was a robed figure, its hood partially pulled back. Ulysses strained to see the face.

"Greymeade, zoom in and highlight the robed figure," Ulysses requested quietly. The image was altered in the manner asked.

"I don't believe it," Ulysses whispered, as both he and Ms Jax stared at the blown up image of Heinrich Perigord.

"He's back," Ulysses said.

About the Author

BORN IN 1972, Katherine, NT, Australia. Married with three children I have always loved to read in particular fantasy fiction. My favourite authors include JRR Tolkien, Robert E Howard, Stephen King, Raymond E Feist and the awesome Matthew Reilly. Growing up I was always a bit of a geek, in particular my love of comics and horror movies, something that has stayed with me well into my "mature years".

I was a soldier in the Australian Defence Force for nearly 20 years, having served on operations in Rwanda and East Timor, and later an instructor at the School of Infantry. I'm a qualified cinema graphic make-up artist, having trained under Oscar winner Peter Frampton. I had high aspirations of being the next Tom Savini. I enjoy keeping fit, reading and annoying my kids.

I still love cheesy B grade movies in particular anything with zombies and I love hanging out with my brothers every chance I get, both of whom are successful writers in their own respective fields.

Writing Perigord has been an immensely satisfying journey and one that has yet to reach its final destination.